Australia
BUNDLES OF JOY

Nicola
MARSH

Amy
ANDREWS

Lilian
DARCY

MILLS &
BOON

Mills & Boon, an imprint of Harlequin (UK) Limited, Eton House, 18-24 Paradise Road, Richmond, Surrey TW9 1SR

ISBN: 978 0 263 90608 0

010-0713

IMPOSSIBLY PREGNANT

Nicola
MARSH

THE AUSTRALIA COLLECTION

March 2013

April 2013

May 2013

June 2013

July 2013

August 2013

Nicola Marsh has always had a passion for writing and reading. As a young girl she devoured books when she should have been sleeping and later kept a diary whose contents could be an epic in itself!

These days, when she's not enjoying life with her husband and sons in her home city of Melbourne, she's at her computer, creating the romances she loves, in her dream job.

Visit Nicola's website at www.nicolamarsh.com for the latest news of her books.

For Heath,
my littlest hero and very own precious miracle

CHAPTER ONE

'There is no such thing as the perfect man.'
Keely Rhodes, age 19.

'MBA. Nine o'clock!'

Keely Rhodes didn't waste time answering her friend and co-worker, Emma Radfield. Instead, she slowly turned her head ninety degrees to the left, trying to look nonchalant as she checked out the Major Babe Alert.

However, rather than your average, run-of-the-mill babe, who occasionally popped into the sleek offices of Melbourne's premier corporate website agency, WWW Designs, in search of the very best in Internet technology, this guy turned out to be the last person she had expected to see.

'What do you think?' Emma muttered under her breath, far less subtle in her attempt to ogle the guy as she craned her neck and elbowed Keely in the ribs.

I think I've died and gone to heaven, Keely thought, eyeing every glorious inch of the six-foot-three, broad-shouldered frame as he strode towards the reception desk.

Lachlan Brant was one fine specimen—and, by the confident charisma he oozed on the radio, probably knew it too.

'That good, huh?'

Tearing her gaze away from him, Keely fixed her friend with a curious stare. 'Don't you recognise him?'

Emma shook her head. 'Uh-uh. Believe me, if I'd seen that dreamboat before I would've remembered.'

'The name Lachlan Brant ring any bells?'

'*The* Lachlan Brant?' Emma scanned him from head to foot and dabbed at the corner of her mouth. 'Wow, he's got the bod to match that incredibly sexy voice. Excuse me while I drool.'

'Yeah, he's not bad.'

As her friend quirked an eyebrow, Keely grinned. 'Okay, he's pretty cute.'

Emma's other eyebrow joined the first.

'Make that good-looking.'

If Emma's eyebrows shot any higher they would be hidden under her blonde fringe.

Keely held up her hands in surrender. 'Okay, he's hot. Hotter than hot. He's so hot he's burning up. There, satisfied?'

Her friend sighed. 'I would be if a guy like that looked twice at me.'

Keely rolled her eyes. 'Yeah, right. Like you're interested in anyone but Harry Buchanan. Though for the life of me I can't understand why you're still pining over your first love. Get over it already.'

At the mention of Harry, Emma's eyes glazed over as if lost in some precious private memory.

Keely made an exasperated sound akin to a snort. 'Anyone ever tell you you're a hopeless romantic?'

Emma smiled. 'And I wouldn't have it any other way. What do you think he's doing here?'

Filling her cup from the water-cooler and taking several long gulps to dislodge the lump of foreboding in her throat, Keely hoped to God it wasn't for the reason she suspected.

'Who knows? He's probably dating our illustrious leader.'

Or else he'd discovered the real identity of the caller who had given him more than he'd bargained for last week on his popular radio talkback show.

'No way! He'd have better taste than that, surely?'

Keely shrugged, not in the mood to dish the dirt on Rabid Raquel, the boss from hell, as most of her employees liked to call her. Right now, she was torn between wanting to keep an eye on Lachlan Brant and running back to her office and hiding from him.

Besides, she had more important things to think about, like putting the finishing touches to the website for Melbourne's largest athletic company, designing an upbeat site for *Flirt*, the newest women's magazine about to hit the shelves, and planning Emma's surprise birthday party.

'I need to get back to work,' she said, casting one final appreciative glance in Lachlan Brant's direction before turning away.

Emma sighed. 'Yeah, me too. Lunch at Sammy's? Midday? I'll e-mail Tahlia.'

'If she can tear herself away. Our Director of Sales seems tied to her desk these days.'

'She's gunning for that promotion, you know.'

Keely nodded. If anyone understood, she should. After all, wasn't that one of the main driving forces behind her maniacal hours at the moment? She'd coveted the role of Director of Graphic Design for the last year and might have a shot at the job if Nadia would ever announce her pregnancy.

'Fine, but if she misses one more of our lunches she'll become a very dull girl. You know what they say, all work and no play…'

Emma sent her a sceptical look.

Keely chuckled. 'You're right. As if anything about Tahlia could ever be dull.'

Tahlia Moran was brash, effervescent and the life and soul of every party. Throw in gorgeous and confident and it was little wonder that Keely felt like faded wallpaper next to her other closest friend.

'See you at midday.'

However, before Keely could make her escape, Chrystal, receptionist extraordinaire—and all-round good-time gal if the office rumour mills were correct—waved her over.

Thankful she'd worn her favourite power suit today, Keely strolled across the chrome and glass foyer as if facing Lachlan Brant, her would-be nemesis, was something she did every day.

'Keely, Ms Wilson wants to see you in her office for a second before you pop back here and take Mr

Brant up.' Chrystal flashed her an Oh-goody-look-what-Santa-brought-me-this-year smile as she stared up at Lachlan Brant—her next apparent intended victim in the bedroom stakes—with adoration, barely casting Keely a second glance.

Trying to keep her nerves at bay and wondering what Raquel wanted—and why *she* had to show him up to the boss's office—Keely schooled her face into what she hoped was a professional mask and turned to face him.

'Hi, I'm Keely Rhodes. If you'd like to take a seat, I'll be with you shortly.'

Then it happened.

The man she'd publicly berated on radio turned and fixed her with a penetrating stare, the deep blue of his eyes highlighted by a shirt of the same colour.

And her heart lurched.

For the first time in her twenty-six years, the organ she'd managed to shield from breaking by only dating Mr Averages did some weird pumping that sent blood pounding through her body at a million beats a minute.

'Pleased to meet you.' He smiled and held out his hand—her heart didn't stand a chance.

Keely didn't believe in love at first sight. She was a realist who had both feet firmly planted on the ground and it hadn't steered her wrong to date. Why have romantic notions like Emma or follow nebulous predictions like Tahlia? Wishing for something that would never come true was asking for heartache and she had no intention of taking a fall.

Aware that she'd hesitated a fraction too long, Keely quickly slid her hand into his and shook it, the warmth of his touch doing strange things to her insides as his long, tapered fingers closed over hers.

Now she knew for sure. Not only had her heart flipped out, her common sense had joined the party. Since when did a mere handshake feel like an intimate touch designed for her and her alone?

'I'll be waiting.' His deep voice washed over her, so much richer, mellower, in person than over the airwaves.

How many nights had she lain awake listening to this man and the advice he dished out to the masses, listening to his voice for the sheer pleasure of it? She'd imagined an older man, someone with a wealth of life experience, till she'd seen his photo in the newspaper, though Lachlan Brant in grainy print was nothing compared to the man in the flesh.

Mentally shaking herself out of her reverie, she extracted her hand and tried to get a grip—on her wits, not the man looking at her with an amused gleam in those all-knowing eyes.

'Fine. I'll be back soon,' she said, wondering what it was about him that had her so flustered.

So he had a great body, a soulful voice and a lethal smile. That didn't make him God's gift to women. Or did it?

He also had a degree in psychology and analysed

people for a living, a fact she'd rubbed his nose in during her five-minute brush with fame—or infamy—last week. And boy, would she be in trouble if he recognised her as the crackpot who had made scathing fun of him during that call. 'Quack', 'thick as a brick', and 'out of touch' were a few of the insults she'd levelled at him that sprang to mind—and they'd been the tame ones!

Hoping her legs wouldn't wobble, she walked away, resisting the urge to glance over her shoulder and see if he was checking her out.

As if. Since when did guys like him go for girls like her? Though she'd conquered her eating disorder years ago, she hadn't shed her inhibitions regarding her body along with the excess kilos. Though she looked okay, she wasn't a patch on the waif look that most men favoured these days—and never would be.

Reaching Raquel's door, she cast aside her body-image issues, took a deep breath and entered after knocking twice.

'About time you got here. What took you so long?'

Though Raquel Wilson was a competent leader, with enough drive to take WWW Designs into the next decade, her people skills were on a par with those of an angry Rottweiler. In fact, several employees had taken to calling her Raquel the Rottie behind her back, and Lord help them if she ever found out. Keely had a sneaking suspicion that in this case the Rottie's bite would be every bit as bad as her bark.

Keely gritted her teeth and fixed a smile on her face. 'I was waylaid by a client.'

'Lachlan Brant, you mean?' Raquel's eyes took on a predatory gleam, the same look she got whenever a lucrative client set foot in the office.

'Uh-huh.'

'Good.' Raquel threw the pen she'd been holding on top of a pile of paperwork that looked as if it would keep her chained to her desk for the next decade. 'He's your new assignment.'

Oh-oh. When Raquel said 'assignment', it meant trouble. Co-workers avoided one of her special assignments like the plague—she demanded you tail the client like a detective, finding out every nitty-gritty detail to make sure their account was the best and therefore would lure further big business for the company. In a way, that was what kept WWW Designs at the top. However, the thought of wearing the gorgeous Lachlan Brant like a second skin for any length of time had Keely wanting to hotfoot it to the nearest ice cream parlour—and she'd kicked that habit a long time ago.

Resisting the urge to run as fast as her legs could carry her, Keely did her best to look keen. 'Sounds like a wonderful opportunity but I'm kind of snowed under with other accounts at the moment. *Flirt* has just come onboard and I—'

'Lachlan Brant is your number one priority as of

now. I'm sure you'll find a way to juggle the rest.' Raquel stood and walked to the floor-to-ceiling windows that took in an impressive view of Melbourne's latest cultural icon, Federation Square, and the beautiful dome of Flinders Street Station. 'I have every confidence in you, Keely. If you do well, there could be a promotion in this for you.'

Great. Just great.

How could she refuse tailing Lachlan Brant's welltoned tail in exchange for a chance at the big time?

'I'll do my best.' Inwardly sighing in resignation, she knew that in the Rottie's case her best often wasn't good enough.

'See that you do. Now, bring the man in question up here and let's see if we can get him to sign on the dotted line.'

Keely nodded, managed a grin that she knew must look like a grimace, and headed back to the foyer to find her new *assignment*.

Lachlan stood as soon as she entered the reception area and his sheer presence hit her all over again. The man was serious drool material—and, by that cocky grin, boy, did he know it.

'Ready for me now?'

Ha! If he only knew how ready…

She nodded. 'Follow me.'

He did exactly that and she was aware of him every step of the way to Raquel's office. Thankfully, he didn't have a clue to her identity as a moonlighting heckler and she hoped it stayed that way.

'Your name sounds familiar. Have we met before?'

Her hand stilled on the doorknob to the Rottie's office and she gulped. So much for breathing easy.

'I don't think so,' she managed to get out, without a trace of apprehension in her voice.

'Keely is rather an unusual name. I'm sure I've heard it recently.' He fixed her with yet another piercing glare and she could almost imagine him stroking an imaginary goatee, like some Freudian professor trying to discover the meaning of life as he racked his brain to place her.

Stifling a grin at her mental image of the gorgeous psychologist in front of her even remotely resembling one of his ancient predecessors, she knocked on Raquel's door and waited for the usual barked command to enter.

'Come in.' Judging by the decibel level, Raquel was keeping it down to a dull roar in deference to Lachlan's status as prospective 'assignment' material.

'Is this a bad time?' Lachlan muttered under his breath, placing a hand in the small of her back to guide her through the door.

If she'd learned one thing it was never to slander her boss with anyone other than Emma and Tahlia, and especially not with strangers. However, with his innocuous touch burning a hole through her cool wool jacket, Keely lost all rational thought for a moment.

Concentrate, girl. She needed the promotion to Director of Graphic Design, and babbling in front of her boss and her newest project was not the way to go about it.

'Raquel is very busy,' she said, eagerly pushing open the door to escape the intimacy that seemed to envelop them in the deserted corridor.

'I don't speak to prospective clients like that when I'm busy,' he muttered as they entered the airy office, a slight frown marring his brow.

The Rottie bared her teeth in an attempt at smiling and shook his hand. 'Good morning, Mr Brant. Take a seat and let's get started.'

So much for pleasantries. Raquel picked up a folder and slid it across her desk.

'Call me Lachlan. And surely all this paperwork is a mere formality?' He gestured to the folder he'd barely flicked through. 'I've already done my research, and it looks like WWW Designs will suit my needs, so let's dispense with the sales pitch. I'm eager to get started straight away.'

Raquel's eyes gleamed behind her rimless glasses. She was obviously pleased at landing a big client with seemingly little effort. 'Well, that was relatively painless. Glad to see you're a decisive man, Lachlan, and I'm pleased that you've chosen our firm to handle your Internet needs. Why don't you take these documents with you, leave them with Chrystal once they're signed, and let Keely show you where she works her magic?'

Magic? The Rottie must really want to land the Brant account, badly.

'I'm looking forward to it.'

And, just like that, Keely had the sudden urge to bolt, promotion or not. Lachlan stared at her with a hint of speculation in his eyes and, with her imagination working overtime, she could've sworn she read more than an interest in her design skills there.

He continued, giving her valuable breathing space. 'Your company seems to offer exactly what I'm looking for.'

She tried to break eye contact with him and failed, suddenly knowing how a cobra felt, trapped under the hypnotising stare of a mongoose.

Besides, she was obviously reading more into his words. How could a man like him be remotely interested in her?

Clearing her throat, she finally managed to speak. 'If you'll follow me, we can get started now.'

The corners of his mouth twitched again, as if he was having difficulty keeping a straight face, and she could've bitten her tongue. Obviously, he had a different idea to what getting started meant.

Rather than making some wisecrack, as she had half-expected, he inclined his head and said, 'Lead the way.'

She was expecting a parting shot from Raquel, and her boss didn't disappoint. 'Make this your best work, Keely.'

Keely smiled through gritted teeth and nodded. As

if she ever produced anything less! Though the way her mind kept wandering, from the way Lachlan's suit seemed tailormade for his broad-shouldered frame to the way he smiled with his eyes as well as his mouth, maybe the Rottie had a point in reminding her to keep focused on the job at hand?

As she closed the door Lachlan asked, 'Is she always like that?'

Keely resisted the urge to growl and make like a possessive dog over a bone, the way she did with the girls when one of them had a gripe with their boss.

'Raquel is very driven. It's what keeps this company at the top,' she said, hoping that the good Lord would reward her for being so professional—with the big fat promotion she'd coveted for ages.

'Good to hear. I only work with the best.' He smiled and she noticed the fine lines fanning out from the corners of his eyes, lending a tiny flaw to the otherwise model-handsome face. He leaned towards her and for one insane moment she thought he was going to kiss her. 'And it looks like I've got it here.'

'Are you flirting with me?'

Oops! The words had popped out before she could stop them and to her horror, his smile broadened into a fully fledged grin, like that of a starving cat toying with an itty-bitty mouse.

'What if I am?'

That would mean you're interested in me as a woman and it's my lucky day!

Mentally slapping herself for her wayward and wishful thoughts, she said, 'That wouldn't be very professional. We have a lot of work to do and I'd rather not be distracted.'

True to her cat analogy, he pounced. 'You think I'm a distraction, huh?'

Who was the man trying to kid? In the last half-hour she'd thought about his body, eyes, smile and butt—in that order. Well, maybe the latter had been higher on the list, but it wouldn't help to think about that now, when she could hardly string two coherent words together as it was.

'Don't flatter yourself.' *I'm doing enough for the both of us.* Even if it was only in her mind. 'I merely meant that word games aren't my style. I'd rather focus on the job at hand.'

He'd fallen into step beside her and thankfully she didn't have to look at him, preferring to concentrate on the suddenly onerous task of putting one foot in front of the other and not falling flat on her face. She had an embarrassing habit of clumsiness around men who grabbed her interest and she had no intention of adding to his obvious amusement by sprawling at his feet.

'Mmm…interesting. Does that apply to all areas of your life?'

What was with this guy? He might be irresistible but didn't he ever switch off the charm?

'That's none of your business.' She pushed open

the door to her office and waved him in. 'Speaking of which, I think it's time we got down to some.'

'After you.'

She brushed past him, catching a faint waft of aftershave. She usually hated the stuff, but this was a tantalizing blend of fresh citrus that seemed to wrap around her and add to the heady sensation of being in a confined space with the hottest man to enter her sphere in a long time.

Grateful to have a seat before she made a complete fool of herself, she gestured to the one next to her. 'Let's get started.'

His knee touched hers as he folded his long legs beneath the desk, sending heat sizzling through her body and hot-wiring her dormant hormones.

Great. Not only had her mind entered meltdown mode, her body had followed suit.

'I'm all yours,' he said, sitting back and folding his arms, his confident grin setting her heart hammering in her chest.

And as she reached forward to angle the computer screen towards him and knocked over her credenza, sending pens, paperclips and rulers in all directions, she could only think of one response.

I wish.

Lachlan managed to appear interested as Keely prattled on about search engines, uploading pages, hosting companies and web space. However, the sultry brunette's non-verbal cues intrigued him more than anything she was saying.

From her rigid posture and fiddling fingers to her tapping foot, she seemed nervous.

And so she should be.

The sophisticated woman doing her best to impress him with her knowledge had a secret and, though he hadn't said anything yet, he was on to her.

Cops never forgot a face, and in his profession, after three years on the radio, he never forgot a voice. Though his late-night caller last week had sounded intoxicated, he remembered every cadence, every modulation of the melodious voice that had scrutinized his character and found it lacking.

He'd been angry at the time, and now that his beautiful heckler had been unexpectedly dropped in his lap, could've fired both barrels at her. However, he was in a playful mood today. Perhaps he would string her along till he felt like doing a little heckling of his own?

'Do you have any ideas about the image you want portrayed on your web page?'

She picked up a pen and tapped it against her thigh as she waited for his answer, and all he could think about was the way her hazel-coloured eyes sparkled with intelligence, how the trendy black pinstripe suit fitted her curvy body to perfection, and what he would give for another glimpse of the cheeky dimple that appeared like an unexpected bonus when she smiled.

'I've been in radio for a while. Perhaps you've listened to the Brant Show?'

Bull's-eye! He watched her blush, the faint pink staining her cheeks lending her face a glow, and suddenly he wondered if any other activities could bring that tinge of colour to her face.

She nodded and looked at some distant point over his left shoulder. 'I've listened to your show on the odd occasion. It's very interesting.'

'What do you think of my advice?'

To his delight, her blush deepened. 'You seem to know what you're talking about.'

The pen she held increased its staccato tempo against her thigh and, despite the fun he was having in baiting her, he decided to put an end to her obvious discomfort.

'Thanks. The producers of my prospective TV show want to capture some of my expertise from radio while adding a fresh look at the same time. Think you can help me out?'

Tucking the pen behind her ear and swivelling to face the PC monitor, she smiled and his blood pressure rocketed. God, she was beautiful—from her shoulder-length sleek chocolate-brown hair to that adorable dimple.

He hadn't dated anyone in a while, after the last disaster. His ex-girlfriend hadn't tolerated a man who worked all hours and, though he'd spent quality time with her, she'd ended the relationship after four short months.

Maybe it was time to get back into the dating scene? Starting with the lovely Keely, who had switched her attention to the screen in front of her as she navigated through a host of complex computer programs while he studied her.

'I'm sure I can help. Is this like something you had in mind?'

He glanced at the screen, surprised at the speed with which she'd conjured up a pro forma. 'Wow, you're a whiz on that thing.'

She shrugged and turned away, as if uncomfortable with his praise. 'It's what I do. If you don't like the layout or colour scheme we can change it easily, but I thought you might like this?'

She'd chosen a bold template with a black background and royal blue font—very contemporary, very eye-catching.

'I like it. I'm that easy to read, huh?'

Once again, he caught a spark in her eyes that had him itching to close the short distance between them and haul her into his arms. He'd never had caveman tendencies before, but there was something about her that just begged him to show her his club and coerce her into heading back to his cave.

She folded her hands in her lap, probably to stop them fiddling, and looked directly into his eyes. 'It's a talent I have, reading people. It helps in my job, in delivering exactly what the client is after. And you seem easier to read than most.'

'Is that so?'

She nodded, and he resisted the urge to reach out and tuck the strand of hair that swung across her face behind her ear. 'You're a successful man, determined to make it to the top of your profession. Image is everything to you and you don't like people questioning your beliefs. Well-groomed, personable, charming—it's all part of the persona.'

Oh, she was good.

'Anything else to add?'

'I know just the thing to complete the package.'

He leaned forward, eager to hear what she had to say. She'd switched to teasing mode and, with her eyes twinkling and her glossy lips curved in a semi-smile, she had him intrigued.

'What's that?'

She hit a button on the keyboard and the screen became animated with a host of fancy graphics flashing across it.

'Ta-da! The perfect website, of course.' Her proud grin sent a thrill through him. If she got this excited about her work, imagine her enthusiasm for pursuits outside the office...

He smiled, making an instant decision to take a risk.

'I like it, though there's something else that would complete the package much better.'

Her face fell for a moment, as if he'd unjustly criticized her. 'What's that?'

Before he could stop himself, he reached across, tipped her chin up with his finger and stared into her remarkable eyes. 'The perfect woman.'

CHAPTER TWO

'Accessorise wisely. Choose a man with as much care as you would a handbag to go with those divine shoes.' Tahlia Moran, long-time friend and expert on men.

'WHAT happened then?' Emma leaned forward, hanging on every word.

Keely took a sip of her sparkling mineral water and shrugged. 'Nothing. Lucy came barging into my office and we sprang apart like we'd been doing something wrong.' She stabbed the last piece of lettuce from her Caesar salad and forked it into her mouth.

Tahlia swivelled her head between the two of them as if watching a Wimbledon Final. 'So you think he was implying you're his perfect woman?'

Emma frowned and answered before Keely had a chance. 'Of course. What else could he mean? Besides, she said he was flirting with her before then anyway.'

Tahlia ignored Emma's response. 'Em, you'd see the romantic side of two ants meeting on a crack in a footpath.'

Keely grinned as her two best friends discussed

her love life—or lack of one, more like it—as if she wasn't even there.

'Romance makes the world go round.' Emma pronounced it as a fact rather than one of her favourite theories.

'I think you mean money,' Tahlia said dryly, beckoning the waiter over to take their coffee order before they rushed back to the office.

Emma shook her head. 'Not everyone's as money-oriented as you, Miss Director of Sales.'

'I'm goal-oriented, not money-oriented. There's a difference. Nothing wrong with wanting to make it to the top.'

'What about the glass ceiling?' Keely teased, knowing her response was guaranteed to get a reaction out of Tahlia every time and thankful that the focus of the conversation had turned away from her encounter with Lachlan Brant.

Tahlia's green eyes flashed as she waved her hand in a dismissive gesture. 'No such thing, honey. I'm going places in this company, just watch me. All the way to the top.'

'Won't the Rottie have something to say about that?'

Personally, Keely had every confidence that Tahlia would make it to CEO of WWW Designs, and she couldn't wait for the day when Raquel was ousted from the top job. In fact, every employee would throw the party of the decade when that day came.

Tahlia tucked a strand of chestnut hair into her

signature topknot and made an unladylike noise akin to a snort. 'She won't have a chance to say anything. I'll muzzle her before keeping her on a short leash and locked away in her kennel.'

'Meow!' Emma made a clawing action with her perfectly manicured fingernails.

'Hey, I wouldn't be making cat noises around the Rottie. She'd eat you alive and spit out the bones for breakfast.' Tahlia wiggled her fingers in a saucy wave at Andy, their usual waiter at Sammy's, as he handed them the bill.

'I can handle Ratchet Raquel,' Emma said as all three of them leaned back in their chairs and watched Andy walk away, admiring the fit of snug denim to his butt.

'Grrr…' Tahlia growled.

'Aah…' Emma sighed.

'Mmm…' Keely allowed herself to be distracted for a moment—after all, she could appreciate a fine piece of anatomy like the next girl—before her dilemma niggled its way back into her mind.

'So what do you think I should do?' she asked, slipping her money into the folded bill without looking.

She had the same lunch at Sammy's, the hippest café-cum-bar at Southbank—Melbourne's hot spot for all things trendy—almost on a daily basis: sparkling mineral water with a twist of lemon, Caesar salad with low-fat dressing—hold the anchovies—

followed by a fruit platter for one, capped off with a skinny latte.

Though she'd come to terms with her past, the feelings associated with spending years as an over-weight, lonely teenager continued to dog her and she had no intention of ever feeling like that again. The trauma of what she'd gone through when she'd finally lost weight had left a lasting impression, one that she constantly strove to ignore.

So now she had to work hard to stay in shape, unlike Emma and Tahlia who seemed to devour calories without gaining an ounce. They actually joined her in weekly Pilates classes for fun! If they weren't her best friends, she could easily hate their well-toned, under-exercised behinds.

'I think you should weigh up the pros and cons before you jump into anything.' Tahlia delved into her handbag, pulled out a newspaper and quickly flipped to the zodiac page.

'Oh, no,' Emma groaned. 'Put that away.'

Tahlia raised an eyebrow and sent Emma her best 'don't mess with me' look. 'Keeping an eye on what fate may have planned for you isn't a bad thing.' She smoothed out the paper and ran a finger down the column. '"Work brings challenges but your focus will shift to other things. Try to go with the flow."'

Emma sighed heavily.

Keely stepped in before things turned ugly, as they inevitably did when Emma questioned Tahlia's daily reading of the horoscopes. 'Your zodiac stuff seems to have helped in your professional life, but what about in the men stakes?'

Tahlia shrugged, pulling a magazine clipping, featuring monthly predictions this time, from her bag. 'Hasn't steered me wrong in the guy department so far.'

'But you haven't got a man,' Emma pointed out.

Keely had to agree, but didn't want to gang up on Tahlia. Her tall, slim friend, who never had a hair out of place, might have it together in the career department but she wasn't exactly 'out there' when it came to dating.

Tahlia sent them both a scathing look. 'That's from choice, not from lack of prospects.' She turned to Keely. 'Now, do you want to hear what you should do about the sexy psychologist or not?'

What did she have to lose? Keely hadn't had so many sparks with a guy since...well, since...ever. And, if her intuition was correct, Lachlan had been striking a few matches of his own in her office this morning.

But what if he finds out you're the one who gave him grief on national radio?

It wouldn't be so bad. He struck her as a guy with a sense of humour. Maybe she should come clean and tell him the truth?

Yeah, right.

Would he still be interested in her if she revealed her identity as the woman who'd called him a

Freudian fraud, a babbling psycho and a hack who dished out advice like a near-sighted agony aunt?

Somehow, in the cold light of day, she didn't think so.

Whatever Madame Tahlia and her crystal ball had to say couldn't be any worse than telling the truth.

'Okay, let me have it. What should I do?'

Tahlia pursed her lips and nodded like an all-seeing sage. '''A study or work contact could end up being someone you want to do more than just have lunch with. Embrace the goddess within you and watch them fall: your man won't be able to keep his hands off you.'''

She shrugged and stuffed the cutting back in her handbag. 'So there you are.'

'But what does it mean I should do?'

'I don't know, but now you're fully informed.'

'Give me a break,' Emma muttered under her breath.

Tahlia ignored her. 'You're a Scorpio, right?'

Keely rolled her eyes and laughed. 'Libran.'

'Just kidding!' Tahlia smiled as she stood up and swung her bag over her shoulder. 'Your fate's in your hands, kiddo. It's written in the stars.'

Keely refrained from answering. None of the past horoscope predictions had come to fruition yet: she was still waiting for that promotion, she hadn't trav-elled in five years, and she was still waiting for a tall, dark and handsome stranger to sweep her off her feet.

'Thanks, Tahlia.' She turned to her other friend. 'Em, what do you think?'

'Honestly? I think the wise woman over here has it partially right.' Emma sent Tahlia a cheeky grin and Tahlia raised her nose in the air as if ignoring her. 'Seems like fate has dropped this amazing guy into your lap. Why don't you take a chance and see what happens? He could be the love of your life.'

Unfortunately, that was exactly what Keely was afraid of.

Keely stared at the blank piece of paper in front of her, wondering where her muse had disappeared to. Usually when she had a new client she loved to brainstorm on paper, bringing together a host of ideas and inspiration to create the final product.

In this case, the Brant file lay open on the desk to her right, the blank page on her ergonomic incline board and she didn't have a clue. The harder she tried to come up with a concept, the more her mind drifted to the man at the centre of her project and she would start fantasizing, from the way his dark hair curled around the edges of his collar to the unique blue of his eyes.

A beep on her PC indicated she had mail and she clicked on the icon to display her e-mails—anything to distract her from her wayward thoughts.

To: *KeelyR@WWWDesigns.com*
From: *Lucy-PA@WWWDesigns.com*
Subject: New talent
Sorry 2 barge in on U & LB earlier.
Wow! IMHO, he is 2 cute!
U interested?
Luce

Keely smiled, in total agreement with her assistant's
'in my humble opinion' appraisal of Lachlan, though
cute wasn't the first word that sprang to mind when
describing him. Try sexy, irresistible and charming.

She typed a quick response, knowing she needed
to concentrate on work but grateful for the distraction. Anyway, it would be interesting to get another
female's viewpoint on the subject—besides her over-
zealous friends, that was. If it was up to Emma and
Tahlia, she'd be married to the guy already.

To: *Lucy-PA@WWWDesigns.com*
From: *KeelyR@WWWDesigns.com*
Subject: Latest assignment
Speaking of which, working on LB website now.
By the way, LB off-limits 2 U.
Interest level rising—all in the name of business,
of course! U concentrate on Aidan.
K

She had no right to warn Lucy away from Lachlan.
However, she took her job seriously these days, and
if the Rottie told her to shadow the man, she would.

She could shmooze with the best of them, yet somehow the thought of spending up close and personal time with her new client sent her into a tailspin—and she sure hoped she wouldn't crash and burn.

Now, if she could just come up with a novel way to approach the man, without looking too obvious, she'd be well on her way to that hard-earned promotion.

Her phone rang and she picked it up, expecting to hear Lucy's teasing tones.

'Keely, Lachlan Brant here.'

She straightened so suddenly that she almost tipped out of her chair. Silly, really—it wasn't as if he'd walked into the room or anything.

Taking a breath and aiming for casual, she said, 'Hi, Lachlan. What can I do for you?'

He hesitated for a fraction of a second and, with her overactive imagination, the pause seemed laden with promise—maybe he would tell her exactly what she could do for him and, with a bit of luck, it wouldn't involve work?

'I was wondering how the website is coming along?'

She stared at the blank page and screen in front of her, crossed her fingers and said, 'Fine. I've just been hashing around a few ideas.'

'Such as?'

Great. Though she was creative in her job, she'd never been any good thinking on the spot, and having to tell little white lies was not one of her strong suits.

'Uh…well, seeing as you're on the radio, I was thinking of focusing on you to start with. Sort of like getting to know the man behind the voice?' She silently applauded—not bad for quick thinking.

'Sounds good. That's why I'm calling, actually.'

She should've known. For a moment she'd hoped he'd been calling to keep flirting with her or, better still, maybe ask her out.

Get real. Focus. Before he thinks you're a complete ditz.

'I was wondering if you'd like to come out to the station tonight and take a look at where I work. You know, get a feel for what I do, maybe incorporate a few ideas into the site?' His voice dropped lower, the deep tone sending an unexpected thrill up her spine. 'Perhaps grab a coffee afterwards?'

He'd asked her out! He'd actually taken the matter of approaching him out of her hands and she couldn't be happier.

'Bring along my file and we can work on it while we have that caffeine fix.'

And, just like that, her hopes, which had soared to the heavens a moment ago, plummeted back to earth with a resounding thud.

He didn't want to stare into her eyes over the rim of a coffee mug, flirt with her over an espresso or moon over a muffin.

Uh-uh. He'd asked her to have coffee with him to *work*.

She should be rapt he'd given her an easy way to

start her assignment without having to come up with some lame excuse herself. Then why was she disappointed that his invitation had been about business and not a teensy-eensy bit of pleasure?

Instilling the right amount of enthusiasm into her voice, she replied, 'Sounds good. What time should I meet you?'

'Why don't I pick you up? The security at the station can be a bit tough on strangers, particularly for the night shift. There's a lot of crackpots out there who have nothing better to do than heckle me.'

She choked on the sip of water she'd been having, coughing and spluttering while trying to contort her arm to pat herself on the back.

'Are you okay?'

She could've sworn she heard amusement in his voice but dismissed it. What was so funny about the fact that she'd almost choked to death?

'Surely my suggestion to pick you up hasn't got you that choked up?'

'Depends on your version of picking up,' she said, wondering where that had come from.

Darn it, he'd think she was flirting with him— which she was, but why couldn't she be a whole lot more subtle about it?

'Let's start with the standard garden-variety pick-up from your place and see if we can work on the other pick-up over coffee.' He chuckled, the sound of his rich, deep laughter enveloping her in its intimate cocoon, drawing her further under his spell.

And, just like that, he took up where they'd left off in her office, flirting like a pro.

She really shouldn't encourage him.

He was business.

He was a psychologist who could spend a lifetime psychoanalysing her.

He was way out of her league.

'I take your silence as agreement?'

Managing to shake herself out of her fantasy world, she said, 'It's an improvement on the choking, don't you think?'

'Nothing about you needs improving, Keely.'

She loved the way he said her name, drawing out the *ee* sound in its correct pronunciation. Many people called her Kelly and she hated it.

'Thanks. What time tonight?' She knew his show started at seven, which wouldn't give her much time to get home from work and do the usual pre-date routine.

It's not a date, her voice of reason screamed. And she happily ignored it.

'Is six too early?'

Heck, yes! She wouldn't have time to blow-dry her hair, pick out an outfit designed to impress and do a quick tidy up just in case he popped in afterwards.

'No problem. I live in Beacon Cove, Port Melbourne. Apartment 8/24 on the Esplanade.'

'Great. I'll see you at six.' He suddenly sounded

brisk and businesslike and she wondered if she'd just imagined the whole conversation and its undertones.

'Keely?'

'Mmm?'

'I'm looking forward to it.'

He disconnected before she had a chance to respond, which was rather fortunate as it would've been hard to answer him while grinning like a loon.

Keely barely raised her head as Lucy entered her office. She didn't have a moment to waste and, apart from having to head home and get ready, she needed to have something down on paper for Lachlan's file. Otherwise he'd know she was a total phoney. About the only ideas she'd hashed to date were about the two of them getting up close and personal, and she didn't think that would be appropriate to have on his web page, displayed for the world to see.

Lucy perched on the end of her desk, took off her rose-coloured glasses and wiped them with the end of her funky lime-green top.

'What's got you in a tizz?'

Keely placed the Brant file in her tote bag and zipped it shut. 'I have to leave. Now.'

'Hot date, huh?'

She shook her head. 'No.' And, despite her best intentions to stay cool about the evening ahead and not read anything into it, she blushed.

Predictably, her astute assistant pounced. 'You

have got a date! And I bet I know who it's with. Would the initials LB mean anything to you?'

'It's part of my research for his website,' Keely responded, trying not to encourage Lucy. That was all she needed—for Lucy to rev her up even more than she already was.

'Oh, right.' Lucy's eyes narrowed and she pursed her lips, as if pondering a particularly difficult puzzle. 'So that's what they're calling it these days. *Research.*'

'Luce, I haven't got time for this.' Keely picked up her bag and headed for the door. 'Besides, shouldn't you be working on the *Flirt* account?' She clicked her fingers as if remembering something. 'Speaking of Accounts, have you been down there today? I heard Aidan popped in to oversee some discrepancies.'

Keely scored a direct hit as Lucy flushed a deep crimson. 'I may have seen him briefly.'

'Why don't you ask him out? He's perfect for you.'

Lucy slid off the desk and smoothed her skirt down. 'I really must get back to work.' She stopped at the door and wiggled her fingers. 'Have fun tonight.'

'It's *work.*'

'Whatever. I'll expect an e-mail with the details of your *research* first thing in the morning. Bye.'

'It is just work,' Keely muttered under her breath as she followed Lucy out the door, wishing she could believe it.

The doorbell rang as Keely slicked gloss over her lips and took a final look in the mirror.

Not bad—black bootleg pants, burgundy fitted top, hair blow-dried to perfection and just a hint of make-up to make the most of what the good Lord had given her.

Not great, but not bad. Hopefully, Lachlan would be impressed.

As she opened the front door and his eyes lit up she had her answer.

'Hi,' was all she could manage.

If she thought he'd looked impressive at the office that morning, in suit and tie, it was nothing compared with his casual look. The combination of jeans, white T-shirt and black leather jacket had never looked so sexy on a man—and this was no ordinary man.

'You look great. Ready to go?'

She nodded, finally managing to tear her gaze away from the way the white cotton moulded to what looked like rock-hard pecs beneath.

'Just let me grab my bag,' she said, hoping that the bag was all she managed to grab in the next sixty seconds.

As if she hadn't had a hard enough time convincing herself that tonight was only about business, he had to turn up here looking like *that*.

'Nice apartment.' He stood at the door looking in

and she suddenly realised that the minute she'd caught sight of him all rational thought—along with her manners—had flown out the window.

'Come in,' she said, getting more flustered by the minute as she picked up her bag and his file slid to the floor.

Great—she must've forgotten to zip it up earlier, when she'd slid a brush and lippy for touch-ups alongside the all-important folder.

'Here, let me help.' He bent down and reached for the scattered papers at the same time she did, their heads colliding in a sickening crunch.

'Ouch!' She sank back on to the floor and rubbed her forehead, silently cursing. It looked as if her clumsy curse around cute guys had reared its ugly head again.

Thankfully, he laughed and reached out a hand to help her off the floor. 'Do I make you uncomfortable or are you always this graceful?'

'It's you,' she said, and joined in with a rueful chuckle.

'Mmm…first you up-end half your desk when I sit next to you, now you drop your bag when I get within two feet and give me a concussion in the process. It must be me.'

He pulled her up as she placed her hand in his and true to form, she stumbled against him. Totally unintentional, of course.

As she braced herself against his chest—yep, those pecs felt every bit as good as they looked—and he gazed down on her with a tender glint in his eyes, she suddenly didn't mind being such a klutz.

And when he rested his hands on her hips and smiled in that special way he had, as if she was the only woman in the world, she could've quite happily caused havoc by stumbling, upending bags and messing up desks every day of the week.

'If I'm the problem, what's the remedy?'

'You're the doc, why don't you tell me?' Her voice came out all soft and breathy while her pulse raced double-time as his hands tightened their grip, sending bolts of electricity shooting through her body.

So much for playing it cool. They hadn't even made it out of her apartment and the evening had taken on an intimate feel.

'Take two kisses and call me in the morning.'

O-kay. Think quick. Respond with something light-hearted and witty.

However, all she could do was stand there and stare at him while his gaze stayed riveted to her lips, as if he'd like to follow up on the first part of his advice. As he leaned forward her heart jolted at the clear intent in his eyes and she was sure the air crackled with tension around them.

Work…assignment…client…

The words filtered through her dazed mind and acted like an instant dampener and she reluctantly looked away.

'If that's one of your cures, I'm not surprised

you're so popular,' she murmured, managing a weak smile as her gaze fixed on his chest.

What would he think of her almost letting him kiss her? Totally unprofessional for starters, and as for the rest...

He tipped her chin up, gently forcing her to meet his stare. 'Don't second-guess yourself.'

How did he do that? She'd begun to doubt herself the minute she'd averted their near-kiss and he knew it. Despite her intoxicated ranting over the airwaves last week, he did know his stuff. And wouldn't he have a field-day if he found out why she'd been so riled about his advice to the overweight teenager that night she'd given him a verbal blast?

She opened her mouth to respond and he placed a silencing finger against it. 'And, no, I don't dish out that remedy to just anyone.'

'That's reassuring.' She aimed for brevity but her comment came out sarcastic as she pulled away from him completely, needing to establish physical distance between them to gather her thoughts.

Rather than pushing her for an explanation for her erratic behaviour—welcoming his attention one minute, freezing him out the next—as she half-expected him to do, he fixed her with a curious stare before turning away.

'As much as I'd like to cure your clumsiness, we'd better get to the station. I need to be on the air in less than an hour.' He picked up her bag and handed it to her as if nothing had happened. 'All set?'

She managed to nod, follow him out and lock up without further mishap. However, amidst her confused state at what had just occurred, one thought penetrated.

If kisses were part of his cure, she suddenly had a distinct hankering for treatment.

CHAPTER THREE

'Where men are concerned, always adhere to the "try before you buy" policy.'
Lucy, personal assistant extraordinaire.

LACHLAN gave the console a quick once-over to make sure he was off the air, removed his headphones and waved Keely into the booth.

He'd just spent the last three hours watching her through the glass partition, thoroughly distracted and, though he'd managed to present a professional front over the airwaves, he'd had enough. It was time to switch off and relax in the company of a woman who sparked his interest on many levels.

He'd thought by bringing her here to the station she might come clean about her call to him. However, despite ample opportunity, she hadn't confessed and it surprised him. He valued honesty above all else, thanks to his lying, cheating mother, who had left his father with a broken heart after leaching every last ounce of devotion out of him. And he'd vowed to never end up like his dad, a sad old man obsessed with the one woman he couldn't have, pining away for that so-called love of a lifetime.

Though the call hadn't been a big deal in itself,

he wondered why Keely would keep it a secret, especially after the way they'd clicked.

Standing up and stretching, he knew one thing. He wanted to give this woman a chance. Apart from the sizzling attraction that arced between them whenever they got within two feet of each other, he genuinely liked her and would like to get to know her better.

Starting now.

Opening the door to the sound booth, he beckoned her in. 'What do you think? Pick up any ideas for my website?'

He watched her walk across the outer room; she was wearing a classy, understated outfit that looked as if it had been made for her. She moved with an elegance that turned heads, a quiet confidence that would make any man sit up and take notice. And he'd done that the minute he'd first laid eyes on her, strolling towards him in the foyer of WWW Designs.

Usually, he liked to ponder important decisions, but after his first glimpse of Keely he'd been ready to sign on the dotted line with the company as long as she was involved in some part of his website's production. It must've been his lucky day, for not only would she play a role in the production, she was one of the main players working with him directly.

She smiled, drawing his attention to her lips, resurrecting barely suppressed thoughts of how they'd almost connected with his earlier that evening. He hadn't meant to take things so far so fast, but had been powerless to resist her allure.

'I've looked around, spoken to a few of your co-workers and jotted down some ideas.' She picked up a pad from a nearby table and presented it to him like a proud student handing in a prized project. 'See? Enough here to keep me going for a while. Great idea to invite me to your workplace.'

He barely glanced at the pad, more interested in her non-verbal cues. Another part of his job that he couldn't turn off—he read people's unspoken actions all the time, believing they revealed a lot more about the person than first met the eye.

In this case, Keely appeared nervous as she shifted her weight from one foot to another while tapping her fingers on the back of the pad. Were her nerves a result of her little secret about heckling him or caused by something deeper? Was it just him or did all men make her this jittery?

So much for getting to know her better. It would prove extremely difficult if she reacted like a skittish filly every time he got near her.

'Glad it helped. Shall we get that coffee now?'

'Sure.' She practically bolted away from him, grabbing her bag and shoving the pad inside it before heading to the door.

'Would you like to have dinner too?' He usually didn't eat after a show, preferring to grab a light supper while planning the next day's schedule. However, the thought of staring at Keely over candlelight at his favourite seafood restaurant stimulated his appetite in more ways than one.

'I'm not hungry.' She spoke too quickly, as if the thought of sharing a meal with him was the last thing she'd want.

'Let me guess. You're on a diet.' His gaze slid over her curves as he smiled, knowing that couldn't be true. She had a stunning body, and women who looked like her knew it too.

To his amazement, she took a step back and raised her bag over her chest, as if using it like a shield, the golden flecks in her eyes glowing in what he swore was anger. 'And let *me* guess. You think I need to be on one.'

For a psychologist, he could be pretty dumb at times. Though he'd expected to make light of his dinner invitation when she'd refused it, perhaps he hadn't gone about it the best way. Many women were touchy about their weight, and though Keely had no reason to be he'd obviously hit a nerve.

He held his hands up in a friendly gesture of surrender. 'Hey, I didn't say that.'

Her eyes sparked, shooting daggers. 'Not in so many words. Though your meaning was pretty clear.'

He resisted the urge to shake his head. A minute ago he'd been wondering if it was her endearing clumsiness, her strange nervousness, her beauty or a combination of all three that had him hooked. Now, he knew he needed to re-evaluate his interest in the stunning brunette.

Looks were one thing, irrational behaviour another. And, no matter how much he'd like to get to know her better, if she showed this much paranoia over a simple comment now, there was no telling how she'd act later. He'd been burned by a woman like that in the past—his mother, the queen of inconsistency—and he'd be damned if he'd tread down that path again.

'How about we stick to our original plan for coffee and forget I ever said anything about dinner? Deal?'

To his relief, her shoulders sagged and she lowered the bag, giving him a shaky smile. 'Deal. My shout.'

And, as he followed Keely out, Lachlan knew that despite his wariness at her peculiar outburst he still had every intention of discovering what made his beautiful website designer tick.

Keely sipped at her Irish coffee, thankful for the shot of alcohol swirled through the caffeine hit. Anything to calm her nerves, which had seemed to be working overtime since the minute she'd laid eyes on Lachlan this evening. First she'd practically invited his kiss at her apartment, and then she'd made a prize fool of herself by exploding over his diet comment at the station. And, though he'd done his best to put her at ease, she knew it would be hard recovering from two *faux pas* like that in one night.

Even now, the harder she tried to act nonchalant, as if that almost-kiss back at her apartment hadn't happened, the more wound up she got. At least she hadn't dropped anything, stumbled or tripped over in the last few hours. Though he found it amusing the way she reacted around him, it embarrassed her more than she let on.

'Okay, let me have it.'

'Pardon?' Startled out of her reverie, she looked up at him and wondered how she could survive the next hour.

When he'd mentioned coffee to mull over his file, he'd omitted the part about bringing her to Melbourne's hottest new jazz club. Located not far from her office in Southbank, and sprawled over half a block, the Swing Room offered its patrons everything from soulful crooning in several lounges to intimate tables for two in a quieter area reserved for late-night sojourns.

It would've been hard enough pretending this meeting was business at an average, run-of-the-mill café. Here, with the faint sounds of a master saxophonist filtering through the speakers, the dimly lit room just barely illuminated by candles strategically placed on the tables and the rich aroma of speciality coffees lingering in the air, Keely had no hope.

The atmosphere reeked of intimacy, and the man sitting on her right with his knee occasionally brushing hers wasn't helping matters.

He made casual conversation as if they were old friends, putting her at ease with his witty anecdotes about the radio business. However, the more she focused on what he was saying, the more she noticed his lips, which led her thoughts down a completely different path altogether...

'Let me see what you've done so far.'

Hoping that he wouldn't see through her, and notice that her notes had been compiled in under half an hour at the office, she took out his file from her bag and laid it on the table.

'This is only the early stages, where I tend to brainstorm, so it probably looks a bit of a mess.'

Understatement of the year. She'd covered a single sheet of paper with over a dozen Post-It notes, jotting down the few ideas that had sprung to mind when she'd finally managed to concentrate on the task at hand.

'And don't forget that I've gained a whole lot more info from being at the station tonight, so I'll try to incorporate a few more ideas into the basic plan tomorrow.'

Unfortunately, some of the info she'd learned earlier at the station hadn't been all good. She'd let her attraction for the man cloud her judgement; yet with his inadvertent swipe at her weight he'd reminded her in no uncertain terms that he was just like the rest of the male population: obsessed by superficialities like a woman's body shape rather than considering the heart on the inside. She'd copped more than her fair share of fat jokes and snide remarks over the years and, though they'd hurt at the time, none had surprised her as much as Lachlan's dig. She'd expected more from a man like him, which just went to show that he wasn't so perfect after all. Once again, her judgement when it came to the male species was way off and she'd do a darn sight better remembering it. Besides, Lachlan Brant was business and she had no right to even contemplate acting on the attraction that sparked between them.

She resisted the urge to nibble on a fingernail as he perused the file, his face unreadable.

'Uh-huh,' were the only two syllables he uttered as he screwed up his eyes, obviously trying to make sense of her tiny scrawling on the notes.

Just when she was ready to grab her notes and flee, he looked up and smiled. 'I like what you've done so far. Creative, interesting, effective.'

He handed her the file and she wanted to hug him. Her work was her pride and joy and she lapped up praise. Raquel wasn't huge on giving her employees any pats on the back. Not that it usually mattered; Keely's work spoke for itself and her clients were quick to show their appreciation for her efforts.

'If this is what you can do in one day, I can't wait to see the finished product.' He sat back and draped an arm across the back of the chair, his hand resting merely inches from her neck.

The simple action drew her attention to the way the cotton of his T-shirt stretched across his chest, defining a host of muscles just begging to be touched.

She swallowed, desperate for the slightest amount of moisture to wet her throat, which had gone dry the second her mind associated 'muscles' and 'touching' in the same sentence.

'With your input, I'm sure I can come up with something that is suitable,' she said, trying to ignore the fact that if she leant back a fraction his fingers would brush the nape of her neck.

'Sounds good. Now that the business part of this evening is settled, let's have some fun.'

Oh, no. The word 'fun' had the same devastating effect on her psyche as 'muscles' and 'touching'.

'Fun?' she managed to say, though it came out more a squeak than a word.

'You don't mind if we spend a little longer here, just chilling out? I've had a rough week and wouldn't mind unwinding with good music, great coffee and even better company.' He leaned closer a fraction, his eyes beseeching her to agree, while a faint waft of his aftershave washed over her, shattering the last of any lingering doubts.

As if she needed any convincing.

'I'd like that.'

Like it? She'd *love* it. Spending time with a guy like Lachlan would be amazing, and so much more inviting than curling up in bed with her usual thriller, alone and scared half to death. Though she read scary novels by choice, she still hadn't conquered her fear whenever she heard a noise while doing so.

'Good, that's settled. Would you like another drink?'

'A latte would be fine, thanks.'

He raised an eyebrow. 'You sure? All that caffeine is guaranteed to keep you up all night.'

She shrugged. 'I'm a poor sleeper anyway.' Painful memories could do that to a person, as much as she tried to block them out.

'That's too bad. Maybe you haven't tried the right nightcap?'

'I've tried them all. Hot milk, camomile tea, valerian, counting sheep, listening to ocean sounds and heartbeat lullabies. Nothing works.' She refrained from adding that the only time she did manage to get a decent night's sleep was when she'd been involved in a relationship and had the comforting warmth of a male body next to her.

'I might have just the thing for you.'

Oh, I certainly hope so, a naughty voice inside her head whispered, and she deliberately ignored it. 'What's that?'

He leaned closer and lowered his voice, a secretive smile playing about his lips. 'I'm not sure if you'd be up for it.'

The effect of his smile was instant, her pulse picking up tempo and keeping rhythm with her pounding heart. 'Why don't you let me be the judge of that?'

His smile broadened to a grin. 'It involves you lying down, me being next to you and opening your mind to a host of possibilities.'

Oh, boy. She gulped, desperately wishing for something fabulously witty to say. Instead, her mind was a complete blank, apart from the erotic images that filtered across it like a classic movie on constant re-run.

'I'm talking about hypnotherapy,' he said, his soft chuckle making her want to hit him.

'I knew that.'

'Really?' He captured her hand in his before she knew what was happening. 'It looks to me like you had something more...*interesting* in mind.'

She struggled to concentrate on the simple task of speaking while his thumb gently brushed the back of her hand and created havoc in the process.

'I'm not that easy to read.'

'Oh, no?'

The warmth of his hand, combined with the excited glint in his eyes, ignited a fire deep in her belly that spread like quicksilver through her body.

In one short day this man had elicited responses within her that she'd never experienced and never dreamed of having. A confirmed realist, she knew that the whole 'settle down with a nice steady boy, get married, have kids and live in the burbs' fantasy wasn't for her. How could it be, when she couldn't provide one of the vital ingredients in that happily-ever-after scenario?

Right now, she had a career to build, a promotion to gain and a whirlwind social life. Did she have room in her life for a man, a relationship and the possible implications?

He might enjoy a light-hearted affair, but what if he hoped for permanence? She'd have to walk away at the end, resulting in devastation yet again. Despite what they initially said, most men wanted children— part of their quest to prove something to the world— and she couldn't provide that.

She'd learned the hard way—Jon, the only man she'd fallen for enough to contemplate a future with, had run a million miles when she'd had the courage to tell him the truth. She'd been expecting an engagement ring; she'd ended up with more pain than it was worth.

If there was one thing she'd learned—through her overweight, low self-esteem teenage years, the gruelling hours of counselling, the dramatic weight loss and subsequent collapse—it was to protect her heart. Having it bruised, trampled and shattered did nothing for her ego, not to mention her health.

No, this time she'd be more careful.

If Lachlan Brant wanted to flirt with her, fine.

If he wanted to charm her, hold her hand and prescribe the occasional kiss, fine.

If he wanted anything else…Lord help her!

CHAPTER FOUR

'A man will halt your climb up the corporate ladder quicker than his exit at the first hint of the L word.'
Raquel Wilson, all-round cynic and closet man-hater.

'WHAT'S *Keely's Collection* doing out of mothballs?' Emma picked up the scrapbook from Keely's desk and started flipping through it.

'Lucy asked me to bring it in. We're working on a quiz format for *Flirt*, and she asked if I kept any of that stuff.' Keely didn't look up from her PC screen, eager to put the finishing touches to the athletic company's web page before shifting her attention to her latest, and most distracting, client.

'This is amazing. I can't believe you call this a scrapbook. It should be a girl's handbook on surviving the dating scene.' Emma continued to flick pages. 'You've collected quotes and quizzes like most people collect stamps or postcards.'

Keely didn't look up, her concentration not wavering. Pity she couldn't do the same when it came to the Brant account. 'It's a hobby.'

Suddenly Emma let out a squeal. 'Oh, my God, you've even got stuff *I've* said about guys written in here.'

'Nobody's safe,' Keely muttered. 'Now, shut up and let me finish this.'

Emma peered over Keely's shoulder. 'Why are you hell-bent on finishing this today anyway? I thought it wasn't due till next week? I'm nowhere near completion with the animation yet.'

'Too much work,' Keely said, her fingers flying over the keyboard as she typed the last subtitles on to the site.

'Looks good,' Emma said. 'Though you being in such a hurry to finish this wouldn't have anything to do with a spunky new client, would it?'

'Don't be silly. I give all my clients equal billing.'

'Is that why you went to the Swing Room with Lachlan Brant last night? Intending to add some musical accompaniment to his website, huh?'

To her annoyance, Keely felt heat creep into her cheeks. 'How did you know?'

'A certain young woman whose lips are as loose as her morals told me.'

'Chrystal was there?'

Oh, great. Now the whole office would know about her and Lachlan and would want to know details.

'The hottest new spot in town, according to our resident man-eater.' Emma perched on the edge of her desk. 'So, how was it?'

'It was just part of this whole stupid assignment business,' Keely said, trying not to remember the way Lachlan had stared at her during the latter part of the evening, the look in his eyes spelling danger for her peace of mind.

'Sure thing. In that case, you won't be interested in this.' Emma waved a piece of paper under her nose.

'What's that?' Keely tried to snatch it out of her hand and Emma raised it higher.

'Mmm…let me see. It's titled ''My Perfect Man'' and it fell out of your scrapbook.'

'Give me that!'

'Uh-uh, not so fast.' Emma leaped off the desk, held the paper at arm's length and started reading. 'Looks like a checklist. I wonder how many criteria the wonderful Mr Brant fits.'

Keely groaned and shook her head. 'I wrote that when I was nineteen. Can't you leave a girl in peace?'

Emma ignored her and continued. 'According to this, your perfect man would be over six feet tall, have dark hair, blue eyes, a nice smile, a sense of humour, a professional job, a great body, be adventurous, love jazz, appreciate food—read doughnuts—and be a skilled kisser.' She paused for a second, exhaled and rolled her eyes. 'Phew! Not asking for much, are you?'

'It's just a dumb list,' Keely said, remembering the exact day she'd written it.

She'd finally got her life back on track after losing all that weight and collapsing, and the first guy she'd dated, Ray the Rat, had ditched her after three months for a seventeen-year-old. The list had encapsulated every quality that Ray didn't have at the time and, hence, everything she wanted in a man.

Emma smiled. 'That's where you're wrong. I think this list details quite specifically your perfect man and, if I'm not mistaken, it seems you've already found him.'

Heat flooded Keely's cheeks. Strangely enough, she'd been thinking along similar lines as Emma read the list out. It seemed as if Lachlan met every one of her criteria, though she didn't know about the adventurous stuff yet, and she couldn't imagine him pigging out on doughnuts, not with his buffed body. As for his skill in the kissing department, she'd prefer not to go there—not with their near miss still fresh in her mind.

'I don't have time for this,' Keely said, knowing that the more Emma interrogated her about Lachlan, the more she'd want to dissect every look, word and touch from last night. And she didn't want to do that. He was business, attraction or not.

'Pity.' Emma shrugged, slid the checklist back into the scrapbook and placed it on Keely's desk. 'To be that clear on what you want in a guy and then turn your back on him when he walks into your life. Seems a shame to me.'

'Don't you have work to do?' Keely picked up the scrapbook and shoved it into her top drawer, hoping that the old adage 'out of sight, out of mind' might work in this case.

'Sure. See you after work at Pilates class?'

Keely nodded and waited till her friend had left the room before staring at the closed top drawer as if it contained a poisonous snake.

'Perfect man, my butt,' she muttered, returning her attention to the screen in front of her and wishing Lachlan Brant was anything but.

'Can I help you, Mr Brant?'

Lachlan managed to maintain eye contact with the voluptuous receptionist of WWW Designs, whose name eluded him, which was no mean feat considering she had enough cleavage on show to tempt a saint.

'Is Keely free at the moment? I'd like to have a word with her.'

In fact, he wanted to have more than a word with her, but the rest would have to wait. Ever since that almost-kiss last night, his mind had been plagued by images of her—the way she'd looked with her eyes locked on his, how she'd swayed towards him, how she'd sighed softly as she pulled away. Frankly, he'd been able to think of little else, and the only way to gain some peace of mind was to tackle the 'problem' head-on.

The woman had got under his skin in one day, a record when it came to a man who played his emotions close to his chest. He never fell for a female that quickly, even one as spectacular as Keely Rhodes. Thankfully, they'd got past that little 'moment' after his shift had ended quite quickly, and had moved into an easygoing camaraderie over coffee at the Swing Room, leaving him wondering if he'd imagined her angst.

Either way, he'd put his niggling doubts behind him for now and was eager to see where they went from here.

'I'll check if Keely's free.' The receptionist punched a few buttons on a console and spoke discreetly into a headset.

She'd better be free, in all senses of the word. The fact that Keely might have a significant other in her life hadn't crossed his mind and, though she didn't seem the type to encourage him while involved with another man, one never knew. Look at his mum.

'Keely will see you in her office now. Would you like one of these?' The receptionist held up a plate of cinnamon doughnuts that smelled delicious, somehow making the innocuous question sound as if she was offering more.

He'd had his fair share of women throw themselves at him, yet he'd always preferred the more subtle charms of a woman who acted as if she didn't possess any compared with her overtly voracious counterparts.

However, that didn't mean he had to be rude. He smiled and took one of the doughnuts. 'Thanks. Let's hope it doesn't go straight to my hips.'

'Nothing wrong with your hips from where I'm sitting,' he heard the receptionist mutter before she plastered a professional smile on her expertly made-up face and turned away to answer an incoming call.

Let's hope the beautiful Miss Rhodes thinks so, he thought as he half demolished the doughnut before knocking on her door.

'Come in.'

He pushed the door open, wondering how Keely would act after last night. Would she pretend nothing had happened between them or would she make a joke of it? Personally, he hoped she'd had as good a time as he had and would want to repeat the experience.

'Hope you're not too busy. Thought I might run a few ideas past you for the website...' He trailed off at the stunned look on her face. 'What's wrong?'

Keely tried not to stare, but the sight of Lachlan eating a cinnamon doughnut, one of the few criteria for the perfect man she'd assumed he wouldn't possess, floored her.

As if it wasn't bad enough he had to match every other quality on her checklist!

Pulling herself together, she managed to say, 'You like doughnuts?'

A sheepish smile spread across his handsome face. 'It's a weakness.' He shrugged, looking like a cheeky schoolboy rather than a renowned psychologist. 'What can I say?'

You can say something rude or obnoxious again, something designed to push me away.

However, she knew it was useless. Falling for a

guy like Lachlan—the perfect man, according to her stupid checklist—seemed inevitable.

So much for being a realist.

When it came to her heart, it was ironic that she could be as gullible as Emma, a true romantic.

'Do I have sugar covering my lips or something?'

She bit back her first retort of *or something; preferably me*. 'Sorry if I appeared distracted. I was in the middle of all this.'

'And here I was, hoping that I was the distraction.' He smiled, the simple action illuminating his face. She'd never known a guy to smile like that, his eyes lighting up as if the world was a great place to be. If she was truly delusional, she'd like to think that she had that effect on him.

'You are.' The words popped out and his grin broadened. 'I mean, I was putting the finishing touches on another client's site, and now I need to switch my thinking to you.'

Lame, even by her standards, and by the amused look on his face he didn't buy it for a minute.

'Did you enjoy last night?'

Oh, heck. Was he referring to the radio station, the jazz club or the physical attraction that had zinged between them?

Rather than come up with more pathetic excuses, she decided to keep her answer simple. 'Yes, I did.'

'Good. It makes what I have to suggest now all the more appropriate.'

Oh-oh. The only suggestions he could possibly

make that sprang to mind were highly inappropriate and she could only wish.

'Sounds interesting,' she said, resisting the urge to swing on her chair. Knowing her luck around him, she'd lean back too far and fall off it.

'It is. How would you like to gain real insight into the man behind the voice and put a few masterful touches on my website in the process?'

'I thought that was what last night was about?'

'It was only the start. What I had in mind was you spending time with me in various aspects of my life, watching me interact in different situations, getting a feel for what I want on my website. Look at it as a way to gain firsthand knowledge of what makes Lachlan Brant tick.'

Keely struggled to maintain a calm façade while she composed her thoughts. Funnily enough, she had been about to suggest something similar, though hadn't quite come up with the right words to approach him. This assignment was important to her and she'd make it the best work she'd done if it killed her—though with a guy like Lachlan by her side 24/7, what a way to go.

'Let me get this straight. I get to spend time with you away from work to gain insight into your personality? What situations did you have in mind?'

He crossed his arms, drawing her attention to his broad shoulders and the way his pale blue business shirt stretched across them. 'I like to surf, bushwalk and barbecue to chill out and de-stress, so I thought you could hang out with me, ask some in-depth questions, make a few notes.'

He strode across the room, closing the distance between them in an instant, and crouched down next to her. 'All strictly professional, of course.'

She inhaled deeply, trying to get oxygen to her befuddled brain in a hurry. Instead, his aftershave tempted her to lean closer to him and savour the crisp, clean smell that blended with his pheromones to entice her further.

To make matters worse, he stared at her with an intensity that took her breath away.

'Call it research.' He rested his hand on the back of her chair.

She cleared her throat, wishing he'd stop looking at her like that. How was a girl supposed to think with the bluest eyes she'd ever seen glued to her? 'Sounds good. Do you have any of that adventurous stuff planned for this weekend?'

He laughed, and the spell that enveloped them cleared in a second. 'Not into the outdoors, huh?'

Not unless it involved cuddling under a blanket on a windswept beach with the man of her dreams. As if that was going to happen in a hurry! 'What gave it away?'

'The frown, the way you wrinkled up your nose. Didn't I tell you I'm an expert on body language?'

Girl, don't go there! A host of wicked responses sprang to mind about exactly how he could read her body—by touch, being the primary choice—and she bit back every one of them.

What had got into her? Her hormones were clouding her judgement. She wasn't supposed to like the man, remember? He professed the same textbook psychobabble as the rest of his profession; he had dished out his baloney to that overweight teenager as if he knew how the poor girl felt.

Yeah, right. Since when had a guy who looked like him ever sought solace in food, gorging on sweet things to fill the empty void in his life? Try never. He wouldn't have a clue about being unpopular because of one's size, or the accompanying feelings of embarrassment, worthlessness and soul-destroying loneliness.

His caller that night had been reaching out to him, probably plucking up what meagre supply of courage she possessed to ring him, and what had he done? He had given the girl a two-minute quick fix, incorporating the standard line about joining a gym, exercising more, eating less and making new friends.

Keely's heart had bled for the girl. She'd been there, done that and burnt the T-shirt a long time ago. Hearing Lachlan's trite advice, no matter how good his intentions, had sparked her into reaching for her mobile and giving him the verbal spray he'd deserved.

As for her reaction to his diet comment last night, guys with buffed bods who looked as if they'd stepped off the cover of a magazine shouldn't go there. Ever.

Logically, she shouldn't be attracted to him. She'd never measure up. Physically, she wanted to get as close as she could and stay there for the remainder of her assignment.

'Hey, I won't make you jump off any cliffs or anything. You can just sit back and watch.' Concern had replaced interest in his eyes and she wrenched her attention back to the present, slamming the door on her self-esteem issues, wishing she could lock it and throw away the key for ever.

'Fine. I'll be in touch. Now, I really have to get back to it.'

Though she wasn't fine. Not by a long shot.

And she had a feeling that the more time she spent in Lachlan's company, the more the protective wall she'd built around her heart could crumble, one brick at a time.

CHAPTER FIVE

'It doesn't matter if he has two left feet as long as he's an expert at horizontal folk-dancing.'

Chrystal, serial man-eater.

'YOU two are dating,' Tahlia muttered under her breath as she stretched forward, her head almost touching her knee.

'Spending time together as part of a work assignment doesn't constitute dating,' Keely said, wishing the Pilates class could go on for ever. That way, she wouldn't have to think about Lachlan Brant and the chaos he'd turned her life into. Concentrating on her aching muscles proved an excellent distraction, for all of two seconds.

Emma stood in one smooth movement and held out her hand to pull Keely up. 'But it's more than work. What about the flirting? And all this time you'll be spending together as research? Don't forget it was his idea, even though you were going to suggest it anyway.'

Keely had been pondering the very same question all day and, though she'd managed to finish the bulk of her work, her mind had constantly drifted to Lachlan and the way he made her feel in his presence—uncertain, excited, like being on a rollercoaster and not knowing when the next exhilarating plummet would be.

She'd tried to ignore her erratic hormones and focus on work. Nadia had finally announced her pregnancy and Keely was sure it was no coincidence that Raquel had entrusted this account to her. If she succeeded in satisfying Lachlan Brant as a client, she had a sneaking suspicion the promotion was hers.

'It's just that. Research. I learn more about the man; his website will reflect my efforts. Obviously, he wants it to be top-notch too; that's why he came up with the idea for me to spend time with him.'

Tahlia finished her stretch and stood, taking a deep slug from her water bottle. 'I know this promotion is important to you but don't kid yourself. This man has the hots for you and, if I'm not mistaken, the feeling is entirely mutual.'

Keely hated it when her friends were right.

'So? What's wrong with having a little fun? It's not going to affect my work. In fact, it's going to enhance it.'

Emma lifted her long blonde ponytail, draped a towel across her neck and smiled. 'Sweetie, there's nothing wrong with having fun. I just think there's more to it than that. If the guy was only interested in a quick roll in the sack, he wouldn't be going to all this trouble.'

Expecting an argument from the ever-practical Tahlia, Keely looked at her.

To her surprise, Tahlia shrugged. 'Sorry, I have to agree with the romantic one on this.'

'Great,' Keely said, 'that's all I need. You two agreeing for once.'

'We're just being objective.' Emma handed her a sports drink and Keely drank deeply, hoping the electrolytes would help replenish some of the brain cells she seemed to have lost since she'd first laid eyes on Lachlan.

'Which is probably difficult in your case, seeing as he keeps finding excuses to see you. Must be terribly distracting.' Tahlia grinned and tossed her empty drink bottle into a nearby bin.

'Remind me never to tell you two another detail about my love life.' Keely slung her gym bag over her shoulder and headed for the showers.

'Love life?' Emma pounced on the words once they left her mouth as the girls fell into step beside her.

Keely bit back a groan. She shouldn't blame her friends for encouraging her. She was doing enough fairy tale building in her own head.

'Okay, you got me. I like the guy. He's perfect. There. Satisfied?'

'Not as much as you're going to be if Lucky Lachlan has his way with you over the weekend away,' Tahlia said, trying her best to look innocent while holding the door to the locker room open.

Emma giggled and Keely rolled her eyes, a small part of her hoping that her friend's prediction would come true.

Lucy's e-mail was the first Keely opened on Friday morning and, unfortunately, it didn't help her frame of mind.

To: *KeelyR@WWWDesigns.com*
From: *Lucy-PA@WWWDesigns.com*
Subject: The Perfect Man
K,
Have completed formulating quiz for *Flirt* site.
Keely's Collection was inspirational 4 the perfect man quiz.
Thought U might like to check out my work?
Maybe apply questions to LB, your PM, and get the answers back to me?
Luce

She stifled a groan. Not Lucy too! Emma and Tahlia egging her on were bad enough, now she had her trusty assistant on the case.

Quickly scanning the list of quiz questions, she couldn't help but chuckle.

The Perfect Man's most desirable asset is:
a) great pecs
b) great biceps
c) great butt
d) great 'package'

Does the Perfect Man prefer:
a) boxers
b) jocks
c) thongs
d) free-balling it

The Perfect Man looks best in:
a) a suit
b) jeans
c) underwear
d) nothing at all

The Perfect Man's best accessory is:
a) his cuff-links
b) his Palm Pilot
c) his tie-pin
d) you

Though she was tempted to answer 'd' to all of the above for a laugh, she typed a quick response.

To: *Lucy-PA@WWWDesigns.com*
  From: *KeelyR@WWWDesigns.com*
  Subject: The PM fallacy
Luce,
In my case, no such thing.

Nice work, though. Perhaps applying these questions to Aidan might be more appropriate?
Isn't he your PM?
K

For someone who loved her scrapbook, and who had enjoyed jotting down quotes from her favourite people her entire life, she suddenly wished she'd ditched *Keely's Collection* for a more practical guide. Perhaps something like *Real Men Aren't Perfect. Evaluate every relationship you've ever had and find out why.*

She'd devised her checklist as a tongue-in-cheek exercise when dumped by Ray all those years ago, though she'd forgotten to apply it when Jon had come along four years later and she'd really fallen hard. Maybe if she'd remembered it she wouldn't have gone through the heartache of losing a man she'd thought she loved at the time. She'd also realised that if a guy who'd openly professed his love for her could then run out on her after discovering her inability to have kids—then any man could.

Now, the fictitious man she'd described in her list had walked into her life. From his dark wavy hair and bluer-than-blue eyes to his fondness for doughnuts, he appeared perfect in every way.

And what was she going to do about it?

'Damned if I know,' she muttered as she scanned a few inter-office memos.

Lucy's response came in just as she'd deleted the last one.

To: *KeelyR@WWWDesigns.com*
From: *Lucy-PA@WWWDesigns.com*
Subject: R all the good ones taken?
K,
Aidan is an accountant, therefore can't be PM material
Luce

Shaking her head, she wondered when Lucy was going to wake up, take off her rose-coloured glasses—literally—and take a good look at what was right in front of her. Aidan seemed an ideal match for her and, though he appeared conservative at first glance, she knew he harboured a wild streak. After all, she'd seen the car he drove, and a maroon convertible sports car with cream leather seats didn't seem too boring to her.

Add to that the abseiling equipment she'd glimpsed in the rear seat and there were definite possibilities there.

The guy seemed to have it all—good looks, a great job, he was polite and genuinely interested in Lucy. What more did the girl need?

Promising herself this would be the last e-mail she sent before settling down to work for the day, she responded.

To: *Lucy-PA@WWWDesigns.com*
From: *KeelyR@WWWDesigns.com*
Subject: Perish the thought!
Luce,
That makes him into figures. Particularly yours if
I'm not mistaken.
Your PM is due in today.
Y don't U follow up?
K
(PS Get back to work!)

Taking a leaf out of her own book, she clicked on
the icon to bring up Lachlan's website and hoped she
could focus on work and not on the weekend ahead.
Though the logical part of her brain knew that spending time with Lachlan at his beach house was work,
she had a sneaking suspicion that her romantic side
was telling her otherwise.

Keely had watched Lachlan ride monstrous waves
perched on an impossibly small piece of fibreglass
for the last hour, her heart pounding most of the time.

However, it was nothing compared to the way it
thundered in her chest as he jogged up the beach
towards her.

The water-slicked wetsuit moulded to him like a
second skin, delineating every last muscle of his
toned body as he carried the surfboard under one arm
as if it weighed nothing at all. He'd run a hand

through his hair, sending dark spikes in all directions, while the deep blue of his eyes reflected the cloudless Torquay sky.

As he got closer his boyish grin lit a fire within her, its heat licking along every nerve-ending in her body, heightening her awareness till nothing else existed but this man, this moment.

'So, what do you think?' He planted the surfboard in the sand and leaned against it, looking like an irresistible advertisement for the sport.

'I think you're nuts for balancing on that little board and inviting the sharks to nibble at your toes.'

His smile broadened. 'Care to try?'

'The balancing or the nibbling?' The words popped out before she could stop them and his smile turned to laughter.

'I didn't know you had a foot fetish. Lucky I'm a psychologist.'

She rolled her eyes, enjoying the light-hearted banter they'd been trading all day. The drive from Melbourne to Bell's Beach had taken just over an hour, and her initial nervousness at spending so much time confined in his car had vanished as they'd made small talk.

'Then colour me crazy.'

He squatted down beside her, effectively blocking out the sun, and tucked a strand of hair behind her ear. 'Care for an in-depth one-on-one consultation?'

His voice dropped lower, its tone seductively

husky, and she knew without a shadow of a doubt that he wasn't offering her a professional evaluation.

She leaned back on her outstretched arms in an attempt to put some distance between them. If she'd been hot before, having him this close ensured she entered meltdown.

'Maybe I'm too complicated for you to figure out?'

'Maybe I like a challenge?'

'Is that what I am to you?'

He shook his head, showering her in a fine spray of seawater droplets, a welcome relief of cool against her fiery cheeks. Whatever made her think she could match wits with this man, trade quips with him like an experienced flirt?

Though she prided herself on being a savvy city girl, she was still an inexperienced amateur when it came to the male sex.

'You're an intriguing woman, Keely Rhodes. One I'd like to get to know a whole lot better.' He tilted her chin up and brushed his thumb along her bottom lip, his gaze locked on hers.

'We're here to work, not socialise,' she blurted out, eager to say anything to distract herself from the hypnotic intensity of his stare or the way her lips still tingled after his brief contact. 'Isn't that what you had in mind when we initially discussed this?'

She expected him to break eye contact, look guilty and lie through his teeth.

Instead, he surprised her.

'Why can't we do both? I thought you'd gain valuable knowledge for the website by spending time with me. You know, give it a personal touch.' He captured her hand in his, intertwining fingers in a possessive gesture that quietly thrilled her. 'However, I admit to wanting more from the weekend.'

'I'm not going to sleep with you.' She pronounced it more as a statement to convince herself rather than a warning to him.

Instead of dropping her hand, he tightened his hold. 'Wow, some guy really did a number on you, didn't he?'

To her annoyance, she blushed. Now wasn't the time or place to talk about her disastrous history with men, her self-esteem problem and the ensuing damage it had caused. If she got started, he'd be compelled to charge her by the hour! Besides, psychologists hadn't been her favourite people following long and tiresome hours spent in counselling and, though her hormones were clouding her judgement when it came to this guy, she had no intention of losing her wits completely and trusting him.

'I'd rather not talk about it.'

To her relief, he nodded. 'Fine, then I'll talk and you listen. I'm not one of your slick city guys. Sure, I like Melbourne and its vibe, but I'm a country boy at heart. I love the fresh air, the bush, the ocean.' He gestured to the vista behind him as if reinforcing his words. 'I'm not into lies or pretence. I value honesty above all else, and when I like something I acknowledge it.'

Rather than soothing her, his words sliced into her heart. Honesty? Great. What would he say if she revealed her secret to him?

Which one? a tiny voice in her head prompted— the fact that you heckled him and slandered his professional character or the one you use to push away every man who tries to get close to you?

'And I like you. That's what this is all about.'

She swallowed, buoyed by his refreshing attitude and terrified beyond belief. No man had ever been that up-front with her. And it scared her. A lot.

Searching for the right words to deflect his attention—which she liked way too much—she bumbled along in predictable fashion. 'I'm flattered, but right now I need to focus on my career. I haven't got time for anything else in my life. I'm thinking business and you're—'

'Thinking pleasure?' he interrupted, raising her hand to his mouth and nibbling on her fingertips with small, precise nips.

'Mmm...' She sighed and closed her eyes for a moment, instantly forgetting all the reasons why she shouldn't be doing this.

'Stop analysing and just feel,' he murmured, the soft touch of his mouth against her palm sending bolts of electricity shooting up her arm.

Suddenly her voice of reason gave her a big, loud wake-up call—*so much for business*—and she pulled her hand away before he could undermine her stance to keep things between them strictly professional any more than he already had. 'That's rich coming from you, the king of analysis.'

He shrugged. 'Work's work. You and me, that's something else entirely.'

She took a deep breath, hoping a lungful of sea air would clear her mind, for the longer he stared at her as if she was the only woman in the world for him, the harder it was for her to respond.

'I'm not sure what you want from me,' she said, making a lightning-quick decision to tell him exactly how she was feeling. He wanted honesty? She'd give it to him, at least for the moment.

'I want a website.' He smiled, obviously trying to lighten the mood.

'And?' she persisted, unable to shake the feeling that they'd reached an important crossroad in their brief relationship. *Working relationship*, that is.

She didn't have time for mix-ups or games. If he wanted more from her than a fabulous website, now was the time for him to speak up. And for her to run for the hills as she usually did.

His grip on her hand tightened. 'I want to get to know you better. Nothing more, nothing less. Think you can handle that?'

'As long as we don't lose sight of the real reason I'm here. And that's to work.'

Despite her false bravado, a small part of her was scared out of its wits.

She could listen to her self-talk about *He's work, he's a means to an end, he's the best opportunity for that promotion you've ever had.*

However, what would happen if she switched off the rational, clear-thinking voice inside her head and followed her heart for once?

While spending the weekend away, with him in her face all the time, it didn't bear thinking about.

CHAPTER SIX

'Is a sensitive, considerate man: a) a myth,
b) an oxymoron, c) a moron?'
Lucy, looking for Mr Right in all the wrong places.

LACHLAN flipped the steaks on the barbecue and watched Keely rustle up a salad through the kitchen window. Even with a slight frown marring her brow as she concentrated on getting the right mix of olive oil, lemon and balsamic vinegar, she looked beautiful.

He'd had a hard time concentrating on riding the waves earlier that afternoon, his mind wandering to the woman sitting on the pristine sand, watching him. He'd almost been wiped out several times but had rallied at the last moment, only to be wiped out in earnest when he'd finished surfing and seen the look in her eyes as he jogged up the beach towards her.

She'd looked at him like a woman starved, with her eye on the entrée, main course and dessert all rolled into one. He'd been flattered. Hell, he'd been ready to rip off his wetsuit and take her right then and there in the sand, discomfort be damned.

However, Keely had secrets, and not just the one about her being his late-night heckler. He'd glimpsed vulnerability, uncertainty, and what he could almost label fear in her eyes whenever he mentioned his interest in her.

Not that he'd pushed too hard yet. He wasn't a complete fool. Sure, he wanted to get to know her better, but he had a feeling that if he rushed her she would bolt quicker than his mum had at the first offer from one of her numerous lovers.

'By the look on your face, this barbecuing business is serious stuff.'

Quashing the sharp stab of pain that memories of his traitorous mother never failed to raise, he brandished the stainless steel tongs at her. 'It is. Wouldn't want you to complain about the rump being too rare.'

To his delight, she sent a pointed look at his butt and raised an eyebrow. 'Nothing wrong with a bit of rare rump. It's pretty hard to find these days.'

He laughed and wiggled the piece of anatomy she was eyeing. 'Don't go getting any ideas to sink your teeth into this just yet.'

'I wouldn't dream of it,' she said with a mischievous glint in her eyes, picking up the tongs and aiming a pinch his way. 'I'm very selective with my rump. It takes a lot of handling and careful weighing before I select the best piece.'

He sidestepped the tongs and made a grab for them in one swift movement. 'Glad to hear it. Now, if you don't mind, *this* rump is ready.' He gestured to the grill before filling a platter with two steaks, several prawn skewers and corn on the cob.

'I'm starving.' She reached for the plate, her hand brushing his, and for a split second when he raised his eyes to meet hers he read desire.

Or maybe it was a reflection of his rampant need mirrored there?

Rather than give in to the impulse to ditch the plate and haul her into his arms, he used every inch of willpower to step away and keep his response light.

'Good. I'm famous for my culinary skills.'

She followed him into the kitchen and the intensity of the previous moment dwindled away till he wondered if it had been a figment of his imagination.

'Is there anything you're not good at?' She placed the salad and herb bread on the table next to the mixed grill while he poured the merlot. 'Because, from where I'm sitting, you're almost too good to be true.'

He paused, surprised by her swift change in mood from playful to serious. In the past, he'd been labelled with the tag most guys hated, the dreaded 'nice', though the women he'd dated hadn't seemed to mind. In fact, he'd been complimented on his manners and the way he'd treated them in general. It hadn't been his fault those relationships had failed. Supposedly, nice guys always finished last, and the women he'd been involved with had seemed to reiterate the fact.

He smiled and raised his wine glass to her. 'Give me a few hours. I'm sure I'll think of something.'

She clinked glasses with him, her eyes glittering

in the muted light. 'My friends have labelled you Mr Perfect.'

'You've been talking about me with your friends?'

This was good. Very good. That meant she was more interested than she let on, though he wondered about the 'perfect' tag. No way could he live up to those expectations.

Despite their instant, intense attraction, she hardly knew him, so what had he done to deserve the accolade?

'I might've vaguely mentioned something to them, you being a new client and all.' She speared a prawn and waved her fork around as if her comment meant nothing. 'Though I wouldn't read too much into it.'

'And here I was thinking you might be falling for my charm.'

She chewed and swallowed before answering, a smile playing around the corners of her mouth. 'Sorry to disappoint. Maybe you need to brush up on your technique?'

He liked the switch back to playful and he fully intended to keep the mood light for the rest of the night.

'Oh, I fully intend to.' He reached across and ran a fingertip across her bottom lip, watching her eyes widen, the dark pools tempting enough for any man to lose himself in their depths. 'How do you think I'm doing so far?'

He could've sworn her lip trembled beneath his light touch before she leaned back slightly and broke the contact. 'Needs some work but you've got potential.'

'Thanks. That's all the encouragement I need.'

He stared at her over his wine glass, trying to gauge her reaction to his comment. He'd made his intentions more than clear over the course of the day, and if she opted out now he'd be disappointed.

She reached over and lightly tapped his glass. 'Good luck, Doc. With me, you're going to need it.'

'Sounds like a challenge.'

She laughed, a light-hearted sound that warmed his heart. It had been too long since he'd unwound in the company of a beautiful woman, especially one who sparked his interest on many levels. 'Why do all men get that gleam in their eye at the thought of a challenge?'

'Because it brings out our competitive side.'

She rolled her eyes. 'Men!'

Enjoying their teasing, he decided to push his luck. 'Speaking of my Y chromosome, when am I going to see you in a bikini? After all, we're at one of the best beaches in the world, and members of the weaker sex such as me look forward to seeing the latest in surf fashion.'

And, just like that, the shutters descended over her eyes, cloaking them in a haze of emotion he could only label as disappointment.

'Dream on.' Though the corners of her mouth tilted up in a tight smile, the action was far from a happy gesture.

Okay, so she wasn't big on bikinis. Maybe he'd try a different tack to lighten the moment. 'Hey, can't blame a guy for trying. With a body like yours, seems a shame not to show it off.'

If the shutters had descended seconds earlier, this time the blinds well and truly snapped shut. She shrugged and toyed with the napkin at the side of her plate. 'Sorry to disillusion you, but remember those old neck-to-knee swimsuits? They're skimpy compared to mine.'

She managed a short laugh but it didn't fool him. He'd made her uncomfortable and, once again, she had him confused. This Jekyll and Hyde thing she had going on was frustrating the hell out of him and putting a real dampener on his eagerness to get to know her better.

Keen to defuse the tension that suddenly enveloped them, he raised his wine glass to her. 'I've always stuck by the more is less theory, so I look forward to seeing it. Now, let's eat.'

However, as he passed her the salad he had the distinct impression that eating was the last activity she wanted to do and, for the second time in as many minutes, wondered what deep, dark secrets Keely Rhodes harboured.

Keely trailed her fingers over the book spines, reading the titles but not really absorbing them. If she'd been nervous earlier, it was nothing compared to now. Dinner had been a breeze, with Lachlan switching to small talk after their initial hiccup over his bikini joke and she'd soon relaxed.

However, she'd known it wouldn't last, and as the evening drew to a close the butterflies in her stomach took flight. Though he'd deposited her overnight bag in the spare room when they'd arrived at his beach house, she knew that didn't necessarily mean she would be sleeping in there.

She hadn't been this attracted to a man before, and though she continued focusing on work—apart from her earlier lapse into flirt mode while he barbecued— her mind kept drifting to fantasies of getting intimate in the bedroom.

He hadn't helped matters much, stripping out of that wetsuit back at the beach and asking her to hold his towel up as a shield from prying eyes as he changed. The only problem with that was *her* eyes had been the ones doing most of the prying! Though she'd done her best to avert her gaze, she was only human and couldn't help but take a peek.

And, boy, had it been worth it!

An expanse of tanned skin covered rippling muscles that belonged on an elite athlete rather than a psychologist who surfed part-time. And that butt...

She was sure the towel had slipped a notch as her hands shook while she checked out the doc's hidden talents.

'See anything that interests you?'

She jumped as he entered the lounge room, knocking half a dozen hardback novels off the shelf in the process.

Rather than rushing to her aid, as she'd expected him to do, he chuckled and sat down. 'I'd offer to help, but one concussion a week is more than enough for me.'

'Very funny.' She bent to pick up the books, wondering if she'd ever be cured of her clumsiness. The way he intruded on her thoughts constantly, she doubted it. 'Thanks for dinner, by the way. It was delicious.'

'No problem. Wait till you see what I've got for dessert.'

She almost upended the books a second time. So much for putting a dampener on her imagination. With his words, she conjured up an instant vivid image of strawberries, whipped cream and the two of them sharing dessert…in very inventive ways!

'I haven't really got a sweet tooth,' she said, aiming for nonchalant when she knew she could easily forgo the edible dessert in favour of something much more enticing—like him on a platter.

'Couldn't be weight-related.'

And, just like that, the cosy atmosphere shattered.

Thankful he couldn't see her face as she rearranged the shelf, she swallowed the lump of emotion that lodged in her throat, mentally kicking herself for believing a guy like Lachlan could be different.

Every man she'd ever known had been obsessed about looks and weight, often making jokes about 'fat chicks' who didn't care about their appearance, or chuckling over advertisements for weight loss centres. She'd learned to steel herself against their cruel judgements, despite the urge to smack them silly.

As for taking a swipe at her own eating habits, only one guy she'd casually dated had ever made that mistake—and she'd let him have it, after accidentally spilling her wine over his crotch.

Lachlan had made several remarks about her body since they'd met and, though he probably saw them as innocuous, she knew what they really were—a sign that he was just like the rest of the guys she'd ever known, hung-up over looks and little else. Not to mention a clear indication she shouldn't get involved, no matter how much her body kept telling her otherwise.

He didn't pick up on her stiffening or, if he did, he didn't let on. 'You don't need to worry about that, you look great. Trust me, you'll love this.'

His qualifier didn't help. What if she didn't *look great*? Would he even give her the time of day? She doubted it. No male had, not till she'd shed half her bodyweight and almost died in the process.

As for trust, she'd believed in it too many times to count and had been let down every time. People, especially men, were notorious for saying the T word and then doing their best to give you reasons to *mis*-trust them.

Lighten up. Before he takes his business and your chance at promotion elsewhere.

Taking a steadying breath, she turned to face him. 'What is it?'

'Close your eyes and let me guide you to it.'

'This better be good,' she said, allowing him to guide her through the room and out the door. When in actual fact she felt like bolting through it and not looking back.

'Oh, it's better than good.'

His hands were lightly resting on her hips as he gently propelled her forwards, and her skin fairly sizzled where he touched her. Damn her hormones! One minute she thought he was an insensitive clod, the next she wanted to jump him. She needed to get a grip on her wayward emotions—and fast—before she got a grip on him.

'Just a few more steps… Okay, open your eyes.'

'How did you know?' She looked at the plate piled high with doughnuts of every description, from cinnamon-dusted to choc-iced, her mouth watering at the sight.

Okay, so he'd actually meant dessert when he'd said it. Then why did she feel like a child who had just been told that Santa Claus didn't exist?

He grinned and offered her the plate. 'I saw the way you were eyeing off my doughnut the other day. If I hadn't eaten half of it already, I reckon you would've snatched it out of my hand and gobbled it in one go.'

'Very observant.'

If he only knew. She hadn't just been staring at the

doughnut when he'd walked into her office, but at the way his lips had been dusted in sugar and cinnamon, shaken by how much she wanted to lick it off.

'I've heard the way to a woman's heart is through her stomach.' He demolished two doughnuts to her one and she chuckled at his genuine enjoyment. 'So, sweet tooth or not, dig in.'

Choosing to ignore his earlier jibe about weight for the sake of her job, she selected a choc-iced, silently vowing it would be her one and only. Though she could've quite happily eaten the whole plate, her weekly allocation would be blown. She'd have to attend a Pilates class every day of the week to keep in shape.

Though she'd come a long way from her overweight days, the scare she'd received after collapsing, and the resultant devastating news that she wouldn't bear children, acted as a constant reminder to nurture her body rather than abuse it.

These days she enjoyed every morsel of food that passed her lips, exercised regularly and accepted her body shape—three things she wished she'd done as a vulnerable teen.

'If you're trying to butter me up for something, you're going about it the right way.'

Wiping his hands on a dishcloth, he said, 'Why do you always suspect an ulterior motive?'

'Because men usually have one.' She pronounced

it like the fact she knew it to be, at least in her experience.

'I'm not like all men.'

Well, he'd got that right. 'Appearances can be deceiving.'

If anyone should know, she should.

'What you see is what you get with me.'

Her gaze flickered over him, taking in his relaxed posture, one leg crooked over the other, his hands braced at his back. He was propped against the sink, looking sinfully handsome in denim which hugged his hips and a black polo shirt that moulded his torso as if it had been made for him.

If what she saw was what she'd get, she'd be a lucky girl indeed.

'And what's that?'

Though she wasn't in the mood for word games, she had a feeling that the developing tension between them needed to be addressed before she did something crazy, like fling herself at him.

Or, worse yet, sleepwalk right into his bed.

'Apparently, I'm Mr Perfect.' He smiled, though she noticed the way he shifted, as if uncomfortable with the tag. 'Or so you tell me.'

She sighed, wishing she'd never told him that.

'I might've mentioned something along those lines in a moment of weakness, but don't hold me to it.'

He shrugged, drawing her attention to the breadth of his shoulders. 'Don't worry, I won't. Living up to a title like that would be hell.'

No, hell would be taking a chance on a guy like you.

Trying to ignore her racing pulse, she crossed the kitchen and stood in front of him, torn between wanting to melt into his arms or walking straight past him—and temptation—and out the back door.

'As much as I'm enjoying this conversation, I'm beat. I think I'll go to bed.'

She didn't move a muscle as he leaned towards her, her heart hammering against her ribs. Though she hadn't meant it as an invitation, she realised her declaration had sounded like one, and her body quivered with anticipation, every fibre alert to a possible incoming sensual assault.

'Pleasant dreams,' he murmured, brushing a soft, lingering kiss across her lips, a kiss that left her breathless and yearning.

However, before she could blink, he ran a hand lightly over her hair, cupped her cheek for an instant and walked away.

CHAPTER SEVEN

*'Most men I know are like mascara. They run at
the first sign of emotion.'*
Tahlia Moran, best friend and cynic.

'How was the weekend?'

Keely plopped on the couch next to Tahlia and
hugged a cushion to her chest. 'Good.'

Tahlia quirked an eyebrow. 'And I thought Librans
were supposed to be well-balanced, eloquent individ-
uals.'

'What can I say? He lived up to his perfect reputation.' Worse luck.

'*In* and *out* of the bedroom?' Tahlia leaned forward, her eyes gleaming at the promise of gossip.

'I can only vouch for outside of it.'

Her friend's eyes almost popped out of her head.
'You mean he didn't make a move?'

Keely shook her head, mentally kicking herself for
being disappointed.

'Let me get this straight. This guy goes to all the
trouble to get you out to his love-nest by the ocean,
practically strips naked in front of you, cooks you
dinner and then nothing?'

Keely reached for her wine and took a sip before

answering. 'Nice twist, but in actual fact it was his beach house, he had to change after surfing, we shared cooking duties and—'

'Nothing, right?'

Keely sighed and nodded. 'Yeah, nothing.'

'I don't get it.' Tahlia flicked her strawberry-streaked fringe out of her eyes and popped several chocolate-coated peanuts into her mouth before continuing. 'The guy oozes sex appeal, he definitely has the hots for you, you're keen on him and you're two consenting adults. You do the math!'

'By my calculations, I scored a big fat zero.'

Keely had relived that sequence in the kitchen after dinner a thousand times in her mind. She'd been torn at the time between wanting to shrug off her reservations and get physical with Lachlan and holding him at arm's length. He'd annoyed the heck out of her with his cracks about bikinis and watching her weight, yet when he'd followed up with a compliment she'd been putty in his hands again.

When she'd crossed the kitchen and told him she was going to bed it had almost been a challenge, and his reaction hadn't been what she'd expected.

A chaste goodnight kiss, albeit on the lips, hadn't satisfied her. Not by a long shot. And what had she done about it?

Nothing.

She'd muttered something about being exhausted and rushed out of the room before she—or he—could change their minds.

His behaviour puzzled her. Despite the vibes she kept getting from him, he hadn't laid a finger on her. The guys she'd dated in the past would've taken advantage of the situation in a second. However, Lachlan Brant was living up to his reputation as Mr Perfect more and more every day, a fact that wasn't good for her peace of mind.

'Are you sure he's not gay?'

Keely glared at Tahlia. 'What do you think?'

An impish grin spread across her friend's face. 'Nah.' She dipped into the bowl again, managing to throw several nuts in the air, tilt her head back and catch them in her mouth. 'So, where to from here?'

Keely laughed. 'Nice to see our Director of Sales hasn't lost her touch. Where do you learn those tricks anyway? Another one of your courses?'

As if her friend wasn't busy enough, she also frequented business courses in her spare time, always pushing herself in all facets of her life, as if making up for a lack of something.

Tahlia sniffed and repeated the performance, this time managing to capture two peanuts in her mouth at once. 'They don't teach you this in Business Etiquette 101.'

'Does the college run courses in How To Read Men 101? And, if so, where do I sign up?'

Tahlia munched on the peanuts for a moment, her brow furrowed. 'Maybe he thinks you're not all that keen. After all, you've been sending him mixed messages.'

'Flirting is one thing, sleeping with him another. Besides, I thought he had a right to know up front so there'd be no misunderstandings later.'

'But I thought you wanted more?'

'Yes…no…I don't know! Stop confusing me!'

Tahlia chuckled. 'I think you're doing enough of that for the both of us. Why don't you just go for it? Don't forget, that's what your horoscope said.'

'They're called that for a reason. In my case, it's a horror-scope.'

'Don't mess with the stars.'

'Don't mess with my head.'

'Hey, that's the Doc's job, not mine.'

Keely stood and crossed the room, staring out at the stunning bay view. She loved watching the world go by from her sixth-floor apartment, particularly at dusk when the water took on a mauve hue.

Tahlia was right. She should stop procrastinating and go for it with Lachlan. What did she have to lose? It wasn't as if she was expecting happily-ever-after or anything remotely like it. They could date, have fun, and make the most of every day as people her age should be doing.

Why did she need to constantly overanalyse every situation?

Because you're in deeper than you think.

Telling her voice of reason to shut up, she turned back to Tahlia.

'Thanks for the advice, Dear Abby. Now, how

about we get down to the business of planning Em's surprise party?'

Tahlia scrutinised her for a moment before shrugging her shoulders. 'Nice change of topic. I'll buy it.' She picked up her pocket organiser and started flipping pages. 'I've booked Sammy's, organised the finger food with Andy, and drinks will be buy-your-own over the bar. How is the guest list coming along?'

'All done, though she's going to be pretty bummed that Harry isn't going to be there.'

'Time she got over him. Who pines after their first love for that long anyway? Men are all the same; they just have different faces so that we can tell them apart.'

Keely chuckled at her friend's cynicism. Though Tahlia had men falling at her feet, she seemed oblivious, hell-bent on conquering the world rather than the male species. Despite the way she ignored them, they still flocked.

'I think it's romantic. And, from the photos I've seen of the guy, can you blame her?'

'Point taken. What about a present?'

Keely picked up a magazine from the coffee table and flipped it open. 'I know this is kitschy, but what do you think?'

Tahlia took one look at the page and almost fell off the couch laughing. 'A Barry Manilow figurine? You've got to be joking!'

Keely joined in the laughter. 'But she loves the

guy almost as much as Harry!' She looked at the picture of pint-sized Barry and cracked up again. 'I think he's kinda cute.'

'And I think you're kinda crazy. Besides, I have a better idea. What about that toe ring she was eyeing off in the jeweller's window the other day?'

'The one with her star sign on it?'

Tahlia nodded. 'I think our Miss Conservative is going through a rash patch at the moment. She's never worn a toe ring in her life.'

Keely clicked her fingers and practically bounced around the room in her enthusiasm. 'Great idea. She's definitely after a change of image, so we can also do a makeover. Clothes, make-up, hair, the works!'

Tahlia's eyes fairly gleamed. 'Now you're talking. We can—'

The loud peal of the security buzzer stopped her mid-sentence and Keely glanced at her watch, wondering who her visitor could be. She rarely had company on a Monday night, apart from one of the girls, and the only reason they popped in so early in the week was usually to discuss some man problem from the weekend before.

She pressed the intercom button and said, 'Who is it?' And almost jumped back when Lachlan's deep tones filtered through the static speakers.

'Sorry to barge in on you like this, but do you have a minute?'

Keely turned to look at Tahlia, who leaped off the couch and gathered up her stuff in record time.

'Don't mind me, I'm outta here. Let the man up, for goodness' sake,' she mouthed while heading towards the door.

Keely glanced down at her candy-pink sweatpants and matching hood top and grimaced. 'Look at me. He can't see me like this. I look like fairy floss!'

Tahlia's wicked grin didn't reassure her. 'With any luck, he might eat you.' She gave her a saucy wave and sauntered towards the door. 'And I want details. Don't worry about buzzing him up. I'll let him in on my way out. Later.'

Keely groaned and shooed her away and, as Tahlia left, she rushed around the room frantically trying to clean up. Housework wasn't one of her strong suits, and as she'd been away for the weekend she hadn't had time to devote her scant hour to the usual once-over.

Resisting the urge to shove everything under her couch, she settled for making a few neat piles of magazines and clearing away the remnants of the girlie feast Tahlia had been devouring—wine, pretzels and chocolate-coated peanuts—just in time for Lachlan's knock at the door.

Smoothing back the wisps of hair escaping from her ponytail, and biting her bottom lip for a bit of colour, she opened the door. 'Hi. What brings you by?'

His gaze flicked over her and, rather than seeing

distaste, she read approval in the way his eyes lit up. However, it didn't appease her. She knew she looked a fright and wondered what he was playing at pretending otherwise.

'Sorry to drop by unannounced, but I'm going away for a few days on business and thought you might like this info.'

Her heart sank at his revelation. Just when she'd decided to take the plunge and see where all this tension between them was leading, he had to go away?

'Where are you going?'

He smiled, the simple action illuminating his face and speeding up her heart-rate in a second.

'I'll make you a deal. If you ask me in, I'll tell you.'

'Oops, sorry.' She stepped back, wondering why her manners deserted her whenever he set foot on her doorstep. It probably had something to do with the way he looked, and sounded, and smelt, but that was no excuse.

'Did I catch you in the middle of something?'

She closed the door behind him and resisted the urge to lean against it and sigh. He looked amazing in a dark grey suit, white shirt and burgundy tie— every ounce the consummate professional—and she looked like fairy floss! Not fair.

Smiling, she strolled across the room as if he popped in to see her every day of the week—she wished—and indicated he take a seat before plopping down into one herself. 'No, not really. Tahlia and I were just planning a surprise party for a friend.'

'Was Tahlia the stunning woman who let me in?'

A shaft of jealousy pierced her gut. Okay, so it was true, but did he have to notice that Tahlia's tall, slim figure could grace the cover of a magazine?

She nodded and wished she hadn't removed her make-up and changed when she'd got home. Tahlia had come straight from work and still looked a million dollars in her red power suit, with not a hair out of place at the end of the day.

'Tahlia is Director of Sales at WWW Designs. We've been friends for ages.'

He looked suitably impressed. 'Must be a rule at your workplace to only employ beautiful women.' He paused and allowed his glance to slide over her, very slowly, from head to foot. 'I like your casual look, by the way.'

She tried to detect a hint of sarcasm and came up lacking. He thought she was beautiful? Looking like *this*? Now she knew for sure. The Doc needed *his* head examined!

'Wish I could get out of these clothes,' he said, sticking a finger between his collar and tie in an attempt to loosen it.

You can.

She stared at him for a long silent moment before swallowing those two little words and turning away.

'Would you like a drink?'

'I'd kill for a coffee,' he said, following her into the kitchen. 'So, whose birthday party is it?'

'I'll trade you. You tell me where you're going—' *and why you're really here*, she thought '—and I'll tell you about the party.'

He leaned against the benchtop as she switched on the percolator and she wished he wouldn't look so at home in her apartment. It would make it hard to forget him when the assignment finished. And even harder if they started something that didn't involve work. She wouldn't be able to stand it when the inevitable split came—and it would. No matter how close they got, how well they clicked, he'd bolt like the rest the minute he learned the truth.

'Fair enough. The TV station hosting my new show is sending me to Sydney for a couple of days to check out something similar they screen up there.'

'Sounds interesting.' She poured coffee and added milk and two sugars to his, thinking how strange to find a man with a similar sweet tooth to hers, even if she'd told him otherwise. However, she added an artificial sweetener to hers, forgoing her passion for sweetness in exchange for zero calories.

While she had her head stuck in the cupboard, looking for some chocolate biscuits for him, he said, 'So what's the deal with the party? Is it some old boyfriend you don't want to talk about?'

She lifted her head too quickly and clunked it on the shelf above, cursing silently. There, that had to be another fault; he sounded jealous. Though, in a way, she should be flattered rather than annoyed.

'The party's for Emma, another friend I work with. And, as for not wanting to talk about boyfriends, that's true. I'm not one to kiss and tell.'

To his credit, he let that last comment go. She'd said it as some weird sort of challenge, almost daring him to ask about her previous relationships, though for the life of her she couldn't figure out why.

'That's good to know.' He took a sip of coffee before placing the mug on the counter. 'I like to keep my business private.'

Huh? Had he just said what she thought he'd said?

Rather than taking the easy way out and laughing off his comment, she pounced. 'Are you implying that you'd like to be my boyfriend?'

He fixed her with a stare that bored straight down to her soul, as if trying to probe into her innermost feelings. 'I'm not implying anything; I'm stating a fact.'

She hadn't moved since he'd dropped his little bombshell, her feet rooted to the spot, and he crossed the kitchen in a second.

'Pretty confident, aren't you?' She tilted her head up to meet his gaze, her pulse tripping as his eyes darkened to midnight.

'I call it how it is.'

A little demon lodged in her mind and prodded her with its pitchfork, urging her to provoke him further.

'And how's that?'

'You, me, dating. Seems straightforward to me.'

She didn't resist as he lowered his head towards her with infinite slowness and, with a sigh, closed her eyes. She'd been waiting for this, hoping for it, since that first time in her office when she'd been sure he wanted to kiss her. And if she'd thought the brief, gentle peck he'd delivered at the beach house at the weekend had been good, it wasn't a patch on this.

The minute his lips touched hers, it felt as if a match had been touched to a bonfire and whoosh! They both went up in flames.

Heat sizzled between them as she plastered her body against his, her hands delving into his hair in an effort to pull his head closer. He didn't disappoint, moulding her to his body with hands that wandered everywhere with skilled precision, stroking her till she gasped out loud.

Angling his head, he slid his mouth across hers in an erotic fusion, leaving her breathless. She melded into him, forgetting every last rational reason why she shouldn't be doing this.

His arms tightened around her and she felt his hard chest muscles tense beneath her hands. The fact he must work out was a fleeting thought. He felt so good, tasted so good, that she didn't want this moment to end, ever.

'Wow,' she murmured as his mouth left hers to

trail hot, open-mouthed kisses to her neck and back up again.

A shudder rippled through her as his hand slipped under her top and cupped her breast, sending fiery sparks of pleasure shooting to her core.

He broke the kiss to whisper against her mouth. 'What do you think of this dating thing so far?'

She clutched at the lapels of his jacket, knowing that if she let go she'd slide in a molten heap to the floor. 'Not bad.'

A smile tugged at the corners of his mouth, drawing her attention to those masterful lips and the fact that all he had to do was twitch them in her direction for desire to pool deep within.

'Mmm…maybe I need to brush up on my technique?'

Exhaling a shaky breath, she leaned her head against his chest. 'With me?'

Those two little words came out soft and needy, when she'd sworn never to be like that ever again.

She didn't *need* anyone. Needing only led to pain. And loss. And devastation.

He toyed with the strands of her ponytail while holding her close with his other arm.

'If you're volunteering for the job, it's all yours.'

Say no! A thousand reasons flashed through her foggy brain in a second.

He's toying with you.

He'll bolt when he learns the truth.

He's too darn perfect and you'll never satisfy a

man like that. Once he sees the real you, he'll dump you quicker than he can say love handles.

Ignoring her fears, she lifted her head, looked him in the eye and managed a mute nod in response.

Lachlan grinned as he left Keely's apartment building, more wired than he'd been in ages. He needed to get home ASAP and go for a long bike ride, desperate to take the edge off his physical hunger for the woman who tied him up in knots.

He'd hoped to steal a quick goodbye kiss before heading interstate and it must be his lucky day, for not only had his wish come true, it had blown his mind in the process.

Attraction was one thing, off-the-scale rampant need was another, and the minute his lips had touched hers he'd known he wouldn't be satisfied till they shared more than a kiss, their bodies entwined, slaking a thirst that had him parched. For her.

However, in the midst of his fantasy, a tiny doubt sprouted and took root. Keely had shown him a side he didn't like, a side that reminded him too much of his mother. She'd blown hot and cold too, all over him one minute, walking out the next, and taking a big part of his heart in the process.

As much as he wanted to explore the attraction between him and Keely, he'd better watch out. He didn't have room in his life for a fickle woman, no matter how attractive.

In fact, if he were giving a caller advice, he'd

probably warn him to stay well clear of a woman who looked eager to devour him most of the time yet could change into the Ice Princess in a split second. And, though he'd admit to inadvertently arousing her anger by his throwaway attempts at humour, he knew her mood swings would get on his nerves after a while. A short while.

However, in this case, he had no intention of practising what he preached. He didn't want to stay clear of Keely; he wanted to get closer to her. The closer the better.

And if her mood pendulum swung once too often he'd walk away, heart intact.

CHAPTER EIGHT

'A good man is like quality coffee. He's rich, warm and can keep you up all night long.'
Chrystal Jones, a woman who should know.

'NO OFFENCE, but this idea for *Flirt* sucks!'

Keely looked at the sheet Tahlia handed her and raised an eyebrow. 'But that's the image they're after. Bold, contemporary, out to make a statement. They're a new magazine and they want something totally different so I went all out.'

Tahlia merely shook her head in response and handed the draft to Emma.

To her surprise, Emma's brow crinkled in a frown. 'You've done that all right,' she muttered, following the flow chart with her index finger before coming to an abrupt stop. 'Sorry, sweetie, I have to agree with Tahlia. This idea will be impossible to animate, let alone sell. And that's the bottom line here, making *Flirt* look as attractive as possible to the Heads.'

Emma placed her draft on the conference table between them and reached for a doughnut. 'And, unless you want ours to roll, I suggest we come up with a new design before the Rottie starts snapping at our heels.'

Keely sighed, ignoring the doughnuts for once, and took a long sip of her Macchiato. 'Maybe I'm losing my touch?'

'More like losing your mind over you-know-who,' Tahlia muttered, cradling a steaming cappuccino in her hands.

Keely ignored the jibe. They were meeting to brainstorm ideas for *Flirt* magazine, their newest and biggest client, not dish the dirt on her status with Lachlan.

'When you said meet for a D&M, I assumed you meant the usual doughnuts and Macchiato, not the deep and meaningful conversation that often accompanies any one of us getting involved with a man.'

Though she needed to focus on her work—she could almost reach out and touch the promotion to Director of Graphic Design—the temptation to talk about Lachlan hovered in front of her. However, she knew that if the girls got her started she'd probably never stop.

'Do you want to talk about it?' Emma asked, the worried frown on her brow deepening. 'This stuff can wait.' She waved at the *Flirt* file as if it meant nothing, which they all knew wasn't true. If they ever lost an account like this one, it would probably mean their jobs would disappear quicker than a click of a mouse button on a delete key.

Keely glanced at Tahlia, knowing that out of the three of them she was the most driven. Her career meant everything to her, and if they veered from work during these regular meetings she would pull them back into line.

Today, Tahlia threw both hands in the air. 'What the hell? I'm up for all the gruesome details if you are.'

Keely placed her cup on the table, leaned back and folded her arms. 'Well, there isn't a lot to tell. He's a man, I'm a woman, and we're dating.'

'You're *what*?' Emma screeched, and grabbed her arm. 'When did all this happen? How did it happen? How far have you gone? What—?'

'Whoa! One question at a time, Em.' Tahlia leaned forward like a co-conspirator. 'Did you do the deed yet?'

Keely laughed and made a zipping action over her lips.

'Your lips are sealed, huh?'

She nodded at Tahlia, a smirk spreading across her face at the expression on Emma's.

'Now see what you've done,' Emma said to Tahlia. 'Ask one crass question like that and she clams up. Now what are we going to do?'

Tahlia winked at Emma. 'We could always go directly to the source and ask him. I'm sure Lachlan would love a phone call to his talkback show, asking about his latest love.'

'You wouldn't!' Keely burst out, knowing her friends were joking and enjoying it.

After her lonely teenage years, she'd thanked her lucky stars when she'd met Emma and Tahlia and for the instant bond that had sprung up between them. She valued their friendship more with each passing day and looked forward to their teasing as much as their kooky sense of humour and their loyalty.

Emma nodded. 'Yes, we would. Unless you give us some small titbit of gossip so we can live our lives vicariously through you.'

'Fine.' Keely took a moment to refill her cup from the coffee machine before responding. 'We're going away this weekend to Hepburn Springs for a little R and R. He's away on business in Sydney till then so in a way, it's our first official date.'

Tahlia rolled her eyes. 'Yeah, right. As if you haven't been dating for the last week anyway.'

Keely glanced at Emma, expecting her friend to say something. To her surprise, Emma chewed on her pen, a slight frown creasing her brow.

'What's up, Em?' Keely had enough doubts swirling through her head without her friends joining in. If something was bothering Em, the romantic dreamer of the three of them, it had to be serious.

'You really like this guy, don't you?'

Keely nodded, still a little stunned herself at the swiftness of the whole thing. Lachlan had entered her life just over a week ago and swept her off her feet. She never dropped her guard that quickly, though with Mr Perfect bombarding her with his presence on a daily basis, what choice did she have?

Thankfully, this time she had no intention of letting her heart rule her head. She knew the score: date a gorgeous guy, have some fun, don't get serious. No need for messy confessions about her past, no qualms about calling it quits. Simple.

Emma leaned forward and the frown deepened. 'I thought so. I've never seen you like this over a guy. Just don't get hurt, okay?'

Emma's concern puzzled her. She'd thought her friend would be doing cartwheels instead of doling out dire warnings.

'I really like him, Em, but I'm not about to do anything stupid.' *Like fall in love.*

No, this relationship would be light-hearted, casual, fun. They were dating, not on trial for potential marriage, and in that case her secret wouldn't even come into play.

'If you want my opinion, I think it's about time you lost it over a guy. All this realism garbage you spout gets a bit boring after a while.'

Keely smiled at Tahlia, knowing she could count on her for an honest update of the situation.

'On that note, I think we should get back to business. *Flirt* magazine should be our number one priority right now.'

At least during business hours.

She would have to make a conscious effort to concentrate on work for the rest of the week and banish the thought of her weekend away with Lachlan. Having him interstate and not popping up on her doorstep would certainly help, though her insomnia had taken a turn for the worse lately, and all she could think about while lying in bed at night was how far she was willing to take this dating business—and the possible repercussions—if the unthinkable happened.

By the way her emotions had been careening out of control around him she knew she had to tread carefully.

Dating Lachlan would be fine, loving him disastrous.

Though for the life of her she couldn't back away now. She deserved some happiness, however fleeting, and dating Lachlan promised to deliver in that department. In spades.

If anything, this weekend would be fun, and it had been too long since she'd had any with a man. Sure, her life as a city girl was rewarding, but she'd be lying if she didn't admit to a certain emptiness, a yearning for something more. And, right now, she knew Lachlan could fill that void—and how!

Keely jumped as Tahlia clicked her fingers in front of her face. 'Snap out of it, dating girl. Focus.'

Keely sent a sheepish smile her friends' way, banished thoughts of Lachlan from her mind and tried to do exactly that.

'You don't do things by halves, do you?' Keely glanced around the mud-brick cottage, admiring the antique furniture, the plump throw-cushions and a fireplace that just beckoned to be laid in front of. 'This place is beautiful.'

Lachlan deposited their overnight bags inside the door and looked up, his stare doing strange things to her insides even at a distance. 'You're beautiful.'

Though she knew his compliments were part of his charisma, as natural to him as breathing, a small part of her couldn't help but wish he truly meant them. Before a larger part told her to wake up! She looked in the mirror every morning, certain that her peculiar hazel eyes, brown hair and curvaceous body were nothing special. And far from beautiful.

She stood there, transfixed, as he crossed the room. Her brain—not to mention her body—had gone haywire the minute he'd picked her up from her apartment, his sizzling kiss a greeting she wouldn't forget in a hurry.

He'd said he'd missed her, but not half as much as she'd missed him. Was she insane? She'd known him less than two weeks. She'd recited 'don't fall in love…don't fall in love…' enough times over the last few days in the hope it would make a lasting impression. It hadn't, and she was at serious risk of losing her heart to this man.

If she hadn't lost it already.

'Nothing to say?' He tilted her chin up with his index finger while his thumb created havoc by brushing gently over her bottom lip. 'That would be a first.'

She stared into his eyes, knowing that whatever

happened between them she'd never forget that unique shade of blue. 'Are you suggesting I have a big mouth?'

His gaze dropped to her lips. 'There's nothing wrong with the size of it from where I'm standing. Nor the rest of you, for that matter.'

Oh-oh. There he went again. Another throwaway comment about her body. Sheesh, what was she thinking, losing her heart to a guy who was probably only interested in a svelte figure?

The minute his arms slipped around her she had her answer. She *wasn't* thinking. And it could prove her biggest downfall yet.

Just shut up and kiss me, she wanted to yell. Anything to distract from her doubts.

'Why don't you show me how much you missed me?' she said, sending him a coy smile designed to tempt.

'Again? There's no pleasing some women.'

She snuggled into him, inhaling his scent and allowing it to wash over her in welcome waves. She had to discover the soap he used and buy a cake of the stuff to keep next to her pillow. Maybe if she didn't have his body near her at night, his smell would be the next best thing to help her drift off to sleep?

'On the contrary, I'm very easy to please.'

He stroked her back, his hand burning a scorching trail through the thin fabric of her top. 'Tell me how.'

'Well, seeing as we're in Hepburn Springs, aka spa

country, why don't you start with drawing me a mineral bath, followed by a massage, topped off with a facial?' She accompanied her words by burying her face in his neck and nipping a light trail to his jaw.

'I hear the nearby spa facility offers all that and more.'

His hand stilled in its exploration of her back as she planted a row of tiny kisses along his jaw and upwards, till she reached the outer corner of his mouth.

'Who needs to go to a facility for all that pampering? I can offer you *all that and more* right here.'

He turned his head ever so slightly, fusing his lips to hers with the lightest touch.

The slow, burning kiss affected her more than any they'd shared before. As he deepened it, and she plastered her body against his, she wondered if this amazing toe-curling experience and its accompanying feelings indicated she'd already fallen for him, despite her vows to do anything but. Or could it just be plain old-fashioned lust?

'Stop thinking and just feel,' he murmured, caressing her body with skilled patience till she almost purred.

'Feeling is scary,' she said, arching against him despite herself, unable to stop the powerful surge of emotion that she didn't dare label love that drew her to him.

'I won't let you down.' He pulled away slightly,

cupped her cheek and stared into her eyes, and for one endless moment, she almost believed him.

'Can we slow things down a bit?' As the words left her mouth, she wanted to take them back.

She'd taken things slow her entire life, pulling away from people, sabotaging relationships with men, not willing to get too close. And where had it got her?

Alone. Unable to sleep at night. And still hoping for the perfect man to walk into her life and rescue her from all the insecurities that plagued her as a result of knowing the one thing she couldn't be in this lifetime—a mother.

Now the man of her dreams had come along and she was still balking, still holding back. Why? Wasn't he worth taking a risk for?

And in that moment she knew without a shadow of a doubt that she wouldn't think, analyse or hold back this weekend. She would 'go for it' as Tahlia had advised, and damn the consequences.

'Whatever you want.' He hugged her tightly and she relaxed, knowing that at least for the next two days everything would be all right.

Despite her fears, she did trust him. He seemed to be more intuitive than most men she'd known, so why shouldn't she take a chance and see where it led her?

'The girls were right. You are Mr Perfect.'

He smiled and planted a quick peck on the tip of her nose. 'In that case, I'd better start living up to my reputation. How about I draw you a mineral bath first and organise that massage you crave?'

'Mmm…sounds like heaven,' she said, knowing the only thing she really craved right now was him, but too scared to let go of all her reservations at once.

He released her and she immediately felt cold, bereft. 'Why don't you get changed and I'll call you when the bath's ready?'

She touched his cheek briefly, hoping he could read the clear signal in her eyes, the one that said *I like you. A lot.*

'Thanks for inviting me this weekend. I'm really looking forward to it.'

'So am I.' He looked ready to drag her back into his arms and she didn't move, already recognising it as a haven she could easily get used to. Instead, he gave her a gentle tap on the bottom. 'Now go.'

She grabbed her bag and headed into the bedroom before the anticipation of sharing more than a kiss with Lachlan sent her sprawling. Or, better yet, breaking one of the priceless antiques in his friend's holiday home.

Now wasn't the time for clumsiness. She'd come to the decision that this weekend was about romance and she had every intention to enjoy it.

Lachlan glanced around the bathroom for the final time, hoping Keely would like it. He'd always thought candles and flowers were reserved for a dinner table, but Will, his friend who owned this place—and a regular Romeo with the ladies from all accounts—had insisted the way to make a woman feel special was to use stuff like that in the bathroom.

So he had and, though it wasn't his thing, he had to admit the room looked pretty amazing. He'd never done anything like this before, but then he'd never liked a woman this much before.

It had taken every ounce of his willpower not to drag Keely into his arms and never let go earlier. The expression in her eyes had almost begged him to, in stark contrast to her whispered words to take it slow.

Despite her sassy attitude she appeared nervous, and the last thing he wanted was to scare her away. She meant too much to him and, though he might not ever take the relationship past the dating stage, who said they couldn't date for months? Maybe years, if he was lucky?

Marriage wasn't for everyone, and he knew plenty of people who remained in partnerships without an official piece of paper their entire lives. Hell, he'd counselled more married couples than those who weren't, and even if he hadn't seen the devastation the institution could wreak first hand with his parents, he would've probably stayed away from it anyway.

However, that didn't mean he couldn't enjoy a woman's company in exclusivity and he had every intention of making the most of his time with Keely. If she let him.

He'd glimpsed the vulnerability in her eyes repeatedly, as if she wanted to trust him but couldn't, and, though they hadn't discussed it yet, he had a feeling there was more to it than a past boyfriend. She retreated inwards at times, to a place she wouldn't let anyone else into and, though he respected her privacy, he needed to discover the reason behind her occasional aloofness before it drove a wedge between them.

Thanks to his deceitful mother, he stuck to the old adage 'honesty is the best policy' with an almost obsessive intensity and, though it might be too early to pry into Keely's secrets, he needed to know the cause of that fearful expression in her eyes at times—and who, or what, had put it there—before they got in too deep. As for her strange withdrawal from him when he made the occasional joke, it hadn't happened for a few days now and he'd lowered his guard, liking her warm, spontaneous side more and more.

A soft knock at the door had him casting one last critical look around the bathroom before he opened it.

'I thought you might've fallen in,' she said, pulling the robe she wore tighter across her front.

He tried to concentrate on what she'd just said, he really did, but it proved impossible with her standing there in a pale blue cotton robe looking like a cross between a knowing temptress and Orphan Annie.

He'd never known a woman so full of contrasts—

one minute the savvy city girl, the next a defenceless waif who looked ready to bolt at the first sign of trouble.

Luckily, the only trouble she would encounter here would be if he couldn't control his raging libido. He felt like a teenager around her, a totally foreign feeling. He was usually a man in control, a man who prided himself on being so. Though right now, with Keely standing in front of him looking good enough to eat, he was having a damn hard time remembering it.

However, if she wanted to take things slow, he would, even if he died of lust in the process.

'No, just making sure everything was ready for you.' He opened the door wider and gestured her in. 'Come in.'

She stepped past him and he caught a faint waft of apples. She used a fruity shampoo, and when he'd been away in Sydney he'd found himself consuming apples by the basketful just so he could enjoy the smell of them and remind himself of her. Pathetic, really, but who could blame him? She'd got under his guard so quickly and so thoroughly his head spun.

He watched her mouth open slightly as she looked around, enjoying her reaction. Despite his feeling silly about the candles and flower petals, the appreciative gleam in her eyes vindicated his actions and made him feel ten feet tall.

'This is incredible,' she murmured, reaching out

to take hold of his hand. 'No one's ever done anything like this for me before. Thank you.'

He squeezed her hand before raising it to his lips and kissing it. 'Take your time in here. Enjoy.'

Keely stared at Lachlan, the muted light cast by countless candles illuminating his face in a sensual glow.

The trouble he'd gone to in here had blown her away: the candles, the scented bubble bath, the rose petals floating on the water's surface, the fluffy white bath sheet hanging on a towel warmer and the soft jazz playing in the background. The room almost drugged her with its ambience, yet she had to remain focused if she were to thank the man responsible properly.

'Lachlan, I...I—'

'Shh...I know.' He held a finger up to her lips, effectively removing the need for her stuttered thanks. 'See you when you get out.'

Tears sprang into her eyes as he shut the door and as she stepped out of her robe and sank into the blissful warmth of the bath, she didn't know if they were tears of gratitude or—dared she admit it?—tears of a much deeper emotion she'd vowed to avoid.

CHAPTER NINE

'It's not the size of the wand that's important, it's the way the magician wields it.'

Chrystal, an expert on wands.

KEELY had tried to switch off her thoughts as she soaked in the bath. She'd imagined floating on an endless blue ocean, sitting beside a tinkling waterfall and swimming with playful dolphins. However, her relaxation techniques had had the same effect as they usually did when she tried them at home to drop off to sleep: nothing.

Instead, every time she'd closed her eyes Lachlan's image had popped up in front of her—his smile, the way his eyes crinkled in the corners when he laughed, how his eyes glowed after he'd just kissed her. Endless images that flitted across her mind, reminding her of how much she wanted him.

And how much she wanted to let go of her reservations and love him.

Yes, she'd finally admitted it. Despite being a realist with both feet firmly planted on the ground, despite all her silent protestations, and despite the fact that falling for a man like Lachlan would only end in heartache for them both, she was inches away from falling in love.

Women in love did stupid things. She'd seen it time and time again with her friends and office colleagues, not to mention first hand. Though, strangely enough, what she was about to do couldn't be termed stupid. In fact, the tension between Lachlan and her had been building towards this since they'd first met. If she believed half the cosmic stuff Tahlia was into, she would almost say it was fated.

Taking a deep breath and tying her robe together, she ventured out of the bathroom. This was it. No backing down, no chickening out. No doubts about what he'd think of her body and whether she'd turn him on or not.

She wanted him and was determined to show him exactly how much. And if he was half the man she thought he was, despite his occasional insensitive comments, he'd accept her just the way she was.

'Lachlan?'

The house seemed strangely silent. Dusk had fallen while she'd been soaking in the tub and no lights had been switched on yet.

'In here.' She heard a muffled reply and followed it into what she'd assumed was a third bedroom.

'What are you up to now...?' She trailed off as she opened the door and stepped into another fantasy.

'Thought you might like a massage after your bath,' he said, gesturing to the table set up in the middle of the room, covered in thick towels.

She stepped into the room, shaking her head in amazement. If she'd thought the bathroom had been impressive, it had nothing on this—a slow-burning fire, champagne on ice, lavender permeating the air from an oil-burner and soulful sax playing in the background. All in all, she could've spent a month in this room, as long as the man standing in the centre of it, with a proud grin on his handsome face, came with it.

'If you're trying to seduce me, you're doing a good job.' She smiled and crossed the room, standing on the opposite side of the massage table.

He shook his head. 'This isn't about seduction.'

'Then what's it about?' Her heart thudded as he walked around the table and traced her cheek with the back of a finger.

'I wanted to do something nice for you, to make you feel half as good as you've made me feel since I met you.'

'But I haven't done anything.' She shook her head slightly, wondering if the prolonged soak had fogged up her brain as well as the bathroom mirrors.

'You don't need to.' His hand dropped to her shoulder, where his fingers toyed with the collar of her robe, lightly skimming her heated skin beneath it. 'You've made me happy just by being you. I haven't dated in a while and have forgotten how special it can be with the right person.'

She stared at him, speechless. In all the years when

her self-esteem had taken a beating, where had a guy like this been?

Correction, where had *this* guy been?

She'd been through the wringer with her weight issues, the accompanying hang-ups, the brush with an eating disorder that had ruined her chance at having children and the subsequent ramifications on her relationships with men since. Not to mention the hours of counselling that had left her questioning her own belief system rather than helping her overcome her problems.

And here, now, with just a few words, he'd made her feel whole again.

She blinked back the tears that had sprung into her eyes and reached up to twine her arms around his neck. 'You know what I said earlier, about taking things slow?'

He slid his arms around her, the heat radiating off him warming her better than the slow-burning fire. 'Yeah?'

'I've changed my mind.'

And she set about showing him exactly how.

Keely floated into the office on Monday morning. She'd had the barest minimum of sleep for the entire weekend and didn't care. She'd never felt so alive, so animated, as if she could take on the world and still have enough energy left over to tackle the solar system.

She had a pile of work to get through this week

and, as she dumped her satchel and booted up her computer, all she could think about was Lachlan.

She would have to add one more criteria to her checklist for the perfect man: incredible lover.

If she'd thought his skill at kissing was impressive, it had nothing on his performance in the bedroom. And the lounge room. And the kitchen.

And if she'd thought massage was mainly used as a relaxation technique, she'd had to think again.

Scanning her e-mails quickly, she ignored the inter-office ones and opened Emma's.

To: *KeelyR@WWWDesigns.com*
From: *EmmaR@WWWDesigns.com*
Subject: D&M
Hi Sweetie,
Got time for a D&M in the conference room?
Need a few details for *Flirt* website (and a few from your weekend away?)
C U in 10?
Em

Keely grinned. She knew her friends would be dying to hear the gossip from her weekend away with Lachlan and, despite the urge to keep them guessing, she fired off a quick reply.

To: *EmmaR@WWWDesigns.com*
From: *KeelyR@WWWDesigns.com*
Subject: Only 10?

Em,

Surprised you can wait 10 minutes.

Ideas for *Flirt* website coming along nicely.

Will bring my revamped work.

Have doughnuts and Macchiato at the ready.

C U soon.

K

Gathering up the *Flirt* file, she heard two beeps from her PC. The first e-mail was from Tahlia, reiterating what Emma had said and wanting 'all the gory details', the next from Lucy.

To: *KeelyR@WWWDesigns.com*
From: *Lucy-PA@WWWDesigns.com*
Subject: PM sucks!

K,

Took your advice, asked Aidan out for coffee.

Put the PM quiz to the test and he bombed, big time.

Wolf in sheep's clothing doesn't come close to describing him. How about ravenous wolf who devours his prey?

Dating is the pits.

How many men does it take to screw in a lightbulb?

Three: one creep to screw in the bulb and two to listen to him brag about the screwing part. That sums up Aidan—Yeuk!

Luce (reformed dater)

Aidan a sleaze? Keely shook her head, hoping her lousy judgement in men didn't extend to all facets of life. She could've sworn Aidan seemed like a nice guy, though appearances weren't everything.

Feeling more than a tad responsible for urging Lucy to ask Aidan out, she typed a quick reply.

To: *Lucy-PA@WWWDesigns.com*
From: *KeelyR@WWWDesigns.com*
Subject: Forgetaboutit!
Luce,
Sorry Aidan the Ass turned out to be just that.
The solution? Get back out there. Your PM could be just around the corner.
Drinks, this Friday after work. Be there.
Let the search recommence…
K

Hoping that Lucy wasn't too devastated about the Aidan fiasco, Keely headed out of her office, ready to face the music with her friends.

Several hours later, Keely sat in front of her PC and brought up the newest account that had just landed in her lap. *Bountiful Babes* promised to be a one-stop website for parents who needed the low-down on the joys of having children. Initially, she'd been reluctant to take it on—the fact that she loved kids and couldn't have any rubbed in her face wasn't good—

but with the Rottie breathing down her neck she'd had no choice.

Besides, she'd sensed something else behind the Rottie's urgency, almost as if they needed these new accounts to survive. Which was silly really, considering WWW Designs was one of the largest firms of its kind in the country.

However, she'd never juggled three prestigious accounts at once before, and this, plus the Brant assignment, added to her suspicions that something wasn't quite right. The Rottie had been snapping at everyone's heels for the last few weeks, raving on about deadlines and efficiency, and though she'd held her tongue because of the promotion she coveted, Keely had almost told her to shove it several times.

She'd managed to placate the Rottie with a pat on the head—figuratively speaking—and news that her assignment with Lachlan was proceeding extremely well. She'd just left out the part where her shadowing him had turned from business to pleasure.

As the preliminary work she'd done for the site flashed across the screen, she swallowed the lump of emotion that inevitably rose when she saw anything to do with babies. The motif she'd designed as a border for the web page—a chubby, chuckling baby in various poses—brought a smile to her face. From his ten perfect fingers and toes to his rosy cheeks and dimpled skin, he was adorable, and a stark reminder of what she could never have.

Sighing, she made an angry swipe at a tear escaping from the corner of her eye and turned away as someone knocked on her door.

She sat up straighter and fixed a smile on her face. Just her luck for the Rottie to come bounding in here and catch her sniffling. 'Come in.'

'How's my favourite graphic designer?' Lachlan strolled into the room and handed her a bag. 'I come bearing gifts. Thought you could use something to boost your energy levels.'

She opened the bag and inhaled deeply, the seductive aroma of fresh cinnamon doughnuts making her salivate, before casting him a coy look from beneath her lashes. 'I'm fine and there's nothing wrong with my energy levels. In fact, I haven't been this *energised* in ages.'

He laughed and chose one of the doughnuts from the bag she proffered. 'Glad to hear it.' He rolled his neck around as if trying to work out a kink. 'I'm in dire need of another *massage*.'

Heat crept into her cheeks at his emphasis on the word 'massage'. She'd done all that and more to him on the weekend away, displaying a brazen side she hadn't known existed.

As Tahlia had laughingly pointed out after she'd given the girls a very brief version of events, she was working in the right place: WWW Designs could stand for Wickedly Wanton Woman or Wonderful Wowsing Witch. Both labels seemed appropriate at this stage!

She interlocked fingers and stretched forward, as if limbering up. 'For you, any time.'

As desire arced between them and he crouched down beside her chair, she placed both hands on his chest and held him back. 'However, right now I need to do some work.'

He captured her hands and held them against his chest till she itched to slide her fingers between the buttons of his ivory business shirt and caress the firm skin underneath.

'I thought my website was nearly finished?'

She nodded, trying to think 'work' while this close to the man who had rocked her world repeatedly over the weekend. 'It is.'

'So what's this you're working on?'

He peered over her shoulder, ignoring her muttered, 'A client's work is confidential', his face breaking into a huge smile.

'That's one cute baby,' he said, his eyes glowing with a tenderness she'd never seen before.

She pulled away and swivelled her chair towards the screen, rattled by his reaction.

'You like kids?' she asked, trying to instil the right amount of casualness into her voice while hanging on his answer.

'What's not to like? They're amazing, taking over your life and wreaking more devastation than a cyclone. And I wouldn't have it any other way. I helped raise my younger brothers and sisters and, though challenging, it was the most rewarding thing I've ever done.'

His words drove tiny daggers of pain into her heart, opening up wounds she'd thought healed. She had to ask the next question, knowing his answer would seal the fate of their relationship, one way or the other.

'Do you want kids of your own?'

'Absolutely. If the right woman came along, I reckon I'd like at least half a dozen of the little tykes.'

And, just like that, reality crashed in, leaving Keely struggling for air.

She'd known that dating Lachlan could prove disastrous but she'd gone ahead and done it anyway. Despite her feeble protestations, he was business; she'd fallen for him, and labelling their relationship 'dating' had been a lie on her part.

She loved him, had probably loved him before she knew what had hit her, and therefore had ignored every warning that she shouldn't get in too deep. When relationships went too far, certain expectations came into play, and now she'd heard it for herself.

He wanted the one thing she could never give him.

And it would ruin them in the end.

Struggling to keep her voice steady, she said, 'Why settle for half a dozen?' She managed a brittle laugh before shuffling the paperwork on her desk. 'Now, it's nice of you to drop by, but I really have to get back to this.'

He frowned and stood up. 'Is something wrong?'

She shook her head and tried not to blurt out *Everything is wrong.*

'No, just the usual jitters that deadlines bring.' She looked away, only to be confronted by the computer screen and the evidence of what she couldn't give him, the pain ravaging her anew. 'Raquel wants this done ASAP.'

He didn't budge. 'Are you sure this is about work?'

She had to meet his gaze, if only to convince him that she needed to be left alone before she burst into tears. 'Of course.'

His direct gaze bored into hers, as if trying to see into the windows of her soul and read the secrets there. For now, she sure hoped the shutters were down.

'I'll leave you to it, then. Call me when you have a minute?'

She nodded and faked a breezy wave as she focused on the screen again, hoping he'd been fooled.

By the dubious look he cast her on the way out, she doubted it.

Lachlan slipped the headphones off and leaned back, grateful for the four-minute break a song from some boy band offered. He needed time to think and hadn't had much opportunity lately, what with the new TV show, the publicity demands and continuing with his radio talkback show, which had reached the number one ratings spot over the last few weeks.

Professionally, he had the world at his feet. Then why did he feel like a tightrope walker teetering on the brink of a big fall?

He rubbed his eyes and took a sip of the disgusting brew the station labelled coffee, knowing exactly why he felt so out of control these days.

Keely.

He'd thought he'd been dating the woman of his dreams. So how had their relationship turned into a nightmare?

Ever since their weekend in Hepburn Springs, which had been incredible, she'd withdrawn from him slowly but surely. Back then, she'd reciprocated his passion and they'd connected on many levels, so what had gone wrong?

She'd cited work pressures as being the cause of their sporadic contact, but he knew better. The secrets Keely harboured seemed to grow bigger with every passing day. He'd glimpsed sadness tinged with something more akin to despondency in her eyes on the few occasions they'd caught up, and despite gentle prodding she hadn't opened up.

Either that or she was snapping his head off for the smallest thing, and he'd had a gutful. It didn't take a genius to figure out she had some self-esteem issues and he'd been careful not to make any references to her body since the first few outbursts which had put him on the outer. He'd been patient with her, yet she'd pushed him away at every opportunity anyway.

And it annoyed him. Hell, it had him so riled he could hardly think straight. Here he was, a psychologist at the top of his profession, offering help to thousands over the airwaves, yet he couldn't breach the emotional walls of the one person he wanted to.

He'd reached out to her repeatedly over the last ten weeks, persisting when he could've given up. He'd grown to like her a lot, and she made him happy like no woman ever had. However, she'd eroded his patience. Being stuck in a one-way relationship when the other person's interest had cooled wasn't his style. He'd seen what that did to a man firsthand with his dad and, dammit, he wouldn't wish that on his worst enemy, let alone himself.

Unfortunately, as hard as he tried not to compare Keely to his erratic mother, her behaviour drew frightening parallels that had him ready to call it quits.

Just yesterday she'd flared up over an innocent question he'd asked about how her websites for other clients were coming along, mentioning the cute work she'd done for that baby site. He'd been trying to show his interest in her career, she'd taken offence, and when he'd retaliated with a rather abrupt 'Calm down', she'd stormed out of the café, leaving him gobsmacked.

Another nasty similarity to his mother; she had run at the first sign of trouble. If an inconsequential spat that hinted at the rumbling volcano about to blow their relationship sky-high could make her walk, imagine what would happen if things got really serious between them. She'd flee quicker than he could say, 'It's over.'

When she'd run out of the café, he'd been ready to chase after her and end it right there and then, before an incoming call on his mobile from the producers of his new TV show had distracted him long enough to cool off.

'Lachlan, twenty seconds.'

He looked up at the station manager and nodded, reaching for the headphones.

He needed to focus on work for now, but come Friday night at her friend's party Keely owed him some answers. He'd tired of her games and was more than ready to pick up his bat and ball and head home. Alone.

Keely clutched her belly and groaned. 'This bout of food poisoning is lingering too long. That's the second time in the last few days I've been sick.'

Emma handed her a glass of water. 'Here, drink this. You'll feel better.'

Keely took several sips before her stomach rolled again and nausea washed over her in sickening waves.

'Oh-oh, here we go again.' She made a mad dash for the toilet, vowing to avoid Peking duck for ever.

She'd never been this sick and, added to her lethargy, it made her want to crawl into bed for a week. Work had been manic, explaining her tiredness, but she'd eaten the Chinese food days ago and should be over it by now.

Bracing herself for the meeting with Emma and Tahlia to discuss her final presentation for *Flirt*, she staggered back into the conference room and fell into the nearest chair.

'Feeling better?' Emma had refilled the glass with water and handed it to her.

Keely nodded, wondering if she could beg off the meeting and head home. However, the Rottie had insisted they present her with the work done on the magazine's website—like yesterday—so she'd been up till all hours putting the finishing touches on the design stuff and needed to run it by her colleagues before the presentation.

Emma reached over and squeezed her hand. 'It'll be over soon and then you can go home, okay?'

'Sure,' Keely said as her stomach somersaulted for an encore.

Tahlia breezed into the room at that moment, looking fabulous in a new trouser suit. 'I wouldn't sit in that chair if I was you.'

'Why?' If Keely hadn't already been a pale shade of green she would've turned it anyway. Her friend wasn't just dressed to impress, she had the perfect hair and make-up to match. Little wonder the Rottie rarely picked on Tahlia; her professional look would intimidate the scariest of bosses.

Tahlia sniggered as she grabbed a coffee and sat opposite. 'Because that's the preggers chair.'

'Huh?'

'Every woman who sits in that chair falls pregnant.' Tahlia counted the list off on her fingers. 'Nadia was the latest, then there was Shelby before her, Annie from Accounts, Maggie in Animation and Sue from Marketing.'

Tahlia paused, smug grin in place. 'So you see, it must be the chair. And, seeing as you're now engaging in activities that would make that chair a danger to you, I'd be very careful if I was you.'

Keely managed a weak laugh as her mind started jumping to all sorts of impossible conclusions.

'Leave her alone; she isn't feeling well.' Emma placed a jug of water in front of her before taking a seat.

'See? It's worked already.' Tahlia laughed at what Keely knew must be the bemused expression on her face.

Her friends didn't know about her past; she'd been too ashamed, and, though they would understand, she'd rather relegate that sad time in her life to past memories where they belonged.

Therefore, Tahlia had no idea that the one thing she teased her about could never happen. Then why did she keep thinking that there could be more to this bout of food poisoning?

She'd skipped a period but that was nothing new. Her periods had never been regular and she'd put it down to work stress. It had happened in the past, thanks to her erratic hormones. But now, combined with the other symptoms she'd been having, a tiny seed of hope had been planted in her brain.

Could the doctor have been wrong all those years ago?

Sure, Lachlan used protection, but that method had never been foolproof. Just ask Nadia, her immediate superior and career woman, who had sworn to never have kids. She'd threatened to blow up the local rubber factory that produced condoms when she'd first found out the news.

Despite her stomach continuing to dance the Macarena, Keely managed a small smile. If there was even the slightest chance she was pregnant, she wouldn't blow up the factory—she'd personally kiss each and every employee who worked there.

'What are you grinning at?' Tahlia asked, holding her hand out for the *Flirt* file.

'Nothing,' Keely said, trying to ignore the urge to leap out of her chair and rush to the nearest pharmacy to buy a pregnancy test.

Emma stared at Keely. She'd always been the more perceptive of her two friends and Keely knew that her confusion must show on her face, besides the fact that she'd gone from puking her guts up to grinning like a madwoman in less than a minute.

'Are we still on for drinks this Friday night?'

Keely met Tahlia's gaze for an instant before looking away. Otherwise she'd probably burst out laughing and give the game away. They'd planned Emma's surprise birthday party for the end of this week and had everything arranged. Now all they had to do was get her there.

'Well?' Emma looked at Tahlia, obviously giving up on Keely.

Tahlia nodded. 'Yep. Are you still interested in that makeover before your birthday next week?'

Emma wrinkled her nose. 'Don't mention the B word. This year I'm not interested in celebrating.'

'Is it the age thing? After all, twenty-four is ancient,' Tahlia teased, and though Emma laughed, Keely knew there was more to it than that.

With every year that passed Emma continued to pine for Harry Buchanan, and the fact that he wouldn't be around this year was probably the cause of her friend's reluctance to celebrate.

'I don't care what you say, you're getting that makeover on Thursday night.' Tahlia rubbed her hands together in glee. 'Leave everything to me.'

'What do you think?' Emma glanced across at Keely and she gave her a thumbs up.

'It's a great idea. A change is as good as a holiday, some wise person once said.' And, if that was the case, she'd be in for the equivalent of an around the world trip if her wild suspicions were confirmed.

'Okay,' Emma said, running her hands through her long blonde hair as if already ruing the fact that it would probably be the first to go. 'Now, can we get down to business?'

Keely nodded and clutched her stomach under the conference table, silently praying for a tiny miracle.

CHAPTER TEN

'My definition of a bachelor? A man who has missed the opportunity to make some poor woman miserable.'
Raquel Wilson, obviously single and not loving it.

KEELY stared at the small plastic stick with two blue lines for the hundredth time that week, her reaction the same. Joy. Pure, unadulterated joy, that swept through her body and lifted her spirits to a place they'd never been before.

'I'm pregnant,' she whispered, when in fact she wanted to run up the stairs of her apartment building and shout it from the rooftop.

The doctor had confirmed it yesterday and she'd been floating ever since. She hadn't bothered asking how and why, when she'd been told this would never happen by another member of the esteemed medical profession all those years ago. Instead, she viewed this miracle as a gift and would treat it accordingly— she'd treasure, cherish and love the little human inside her with every fibre of her being.

And tonight she would share her news with Lachlan. Sure, he probably hadn't thought of starting a family this early, but she was confident he'd come around. After all, hadn't he said he wanted a half-dozen of the little cherubs? The only blight on her happiness was the memory of his words, *'if the right woman came along'*.

When he'd said that, she'd half-expected him to glance meaningfully at her, to smile that secretive smile he reserved especially for her, intimating that he'd already met the right woman—her. However, he hadn't done any of those things. Instead, he'd calmly announced that he'd want six kids *if the right woman came along*. Though it shouldn't come as any surprise, he obviously didn't think she fitted the bill.

She'd known it from the start, the fact that she'd never be good enough for a guy like him. And now, when the most amazing thing had happened, she had no idea if he'd be happy about it or not.

She'd been holding him at arm's length for weeks, ever since she'd heard his wish for children. What was the point of developing their relationship when she couldn't give him a family? The more he'd pushed, the more she'd begged off, citing work as an excuse.

He hadn't called for a few days, his silence a clear indication she'd almost succeeded in her plan. After going off the deep end at lunch earlier in the week and walking out on him, she knew the end was in sight. She'd been deliberately treating him badly, hoping he'd take matters out of her hands and end the relationship, leaving her to mend her broken heart in peace.

For the life of her, she couldn't fathom why he'd stuck around this long after the way she'd treated him. The more she gave him the brush-off, the more determined he seemed. Perhaps it was the psychologist in him, trying to figure her out? If that were the case he'd sure have his work cut out for him!

Thankfully, she could now stop behaving like an irrational cow—an irrational hormonal cow!—and hope that he hadn't given up on her.

Things would change, starting tonight. And, though she wasn't completely delusional, expecting a profession of undying love, she hoped that he'd be happy with her news and could hardly wait till after Emma's party to tell him. Though she would've preferred to tell him beforehand, he had to work and had said he'd meet her at Sammy's.

And, seeing as the father-to-be needed to hear the news first, she would just have to wait.

Placing the pregnancy test back in its plastic bag and into the top drawer of her medicine cabinet, she closed her eyes and sent a silent prayer heavenward that Lachlan would see this baby as she did, as a testament to their love and the beginning of a future together.

Keely waved to Emma and Tahlia as they strolled into Sammy's, before glancing over her shoulder into the room they'd hired and silencing everyone with a finger over her lips.

'She's coming,' someone hissed, followed by a tittering of giggles.

A slight frown creased Emma's brow as she reached the back. 'What are we doing hiding in this corner? Our usual spot is over—'

'Surprise!'

Keely stepped back as the chorus of voices sang out, enjoying the stunned expression on her friend's face.

'What the...?' Emma's head swivelled between Keely and Tahlia while people from work swarmed around her, everyone talking at once.

Keely leaned over and squeezed Emma's arm. 'Happy birthday, Em. We know how much you love surprises, so...surprise!'

Emma smiled, a dazed expression on her face. 'I can't believe you did this and I didn't twig. You're usually lousy with keeping secrets.'

Keely returned her smile and thought, *not any longer*. She could keep a secret and it was a doozy!

'Enjoy the night, sweetie. You deserve it. And you look fabulous, by the way.'

Emma patted her hair self-consciously. 'I like this bob, even if I do feel bald.'

Keely chuckled. 'It's not just the hair, it's the whole package. Your clothes, your make-up. Watch out, next you'll be moving out of home!'

Emma rolled her eyes. 'And not a moment too

soon. I'm twenty-four now. Time to grow up, don't you think?'

Keely nodded, knowing her friend wasn't the only one with growing up to do. She was going to be a mother—a sure-fire way to guarantee she grew up, fast.

'Your man's arrived.' Tahlia pointed towards the front bar and Keely eagerly turned, barely restraining the urge to run across the crowded room and fling herself into his arms.

However, she needn't have bothered. Lachlan had his arms full already. With Chrystal.

'Oh-oh, trouble in paradise,' Tahlia muttered.

Keely handed her the fruit cocktail she'd been drinking and said, 'Hold this.'

'Before she flings it at her,' Keely heard Emma add as she stalked away.

Lachlan looked up as she neared and had the audacity to grin sheepishly and shrug.

There was nothing sheepish about Chrystal's response and the predatory way her eyes glittered in the dim lighting. 'There you are, Keely. Look who I ran into. The doc was just seeing if I had something in my eye.'

Gritting her teeth and refraining from putting something in Chrystal's eye—like her finger—Keely said, 'You should be okay.' *After all, you're wearing enough mascara to shield them from a dust-storm.* 'Want me to take a look too?'

Chrystal shook her head—and her huge chest followed suit—though, thankfully, Lachlan had the sense not to look in that direction. If he had, there was no telling what she might've done. She'd never been the jealous type, though her hormones seemed to have kicked in with a vengeance, her temper spiking to irrational in a second.

'See you later, Lochie,' Chrystal purred, a triumphant smile on her face as she sashayed away.

'Lochie?' Keely stood in front of the man she loved, torn between wanting to kiss him and slap him. 'Well, isn't this cosy? You two progressed to nicknames already?'

A puzzled frown creased his brow. 'She's harmless.'

The little demon that put in a regular appearance in her mind prodded her with its pitchfork—hard. 'Yeah, as a tiger snake. What do you call her, *Lochie?*'

Rather than laughing off her jealousy, as she'd expected him to do, he folded his arms and glared. 'Don't.'

'Sorry?'

Though they hadn't seen each other since her childish display at the café, she'd taken his agreement to attend Em's party as an indication he was ready to forgive her. Obviously, she had been wrong.

He held up his hand as if staving her off. 'Don't

do the jealousy act. It would be hypocritical coming from you at the moment.'

She almost reeled back, shocked by his words. 'What's that supposed to mean?'

This had to be a joke, right? Some sort of payback for holding him at bay? He'd laugh any second now and say, *Fooled you.*

He didn't. 'You need to care to be jealous and I don't think you do. Care, that is.' He ran a hand through his hair, sending dark waves wayward. 'We need to talk.'

Oh-oh. She knew what those four little words meant. He talked, she listened, he walked, she crumbled. Nothing new in the scenario, just new players. Unfortunately, she seemed to have a starring role every time, with a different leading man to break her heart.

'About?'

'I'm tired of playing games. You've given me the cold shoulder for weeks now and, rather than be honest about wanting out, you hide your feelings along with the rest of your secrets.'

Icy dread stole through her veins. This didn't sound like a man who would welcome news of her pregnancy. This sounded like a man aiming to end their relationship, just as she'd suspected.

'If this is about our fight in the café, I'm—'

'That's only part of it.' He cut her off before she could apologise. Not that it would do any good. He had a determined glint in his eyes, as if he had his farewell speech already worked out. 'You're all over me one minute, barely speaking to me the next. I thought by coming here tonight we could see if there was any hope for us but I can see there isn't.'

Fury surged through her, replacing dread in an instant. 'And when did you figure this out? Before or after Chrystal thrust her enhancements in your face? Nothing like a killer body, is there? Pity mine didn't match up, what with you thinking I need to watch my weight and all.'

He stared at her as if she'd sprouted horns. Which was appropriate, considering the demon in her brain hadn't let up. 'I have a friend who can help you.'

'Help me?'

'Sort through the issues you have.'

Great. Rather than offering her his love, he thought she needed a shrink. And, worse, he wasn't volunteering for the job, which showed exactly where she stood with him.

'Never mind.' She shook her head, wondering how what should've been the happiest night of her life had turned into a disaster before it had even started.

'Look, I don't think—'

'No, you don't, do you? If you did, you'd accept it when I say I have work pressures and can't see you. You'd understand why I'd be jealous to see the office tart draped all over you.'

He shook his head, casting her a pitying glance.

'Maybe that's the first honest thing you've said to me. What about the rest?'

'The rest?' She gaped at him, wondering if she could blame the fog clouding her brain on hormones too.

'You've got secrets, Keely, starting with that phone call you made to my show a few months ago.'

'You know…' She trailed off, feeling a fool for not confiding in him earlier. She'd thought he would laugh it off, and maybe he would have if she'd told him herself. However, in the heat of the moment, her silence looked incriminating. What would he think about the rest?

He frowned, looking more foreboding than she'd ever seen him. 'I've known since the start. I remembered your voice straight away and thought it was pretty funny at the time. However, the closer we got, the more you clammed up. I saw the shadows in your eyes all those times you pushed me away and it made me wonder what else you were hiding and why you couldn't tell me about something so trivial.'

She almost reached out to him, then thought better of it. He didn't exactly look receptive at the moment, and if she didn't tell him the truth she could lose him.

'I wanted to tell you but would've been forced into dumping the rest on you and I didn't want to scare you off.'

She glimpsed a softening in his expression. 'Do I look like the type of guy to run?'

She shook her head and sighed, wishing she'd had the sense to do what he'd asked her at the start—to trust him. 'You're right; I do have issues. I thought I'd got past them, but I'm still oversensitive at times. That night I made the phone call to your show was the anniversary of a particularly difficult time in my life and I'd had a few drinks. When I heard you dishing out advice to that overweight teenager, some-thing inside me snapped and I called up.'

She paused for a moment, wondering how far she should take her explanation. Not a muscle twitched on his face as he stared at her in stony silence, and in that instant she knew she would have to tell him everything or risk losing the love of her life.

'Her plight was too close to home. I was that teen-ager years ago, desperate for help and finding none. My parents didn't care, I didn't have any friends, and my psychologist spouted a whole lot of garbage when I needed help the most. That night on the radio you said something that triggered a reaction and the rest...' She spread her hands before him. 'Well, I guess you remember the stupid names I called you.'

'And you didn't tell me all this because you thought I'd run?' He didn't reach for her as she'd hoped. He didn't smile or touch her. Instead, he con-tinued to stand there with his arms folded, looking unmoved, and the flicker of alarm that had shot through her when they'd first started talking turned into full-scale panic. 'What sort of a man do you take me for?'

Before she could answer, he said, 'Don't answer that. You've already made it perfectly clear.'

He picked up his jacket from a nearby barstool and shrugged into it. 'Look, I'm sorry for what you went through all those years ago, I really am. However, I asked for honesty at the start of this...whatever it is we were involved in...and I didn't get it.'

She felt the blood drain from her face at his use of the past tense 'were'. 'It's called a relationship.'

He shook his head. 'To you, maybe. To me, we were just dating.'

Pain lanced through her and she held a hand against her stomach in a purely reflex gesture, as if trying to protect their child from hearing its parents argue.

'So you weren't ever interested in anything long-term? What about all that stuff you said about having kids?'

She saw the hurtful truth in his eyes before he nodded. 'Dating is as far as it goes for me, as far as it ever would've gone. To bring kids into this world I'd have to be damn sure I could trust the mother of my children and, by the way all this has panned out, that woman isn't you.'

'I see.' Her words came out a whisper as her grip

around her belly tightened. However, before she could say anything else, his mobile phone rang.

Torn between wanting to walk away from the best thing that had ever happened to her and fling her news in his face to get a reaction out of him, she watched him pale and clench the phone against his ear.

She heard him say, 'When? Which hospital? I'll be there in fifteen minutes,' before hanging up and thrusting the phone back in his pocket.

She laid a hand on his arm without thinking. 'Is everything okay?'

He looked down at her hand, as if wondering what it was, before shrugging it off. 'I have to go. My dad has had a heart attack.'

'I'm so sorry,' she said, wanting to be by his side despite his callous words a few moments earlier. 'Would you like me to come with you?'

He fixed her with an icy stare. 'I don't think so. You haven't exactly been the most supportive girlfriend the last few months. What's changed now?'

This was her opportunity to tell him about the baby but she stalled, knowing it wasn't the right time. 'I'll tell you later.'

He shook his head and started to move away. 'I haven't got time for this and, as far as I'm concerned, there won't be a later. Let's just end it here and move on.'

In that instant her fickle hormones surged again,

jump-starting her brain into first gear along with her temper. 'Is that right? You think we were *just dating* and now we *just end it*?'

'Yeah.'

'What if I love you? And what if I said I was *pregnant*?'

If he'd been pale before, he positively blanched now. 'I'd say you'd go to any lengths to trap your idea of the perfect man and, just for the record, I'm not him.'

He practically ran out the door, leaving her standing there with tears streaming down her face and her hands clutched over her stomach, alone with her baby who would never know its father.

CHAPTER ELEVEN

*'Lachlan isn't afraid of commitment. He's
monogamously challenged.'*
Emma, a supportive friend.

LACHLAN rushed into his father's hospital room, expecting to see a sick, shaken man. To his surprise, Derek Brant sat up in bed, scowling at the various leads hooking him up to countless monitors.

'About time you got here. Look at me, trussed up like a turkey. Can't you do something about this?'

Lachlan exhaled, unaware he'd been holding his breath, as he entered his dad's room. He'd been expecting the worst, despite what the doctor and nurses had said, yet here his father was, sitting up and looking ready to unhook his shackles and escape.

He crossed the room and bent down to give his dad a hug. 'You've had a heart attack, you need to be monitored, so just leave those trusses alone, okay?'

His dad returned his embrace for all of two seconds before pulling away. 'What took you so long? I could've been dead and on a slab downstairs by the time you got here.'

Lachlan bit back a smile. His dad hadn't lost his

gruff manner and was obviously going to be fine. 'I was at a party and came as soon as I heard.'

His dad snorted. 'Off gallivanting with that pretty young thing of yours, eh?'

Lachlan had tried to block Keely from his mind as soon as he'd left the party, determined to concentrate on reaching his father. However, now that he'd seen his dad was okay, the full impact of what she'd said hit him with renewed force.

'She's not mine any more,' he said, wondering if anything she'd told him tonight had been the truth.

He'd seen the pain in her eyes when she'd discussed her weight problem and her empathy for his teenage caller, so he could safely assume she'd been honest about that. Besides, it explained her bizarre behaviour every time he mentioned anything remotely connected with body image.

But what was all that baloney about loving him after he'd ended it? Not to mention bringing up a possible pregnancy?

He shook his head, well acquainted with the lengths some women would go to to trap their man, his mother being a prime example.

'What happened?' His father fixed him with one of his infamous *don't think about fobbing me off, boy* looks.

'She reminded me of Mum,' he blurted out, before silently cursing himself for bringing up the one topic known to wind his father up, especially at a time like this. 'Fickle, unpredictable and totally incapable of maintaining an honest relationship.'

To his surprise, his father didn't swear and flush an angry crimson as he usually did when the subject of his ex-wife arose. Instead, he sighed and leaned back against a mound of pillows. 'I think we need to talk, son.'

Lachlan shook his head. 'I'm sorry I brought her up, Dad. This isn't the time. You need to concentrate on getting well, not getting worked up.'

His father stared at him with the familiar stubborn glint in his eyes. 'I'm fine,' he snapped, 'and you need to hear this.'

Lachlan sat back, knowing it was useless to argue when his father was like this. It would be easier to remain calm, hear him out and change the subject, quickly.

'Why do you say your young woman reminded you of your mother?'

Lachlan tried to ignore the pain he knew his explanation would resurrect. Despite his vow to never commit to a woman long-term, let alone think of marriage, that was exactly what he'd done within a month of dating Keely. He'd fallen in love with her, going as far as buying a house recently in the hope of convincing her that they could live happily ever after.

And what had she done? The closer he'd wanted to get, the more she had pushed him away with pathetic excuses and loaded silences. Even then he'd made allowances for her, had given her breathing space, yet it had all been for nothing. Tonight, when she'd done the whole jealousy routine that women had down pat, on top of her recent walk-out, something inside him had cracked and what she did or said didn't matter any more.

Okay, if he were completely honest, he'd gone to the party looking for an excuse to end it anyway. Picking that fight courtesy of her jealousy had made it all the easier. And, even as she'd spoken of telling him the truth, he'd seen the secrets behind her eyes. He couldn't live with a woman like that, couldn't trust her with the one thing he'd sheltered since his mum abandoned him all those years ago—his heart.

He could've predicted her protestation of love at the end. Most women would say anything to hold on to a man, even if it was a lost cause, but her words of a supposed pregnancy shocked him the most.

After his mother had left all those years ago, he'd overheard his aunt and father talking about how she'd trapped his father into marriage with her pregnancy. His aunt had said it was the worst thing a woman could do and his father hadn't disagreed.

'And what if I said I was pregnant?'

Keely's words, flung at him like barbs intended to wound, had brought back memories of his mother's treachery, and he wanted nothing to do with a woman like that. He'd get over her and never, ever, be duped again.

His father reached out and placed a gnarled hand on top of his. 'Tell me, son.'

'She blew hot and cold all the time, just like Mum. And when the going got tough she ran like Mum too. Then, after I'd ended it, she tried to hold on to me by saying she loved me and insinuating she could be pregnant, like Mum trapped you.'

'Ah, hell,' his dad muttered and, before Lachlan could stand up, tuck the bedclothes around him and bring an end to this conversation, his dad tightened his grip.

'Your mother didn't trap me, son. It was the other way around.'

'What?' Lachlan leaned closer, not sure if he'd heard the almost-whispered words correctly.

'I'm not proud of what I did but it happened. And, though I should regret it, I don't, because I look at you kids and thank God every day that I did it.'

Lachlan shook his head, wondering how much morphine his father had in his system. 'You're talking in riddles, Dad.'

'When your mother told me she was pregnant I forced her into marriage, even though she said she didn't love me. She was happy for a while after you came along but I could see that her heart just wasn't in the marriage. So, to bind her closer to me, I insisted we have more kids.'

His father rubbed his free hand over his eyes, as if trying to wipe away a host of unpleasant memories. 'I think she did it out of pity for me. The more I tried to make her love me, the further she pulled away. That's why she acted like she did most of the time. I drove her away, son, with my obsession for her. When she left, it was as much my fault as hers.'

Lachlan sat back, stunned, grasping for the right words to say and coming up empty.

'So, you see, your young woman...Keely, isn't it?...she's nothing like your mother. If she said she loves you you hold on to her tightly and never let go. Having the genuine love of a good woman would be the greatest gift a man could ever have.'

Spent, his father finally leaned back on his pillows. 'Now, leave an old man to rest in peace, figuratively speaking, hopefully, while you convince Keely to take you back.'

Lachlan wanted to ask his father a thousand questions about the past but now wasn't the time. His dad was right. He had to win back the love of his life. Though, after what he'd put her through, he knew words or small peace offerings wouldn't cut it. He needed to make a grand statement and hope to God she'd forgive him.

Suddenly, he knew just the way to do it.

Keely had barely entered her office on Monday morning when Lucy pranced in, looking like a perky zebra in her black and white striped ensemble. She usually loved her assistant's funky taste in clothes, but not today. Even the sight of Lucy couldn't cheer her up.

'I'm the bearer of bad news.'

'So what's new?' Her whole life could be an advertisement for bad news, all except the little life growing inside her, of course.

'The Rottie just cornered me, saying that the TV execs producing Lachlan Brant's new show need to see his completed website. Today.'

Keely swallowed the lump that rose in her throat and blinked furiously, not willing to shed one more tear over her Mr Not-so-perfect. She'd done enough crying over the weekend to last her into the next century, but no more. He wasn't worth it.

Despite their goodbye, a small part of her had hoped he would contact her over the weekend, just to see if she was okay. Instead, her phone hadn't rung and the only visitors she'd had were Emma and Tahlia, plying her with cups of tea, tissues and doughnuts as they cursed all men in general.

And, by Lucy's careful expression as she mentioned Lachlan's name, she knew that the girls must've filled her in on the situation.

'It's not so bad,' Keely said, determined to put on a brave face, at least during office hours. 'The website is finished. When are they coming in?'

Lucy grimaced. 'They're not. They want you to go to them, some place in Albert Park.'

Keely sighed and wondered where she'd gone so wrong. Was she so horrible that Lachlan couldn't even bear to see her? Was that why he'd probably gone to the TV station and coerced them into viewing her work rather than checking it himself?

So much for love. So much for Mr Perfect.

The first thing she would do when she arrived home tonight was tear up that stupid checklist. And burn the rest of the collection.

'Fine, I'll do it. E-mail me the address. What time did they say?'

'Three o'clock.' Lucy paused on her way out and swung around to face her. 'Don't bother coming back to the office. I can handle things here.'

Keely leaned back and shook her head. 'You know, don't you?'

Lucy nodded. 'Yeah, Emma told me about the break-up. She said she didn't want me blundering around in here, putting my big foot in my mouth while I blathered on about Lach—' She clamped her hand over her mouth, her eyes wide.

Keely managed a shaky laugh. 'It's okay, you can say his name. You did before anyway.'

'But that was business,' Lucy garbled through her fingers before lowering her hand. 'Seeing as you brought him up, I just want to say that I'm here for you if you need anything. Like a voodoo doll of the guy, a few sharpened pins, a dartboard with his photo in the bull's-eye... Get my drift?'

'Thanks, Luce, but I'll be fine.'

Lucy sent her a sceptical look that read *Are you insane?* before waving and shutting the door behind her.

I'll be fine.

She'd hoped that by now, after repeating the words time and time again over the weekend, she would start to believe them.

Instead, they sounded as hollow and empty now as they had then.

Just like your heart.

Ignoring the pain that knifed into the organ that Lachlan had broken without trying, she looked down at her flat stomach and murmured, 'Looks like it's just you and me, kid.'

Clutching her satchel and laptop, Keely knocked on the door of the stately mansion. Nice place, if you could afford it. TV execs must earn a squillion to afford something this extravagant in the upmarket suburb of Albert Park.

She just hoped they liked her presentation so she could get this ordeal over as quickly as possible and erase the name Lachlan Brant from her memory banks for ever.

'It's open,' a muffled male voice shouted from somewhere out the back.

Shouldering her load, she opened the door and admired the polished oak floors in a hallway that stretched as far as the eye could see. She wandered in, surprised at the airy feel of the place. Some of these dignified old homes tended to be dark, dreary places but not this one. Personally, she preferred the contemporary feel of her trendy apartment, but this old place had a lot of charm.

As she looked up at the ornate ceiling and cornices, the hair on her nape prickled, the same way it usually did when one man was near.

'Hey, Keely.'

Her gaze drifted slowly downwards. She needed to confirm what she'd just heard wasn't an auditory hallucination.

'Thanks for coming.' Lachlan stood in a nearby doorway, looking every bit as good as she remembered. Black shirt, black jeans, with his hair mussed in that way that made her fingers itch to smooth it.

However, after the way he'd trampled over her heart, surely that itch in her fingers was to slap him rather than run them through his hair?

'What are you doing here?' The words came out sounding a lot calmer than she'd expected as she carefully placed her laptop and satchel on the ground, before she was prompted to do something crazy— like fling them at him Frisbee-style.

'I needed to see you.'

Her gaze darted to the door as she wondered how quickly she could escape. However, he was a smart man. He hadn't taken a step towards her, for if he had she would've been forced to flee, professionalism be damned. In the past, she might've stood her ground and fought for the man she loved, but not this time. She'd bared her soul to this guy and what had he done? Dismissed her like yesterday's news.

As she'd originally thought when they'd first met, she wasn't good enough for him. He'd made that patently obvious by saying she couldn't be the mother of his children. Well, she'd show him. She didn't need some uptight, pretentious psychologist to parent her child. She would do a fine job of raising her child on her own, without the input of a man who thought she didn't measure up.

Instilling the right amount of *I don't give a damn* into her voice, she said, 'Naturally, you'd want to see the finished product. If you'd show me to a table, I can boot up the laptop and you can take a look at your new website.'

'That's not what I meant.' He made the mistake of moving towards her then and she held up her hand to hold him off.

'I'm here for one reason only and that's business. If you want to discuss anything else, I'm not interested.'

'We need to talk.' He stopped two feet in front of her, two feet too close.

She could smell his soap, as if he'd recently showered, and it resurrected painful memories she'd rather forget—like the first time she'd got close enough to smell it, the way its scent had clung to his pillow the morning after they'd first made love and how she'd buried her face in that pillow, unable to get enough of him.

'That's becoming your catch-cry, isn't it?' She

shook her head. 'I think you've said enough. Now, the website?'

'Forget the damn website!' he muttered, reaching towards her.

She backed away, almost tripping in her haste, and he thrust his hands in his pockets instead, cursing softly.

'This isn't going to happen, Lachlan. Not now, not ever.'

To her amazement, he strode past her, locked the front door and pocketed the key.

She laughed, a bitter sound that sounded nothing like happiness. 'You think you can lock me away like Rapunzel? Well, I've got news for you, mister. This isn't a fairy tale and you sure as hell aren't Prince Charming.'

'You're right. I'm not Prince Charming, Mr Perfect or any other fictitious character you care to label me with. I'm not some dream man who won't put a foot wrong, who won't ever say or do the wrong thing.' He reached for her and grabbed her upper arms and she stood there, too surprised by his outburst to move.

'I'm just a normal guy who's so head over heels in love with you that he can't think straight, let alone say the words you want to hear.'

Her heart leapt at his words, before settling into misery again. His sudden turnaround had to be about the baby. He'd thought about it over the weekend and had decided that having a child of his own was worth putting up with her for, even if she wasn't good enough to be the mother of his children by choice.

As much as she loved him—and as much as this baby deserved a father—she wouldn't risk her heart again. He'd had his chance to love her for *her*, and he'd blown it. Big time.

Shaking her head, she blinked back tears. 'You'd do anything for this baby, wouldn't you?'

He dropped his arms, a stunned expression on his face. 'You really are pregnant?'

'Of course,' she snapped, wondering if his short-term memory was functioning. 'I already told you at the party, remember? Around the time you dumped me? Ring any bells?'

Confusion clouded his eyes as he stared at her. 'But I thought you were just posing a question.' His eyes narrowed, as if trying to remember her exact words. 'Didn't you say something like "What if I said I was pregnant?" That sounded like a big "what if" to me, not a declaration.'

'You're splitting hairs,' she said, trying not to agree with him. Perhaps she hadn't made it clear that night. Not that it would've made a difference. He'd walked away from her anyway. Worse, he'd accused her of using something like that to hold on to him, which showed exactly what he thought of her. 'Besides, what difference does it make? I opened up to you, you rejected me. End of story.'

However, she couldn't ignore one salient point. If

he hadn't known she'd been serious about the baby, why say he was in love with her now? What did he hope to gain?

He tilted her chin up and, despite her efforts to look away, her eyes were drawn back to his. 'This is the beginning for us, not the end.' He smiled and it lit up his entire face. 'We're really going to have a baby? That's incredible.'

She wouldn't be swayed by his tenderness or smooth words. The time for saying the right thing had passed and she'd be better off concentrating on building her own future rather than dwelling in the past.

'You blew it, and as far as I'm concerned there's no going back.'

You hurt me, she wanted to scream, but swallowed the words like she always had, preferring to bottle up her feelings and withdraw from those who cared rather than risk being let down.

It had happened to her repeatedly as a teenager, and she'd learned to be self-sufficient and not rely on the approval of others to get through life. Now Lachlan, the man she loved, had let her down at a time she needed him the most and she'd be damned if it happened again.

'Tell me how you feel. Please.' He slid his hand around to cup the side of her face, its warmth a comfort that she'd missed.

Her first instinct was to pull away and run, but the

sad expression in his eyes beseeched her to stand and deliver.

'I've already tried and you didn't listen. Why is it different now?'

He wiped away the tears that spilled down her cheeks in slow rivulets before hauling her into his arms and burying his face in her hair. 'Please don't cry. I can't bear it. I'm so sorry for hurting you.'

She stiffened at the first contact of hard chest wall but soon relaxed into him, melding against his body as if she was made for it. And the last of her resistance melted away as he held her close and whispered into her ear, 'I love you so much. You're my world, my everything. I know I don't deserve it but please hear me out.'

She snuggled into him as her tears subsided, too drained to reply. His masculine scent filled her nostrils, calling to her receptors on a deeper level, beckoning her to fill herself with this man in every way.

His words filled her with a hope that begged to give him a chance.

Leaning back slightly, she looked up. 'What happened with us? What went wrong?'

The sadness she glimpsed in his eyes made her want to hold on to him for ever. 'A combination of things, starting with a major hang-up I've had about my mother for most of my life.'

Oh, great. He was a mummy's boy?

'Though I'll never forgive her for running out on

my dad and breaking his heart, I recently learned a few truths that set the record straight.'

Her hand flew to her mouth. 'Your father! How is he?'

'He's fine. In fact, I owe him a lot for making me see sense. For a psychologist who prides himself on reading people, I really botched up with you, didn't I?'

She shrugged and smiled for the first time since Friday night. 'Hey, I've already told you what I think of your counselling skills. On national radio too!'

He laughed and scooped her closer. 'And my ego hasn't recovered since.' His smile faded as he tucked a strand of hair behind her ear. 'You must've gone through hell growing up. I'm sorry for dismissing it the other night.'

'You don't know the half of it,' she said, understanding she would have to tell him everything for a fresh start.

As she opened her mouth to speak, he held a finger up to her lips. 'You don't have to tell me if you don't want to. I trust you, and it took the fact that I almost lost you to wake me up to it.'

She kissed his finger before pushing it away. 'I need to do this for me.'

'Okay, but why don't we sit down?' His eyes lit up as he placed a hand on her belly. 'After all, you're carrying precious cargo in there.'

At the possessive look of love on his face, her

heart slammed against her ribs. This man loved her and their baby. What more could she ask for?

Sure, he owed her an explanation for the rotten way he'd treated her, but how could she blame him when she had enough hang-ups to keep him occupied till their fiftieth anniversary?

He led her into a sunny family room adjacent to the kitchen, where she glimpsed champagne chilling in a bucket next to two flutes.

She quirked an eyebrow and looked at him. 'Cocky, weren't you?'

'Hopeful, not cocky. There's a difference.'

He made a move to uncork the bottle before glancing back at her uncertainly.

'Water will be fine.'

'Cheap date,' he muttered as he filled two glasses from the tap and added a slice of lemon to each.

'But you love me anyway,' she said, sending him a coy smile as he handed it to her.

'Now who's cocky?' He sat next to her on the couch, his hand resting on her knee, sending heat streaking through her body. 'Where were we?'

Rather than her hunger for him abating with the enforced absence of the last few days, it had grown to monstrous proportions and it took all her willpower not to jump him.

'We're discussing how screwed up we both are. Shall you go first or shall I?'

He tilted his glass towards her and smiled. 'Ladies first.'

'Okay.' She settled back on the couch, wishing they'd done this weeks ago. If so, it would've saved her a lot of stress—and a fortune in doughnuts and tissues. 'You know about my weight problem, right? The part I didn't tell you was that I became so obsessed about losing weight that I went the other way, losing so much I collapsed.'

His grip tightened on her leg. 'Were you anorexic?'

She shook her head. 'No, thank goodness, but almost. When I collapsed, I spent some time in hospital, and that was enough to get me back on track. I absolutely hated the place and would've done anything to get out so I started eating and actually began to feel good about myself. However, the medical team told me something that changed my life.'

She closed her eyes, wondering how many times she'd relived that fateful moment over the years and wishing she could find that doctor right now and shove her pregnancy test in his face.

Taking a deep breath, she opened her eyes. Lachlan hadn't moved a muscle—he didn't push her or demand to know the truth. Instead, he waited patiently.

'They told me I'd probably never have children.'

'*What?*' he exploded, his anger surprising her.

'I suppose they thought it was true at the time. However, it changed my life. At least how I related to men,' she rushed on, before she lost her confidence to tell him everything. 'Most men want a child to prove their potency to the world and that's the one thing I thought I couldn't give them. The first guy I really fell for did a runner when I told him the truth, despite vowing to love me for ever, so I picked up the pieces of my fragile self-esteem again, and moved on. The second—well, he was just as bad. I've only dated casually since, for that very reason. However, when you came along…' She shrugged and covered his hand with hers. 'Despite my intentions to hold you at bay, I fell for you.'

He clicked his fingers in a lightbulb moment. 'That's why you backed off from me, isn't it? That day I came to your office I prattled on how about how much having a large family meant to me. And you thought you couldn't give me that?'

She nodded and he hauled her into his arms.

'You put my feelings ahead of your own?' He stroked her hair, a soothing gesture she would never tire of. 'You're a remarkable woman, Keely Rhodes. Our child is going to have one very special mother.'

She wriggled out of his embrace. 'Hang on a minute, buster. That's me off the hook. How about you?'

'Like I said, my mother left me with enough emotional baggage to weigh down a jet plane. She lied, cheated and generally devastated my father before walking out on us. Hence my obsession with honesty.'

'Go on.' She watched a myriad emotions flicker across his face, knowing how painful this must be for him but needing to hear it anyway.

'When you were holding out on me these last few weeks, I was going out of my mind. If you couldn't tell me about that phone call, I wondered what else you were hiding. Add to that your walk-out at the café, plus the way you kept clamming up or over-reacting over what I thought were innocent comments, and I was ready to throttle you. Then Chrystal mentioned something about you and some guy Aidan the other night and I lost it.'

'I'll kill her,' she muttered under her breath. 'Aidan is this loser who pops into Accounts on occasion. I thought he'd be perfect for my assistant, Lucy, which turned out to be false anyway. Why would Chrystal start a rumour—?'

She burst out laughing and refrained from slapping her head to knock some sense into herself. 'You're her next victim and she wanted me off the scene! Why, the little scheming tramp. And you believed her?'

He had the grace to look sheepish. 'In all honesty, I was probably looking for an excuse to have it out with you, so I latched on to her words and they fuelled my own insecurities. Your jealousy act set me off; that's what I thought you were doing, acting. When I heard about this other guy it reminded me of my mother, and when you flung that bit about a possible baby at me…she'd done the same thing to my dad. Or so I'd thought. Dad set me straight and made me see what a mess I was making of my own life, blaming you when you're nothing like her.'

She could strangle Chrystal with her bare hands, but in a way she owed her. If she hadn't interfered, Keely might've danced around her past for months yet, driving a bigger wedge between them, and Lachlan wouldn't have discovered the truth about his mother.

'You said you loved me; my mother never loved my father.' He rubbed a hand over his face, as if trying to erase the past. 'I was so ashamed for flinging your declaration back in your face that I stayed away on the weekend, trying to concoct a scheme to win you back.'

'And this is it?'

He grinned, the warmth of his smile sending her pulse racing. 'Partially. Lucy helped get you here and I hoped the truth would do the rest.'

'You're getting there. Keep going.'

Lucy would have a lot of explaining to do tomorrow. Though how could she fault her assistant for bringing the man she loved back into her life? She should give her a rise rather than a scolding.

'What do you think of this house?'

His question came from left field, though nothing should surprise her in this all-round weird week. Over the last seven days she'd discovered she was pregnant, been dumped and then reunited with the love of her life, and, if the rumours were correct, gained that promotion she'd been hankering for.

Raquel had scheduled a meeting with her for the end of the week, and she hoped the Director of

Graphic Design position would be hers. She'd done a damn good job with the Brant assignment, even if she had taken the shadowing bit to extremes! Though how the Rottie would react when she learned she'd lose a second director to motherhood didn't bear thinking about.

She glanced around the room, admiring the airy open plan with afternoon light spilling in from the floor-to-ceiling windows, the comfortable furniture, the mix of modern with eclectic.

'I love it from what I've seen of it. My apartment is the antithesis of it, but this place feels welcoming, like a real home.'

The corners of his mouth twitched. 'Good, I'm glad you like it. I bought it weeks ago, with us in mind. Think you could live here?'

'Huh?' The idea that he'd had so much faith in their relationship made her feel guilty all over again for holding him at bay.

'I'm the new owner, and I'd hoped my future wife would love it as much as I do.'

Her mouth dropped open and his soft chuckles echoed in the silence as he cupped her chin and gently closed it.

'That's right, Keely. I'm asking you to marry me.' He kissed her, a slow, lingering kiss that lit a fire deep within. 'I love you, and would be honoured if you'd agree to be my wife.'

'I love you too,' she whispered, her heart tripping with the extent of how much, 'and the answer is yes.

Though I don't know if I can live with a man who isn't perfect.'

He closed the short distance between them by pulling her on to his lap. 'In that case, you'd better concentrate on the bits that are perfect.'

He lowered his lips to hers. 'Starting with this.'

EPILOGUE

'Note to self: ditch Keely's Collection. *Perfect man found—and he's amazing.'*
Keely, new convert to the 'happily-ever-after' philosophy.

KEELY strolled into the conference room, using every ounce of self-control not to do a happy dance and blurt out the truth as soon as she saw her friends.

'Hey, how are you, sweetie?' Emma joined her at the coffee machine and refilled her cup. 'Over that bug yet? Feeling okay about everything else?'

Keely nodded and smiled, resisting the urge to blab to the world that she wasn't just feeling okay, she was feeling downright amazing. The love of a good man, a marriage proposal and an unexpected baby on the way would do that to a woman.

'I'm fine. Though I have got some news for you.' She bit back a grin at the anticipated reaction from her romantic friend. Not just the fact that she'd reunited with Lachlan but they were starting a family to boot.

She'd omitted that pertinent fact when crying on the girls' shoulders over the weekend—she hadn't wanted them to rush over to Lachlan and do something crazy—like dragging him back to her hand-cuffed and forcing him to marry her. Though now that she came to think about it...it would've speeded up the whole process and saved her days of heart-breaking misery.

Tahlia walked into the room at that moment and headed over to join them. 'I hope it's got nothing to do with that louse Lachlan. Good riddance to bad rubbish, no matter how gorgeous.'

Keely filled her mug with hot water and camomile tea, knowing her caffeine withdrawal was going to be hell but willing to do anything for the precious life inside her. 'Actually, it has got something to do with him.'

Tahlia's eyes narrowed as her gaze swept from Keely's tea up to her face. 'What's going on? I thought he was history? And why are you drinking *that*?'

Keely sipped at the tea and tried not to grimace, failing miserably. Maybe she'd try peppermint or raspberry tomorrow.

'You're pregnant, aren't you?' Emma blurted out, her eyes twinkling with barely suppressed excitement.

Keely's eyebrows shot up. 'How did you know?'

Emma let out a whoop and smothered her in a ferocious hug while Tahlia gaped in open-mouthed amazement before muttering, 'I need to sit down.'

Laughing at her friends' reactions, she disengaged

from Emma's arms and gestured at the table. 'Why don't we all have a seat and I'll explain everything?'

'Good idea,' Tahlia said, shaking her head and looking totally perplexed while Emma grinned as if she'd just won the Lottery. 'I take it you're happy about the news, despite the louse's defection?'

Keely filled a glass with water, deciding to ditch the herbal tea for now. It would have to grow on her, as everything else about her would grow in the next few months.

'I'm ecstatic,' she said, hugging a protective arm around her middle. 'Oh, and I'd prefer it if you'd stop calling my future husband a louse.'

This time Emma joined Tahlia in the open-mouth stakes, before screeching, 'You're getting *married*?'

'Yeah. It's great, isn't it?'

Emma let out an excited squeal and clapped her hands together. 'This is fantastic! How romantic. When did all this happen?'

'On one of those dirty weekends away, I'd imagine,' Tahlia said, sending Keely a wicked smile.

Emma waved away Tahlia's comment. 'Not that part. Last thing we knew, you were sobbing all over us, telling us what a jerk he'd been in dumping you. And now you're getting married?'

'I was kind of premature about the jerk bit. He's still pretty perfect.'

'The marriage isn't just about the baby, is it?' A slight frown marred Tahlia's brow, her ever-practical and blunt assessment of the situation leaving Keely in no doubt as to how much her friend actually cared.

'Uh-uh. He'd already said he loved me before he knew about the baby. And he'd bought us a house to prove it.' She patted her belly and smiled. 'I guess this little person will just hurry along our wedding plans, that's all.'

Emma sat bolt upright and rubbed her hands together. 'Fabulous. We've got a wedding to plan.'

'And a baby shower,' Tahlia added, leaning over and hugging Keely tightly.

Keely laughed and blinked back tears. She could blame her swinging emotions on hormones, but she'd rather attribute the sudden waterworks to her best friends and their unswerving loyalty.

For someone who'd been alone and floundering for so many years, she wanted to pinch herself now to see if all this was real—great job, wonderful friends, and now the perfect man and their precious miracle.

'Thanks, you guys. For everything.' She dabbed at her eyes, thankful for waterproof mascara, and pointed at the files on the table. 'Now, we'd better get stuck into work before the Rottie gets stuck into us. Any other goss from you before we get started?'

Emma's eyes glowed briefly before she opened the file in front of her and started shuffling papers. 'Harry's coming to town for his yearly visit soon, so I'm kind of looking forward to that.'

Tahlia hooted. 'Kind of? Bet you can't think of

anything else, you're so obsessed with the guy.' She paused and winked at Keely. 'Though I reckon he's a figment of your imagination. We've never seen him in the flesh, so to speak.'

'And you won't, with that attitude,' Emma said, blushing furiously.

Still caught up in her own love fest, Keely understood exactly where Emma was coming from. If she loved the guy, she should go for it. After all, look where that philosophy had got her.

'We'd really like to meet him, hon. And if he's as special as you say he is why don't you throw caution to the wind and tell the guy how you feel?'

'Yeah, why don't you jump his bones already?' Tahlia chimed in, a smirk on her face.

'I'll think about it,' Emma muttered, her blush deepening.

Tahlia shrugged and reached for her file. 'If you don't do it, we will.'

'You wouldn't dare!'

'Just try me,' Tahlia said, patting Emma's cheek before settling back in her seat. 'No goss from me, so let's get to work.'

Keely chuckled, loving the familiar banter and knowing she was going to miss it while away on maternity leave. Though she knew the girls would be visiting on a regular basis, it wouldn't be the same as their D&Ms in the conference room. Not that she'd have time to worry about it; her little bundle of joy would be monopolising all her time as she discovered what motherhood was all about.

'Here's the finished product for *Flirt*,' she said, handing copies to Emma and Tahlia.

However, before they could take a look, Lucy stuck her head around the door. 'Sorry to interrupt, ladies, but you have a client waiting in your office, Keely. I told him you were busy, but he said it would only take a minute and he wouldn't take no for an answer.'

Keely bit the inside of her cheek to stop herself from laughing as she noticed Lucy's wink and 'come here' hand gesture, which could only mean one thing.

Her *client* needed some immediate attention, and she was more than ready to give it to him.

'Back in five, girls,' she said, casually strolling to the door when in fact she wanted to pick up her feet and fly to her office.

However, she forced herself to walk sedately down the corridor, her anticipation mounting with every step. It had only been a few hours since she'd kissed her new fiancé goodbye, but one could never have too many kisses from a man like Lachlan.

Reaching her door, she schooled her face into a professional mask with effort and entered the room. 'I hear you have some important business to discuss. What can I do for you?'

Lachlan spun round from the window and crossed the room in two seconds flat, hauling her into his arms so quickly that all the breath rushed out of her.

Not that she minded; she was getting used to feeling breathless around him.

'You can start by wrapping up whatever you're in the middle of and coming to lunch with me.' His hands played in a leisurely way along her spine, sending electrifying tingles shooting every which way.

'I have work to do.' She tried a mock frown and failed dismally.

He ran a finger slowly down her cheek, letting it rest against her bottom lip, which practically quivered under his touch. 'How about you *work* on me?'

She shook her head and chuckled. 'Doc, you're crazy.'

His lips brushed hers in a sweet, lingering kiss, the kind that she could get used to for the rest of her life. 'Crazy in love with you.'

TOP-NOTCH SURGEON, PREGNANT NURSE

Amy
ANDREWS

Amy Andrews has always loved writing and still can't quite believe that she gets to do it for a living. Creating wonderful heroines and gorgeous heroes and telling their stories is an amazing way to pass the day. Sometimes they don't always act as she'd like them to—but then neither do her kids, so she's kind of used to it. Amy lives in the very beautiful Samford Valley, with her husband and aforementioned children, along with six brown chooks and two black dogs. She loves to hear from her readers. Drop her a line at www.amyandrews. com.au.

To my dearest friend, Leah. Who knows.

CHAPTER ONE

BETH ROGERS stared at her office wall, reliving Friday night over again in all its horrifying splendour. She blew on her tea as she absently tucked a stray strand of blonde hair back into her theatre cap.

A pair of vivid green eyes, the exact shade of the peridot in her favourite pair of earrings, had haunted her all weekend. Crinkly caramel hair styled into a trendy just-got-out-of-bed fashion had continually flashed on her inward eye. A well-modulated English accent had replayed relentlessly. The aroma of popcorn, coffee and shortbread lingered even now.

How could she have done that? She'd never had a one-night stand in her life. Never.

At thirty-eight, no doubt there were some out there that would think that terribly boring. But having had her life defined by an even worse error of judgement at fifteen, she'd always shunned the casual sex scene. At least this time round she'd made sure they'd used protection.

'Here she is.'

'Where else would she be at seven in the morning, even though as NUM she doesn't start till eight?'

Beth looked away from the very fascinating wall to find her two sisters lounging in her doorway. She smiled at them, plastering an all-is-well-with-the-world look on her face and banishing those peridot eyes. 'Good morning to you both, too.'

Rilla and Hailey entered and threw themselves down on the low lounge chairs that sat against the wall opposite the desk.

'Well, I know why I'm here this early—' Beth began.

'Because you're a workaholic,' Rilla interjected.

Beth ignored her. 'But why are you both here so early?' Like she needed to ask. Rilla and Hailey had been hovering for days. 'I thought you were on days off, Rilla. And, Hailey—you don't start till one. Wet the bed?'

The sisters looked at each other. 'Come on, Beth. We're just worried about you,' Hailey said, putting all her best counseling skills into the conversation. 'We're family. When you hurt, we hurt.'

'Yes,' Rilla agreed. 'We've been fretting all weekend about you.'

Beth looked at her sisters and felt their love and concern. They were so different from her. She was lanky and blonde, like the few photos she'd seen of her mother. They were darker and curvier, like Penny, *their* mother. But she'd been part of the Winters family for over twenty years and, blood bond or not, she was as close to them as any sisters.

She shook her head and smiled at them. 'I'm fine guys, really. This is a tough time of year for me. I know you know that better than anyone else and I appreciate your concern.'

The sisters exchanged looks again. Beth's words were reassuring but they knew how bruised her heart was still, even twenty-three years down the track. Had lived through that tumultuous time all those years ago as well and even though they'd both been quite young, Beth had been unbearably sad and it had left a lasting impression.

'So did you go and see that movie Friday night?' Hailey asked.

Friday night. No, she was trying not to think about Friday night. 'Yep,' she said, hoping to sound nonchalant.

Rilla looked at, Beth waiting for more information. None was forthcoming. 'Was it able to distract you like you hoped?' she prodded.

The movie hadn't but what had happened afterwards certainly had! It had kept her distracted all weekend. 'Yep,' she said again.

Rilla and Hailey exchanged yet another look. 'I didn't think an action movie would hold your attention for long, you're more a foreign-film buff,' Rilla persisted.

'Oh, yes, all that blowing up stuff.' Beth nodded convincingly, 'very good distraction.'

'What did you do afterwards? I hope you didn't go back to your house and brood all night. You know we would have come over.' Hailey frowned, her concern all too obvious.

Yes, she knew. But she hadn't been able to bear the thought of it. Her sisters' efforts to keep her mind off the baby she'd given birth to twenty-three years go would only have served to focus her mind on it more. They'd been there to witness the aftermath of that turbulent time and their presence alone would have been enough to stir the memories.

Beth decided to throw them a crumb to sidetrack them. 'I actually walked out of the cinema into a medical emergency. A woman had collapsed into a diabetic coma and then she started to fit. This…' Beth paused slightly while she searched for an adequate description. 'Guy and I, rendered some first aid while we waited for the ambulance.'

'Guy?' Rilla and Hailey said in unison, recognising the significance of Beth's hesitation, sensing a juicy titbit.

Damn it! She shouldn't have stumbled over how to explain him. She should have known her sisters would jump on that part of the information.

'What was he like?' Rilla asked.

'What's his name?' Hailey pressed.

'What's he do?' Rilla added.

'Spill!' Hailey demanded.

Hot. He was hot. Amazing green eyes, beautiful mouth and a way with her body that had made her weep in his arms.

'He seemed nice enough,' she fobbed them off, hoping her nose wasn't growing. 'His name is Gabe. He's English. He's a teacher.' They were looking at her expectantly and she knew how tenacious they could be so she threw them another crumb.

'We had coffee.'

And he made me laugh. He made me forget. And he was flirting and he had desire in those amazing eyes and something else, something sad, and when he suggested I go back to his hotel room I did because I couldn't bear to be alone with the memories, and we had sex. All-night sex. Last-night-alive-on-earth sex. Armageddon sex. Until I slunk out of his room at dawn.

'Coffee?' the sisters said in unison again, looking at Beth speculatively.

'Do you fancy him?' Rilla asked.

Beth rolled her eyes. 'He's…younger than me.'

'How much younger?' Hailey demanded.

'Thirty-three.' But he hadn't looked a day over twenty-eight.

'So?' Hailey shrugged.

Her sister's words triggered a Friday-night flashback.

'Look, I'm flattered but you're a little young for me,' she had said and had laughed nervously.

'So?' Gabe had said, staring at her with desire and heartbreak in his eyes.

'Don't you think you should be playing with girls your own age?' she'd practically squeaked.

'No.'

And he'd been so sure of what he'd wanted and yet still kind of vulnerable, her insides had melted and she'd taken his proffered hand and followed him without any further argument.

'Is he married?' Hailey's persistent voice broke into her wandering thoughts.

Beth gave her sister a scandalised look. 'No.'

'So?' Hailey stated again.

Beth looked from one to the other, her head spinning. She was glad her instinct to keep Friday evening's full story to herself had kicked in. For as long as she could remember her sisters had been trying to set her up with men. It was their payback for years of her mothering them. But the last thing she needed was them constantly questioning her about Gabe.

She didn't want to be frequently reminded of her completely out-of-character actions. She already had a son out there somewhere to remind her of that. Her one-night-stand-man was best left at the hotel.

'So nothing. We had a pleasant chat.' Beth waited for a lightning bolt to strike her. 'He's in Australia for seven months. I'm never likely to see him again.'

'What sort of a teacher is he?'

'I don't know. We didn't really talk about our jobs,' Beth said wishing she was wearing a theatre mask to hide the heat she felt rising in her face. *She'd slept with someone she barely knew.* They'd talked about the movies and books and music. *And then they hadn't talked about much at all.*

Beth was saved any further interrogation by the arrival of the Brisbane General's Chief of Staff. She'd never been so happy to see the man who'd been more like a father to her than the man who had actually given her life.

'Ah, not one daughter but all three,' John Winters said, beaming at his girls. He didn't have to ask why they were altogether—he knew why.

'Hi, Dad.' Rilla and Hailey rose to hug their father and he gave them a big grateful squeeze each. He winked at Beth over the top of their heads. 'How are you darling?' he asked gently.

Oh, God, not you too. 'I'm good, John. Really, I'm OK.'

John moved into the office and Beth rose to embrace him. He was tall and broad and handsome still, his hair greying nicely at the sides. She lingered in the circle of his arms, thankful every day that John and Penny had taken her in and given her a second chance at life.

'To what do I owe the pleasure of your hallowed company?' Beth teased. 'It's a bit far down from the executive suites to the bowels of the hospital, isn't it?'

John chuckled and sat on the corner of her desk. 'I'm

just showing the visiting neurosurgeon around. He's meeting me here shortly.'

'Dr Fallon?' Beth asked.

'The English guy? The one who's leading the neuro team to separate the Fisher twins?' Hailey piped up. 'What's he like?'

'He has an impeccable reputation. He's only thirty-three but has a very bright future. He's worked on some real cutting-edge stuff in Oxford and has a very successful private practice. He's been involved with separating two sets of craniopagal conjoined twins already. The Fishers are lucky to have him. The General is lucky to have him.'

'That's not what she meant, Dad,' Rilla said, laughing at her sister.

John's eyes twinkled. He'd known exactly what his youngest daughter had meant. 'Well, he doesn't do much for me but I guess you young things would call him a hottie. Why, interested?'

'No way,' Rilla said vehemently. 'But Beth, on the other hand…' she turned to look at her older sister '…needs a good man.'

'Hey!' Beth protested. 'If anyone needs a man around this joint, it's you. It's about time you started moved on. It's been seven years since Luca left.'

'Absolutely,' Hailey agreed.

'You can't talk,' Rilla said turning to her younger sister to deflect the attention from her. 'How long has it been for you?'

Hailey laughed. 'Give me a break. I only got back into the country eight weeks ago.'

'You're normally faster than that,' Rilla pointed out.

Hailey started to protest and then figured it was a little

rich to be outraged by her sister's comment when it was essentially true. She'd had a string of boyfriends. But things had changed in London. 'I'm mellowing in my old age.' Hailey shrugged.

They all laughed and Hailey joined them. It was good to be back home among the family again. She'd missed them on the other side of the world and their familiarity was like a soothing balm to her burnt-out soul.

Dr Gabriel Fallon heard their laughter all the way down the corridor. He looked up at the sign that jutted out from the wall above the door where all the noise appeared to be coming from. It read 'O.T. Nurse Unit Manager.' Definitely where John had told him to come. *Looked like the Brisbane General was going to be a fun place to work*. It would make a nice change from the gloom he'd left behind in England.

He approached the office and knocked quietly on the door. John was sitting on the desk, two women were sitting in the chairs against the wall and another, behind the desk—John's daughter, he presumed—was obscured from his view by her father.

'Am I interrupting something?'

Beth felt the laughter die a sudden death on her lips. That voice. That accent! She'd know it anywhere. The same voice that had asked her to his hotel on Friday night. The same voice with the sexy accent that had whispered outrageous things to her all night.

'Gabriel,' John said, rising to his feet and ushering the newcomer inside. 'Pardon us. Clan gathering. Meet my daughters. This is Rilla. She's the middle child. She works down in Accident and Emergency.'

'Rilla.' Gabe nodded extended his hand. 'A pleasure to meet you.'

Beth watched Rilla blush under Gabe's gaze and knew exactly how she felt. His accent flowed over her like warm icing on a hot cake. *Oh, God, oh, God!* What the hell was he doing here? Gabe? Teacher Gabe? Her Gabe was the new hotshot from the UK? No wonder he'd been so good with the diabetic. *First-aid course, my fat eye!*

'This is Hailey, the youngest child. She's just started on the kids' ward. She's been away for three years in your neck of the woods.'

'Oh, whereabouts?' Gabe asked, shaking her hand.

'London,' Hailey confirmed.

Oh, God, it's me now. Beth wished she could hide under the table as she watched her father and Gabe turn towards her. Time ground to a halt as their actions appeared to unfold in slow motion.

'And this is the woman in charge around here. She's also done quite a bit of travelling and even worked in Oxford. This is my oldest daughter—'

Gabe's eyes widened as recognition dawned. 'Beth!' he supplied before John had a chance.

Gabe couldn't believe what he was seeing. The woman who'd been on his mind all weekend was standing in front of him. Her hair may be obscured by a cap, her lithe body covered in baggy theatre greens, but he'd remember that flawless complexion, those eyes, that mouth anywhere. *Hell!*

Beth swallowed, trying to moisten her suddenly parched mouth. Nothing had prepared her for the impact of seeing him again. On Friday night he'd worn jeans and a polo shirt. Today he was wearing dark grey trousers, a striped business shirt and an impeccably matching tie. But she knew neither were a match for what lay beneath.

'Hello, Gabe.'

John frowned. 'You two know each other?'

Intimately. Gabe had thought about no one else since he'd woken alone in his bed on Saturday morning. He'd slept with the boss's daughter? A colleague? *Oh, good move, Gabriel!* He saw a burst of panic flare her pupils and her blue eyes darted nervously to John and then back to him. *She didn't want her family to know.* 'We…met on Friday night.'

Beth could see Hailey and Rilla exchange looks in her peripheral vision as his green eyes captivated her, making it impossible to look away.

'You're the guy who helped her with the diabetic?' Rilla exclaimed.

Among other things. Gabe smiled at Rilla and then turned back to Beth. 'Yes. We made quite a team.'

John was looking at Beth and she quickly filled him in with an abridged version of events, ignoring the familiar undertone in Gabe's voice.

'Well, then. No introduction needed,' John said.

Gabe saw a slight hint of pink adorn Beth's high cheekbones. *Definitely no introduction needed.* He wondered if John Winters would have been so welcoming had he known just how well acquainted he was with Beth.

'It'll be a pleasure working with you,' Gabe said.

Beth nodded, unable to speak, trying not to focus on the word 'pleasure'. Was it just her hyperactive imagination or had he emphasised it slightly? Her body was still tingling in places from the pleasures they had shared.

No! This couldn't be happening. If she'd known she was going to have to work with him, she would never have thrown common sense and a lifetime of caution to the winds and slept with him. The one thing, the only thing, she'd managed to comfort herself with over the weekend had been she'd never have to see him again.

'Well, we'd better be getting on,' John said. 'I believe Dr Fallon has an afternoon list, Beth?'

Beth looked at John and nodded. She forced herself to concentrate on only him, ignoring both Gabe's and her sister's speculative. 'Starts at one.' She leafed through some papers on her desk and handed one to Gabe.

'Thanks,' he said softly as he took the theatre list. He watched her intently as she avoided his gaze. 'I guess I'll see you after lunch.'

Beth gave him a quick smile, which she hoped appeared friendly, and made a show of straightening the papers on her desk. Rilla and Hailey were shrewd. Too shrewd. If she ignored him, started acting weirdly, they'd be onto her. She could tell they were already bursting to get her alone.

John gestured for Gabe to exit first. 'See you later, girls.' John smiled at his daughters as they left the office.

Beth sat, her shaky legs dubiously supportive. She adjusted a few things on her desk and then risked a look at her sisters. They were looking at her with grins on their faces.

'What?'

'You didn't mention that Gabe was so gorgeous,' Rilla stated.

'Very sexy,' Hailey concurred. 'Slip your mind?'

'He's OK, I guess.' she shrugged.

'You guess?' Hailey laughed. 'That man is so damn cute I thought about slipping into a diabetic coma just to grab his attention.'

Beth grinned at the image and then sobered. 'Well that man is now apparently a colleague so the rest of it doesn't matter.'

'Thought you said he was a teacher?' Hailey said.

Beth shrugged. 'That's what he told me.'

A great start to their working relationship. Not only had they slept together but he'd lied to her. Had the flirting and flattery been lies too? To get her into bed? He had confessed to her, as they'd eaten from room service at three in the morning, that he'd never done anything so spontaneous before. Had that been another lie?

She had suppressed the impulse to question him further at the time knowing that a few hours in bed with a stranger did not permit her access to the intimate details of his life, and now wished she hadn't. She'd known what had driven her to act so outrageously—what had been his excuse?

Beth groaned inwardly. What did his reasons matter? The more important question was how she was going to work with him. The next six months stretched before her interminably and she wished they were over already.

'Well.' Rilla grinned and winked at Hailey. 'Looks like Gabe's going to be around for a while. You never know what could happen in that time.'

Beth looked from one to the other. Their brown eyes sparkled mischievously at her. 'No.'

Rilla and Hailey's grins widened.

'No,' Beth repeated, more emphatically this time.

'Oh, come on, Beth,' Hailey cajoled. 'I think he fancies you.'

Beth tried not to remember just how much he'd fancied her on Friday night. 'I'm not interested.'

'Liar, liar pants on fire,' Rilla teased.

'I do not date colleagues.'

'Oh, Beth,' Rilla chided. 'You do not date, full stop.' She made a chicken noise and flapped her arms a couple of times. Hailey giggled.

Beth fixed her sister with a glare. 'Rilla, you of all people should know how disastrous relationships at work can be.'

Rilla's smile died and Hailey's laughter cut off abruptly. Her sisters looked at her as if she'd slapped them, and Beth knew she'd stepped over the line. *Damn Gabe Fallon!* She'd done nothing but mother and dote on them since she'd entered their lives twenty-three years ago. Rilla had been seven at the time and Hailey five.

'I'm sorry, Ril,' she said immediately, getting up from behind the desk and crouching beside her sister's chair. 'I spoke without thinking.'

Rilla blinked and smiled weakly. 'It's OK, Beth. I know you didn't mean it that way. Just because it didn't work out for me, it doesn't mean they're necessarily a bad thing. You have to stop punishing yourself. It's been twenty-three years…'

It was both incredible and daunting to have two other human beings who knew everything about you and loved you anyway. Who knew what kind of ice cream you liked or what you wished for when a falling star crossed your path or how you'd cried yourself to sleep for a year. Despite their physical differences, despite their different surnames, Hailey and Rilla were her family. She didn't know what she'd do without them.

Beth looked into Rilla's earnest brown eyes. She took her sister's hand and gave it a squeeze. She reached for Hailey's and did the same.

'Listen, guys. I love you both but I don't need fixing up. I like my life. I have a great job and my own place and I can do what I like, when I like. I'm happy.'

Beth knew it was hard for her younger sisters to grasp. They were both still at an age when marriage and children were possible. Two years off forty, she'd given up on the often desperate need to hold a baby in her arms and her dreams of becoming a mother again. And she'd mourned that for a while but in the last couple of years had found some peace with it.

'Now, come on, you two,' Beth said, breaking away and standing up. 'Thanks for coming but go away now. I have work to do.'

Rilla and Hailey stood and they all huddled together for a group hug, their foreheads touching.

'You could just use him for sex,' Hailey suggested. 'He looks like he'd know some pretty slick moves.'

Rilla burst out laughing and Beth joined in despite shaking her head at Hailey. *You have no idea, sister, dearest!*

'Goodbye you two.' Beth kissed both her sisters and returned to her desk, pleased to be alone again.

She put her head on the desk and groaned. Now what? How was she supposed to see Gabe every day and act like she hadn't seen him naked?

The day got worse. Kerry Matthews, her second in charge and the scrub nurse rostered to work in Theatre Four with the new neurosurgeon, went home at lunchtime with a migraine. The other two nurses allocated to the theatre were junior and as such had had little experience in neurology cases.

Beth had cut her teeth in neurosurgery. She'd worked for two years at the internationally renowned Radcliffe in Oxford when she'd first gone traveling, and had been working there again when she'd come home for Rilla's wedding eight years ago and decided not to go back.

So, with the other theatres staffed and running smoothly, Beth resigned herself to having to scrub in. She stood at the washbasins outside Theatre Four and put her mask on. She could do this, she thought briskly as she tied the paper straps. Just hand him the instruments as he asks for them and try and anticipate his needs. Nothing she hadn't done for any other surgeon in the past eighteen years.

Except she'd never slept with any of the surgeons she'd worked with. And it wasn't like she hadn't had her share of opportunities. Because she had. *But she didn't do that.* She didn't sleep around. At all. And certainly not with colleagues.

Sure, there had been some relationships. But her past had made her very reserved and distrustful so nothing had been successful for long. And no one had got past the detached veneer to the softness beneath.

Letting that go long enough to let someone in was a big step for Beth. Too big. It meant giving up some hard-won control and that terrified her. Too many things had happened in her younger years that she hadn't been able to control. Being fostered by the Winters had put her back in charge of her life and it had been the gift she'd treasured most from her new family.

Beth flicked the taps and pushed the surgical scrub dispenser with her elbow. Green liquid squirted into her hand and she began the three-minute routine she could perform in her sleep, trying not to think about having to stand close to Gabriel Fallon for the next few hours.

'You ran out on me.'

Beth started. She hadn't heard him approach. The hairs on the back of her neck stood to attention as his presence loomed beside her. She turned her head to see him lounging against the sink, applying his mask. Looking at her.

'Yes.' What else could she say?

'I was hoping to…have a late breakfast. Maybe make a weekend of it.'

Beth faltered in mid-scrub. A whole weekend in bed with Gabriel Fallon. The mind boggled.

'You lied to me. You said you were a teacher.'

Gabe turned to face the sink and flicked the tap on. 'I do a little lecturing.'

Beth glared at him over the top of her mask.

Gabe chuckled. 'Look. I'm sorry. I don't usually tell people I'm a neurosurgeon. I'm good at my job but it takes up so much of my life. I have a killer schedule and I so rarely get the chance to socialise. When I do, I like to keep my work at work. And it can get weird. People know you're a doctor and they always want a consultation.' He scrubbed at his soapy hands for a few moments. 'Would you have stayed if I'd told you I was a neurosurgeon?'

She could hear the smile in his voice and she didn't have to look at his peridot eyes to know they'd be laughing. Beth snorted. 'I wouldn't have gone to bed with you if I'd known you were a neurosurgeon.'

He nodded as he scrubbed at his wrists. 'I'm glad I was…economical with the truth, then.'

Beth worked the soap down towards her elbows, ignoring the way the mask muted his voice, accentuating the accent, making it sound husky as hell.

Time for a few home truths. 'I don't do one-night stands.'

He'd known that the minute he'd suggested she go back to his room. He could still recall how totally shocked she'd looked for those seconds before something had changed in her eyes and she had taken his hand. 'I never intended it to be a one-night stand.'

'I don't do two-night stands either,' she said primly, horrified by the leap her pulse took at his statement.

He laughed and the noise caused a flutter inside her and she scrubbed harder at her arms. 'This is not funny. This is a disaster.'

Gabe frowned. 'No, a disaster would have been if we'd slept together and it had been awful. And it wasn't.' He looked down at her and their gazes clashed. 'It was good. It was very, very good.'

Beth heard her breathing go all funny. She couldn't refute it, no matter how much she knew she had to get this conversation back on an impersonal level.

She cleared her throat and turned back to concentrate on her scrub technique. 'Be that as it may, we have to work together for the next seven months so I think we need to establish some ground rules.'

Gabe smiled behind the mask. 'This should be good.'

'One. Forget Friday night happened.' She looked at him for confirmation.

He nodded.

'Two. No references to Friday night—ever.'

Gabe nodded again.

'Three. Be professional at all times. I will call you Dr Fallon and you will call me Sister Rogers. Four—'

'Rogers?' Gabe interrupted, frowning. 'I thought John said you were his daughter? Oh, God…you're not married, are you?' She hadn't mentioned a husband and she hadn't been wearing a ring. Maybe that's why she'd looked so panicked?

'No!' Beth said indignantly. Did he really think she would have slept with him had she been married? 'John is my foster-father. I've been with them since I was fifteen.'

Gabe struggled with relief and curiosity. 'Ah. I see,' he said, even though he didn't really.

Beth pressed on. 'Where was I?'

'Number four, I believe.'

Beth nodded. 'Four. No fraternising outside work—'

'Look, Beth, let me spare you the rest of the list,' Gabe interrupted. 'I happen to agree. Relationships at work should be avoided.'

Not that it was a strict rule for him. He'd had relationships with colleagues before but they'd always known the score. Relationships with women who didn't, women like Beth, were to be avoided at all costs.

'I have no intention of continuing where we left off. I live on the other side of the world. I'm here for seven months only. There would be very little point.' *Except for the pretty amazing sex, of course.* 'You have no need to fear. I will be nothing but professional.'

'Good.' Beth held her arms up under the tap and let the water run down them from her fingertips to her elbows, sluicing the soap off. 'We're both on the same page, then.'

She shut off the taps with her elbow and waited for the excess water to drip off her arms squashing the traitorous flutter of disappointment at his easy capitulation. She flapped her arms, briskly to dispel it altogether, keeping her arms bent. And then she turned on her heel, her now sterile arms held out in front of her.

Gabe watched her go, pushing open the theatre doors with her shoulder, her green theatre scrubs accentuating the length of her thighs and the slimness of her hips and bottom. He shook his head as he watched the last drips of water fall from his elbows.

That morning Beth had been thrown but this afternoon she'd been back in control. All business. Where was the woman who had struck such a chord with her sad eyes on Friday night? Who had come apart in his arms? Who had wept as she had come down from the heights they'd climbed?

Something had been up with Beth Rogers on Friday night. Maybe it had been his own recent grief that had made him sensitive to her inner turmoil but something had made her act completely out of character. Impulsively. As had he.

He'd known after about five minutes in her company that she wasn't the type to sleep with a virtual stranger. And yet after her initial shock she had followed him willingly—surprised the hell out of him—and given him everything she had.

He could still hear the gut-wrenching quality of her sobs as she had curled herself into a ball beside him. There had been such misery in her outpouring. Heartbreak and sorrow and grief. It had come from something buried deep inside. And, with his own emotions still a little raw, it had affected him more than he wanted to admit.

Beth Rogers was certainly a conundrum. Not that he had the time or the inclination to find out what made her tick. She was right. They were colleagues and he didn't need any complications messing with his burgeoning career. Separating conjoined twins was complicated enough.

He flicked off the taps and drew a mental shutter on their one-night stand. He had an aneurysm to clip.

CHAPTER TWO

Two weeks later, Gabe was staring down at the eight-month-old Fisher twins, lying back to back in their pram, fused occipitally. He was still amazed at the rare phenomenon. One in two hundred thousand live births. And craniopagus? Only two per cent of Siamese twins were joined at the head.

Most doctors could go a whole lifetime and never see this condition but in his relatively young career he'd now seen three sets of craniopagus-conjoined twins and had successfully separated two of them. Consequently, he was one of the world's foremost experts.

As the late, great Harlan Fallon's son, the world had expected big things of him, and fate, it seemed, had intervened to ensure that Gabe's career was just as stellar as his father's had been. A tremor of excitement ran through him. In approximately four months he could give these precious babies separate lives.

He hoped. Gabe was aware, more than anyone, of the pressures that were being put on him to ensure a third successful operation. With two positive outcomes under his belt and the Fallon reputation at stake, failure wasn't an option—despite the enormous odds against him. But he'd faced long odds twice already and won. Looking down at the girls now, he hoped his luck wasn't about to run out.

Bridie babbled away while her sister slept. She smiled a dribbly smile at him and he offered her his finger, which she grasped willingly.

'She likes you,' June Fisher commented.

'Well, I do have a way with women,' he joked as he allowed Bridie to suck his finger.

'Oh, yeah, you're real big with the babes.' Scott Fisher grinned.

Gabe laughed and they chatted some more about the op. 'As I explained earlier, the most important thing we can have on our side is time. We'd like to wait until Bridie and Brooke are at least ten kilos before we operate. It's a big operation and we want them to be as strong as possible. Brooke is almost there but her sister…' He stopped and smiled down at Bridie '…is still lagging behind. We'll get the dietician involved and hopefully she should be bang on target for her first birthday.'

'That'd be a great birthday present for them,' a teary June said. 'To be able to see each other for the first time.'

Gabe repeated his warning that while they would do everything they could, it was a long, risky operation and there were no guarantees. They could lose one or both of the girls. Or even if they both survived the rigours of the operation, one or both of them could have brain damage. He was particularly worried about Bridie. Her sluggish weight gain indicated she wasn't as strong as her twin.

'The team's going to be spending these next four months practising every step of the operation. I have all the scans, the MRIs and the angiography, and we have 3D images as well as several plastic models of the girls' heads we're working with so when we come to operate, every step will have been rehearsed.'

Gabe had been consulted in the Fisher case since their birth and, thanks to the wonders of the internet, had been involved with the planning right from the start.

'I want you to come along to the weekly case conferences we'll be having. It's important to me that the whole team meets both you and the girls so we can all get to know each other. It'll be a good forum for any questions you may have too.'

Scott nodded. 'Of course. We'd love to get to know the people who are going to be involved in the girls' separation. Thank you for involving us. You've been great, disrupting your life and career in the UK. We can't thank you enough, Gabe.' He gave his wife's hand a squeeze.

Gabe smiled. 'Don't thank me yet. The other thing we need to think about is that, despite everything, we may have to go for an emergency separation if something unforeseen happens.'

'Yes, we've been told that's a possibility,' Scott said.

Gabe nodded. 'It's obviously something we want to avoid. We want to be able to control as much of the situation as possible so the girls get the best outcome possible. If we have to go for an emergency separation it'll be because one or both of the girls' health is failing, and that's not an optimal condition to be operating under. So keep doing what you're doing. Feed them up and keep them healthy.'

Gabe chatted with the Fishers for a little while longer and then held open his office door as June manoeuvred the pram out. He waved at them as they walked away, shutting the door as they disappeared round a corner. Two lovely people, parents who would go to the ends of the earth for their children—he hoped he didn't let them down.

He stood looking at the scans illuminated on the viewing box. The enormity of the task ahead was staring back at him. Two separate but fused brains, tethered together by networks of wispy fibres.

It would take hours, at least twenty if everything went successfully—many more if it didn't. And involve a team of about thirty people. Several other neurosurgeons, plastic surgeons, vascular surgeons, anaesthetists, radiographers and nurses.

And that didn't take into account the hours of treatments and scans they'd already endured. A month ago plastic surgeons had implanted tissue expanders under the scalps around the operative site. Every week the twins had came back to have saline injections into the expanders so the skin would be nice and stretched and able to be closed over the gaping surgical wound that would remain after the separation.

Gabe switched off the light and removed the scans. He checked his watch. Three o'clock. His outpatient clinic was over for the day. He had time to go down to Theatres and get some more practice in on the Fisher twin model.

He entered the male staff change room and climbed into a set of theatre greens. He donned a blue hat and tied it securely in place at the base of his skull and covered his shoes with the slip-on bootees made out of the same thin, gauzy material as his hat.

He passed Beth's office but noticed she was talking to

a group of people and didn't stop. Their relationship had been cordial, strictly business, their night together a taboo subject. Which was just as well. Neither his career nor the Fisher twins could afford the kind of distraction that could flare out of control should they ever cross that line again.

Except as he snapped the scans in place on Theatre Ten's viewing boards, he realised he did think about her and their night together an awful lot. Too much. Even now, while he was trying to concentrate on the intricate meshing of Bridie and Brooke's cerebral vasculature, his mind was wandering to the room down the corridor.

Damn it! He turned away from the scans in disgust. In a few short months, maybe less if they were unlucky, he had to separate the intertwined circulation—he needed to focus!

Gabe was good at focus. Focus had got him to where he was today. One of the world's foremost neurosurgeons. And at work his mind was always on the job. Always. He was driven. Career orientated. Focused. Nothing distracted him. Certainly no woman. And he couldn't let that happen now.

His father had reached the pinnacle of transplant medicine by never letting anything divert his attention. Not a wife or son or colleagues or a reputation as an arrogant, pompous bastard. Thousands of transplant patients had benefited from the advances Harlon Fallon had pioneered and that was the most important thing. If ever Gabe had felt neglected or had yearned for a little attention, he'd remembered the Nobel Prize his father had won.

His father had made a difference to the course of modern medicine. And that's what he wanted to do. He wanted to be to neurosurgery what his father had been to organ transplantation. And before his death his father had been proud of him. But he couldn't rest on his laurels. He'd gained an impressive global reputation, now it was his job to build on it.

Beth stared at the four student nurses standing in front of her. They looked terrified. She remembered how scary and overwhelming it had been when she'd first been sent to the operating theatres as a student and softened her words with an encouraging smile.

She was giving them her usual spiel about her high standards and what she expected of them. The operating theatres were a dynamic environment where one mistake could have serious ramifications—one careless miscount, one accidental contamination of a sterile field. She needed them to be vigilant.

They all looked impossibly young. They were second years. The three young women didn't look twenty. The young man looked slightly older, maybe twenty-two or three. *The same age as her son.* Her heart ached just looking at David Ledbetter. He was tall and blond with a dimple in his chin, and she found herself wondering for the millionth time what her own son would look like before she ruthlessly quashed it.

'OK, then. Time for a tour. Go round to the change rooms.' Beth pointed to the door through which they'd entered. 'Put on a set of greens, a pair of bootees and a cap and then knock on my door.' She pointed to the door on the other side of her office that led into the theatres.

The four of them stood there, looking nervous. 'Now,' she prompted.

The students darted from her office and Beth relaxed.

For a moment she wished she could be one of those NUMs that she heard the students talk about with affection. The ones who smiled a lot and befriended their students. But she was a little too reserved for that. Her background had taught her to be wary. Detached. So a reticence to get too close or involved was almost second nature to her.

Although Gabe hadn't had any problems getting past her reserve.

And it was difficult to be chummy when she had to ride them over their sterile technique and lecture them on the necessity of the endless cleaning required to keep the ultra-clean environment of the operating theatres as pristine as possible.

Her job required that she be a perfectionist—patients' lives depended on it. It was up to her to set standards and see they were maintained. And in the operating theatres, the standards had to be highest of all. Sterility and safety were paramount and the buck stopped with her. There was no place in her theatres for sloppy standards. And everyone who worked in the OT knew it.

Beth had struggled for years over how to bridge the gap between the person she had to be and the less reserved, more outgoing one she'd like to be. And in the end she'd given up. The people who mattered, who had known her for a long time, knew the real Beth beneath the guarded exterior. And she was fine with that.

There was a knock at the door and Beth opened it, stepping onto the sticky antiseptic mat which removed any dirt that had dared to venture into her office and stick to the bottom of her clogs. She gave a brisk nod of acknowledgement.

'This is the main theatre corridor,' Beth said, looking up and down, launching straight into it.

'Down this side are a couple of offices, the staffroom, change rooms and storeroom. On the other side…' she pointed to the swing doors of Theatre Five opposite '…are the ten theatres.'

She strode down the corridor. 'The theatres are not to be entered from these doors we see here but rather through the anaesthetic antechamber.'

Beth walked through an open doorway into Theatre Eight's antechamber. 'The patient is put under anaesthetic and intubated in here.' Beth indicated the monitoring equipment and stocked trolleys. To the left a double swing door separated the operating suite from the anaesthetic area.

She walked through the antechamber and under another open doorway. 'This is the room where the surgeons and scrub nurses scrub up.' The room housed a line of four sinks and it too had a closed swing door to the left which led into the theatre.

'This door,' Beth said, walking past the sinks to the far side of the scrub room, 'leads to the equipment corridor.' She pushed the single swing door open and indicated for the students to precede her. 'Basic supplies are kept here. It's also where the trays of instruments are sterilised prior to each procedure.' Beth stopped at a large steriliser fixed to the wall, its door open.

'At the end of the procedure, after all the instruments have been accounted for, the instrument trays come back out here and are passed through this window,' Beth pointed to the small double-hung opening behind the students.

'You lift the window, place the tray on the bench and shut it again. This puts the instruments in the hands of the nurses who run the dirty corridor beyond the window. This is the area where the instruments are cleaned, the trays reset and then sent to the central sterilising department.'

Beth drew breath and looked at the students, who all looked like their heads were about to explode with information overload. She saw the lost look on David's face and her heart went out to him.

'It's OK,' she said, taking pity on them. 'It's a lot to take in now but you'll soon get the hang of it.'

It didn't seem to help. None of them looked convinced so she kept them moving back out to the main corridor.

'There are ten operating suites. Two are usually kept free for emergency operations. Today that's Theatres Eight and Ten. This afternoon in the other suites we have three general surgery lists, two orthopeadic lists, an ENT list, one Caesar list and one gynae. Tomorrow you can go in and observe cases.'

Beth noticed the lights ablaze in the tenth suite as she approached. 'This is not acceptable,' she muttered as she strode towards it. 'I try to run these theatres as efficiently as possible. These big theatre lights are hellishly expensive to run,' she lectured. 'Lights must always be out if the suite is not in use.'

Beth entered the anaesthetic area, making a mental note to talk to Tom, the head theatre orderly, about it. It was the orderly's job to do end-of-day cleaning and that involved turning the lights off.

She veered to the left and shoved the double swing doors open with a shoulder, the students following close behind.

Gabe looked up at the interruption to his concentration.

He'd been engrossed in a particularly tricky vessel dissection and was annoyed at the intrusion. Especially as it was thoughts of the woman in front of him that had made it difficult for him to get into it in the first place.

'Oh.' Beth stopped abruptly.

Neither of them said anything for a moment.

'I'm sorry, Dr Fallon, I didn't realise you were in here.'

Gabe gritted his teeth at her formality. Despite agreeing to the necessity for it, he longed to hear her say 'Gabe' again, like she had that night. 'That's quite all right, Sister Rogers. I was just working on the Fisher case.'

Beth nodded. 'I'm showing some student nurses around. They'll be with us three days a week for the next six months.'

'Ah,' Gabe said, loosening a little. He never missed an opportunity to teach. 'They might be here when we separate the twins.'

'The Fisher twins?' Joy, one of the students, asked.

Gabe smiled at her. 'Yes. Come over here. I'll show you the scans.'

Beth stood back a little while Gabe explained the unusual anatomy and answered the students' eager questions. A little too eager, Beth thought. If the girls batted their eyelashes any more they were bound to fall out. Not that she could blame them. The combination of his well-modulated voice with his touch-of-class accent was hard to resist. He should have been working for a phone-sex hotline. His voice stroked all the right places.

'How often are you practising?' David asked.

'I try to do a little each day,' Gabe said. 'But we're having our first multi-disciplinary practice here on Saturday.'

He looked at Beth and she gave a brisk nod. Not something she was looking forward to. Seeing him every day was hard enough, without having to spend hours in his company on what should have been a day off.

'We're starting at eight,' she confirmed.

'And what does the practice entail?' David asked.

'Saturday is mainly big-picture stuff,' Gabe said. 'The logistics of the amount of people involved. Trouble-shooting and contingencies if things don't go according to plan. We have a weekly case conference starting Monday to discuss the intricacies.'

'How many staff will be required on the actual day?' Joy asked.

Beth almost rolled her eyes at the way the student nurse was preening in front of Gabe. She was a pretty redhead with a cute nose and an even cuter spray of freckles across it. Gabe shot her a smile and Beth couldn't suppress the frown that wrinkled her forehead.

'The cases I was involved with in the UK had about thirty personnel helping in one way or another during the separation process.'

Beth could tell each of the students was hoping to get a look-in. 'I'm sorry,' she said to them, 'only the most experienced staff will be on the team.'

Gabe nodded. 'Sister Rogers is right. With so many variables, so much potential for disaster, we need to have only the most skilled people.'

The students asked a few more questions. 'OK, I think we need to let Dr Fallon get on,' Beth broke in, checking her watch. 'We'll continue our tour.' She paused at the door, looking back over her shoulder. 'Don't forget the lights when you're done, Dr Fallon.'

Gabe's gaze met hers. *Business as usual.* 'I won't, Sister Rogers.'

Beth shook off the intensity of his gaze as she took the students to the recovery unit next, explaining the set-up and routine post-op monitoring. She didn't get too detailed. There would be more for them to see and learn next week and she could tell they had already overdosed on information. Before sending them on their way, she handed out their workbooks and briefly explained the competencies they'd be expected to achieve while here.

It was nearly five o'clock when Beth sat back down at her desk. All the lists except for Theatre Three's had finished for the day and Recovery was emptying. She should have gone home an hour ago but she was due at John and Penny's place for the regular weekly Winters family meal and decided she'd work on the roster for an hour and go straight from work to tea.

The roster was the worst part of her job. With ten theatres to staff and eighty nurses to appease, someone was bound to miss out on their requests. She always tried to be fair with the weekend and on-call shifts but invariably she managed to alienate some of her staff.

There was a knock on her door. 'Come in,' she called, not bothering to look up from the spreadsheet on her computer screen.

'Have you got a moment?'

Beth's head snapped up. She hadn't expected it to be Gabe. How was it that the man even made a pair of plain cotton theatre scrubs look good? 'Certainly, Dr Fallon.'

Gabe's brow wrinkled. 'Really, Beth, is it necessary to

continue with such formality when we're alone? I have seen you naked, remember?'

Beth gasped. 'Do you mind?' She got up from her desk and shut the door as images of a naked Gabe filled her mind. 'Yes, it is necessary, Dr Fallon. At work, it's imperative.'

The truth was, Beth was scared stiff that if she called him Gabe, everyone would know they'd slept together. That there would be a betraying catch in her voice that would give her away. 'Gabe' had been what she'd called him when he'd been inside her. 'Gabe' had far too many intimate connotations for her to bandy it around with any ease.

'And I would appreciate it if you didn't use "naked" in any sentence when talking to me.'

Gabe sighed as he lowered himself into a chair opposite her desk. Beth's office smelled of her. The same fragrance that had stayed with him since they'd first met. Like cinnamon doughnuts and a citrus orchard. Whatever it was, it overrode the pervasive antiseptic smell that invaded the operating suites.

'OK then, Sister Rogers…no "n" word. Whatever. I was wondering if you'd given any thought to rostering the nursing team for the big day.'

Beth was relieved he'd dropped the subject and had gone straight to talking shop. Her heart was still galloping madly as she tried to follow his train of thought. 'I was going to look at that on Saturday. I know who we need, it'll be a matter of who's available when the date's chosen.'

Gabe nodded. 'I'm thinking we should set a tentative date. That will help with staffing in all departments.'

'Even if we can narrow it down to an approximate week. If we're looking at four months from now, that's May,'

Beth scrolled through to her annual leave spreadsheet. 'I'll have to rearrange some things. A couple of my most experienced staff are down to take leave during that time.'

'Yes, OK. I'll look at trying to set an estimated date. Will that help?'

Beth nodded briskly, trying to be businesslike when that chair had never been filled so well in all its life. 'I take it you'll want to do this on a weekend? We'll be needing so many staff we won't be able to run other theatres as well. It would leave them too short.'

'Yes, logistically it's the only way to do it,' Gabe agreed. 'Of course, that's in a perfect world. If we need to go to an emergency separation, that could happen on any day.'

Beth nodded. 'We may have to cancel some cases if that happens. Is it likely?'

Gabe rubbed his jaw. 'Bridie is definitely the weaker twin. She's not thriving like her sister. They're both in good health at the moment but if Bridie picks up a bug and can't fight it off, she could jeopardise Brooke's health too. It's a possibility.' He gave her a smile that was half-grimace. 'I guess we have to cross that bridge if we get to it.'

Beth saw a flash of vulnerability in his green gaze and realised the enormity of the job that had landed in Gabe's lap. Sure, the surgery would require a team effort, but he was the leader, the 'expert'. The outcome, good or bad, would be on his head.

She felt a rush of tenderness welling inside her as she remembered the carefree man she'd slept with. How different was the man before her? Dr Gabriel Fallon was an entirely different animal to Gabe, her Friday-night man.

She remembered the first day she'd scrubbed for him,

Dr Gabriel Fallon, eminent neurosurgeon. She'd been worried how it would work so closely on the heels of their one-night stand, but she needn't have been. He'd all but ignored her, demanding perfection from her and everyone in the theatre. Treating her with the utmost in professional courtesy. As if their fling had never happened.

So different from the Gabe of their first meeting. Gabe, the lover. Sure, she hadn't been able to shake the feeling that something hadn't been quite right with him that night either, and he'd all but confirmed that when he'd admitted to his spontaneous behaviour, but he'd still been relaxed and laid back.

And if the whispers she'd heard since about his reputation were anything to go by, that Gabe enjoyed a party and a flirt and the company of women who knew the score.

Beth supposed the pressures of his work almost demanded this type of split personality. His job was highly stressful so it seemed only sensible to release the pressure through playing jack the lad in his downtime.

She opened her mouth to say, It'll be all right, Gabe, then caught herself in time. She pressed her lips firmly together. She didn't want to be part of his downtime. Best not to give him any encouragement.

'Fingers crossed, we won't.' Beth stood. 'Was there anything else, Dr Fallon?' she asked primly.

Gabe contemplated saying something shocking just to rattle her. Beth was one single-minded woman. 'No, Sister Rogers.' He stood also. 'I'll consider myself dismissed.'

Beth watched him go wishing it was just as easy to dismiss him from her thoughts.

* * *

The sun was setting as Beth pulled up at the Bullimba house she'd called home since she'd been fifteen. Her gaze took in its rambling whitewashed exterior. It had been a palace compared to some of the dives she'd lived in on the streets and she'd loved it the second she'd clapped eyes on it.

She was running a little late. She'd done battle with the roster for another hour and then given it up as a bad joke. Gabe's scent, sweet like shortbread, had invaded every corner of her office, making a mockery of her concentration. She'd stopped at the nearby shopping centre and picked up a bunch of flowers for Penny.

Beth walked up the path and was raising her hand to insert her key in the lock when she heard a car door slam behind her and a sexy voice say, 'Wait…'

Beth's heart crashed against her ribs as she turned towards the voice. 'What the hell are you doing here?' she demanded.

Gabe laughed. 'That's no way to speak to a dinner guest.'

He was wearing the clothes he'd worn to work this morning. Chocolate-brown trousers and a purple pinstriped shirt. The tie had been removed, the top buttons undone.

'I hope your family are drinkers,' Gabe said as he drew level with her, holding up a bottle of wine.

His crinkly caramel hair was still a little flat from his theatre cap and despite her absolute horror when she realised she would be sharing the table with him, she suppressed the urge to ruffle it. 'You're having dinner with us?' *Great. She'd drink the entire bottle all by herself!*

Gabe nodded. 'I ran into your father on my way out of the hospital.'

Damn John. 'No,' she said, shaking her head. 'You can't have dinner with us.'

Gabe chuckled. 'Yes, I can. John asked. I accepted.'

'But…Dr Fallon—'

'Beth,' Gabe said sternly, 'I swear to God, if you call me Dr Fallon all evening…'

'Sorry Dr…er…Gabe.' Beth tried not to stumble over the word but she did anyway. 'Look, you don't understand. It would make me feel very uncomfortable.'

Gabe frowned. 'Why?'

She stared at him for a few moments, wondering whether he'd lost his mind. 'Because we slept together,' she said, lowering her voice to a harsh whisper. 'Or have you forgotten that already?'

He grinned at her, remembering in vivid detail. 'So?'

So? So! So she couldn't exchange polite pleasantries with him in front of her family and not give herself away. 'Rilla and Hailey are very shrewd. They'll guess. And I don't need them on my case. They'll try to matchmake and it was a one-off G-Gabe. A one-off. Not to mention that my father is your boss. You want to be sitting across the table from him when he realises just how well you know me?'

Gabe could see the pink in her cheeks as her straight blonde hair brushed her shoulders. He sighed. 'How old are you Beth?'

Beth glared at him. 'Older than you. Old enough to know better than to jump into bed with a complete stranger.' *How could she have been so stupid?*

'I don't care who knows that we slept together, Beth.'

'Well, I do,' she snarled. 'What happened with us is not the way I act. I'm embarrassed by it. I'd like to keep it to myself, if that's all right. I'm worried we might slip up and let the cat out of the bag, especially if we're together socially with my family. They know me too well.'

'Beth, what happened between us wasn't exactly normal for me either. We were both acting out of character. There was something obviously weighing on you that night. Don't forget, I held you while you cried your heart out. It meant something to me that you could let go. Whatever you think, it was more than just a one-night stand.'

Beth shut her eyes. She could hear the sincere note in his voice and wished he hadn't reminded her of how she had broken down. The fact that it apparently meant something to him she couldn't even begin to process.

'Please...' She opened her eyes and fixed him with pleading eyes. 'If it really meant something then I'm asking you to just turn around and leave. I need to be more prepared than this.'

Gabe saw the desperation in her eyes and a hint of the sadness that had afflicted her that fateful night. He handed her the wine and opened his mouth to agree.

The door opened abruptly. 'There you are. Both of you,' John boomed. 'Well, don't just stand there, come on in. Penny is so looking forward to meeting you.'

Gabe shot Beth an apologetic look as he allowed John to usher him into the house.

Beth stood staring after them, wine bottle in one hand, flowers in the other.

Damn it!

CHAPTER THREE

TO MAKE matters worse, Penny sat Gabe and Beth together. She was super-aware of him as they took their places at the table. His body heat radiated towards her, stroking hot fingers across her skin. The occasional brush of his arm against hers caused unwanted flashbacks.

Rilla and Hailey sat opposite, grinning at her. She frowned at them. John and Penny sat at each end of the table, oblivious to any odd vibes.

'So, where in the UK are you from?' Penny asked.

'I grew up in Reading. My mother still lives there. I studied in London. But I live in Oxford at the moment.'

'Oh, Beth worked at the Radcliffe in Oxford for years, didn't you, darling?' Penny supplied.

'It was a long time ago,' Beth said evasively.

'How long have you been back for?' Gabe asked.

Beth concentrated on Penny's divine roast lamb. 'Eight years.'

'Beth's been all over,' Rilla boasted.

It was true. Beth had left on her travels as soon as her training had been complete. Being welcomed into the loving arms of the Winters clan had been her saving grace but memories of her baby boy had haunted her and she'd been desperate to escape them. A decade of wandering the world had helped put them into some perspective.

'How long have you been theatre NUM?' Gabe asked politely.

'Five years.'

Gabe could tell from her tight replies that she'd rather he didn't talk to her. Knew that she'd rather he wasn't here at all. And he did plan on eating his meal and leaving but it seemed rude to ignore her in the meantime.

As if he could have anyway. Given their close proximity, his body was excruciatingly conscious of hers. Every movement she made brought her body into contact with his and he was reminded of the way her skin had felt on *that* night.

'So, Hailey, you've been to the UK too?' Gabe asked, smiling at Beth's younger sister.

Beth let out a relieved sigh and let the conversation flow around her, participating only when required.

'Are you OK, Beth?' John asked, as he stood to clear the dishes, 'you seem very quiet tonight.'

Beth could see the concern in the older man's eyes and could tell he was anxious about the recent anniversary. She gave him a reassuring smile. 'Just preoccupied by the Fisher case. There's so much to organise.'

As Penny served dessert the conversation swung to the case that had captured worldwide media attention.

'You must be under a lot of pressure, Gabe,' Penny said. 'Two successful separations under your belt is quite an impressive precedent.'

Gabe shrugged. 'I suppose so. I try not to worry about

other people's expectations though. My own are high enough.'

'What are their chances, do you think?' John asked.

'It'll depend very much on their shape going into the operation. If we can get the twins to the ten-kilo mark and Bridie and Brooke are healthy, their chances will be much better.'

'And if everything is as you hoped?' John pressed.

Gabe really hated predicting outcomes even though he knew it was the one thing people most wanted to know. Certainly Scott and June were eager for the figure. 'Two healthy girls going in still only gives them about a fifty per cent chance of both of them pulling through. It's a massive operation...too much potential for catastrophe.'

'How does it compare to your other cases?' Hailey asked.

'Well, all three sets of twins have been joined in different parts of their heads so in essence each operation is completely different. I think the Fisher case, however, looks the most technically difficult.'

'Oh, I so hope those little girls pull through,' Rilla said softly.

'Yes,' Hailey agreed. 'They're quite a fixture on the kids' ward. Scott and June pop in for a visit every week when they come to the General. The twins are always so happy and placid, they have this dear thing they do where they hold hands. It's so sad that they're joined at the backs of their heads and can't see each other.'

Gabe had thought so too. 'Well, hopefully they'll be able to look into each other's eyes before much longer.' Gabe smiled. 'I'm going to do everything in my power to make it happen.' *And Fallons didn't fail*.

'So I guess you two will be working quite closely on this?' Penny asked. 'It seems like a mammoth task.'

'We will need to be co-coordinating a lot,' Gabe confirmed, sensing Beth tense beside him.

Gabe caught the speculative look Beth's two sisters exchanged out the corner of his eye. She was right—they didn't miss much. He was struck by how similar they were. Rilla and Hailey were definitely Winterses. Both short and curvy with dark hair and olive skin like Penny's.

Tall, blonde, peaches-and-cream Beth shared no similarities whatsoever. If he hadn't already known that Beth was John's foster-child he'd have begun to suspect the milkman may have had a hand in her conception. Differences aside, there was a lot of obvious love around this table and he felt an unreasonable spike of jealousy needle his chest.

The Winterses personified the type of family he'd always yearned to be part of as a child. Growing up in a household that had been torn apart by his father's slavish devotion to his job, it had never occurred to him that families with a medical background could actually be functional. Certainly his father had always been at pains to drum into him that dedication to medicine and family did not mix. That you could have one or the other. But not both.

And yet he was sitting amidst the living proof that his father had been wrong. John Winters was a successful doctor at the pinnacle of his career. The chief of staff of one of Brisbane's largest hospitals was a very powerful position indeed. And yet he obviously loved his girls, had a great wife and made time for his family. It could be done.

He glanced at Beth, still tense beside him. He felt a

strange urge to reach out and pull her into his side. Rub his hand along where her neck sloped into her shoulder. Knead the tension away. For the first time ever in his life he was seduced by the idea that it was possible to have both. Medicine and a life. Maybe even be more successful with the support of a loving a family.

'Have you scheduled any team practice sessions yet?' John asked.

'Saturday morning is our first,' Gabe replied, looking away from Beth, pulling himself back from his fanciful thoughts. *One hour at the Winterses' dining-room table, sitting next to Beth, and he was forgetting years of hard lessons.*

He sat up straighter. 'We also have our first case conference on Monday morning which involves Scott and June and the girls.'

'How often will the surgical team get together to practise?' Penny enquired.

'That's something we'll need to discuss on Saturday. Once a week at least for the whole team or as much of the team as possible. It'll depend on everyone's schedules, which is why it'll happen on a weekend. No doubt there'll be a lot of smaller group practices going on too. The case conferences will be weekly.'

'Sounds like you'll all know your stuff by D-Day.' Penny nodded. 'It's a good idea really, for team bonding as well. An operation of such magnitude surely requires not only a well-oiled but a close-knit team. Getting to know and trust each other would be paramount.'

Beth, who had been wishing the conversation to end, blushed, thinking about how well she knew Gabe.

'Absolutely,' Gabe agreed. 'The team needs to have a

familiarity with each other and be united towards our common goal.'

Familiarity? Beth dipped her head as she reddened further. They were already too familiar. Their familiarity was carnal!

'Well, good luck. No doubt Beth will keep us up to date and you must come and have tea with us again. Coffee, Gabe?' Penny prattled as she cleared the dessert plates.

Oh, God no. Just go, please, go. Sitting next to him as he talked, their carnality pulsing between them, was shredding her composure. His accent flowed over her like warm butterscotch and every cell in her body demanded she rub herself against him and purr. She could have sworn he had been about to touch her a little while back. She was getting a crick in her back from sitting so straight.

Beth desperately willed him to decline. She looked at him directly for the first time all evening, a plea in her eyes.

Gabe recognised it immediately. Her hair framed her face and her steady blue gaze begged him to leave. She needn't have bothered. Being at the Winterses' was playing havoc with all his previously held opinions. He wanted out too.

'No, thanks, Penny. Actually, I think I might head off now.' He made a show of checking his watch. 'I need to ring one of the Hopkins neurosurgeons in the States and discuss the case.'

Penny and John pressed him to stay, but beside him Beth's relief was almost palpable. He declined and stood to go, thanking Penny for the invitation.

He bade farewell to Rilla and Hailey. 'I guess I'll see you tomorrow,' Gabe said, looking down at Beth's erect posture.

Beth nodded, acutely aware of him standing behind her, his heat almost a physical caress.

'Tomorrow.'

John and Penny showed Gabe out and it was only when she heard the door click shut that she sagged against the chair.

The Saturday morning practice session came round too soon. Beth arrived at seven and tackled the problem of how to staff the operation while she waited for the others to arrive.

There was no scheduled lists today, just emergency cases, so the theatres were running on a skeleton staff. More nurses were on call should extra be required. She could hear laughter drift down the corridor from the staff-room as she pondered the personnel required and how to give them all adequate breaks during an operation of inde-terminate length.

By eight the key players had arrived and they all assem-bled in Theatre Ten. It was the largest operating suite and, as such, equipped to cope with the numbers that would be required on the day.

Today there were four neurosurgeons, two plastic surgeons, two vascular surgeons, two anaesthetists, four nurses and two orderlies. Sixteen people. It was expected there would be almost double that number on the actual day. And theatre ten already seemed too small.

It was a busy morning. They discussed the logistics of the surgery and managing the number of people. Various issues and potential problems were aired and everyone suggested ways these could be overcome. Gabe was a fount of knowl-edge, drawing from his experience, able to troubleshoot and identify areas that no one else had thought of and employ-ing some of the solutions they'd used in the UK surgeries.

They talked over the best ways to manage all the

equipment needed and did a dummy run, one of many they'd do between now and the operation, involving shifting one of the twins to the other table once the separation was complete.

Beth was also keen to set a procedure in place early for emergency resuscitation. The surgery was obviously hugely risky and she wanted everyone involved to know the resuscitation procedure back to front just in case. Gabe was able to advise how they'd managed in the UK and between them they came up with a quick, efficient way to deal with the worst-case scenario. Everyone would know their role in such a situation before the operation even began.

Beth's head was spinning by the time they called it a day four hours later. She had lists of things she needed to organise and follow up. Extra lighting, sufficient of instruments and regular practice days were the most pressing.

Having the theatre fitted with closed-circuit cameras was also something that needed to be sorted out sooner rather than later. Gabe had insisted on the importance of such a set-up. On D-day the tearoom, which would act as the main hub for superfluous staff, would have live footage relayed to its screens so everyone could keep abreast of the progress.

Beth knew that a lot of modern theatres were being built with these systems already in place. One of the newer south-side hospitals had all its theatres fitted out and she made a note to talk to the NUM involved about the intricacies of the system.

They agreed to meet every Saturday as a team and the surgeons would practise the exact techniques both alone and together in addition to the whole team sessions. Beth felt a bit like she was training for an Olympic event except there were more than medals at stake. Two precious lives depended on them. Penny was right—how did Gabe cope with the pressure?

'We're all going to the pub for lunch,' Kerry said as she popped her head into Beth's office. 'Join us?'

Lunch with Gabe? Tea had been bad enough. 'I want to get some of this organised,' Beth said waving her list in the air and picking up the phone.

'Oh, come on, Beth,' Kerry cajoled. 'You work too hard. Have lunch and then come back afterwards if you want.'

Beth looked at the pleading look on her friend's face. They'd known each other for a long time. 'I'll join you later,' she fobbed her off, knowing she wouldn't be doing anything of the sort. 'You going to Barney's?'

Kerry nodded. 'You'd better or I'm going to send Gabe over to drag you here.'

'What am I going to do?' Gabe asked, popping his head in too.

'Beth's passing on lunch.'

Gabe looked at Beth and then back at Kerry. 'Leave it with me. Save us both a space.'

'No,' Beth said, when she'd given Kerry enough time to be out of ear shot.

Gabe sighed. 'You know, Penny was right. We do need to be a well-oiled team. This operation is a hugely stressful event. Socialising will help build rapport and it gives us another forum to discuss the operation. Maybe talk about things we hadn't thought about.'

'Take notes,' she said, and started to dial a number.

Gabe entered her office and pushed the call cut-off button.

'Dr Fallon...' Beth gaped.

'Sister Rogers. I'm afraid I'm going to have to insist. Debriefing is mandatory.'

Beth tried to ignore how her skin erupted with goose bumps at his insistence. His accent slid over her like silk and she felt a pull down low in her abdomen.

They glared at each other for a few moments. Beth looked at his finger still firmly in place. This was ludicrous. There was a huge group of them, she didn't have to talk to him at all.

'Let me make a few phone calls and then I'll join you,' she finally acquiesced.

Gabe smiled at her as he lifted his finger. 'Thank you.' He strolled towards the door. 'If you're not at Barney's in thirty minutes, I'm going to take Kerry up on her suggestion.'

Beth swallowed as his silky threat tantalised more than it terrorised.

Twenty-five minutes later Beth stopped at the kerb, waiting for the green man. She looked to her right. The city skyscrapers loomed nearby. The General had been around for over a century and whoever had chosen this spot had done well. It was prize real estate, with its city views and proximity to the hustle and bustle of downtown Brisbane.

The light changed and Beth crossed the busy road, heading towards the garish neon sign that announced the pub's location. Barney's was a popular hangout for the hospital staff, being situated as it was directly opposite the General.

She stepped into the jovial atmosphere and moments later squinted into the dark recesses as her eyes adjusted from the bright sunshine outside.

'I was just about to come and get you.'

Beth wasn't expecting the sexy low threat growled in upper-crust English so close to her ear and her skin tingled where Gabe's breath fanned her skin.

'We've ordered fish and chips,' he said, ushering her along with him as he balanced three beers. 'What do you want to drink?' he asked, as everyone greeted her and he pulled out her chair.

'Um…' Beth was still catching her breath from his earlier statement. 'Chardonnay, please.'

She listened, slightly dazed, as the conversation flowed around her. Any chance she had of forming coherent chatter died as Gabe joined her, plonking her wine on the table in front of her and sitting down next to her.

He joined in the flow easily, unlike Beth who had developed a sudden case of muteness as her awareness of him rose to excruciating levels.

He was dressed as Gabe. Laid-back Gabe. Not the cool professional he'd been an hour ago, dressed in scrubs and a cap, concentrating and focused on the Fisher case, calling her Sister Rogers. He was in jeans and a polo shirt like he'd been the first time they'd met. His caramel hair looked like it had been carelessly finger-combed, making him look impossibly young, and he was smiling at her. A lot. And calling her Beth.

Oh, god! Despite telling herself not to, despite not wanting to, she had a thing for him. She took a gulp of her drink. How embarrassing. Hadn't she embarrassed herself enough in front of him? Not content to just sleep with him after five minutes' acquaintance, she'd also sobbed like a baby in his arms. Beth took another gulp of her wine. Coming here today had been a mistake.

She was grateful when the meal arrived and people concentrated on eating instead of talking.

'So,' Gabe said, his voice low. 'I enjoyed my time with your family the other night.'

Beth cringed, thinking about how his surprise invitation had thrown her and how uncomfortable she'd felt sitting next to him. She'd been less than polite. 'John and Penny enjoyed your company,' she murmured, trying to make amends for her behaviour.

'Only John and Penny?' Gabe teased.

Beth glanced up from her meal at him and saw his easy grin. She ignored him, returning her attentions to her beer-battered fish. His ego didn't need any massaging.

'How old were you when the Winters fostered you?' Gabe asked.

Beth stopped in mid-chew. 'Fifteen,' she said stiffly.

Gabe noted her reticence. 'I'm sorry. I'm prying. You don't like to talk about it.'

Beth placed her cutlery on her plate carefully. 'Not at all. I just don't see the point in discussing it.'

Gabe laughed. 'It's called conversation, Beth. You know, social interaction? Getting to know each other? We seemed to have put the cart before the horse and I thought it might be nice to get to know each other beyond the…physical.'

His voice lowered on the last word and she shivered. Like she needed reminding of their uninhibited beginning. Talking about her past seemed preferable to hushed references of their night together. 'It's a long story. My mother died when I was six—'

'I'm sorry,' Gabe interjected.

Beth shrugged. It wasn't as if she remembered her. The

only images of her mother she could recall had come from battered old photos. 'I didn't really know her.' Except that wasn't entirely true. Vague, elusive sensations of being hugged and rocked and loved were never far away.

Maybe if her mother hadn't died, the rest of her life wouldn't have gone to hell. And her father would never have insisted she adopt the baby out. But, then, if she'd lived there'd have been no catalyst for the dramatic downward spiral and life would have been very different. Beth probably wouldn't have found herself in the predicament in the first place.

'My father… Things were bad after. He threw himself into his work, shut me out. I think it was too painful to acknowledge me. He was distant and the times he wasn't he was harsh and critical. He remarried. My stepmother… well, she wasn't exactly…kid friendly. I rebelled in my teenage years. We fought a lot. The stricter he got, the more I rebelled. After years of ignoring me he didn't know how to handle me.'

Gabe listened to her tale of woe and could draw eerie parallels with his own life. He was beginning to see why Beth was so reserved, so tightly in control of her actions. Her childhood had been fraught. He remembered how his own parental circumstances had buffeted his life and the constant state of anxiety he'd lived in for such a long time.

'I ran away.' She shut her eyes as the awful isolation and dread of life on the streets revisited her. It had been a harrowing time. She opened her eyes, stirring from the memories, realising she'd given away more than she'd meant to. 'Anyway, I eventually wound up in the foster-care system. And got lucky.'

Gabe wasn't fooled by her quick wrap-up. Somewhere there was a chunk of the story missing. Could it be worse than what he'd already heard? What had happened to her after she'd run away? Had she got into drugs or crime or other things that street kids became embroiled in?

'You certainly did,' he agreed, knowing he'd pushed too much for one day.

But there was more to the Beth Rogers story, of that he was sure. Having this glimpse into her life seemed to throw up more questions. Her uncharacteristic act of sleeping with him seemed even more peculiar, knowing what he now knew. Was there an even bigger demon in her past?

They ate in silence for a few moments. Low conversation buzzed around them. As the silence stretched between them Beth's awareness of him trebled. At least conversation kept her mind off the sensations stroking her skin.

She took a swig of Dutch courage and looked at him. 'What about you, Gabe? What was it like growing up with the great Harlon Fallon?'

'It wasn't dull.'

Beth noted his clipped reply and frowned as a memory flashed a warning light in her head. *Oh, God! Open mouth, insert foot.* 'Damn. Sorry, Gabe. He died just recently, didn't he?'

Gabe felt the heaviness in his chest that had been with him since his father's death intensify. 'A few months ago.' He nodded.

His voice sounded so bleak and Beth saw the same sadness she'd caught a brief glimpse of that first night. So...he had been grieving too. 'Look, sorry, forget it. I didn't mean to pry either.'

Gabe gave her a sad smile. 'It's OK, Beth. I don't mind talking about it.' He forked a chip into his mouth and took a swallow of his beer. 'My parents divorced when I was twelve. Dad was never around and I guess Mum got sick of being a single parent. They argued a lot. Mum accused him of loving his job more than us.'

'Ouch.'

Gabe nodded. 'Unfortunately, Dad didn't disabuse her of it. She married again shortly after. Like you, my stepfather and I never really saw eye to eye.'

So Gabe had his demons too. Maybe that explained her rash attraction to him that fateful night? Maybe she'd recognised a kindred spirit, had identified with his grief and been drawn to him? She looked down at her empty plate. 'I think it takes someone much stronger than a mere child to accept someone new into the picture.'

He nodded. 'I guess I felt it was betraying my father to accept Ronald. We argued a lot. I'm afraid I wasn't very nice.'

Beth remembered back to her own tumultuous teens. She hadn't been nice either. In fact, she'd gone off the rails big time. Being emotionally isolated from her father, she'd felt acutely the loss of the mother she'd never even really known. Was it any wonder she'd wound up pregnant when she'd been so hungry for some love and attention.

'Did you go live with your dad?'

Gabe snorted. 'Dad didn't have time for anyone, never mind a sullen teenager.'

Poor Gabe. The bitterness she heard in his simple statement was achingly familiar to her. Gabe had obviously felt as let down by his parents as she had by hers.

'So you didn't really get on with your dad either? Did you reconcile before he died?'

'I don't know about reconcile. I lived with him when I went to med school in London. He was a complex man. I don't think he'd have let me in even if he'd lived to be a hundred. But I think he was…proud of me…at the end.'

'I'm sure he was,' Beth murmured. She took another sip of her drink, leaving Gabe alone with his memories for a minute.

'Well, you must have been the envy of all your fellow students. Living with the great Harlon Fallon. You must have learnt so much from him.'

'Oh, yeah. I learnt single-mindedness. That any distractions to your career were to be avoided at all costs. That you could be a great doctor but you couldn't be a great father or a great man as well, and you had to make the choice early on. That success comes at a cost to your family.'

Beth stopped chewing. It sounded so bleak. At least the Winterses had shown her that children, even surly teenagers, needed love and had showered her with it. Thankfully she'd had a chance to be a part of a real family. A chance to start over. 'That sounds dreadful.'

Gabe smiled down at her. 'No. It wasn't that bad. I thank him actually. My father may not have been the warm and fuzzy type but in his own way he was looking out for me. He was right—doctors have one of the highest divorce rates of all professions. Surgeons are worse. Neurosurgeons worse again. None of the marriages of my friends who are surgeons have made it past a couple of years.

'Being a product of divorce has helped me prioritise in

my life. I don't think you can have the type of career I want and have a family also. That's just not fair to them.'

Beth looked into his steady green gaze, his accent oozing rivers of sensation all over her, and felt completely horrified. She had a thing for a guy who'd been raised by a robot! Harlon Fallon may have been a brilliant physician, taught his son focus and the importance of a career, but had he ever put his arms around Gabe and told him that he loved him?

She felt absurdly like doing that just now. Not the love thing. But just hugging him. Hugging the lost little boy somewhere inside who just wanted his father to love him. Maybe it was the loneliness of her early years or more likely the unrequited mother in her, but she sincerely hoped that anyone, regardless of what they did for a job, could see that family was more important than anything. Above career. Above accolades. Even above Nobel Prizes.

At least, despite all evidence of her past, she still believed that a happily-ever-after was out there for everyone. Who knew? Maybe it was still out there for her. *If she could ever forgive herself enough to love.* And it could still be out there for Gabe too. As long as he didn't become a chip off the old block.

CHAPTER FOUR

MONDAY morning the majority of the team gathered in a clinical support office on the tenth floor for the first case conference. Subsequent meetings would only involve the main players but Gabe had wanted everyone involved to meet the Fishers at least once. He wanted them to see that through all the hype, all the media coverage, this was what it was about. Two little girls. A family. He wanted to put a human face to the mammoth task that lay ahead of them.

The large room was dominated by a huge oval table and a magnificent view of the Brisbane skyline but when June Fisher pushed the pram through the doors, all eyes were on Bridie and Brooke. Those who hadn't seen the girls before, including Beth, stared in awe. They were truly a sight to behold.

Gabe introduced the team and Beth was impressed he'd remembered everyone's name even down to Tom the orderly.

'Hi.' Beth smiled at June, holding out her hand as Gabe got to her. 'I'm Beth Rogers. I'm the nurse unit manager of the operating theatres.' June and Scott shook Beth's hand. 'If you have any questions at all as we go along this morning, make sure you let us know. You two are as much a part of this team as anyone else.'

'Thank you,' June murmured.

Beth's gaze was continually drawn to the twins as the surgeons discussed the logistics of the case with their parents. Bridie was asleep but Brooke babbled away as she sucked furiously on a rattle. How Bridie slept Beth had no idea. Her sister's vocalising filled the whole room and the surgeons kept stopping in mid-sentence to smile at the happy, normal noises coming from a far from normal child.

The longer she spent in the meeting, listening to all the complex issues, the more she admired the Fishers resilience. There'd been a lot of gossip in the hospital and reports in the media that the Fishers had been irresponsible and should have had the twins terminated when their condition had become evident.

But looking at the two dear little girls Beth knew it couldn't have been that clear cut for Scott and June. Having given up a child herself, Beth knew the terrible gut wrench of such decisions. She didn't envy them their position or judge them for their choice. And none of it mattered now anyway. Bridie and Brooke were here. That was all that mattered.

Bridie started to stir and Brooke automatically reached back to touch her sister. Beth felt a lump in her throat as she watched the innate gesture of comfort. She thought about her relationship with Rilla and Hailey. About their sisterly bond and how strong it was. They *had* to pull both the girls through. After such a close tie, how could either be whole without the other?

Gabe sat opposite and she looked up to find his gaze on her. He was talking to the vascular guys and quickly turned his attention back to them but he'd definitely been watching her. Goose-bumps pricked her skin as his voice washed over her, and Beth found herself wishing they'd started off on a different footing.

It still felt awkward to be around him. She knew—she hoped—that with time and distance it would ease, but the Fisher case was throwing them very much together, not giving her the space she needed to look at him with indifference.

Scott and June departed with the girls half an hour into the meeting, along with most of the team. Beth stayed on and took necessary notes as they pertained to her and her staff's role, conscious as ever of Gabe.

When would it stop? She hoped and prayed that by the time the op came around in four months or so she'd be feeling less on edge around him because the separation would require nerves of steel. There would be no room for this odd jittery feeling. This heightened awareness of him. Gabe seemed perfectly cool with it. Why the hell couldn't she?

Two weeks passed. Two more case conferences. Beth had spent the morning away from the theatres, first attending the case conference and then travelling across the city to the Raymont Hospital to look at the way closed circuit cameras had been implemented into their theatres.

Her head was buzzing with information as she stopped by the cafeteria located in the grounds of the General, to pick up a cappuccino and a sandwich. The twins and the impending operation were uppermost in everyone's thoughts. At least Beth was finally starting to feel a little less like she had 'Gabe Fallon and I slept together' tattooed on her forehead as preparations continued.

He still had the ability to make her breathless from a smile or one word in his smooth accent but he was professionalism personified, focused to the point of obsession about the operation, and it made it easier to put their intimacies behind her.

Beth paid for her food and was passing the tables located outside, her mind on the projected budget John had requested, when she was interrupted.

'Beth.'

Gabe had seen Beth approach as he sat at a table with Scott and June and the girls. He'd run into them when he'd popped down to get some lunch and they had asked him to join them. It was a gorgeous sunny February day and he'd been more than happy to sit with them and soak up some sunshine. Februarys in England were never like this.

'Beth,' Gabe called again, louder this time as she appeared to have not heard him. He'd managed to persuade her that they could revert to first names without giving any secrets away.

The budget figures disappeared into the ether as Beth turned her head towards Gabe's voice as if pulled by a powerful magnet. She spotted him sitting with Scott and June and he waved at her. He looked all sexy and relaxed in a green shirt almost the exact shade of his eyes, a smile making his features even more deadly. Her step faltered. Did she really have to socialise with him? They were together more than was good for her sanity anyway.

But the Fishers were smiling at her and it would be rude to ignore them. She plastered a smile on her face as she approached.

'Do you guys live here?' Beth teased as she drew close.

'Feels like it.' June laughed. 'We had some other appointments and stopped for lunch. We managed to persuade Gabe that a pasty Englishman needed a bit of sunshine.'

Beth joined the laughter. Gabe was a far cry from pasty and they all knew it.

'Have you got time to join us?' Gabe asked, patting the bench seat beside him.

Beth looked at her watch, wishing he hadn't put her on the spot. She shrugged. 'I don't have to be anywhere for half an hour.'

Gabe scooted over and Beth sat. Beside her the twins babbled away in their pram, the visor down to shade them from the midday sun. Beth's eyes were automatically drawn to them as she unwrapped her sandwich.

Two perfect babies. If she hadn't known about their conjoined condition, she'd have thought they were normal babies lying back to back. They were gorgeous. Little bow mouths and blue eyes. Their fused heads were covered in a light smattering of blonde hair and Brooke had a small brown birthmark on her forearm.

'Do you have kids, Beth?' Scott asked.

Beth looked up. How many times had she been asked this question in her life? How many times had it cut her to the quick to deny it? 'No,' she said, taking a bite of her sandwich, feeling the same emptiness she always felt.

They made small talk as they ate, mainly about the girls. It was easy to think of them as one child but Beth and Gabe laughed as June told funny stories about their individual traits. As she finished her coffee Beth had a much better appreciation of the Fisher family and the challenges they faced with the girls' rare condition.

Scott and June were such lovely people. They could

have been bitter about the hand fate had dealt them but they were continually upbeat and unwaveringly positive.

'I know people think we should have terminated the pregnancy,' June said, expertly scooping the girls out of the pram onto her lap. 'But how could we have not known our girls? Even if just for a little while?'

How indeed? Beth knew too well the ache inside from empty arms. She stared at June as she kissed the girls' heads and snuggled them in close, feeling envious. June looked as dedicated and loving as any mother and Beth felt a painful twinge in her chest.

'You followed your heart,' Beth said quietly, wishing she'd had the strength to follow hers.

Gabe heard the wistful note in Beth's voice and was surprised to see a shimmer of tears in her gaze before she blinked them away. The urge to squeeze her hand was surprisingly strong. *Damn it.* Despite knowing he shouldn't be, couldn't afford to be, he was attracted to her.

Luckily for him her reserve and painstaking professionalism made it easy for him to keep a lid on it. But seeing her like this, all soft and...vulnerable, not guarded, he felt it flare out of control. Her mouth was soft and her teeth were pressed into her bottom lip and he remembered how great her mouth had felt under his. How vulnerable she'd been, sobbing in his arms.

'Would you like to hold them?' June asked Beth.

Beth knew she shouldn't. It would be breaking every professional boundary that existed but she felt so bereft at the moment and her arms ached to hold them. And they were babies. The best nurses knew that sometimes boundaries were there to be crossed.

Beth nodded and June stood to hand them over, placing them effortlessly in Beth's lap. Their smell was the first thing that filled her senses and, smiling, she shut her eyes and inhaled their sweet fragrance as she rubbed her cheek against the soft down covering their heads.

'They like that,' Gabe murmured.

Beth opened her eyes to find Bridie smiling a dribbly smile at him. Gabe offered his index finger and Bridie grasped it gleefully. Gabe laughed and Beth felt it go right to her pelvic floor muscles.

He looked up and smiled at her.

'She likes you,' Beth said huskily. Did he have the same effect on the entire female population?

'What's not to like?' Gabe grinned and returned his attention to Bridie.

Indeed. A voice that purred. Mesmerising eyes. Sexy as hell. And a hit with babies. A very dangerous combination.

'You're both naturals.' Scott smiled.

Except she was too old and he was too career orientated. Beth shut her eyes again, revelling in the feel of the two squirming, sweet bundles pressed against her. *She still wanted this*. Damn it. Twenty-three years later, her arms still ached to hold a baby.

Her pager pealed and Brooke jumped. Scott and June laughed as Beth apologised. 'I'd better go,' she said reluctantly as she pulled the pager off her waistband and checked the message.

'Here, give them to me,' Gabe said, holding out his arms.

Beth baulked at the intimacy but after one last cuddle shuffled them onto Gabe's lap and bade everyone a hasty goodbye. Unfortunately, the mental image of Gabe with the two little girls cuddled against his chest stayed with her for hours.

A few days later, due to staffing problems, Beth was standing gowned up next to Gabe, trying not to remember how right he'd looked holding the twins. At least the awkwardness she'd initially felt in his company had started to dissipate and, looking around the theatre now, Beth doubted anyone could tell from their body language that they'd been lovers.

It certainly couldn't be told from Gabe's. He was every inch the neurosurgeon as he concentrated on excising the tumour from the anaesthetised patient's brain. His movements were precise, his touch impersonal, his requests businesslike. She was taking her cues from him and it got easier every day, but part of her still expected someone to point the finger at any moment and expose them.

Beth handed Gabe a swab and noted she was running out.

'More swabs,' she requested, lifting her eyes to David, who was hovering nearby. The students had been allowed to undertake scout nurse duties this week.

David located a packet and carefully opened the sterile packaging, his finger accidentally brushing the corner of the swabs.

'Your hand contaminated the sterile field,' Beth said firmly. 'Get another packet please.' She wasn't angry, just matter-of-fact. It happened a lot, even to seasoned professionals.

But she noted the colour in David's cheeks when he returned. 'It's OK,' she said in a low voice as he opened the new packet with trembling fingers. 'It happens to the best of us. The important thing is to be honest when it happens and realise that sterility is what's important—not ego or pride. This patient needs every one of us to be vigilant.'

David nodded and performed a count of the swabs with her. She watched as he changed the count sheet to reflect the additional pack.

Beth turned back to Gabe. A sudden wave of dizziness assailed her. Her vision blurred and she blinked to clear it as she steadied herself against the table. Nausea slammed into her and she felt sweat bead on her brow. She took a few deep breaths but the mask hindered her and made her feel claustrophobic.

It took a few seconds for the light-headedness to dissipate. She became aware of Gabe asking her for something.

'Beth?' Gabe frowned, looking down at her. 'Are you with us?' he demanded.

Beth blinked and gave her head a slight shake to clear the lingering fog. 'I'm sorry,' she apologised. 'I was… thinking ahead.'

Gabe nodded, not totally convinced. 'Needle holder,' he repeated.

Beth passed it to him and leaned heavily against the table as another wave of dizziness hit. Gabe said something and she looked at him but she couldn't hear the words for the ringing in her ears and her pulse hammering madly through her head.

'Beth?'

Beth continued to stare at him as her vision started to blacken from the outside in. *Oh, God, she was going to faint!*

'Gabe,' she said breathily, before her sight went altogether, 'I think I'm going to faint.'

Gabe could see the spark in her eyes fading and it took a couple of seconds to realise that Beth was teetering on the edge of consciousness.

'David! Catch!' Gabe ordered as the unsuspecting student passed behind them.

A startled David turned just in time to catch Beth as she slumped and fell backwards. The whole theatre stared at the unconscious Beth. The very capable Sister Rogers fainting? Impossible!

'Is she OK?' Gabe demanded. 'How's her pulse?

David placed two fingers against her neck, locating the strong, steady thump of Beth's carotid. 'Good.'

Gabe felt a wave of relief wash over him. He hadn't realised he'd been holding his breath. 'Tom, help David with Sister Rogers,' he told the orderly. 'Get her on a gurney.'

Gabe, satisfied that Beth had just fainted, shut down his concern and returned his focus to the operation. 'Which one of you is going to scrub?' he asked the three nurses standing against the wall, still looking askance at the spectacle.

'Come on, come on,' he demanded. 'Concentrate, everyone, we have a head to close.'

And with that, the operation got back on track.

Beth came to as Tom and David were placing her on the gurney the tumour patient had been wheeled into the theatre on.

She murmured and then her eyes fluttered open. Tom and David's blurry features swam before her coming into slow focus. 'Wh-what happened?'

'You fainted,' David said.

Beth blinked. Huh? Her? Faint? She'd never fainted in her life! She struggled to sit up and immediately felt woozy.

'Whoa there,' Tom said, placing a steadying hand on Beth's shoulder as she swayed drunkenly. 'I'll put the head up.'

He used the handle at the side to adjust the gurney and lift the top to bring Beth into a supported sitting position.

'I'm fine, I'm fine,' Beth protested, as she shut her eyes to stop the room spinning. 'It's probably just my blood pressure.'

David pulled the blood-pressure cuff off the anaesthetic monitor and placed it around a protesting Beth's arm.

'Eighty on forty-five,' he announced when the figure appeared on the monitor.

'See,' Beth said crankily. 'Just a bit of postural hypotension.' Except she really felt like she was going to throw up.

'I've known you since you did your training here, Beth,' Tom said sternly. 'You are not a fainter. Everything all right?'

Beth nodded firmly. 'Of course. I think maybe I just need to eat something. My blood sugar might be a little low.' Beth swung her legs round until she was sitting on the edge of the gurney, pleased that the dizziness had settled.

Tom nodded. 'I'll give you a hand to the tearoom.'

Beth squared her shoulders and looked the orderly, who had been at the General since before her father, in the eye. 'You will do no such thing, Tom Lester. I'm perfectly capable of walking unaided.'

They helped her off the trolley and hovered while she got her bearings. 'Tom, go back into the theatre,' Beth ordered. 'I'm fine now and they'll need you.'

The orderly hesitated. 'David can help me,' Beth assured

him hastily. She wanted to talk to the student nurse about the earlier incident anyway.

Tom looked at David with a measured stare and Beth could tell he was trying to convey a don't-let-her-out-of-your-sight message to the younger man. Then he headed back toward the theatre. Beth wanted to remind the orderly she wasn't a child and she was the boss around here, but the nausea was growing and if she didn't eat soon she was seriously going to vomit.

David accompanied her to the tearoom and Beth indicated for him to take a chair as she grabbed a yoghurt from the fridge and devoured it. The trembling in her hands settled and the nausea stopped as if someone had flipped a switch. She sank back into the chair opposite David and closed her eyes gratefully.

What the hell was wrong with her? Was she coming down with something? Flu? She didn't feel feverish or have a sore throat or aching joints. Had she contracted some horrible virus with a long incubation period all those years ago when she'd lived overseas? She had worked in some fairly dodgy parts of the world.

This wouldn't do. Beth Rogers didn't get sick. In her eight years back at the General she hadn't had one sick day. And she certainly wasn't about to start now. Whatever it was it could just leave her alone. She didn't have time to be ill.

'Sister Rogers? Are you OK?'

Beth heard the slight crack in the younger man's voice and opened her eyes, pleased to find that the room was stable. She looked at the concern on his face. 'Yes, thanks, David,' she said, and smiled to allay his concerned look. 'I am now.'

'You gave us all a scare,' David said.

Beth noticed how his shoulders relaxed and the frown marring his forehead evened out. 'Don't worry, it won't happen again, I promise.'

The look of relief on David's face was almost comical and Beth suppressed a smile. 'What about you?' she asked. 'How are you doing? I hope you're not worried about contaminating the sterile package earlier.'

'No,' David sighed. 'I'm not…but…'

'But?' Beth could tell there was something bothering him.

'There's so much to learn, you know? I really like this specialty. But there's so many instruments and set-ups and procedures. I'm worried I'm going to stuff up all the time.'

Beth nodded, pleased that David was conscientious enough to care about his performance. It obviously wasn't just another rotation for him. She glimpsed a bit of her younger herself in him.

'Relax, David,' she said. 'We all make mistakes when we're first starting. And there is so much to learn. You know what I used to do? I used to spend every opportunity in the storeroom with the trays and an equipment manual, familarising myself with the different instruments. The basic ones and which combinations constituted which set-ups for which operations. I even used to come in on my days off. But I learned pretty quickly that way.'

'Yeah?'

David looked thoughtful and she could tell he was eager to learn. 'And don't forget. I'm here too. As well as the other senior staff. We're your resource people. Use us. OK?'

'OK,' he said, and smiled.

Beth smiled back, pleased with her rapport with the

student nurse and that he seemed so receptive to her advice. 'Now, get back to the theatre.'

Beth shut her eyes again after David had departed, her head lolling back against the wall. She wondered how long it would take the hospital grapevine to Chinese-whisper her little faint into something much more serious.

Beth lurched between feeling perfectly normal and desperately nauseated for the next few hours. Luckily she'd discovered that eating something was a very quick fix to the queasiness and an old packet of chocolate-coated sultanas she'd found in the bottom of her drawer worked miracles.

At one o'clock Rilla and Hailey arrived at her office. About the same time her stomach decided to become unsettled again and the sultanas were gone.

'We came as soon as we heard,' Hailey said, munching on a chocolate bar.

'Why are you still here?' Rilla added. 'You're obviously not well.'

Beth startled at their intrusion and looked up, spying her sister's chocolate bar. 'Quick, Hailey,' she said, standing and pointing, 'break me off a bit, will you?'

'This is my lunch,' Hailey complained.

'Hailey!' Beth practically snarled. 'I'm just asking for a bit. I'll buy you another one later. I need it now!'

Hailey blinked at the savageness of her sister's tone and snapped a bit off, handing it over. Rilla and her exchanged looks as their normally reserved, placid sister did a pretty good impression of the Cookie Monster.

'You OK, Beth?' Rilla asked.

'Sorry.' Beth grimaced, sinking into her chair. 'I've been

close to throwing up all morning and food's the only thing that helps.'

'So you've been feeling nauseated,' Rilla said as she sat in her usual chair, 'and you fainted this morning.'

Beth looked at both her sisters. 'Hell, you heard about that already?' She looked at her watch. Three hours. Even for the General that was fast.

'Well, actually, I heard that you'd had a seizure.' Hailey shrugged, sitting down as well, 'But Rilla assured me it was only a faint.'

'Exactly.' Beth nodded. 'Just a little faint. I think I'm coming down with a virus or something.'

'But you're never sick,' Hailey snorted.

'Maybe I'm a little rundown. I've been really tired the last few days. I'll be fine after a good night's sleep.'

A knock at her door interrupted the conversation and three sets of eyes turned to greet Gabe as he appeared in the doorway.

He exchanged pleasantries with Rilla and Hailey and then frowned at Beth. 'I didn't expect to see you still here. You should have gone home.'

'That's what I said,' Rilla said.

Beth ignored them both. 'You finished the list OK?'

Gabe nodded. 'Are you all right?'

'I'm fine,' she assured him testily. Everyone in Theatres, it seemed, had 'popped in' to check on her and she was getting heartily sick of it.

'Hey.' Gabe laughed, holding up his hands. 'Just asking. If you're going to make a habit of fainting in my theatre, I'd like to be forewarned.'

Beth shot him a thunderous look. She was feeling woozy

again which made her cranky. 'Fainting once in thirty-eight years is not a habit,' she snapped. 'Was there anything else?'

Gabe backed out of the doorway, his eyebrows raised at Beth's sisters.

'What?' Beth demanded moments later as her sisters fixed her with puzzled stares.

'Are you sure you're OK, Beth?' Rilla asked.

Beth sighed. 'Yes,' she said wearily, staving off more nausea. 'I'm just tired and light-headed and feel like throwing up all the time. I don't know what's wrong with me.'

'Well, if it was anyone but you and your non-existent sex life, I'd tell them to do a pregnancy test,' Hailey said. 'You have all the classic symptoms.'

Beth blinked and stared at Hailey open-mouthed. And then she laughed and her sisters joined her. That was completely preposterous!

The next morning, though, as Beth heaved into the toilet, the notion didn't seem so out there. Her period was late. Nothing out of the ordinary for her. She'd always had an erratic cycle. Anything up to seven weeks wasn't unusual for her. She'd been on the Pill to regulate it for years but she'd stopped taking it a while ago, wanting to give her body a break, and hadn't bothered to go back on it.

But it couldn't be possible. She and Gabe had used condoms. Yes, they weren't one hundred per cent infallible but they were pretty damn close. Had there been a faulty one that neither of them had noticed? Surely not. She was thirty-eight, for crying out loud—she should be practically infertile at her age.

Still, a tiny worm of excitement burrowed into her heart as she drove to work. The thought that she might be carrying a baby was overwhelming. The thing she'd wanted most since she'd been fifteen and her baby boy had been taken from her. Pregnant? A second chance? A baby to fill her arms and her life? Was she going to finally get a chance at being a mother?

The nausea haunted her throughout the day and she snacked constantly to keep it at bay. The worm of excitement burrowed deeper as she hugged the possible pregnancy to herself. She tried really hard not to get carried away but it occupied her every thought.

She shouldn't be excited. She knew that. When it turned out to be just a virus, she'd feel like a right idiot. And at her age, with no partner, set in her ways and a fantastic career, a baby should be a horrifying thought. Heaven alone knew what people would say. The hospital grapevine would be rife with rumours and speculation.

And then there was Gabe. She'd learnt enough about him to know that a baby would be an inconvenience to his career plans, as he had been an inconvenience to his father's. That he had a bright future which did not involve a family. She doubted very much whether he would welcome the idea of being a father.

But she knew one thing for sure. If she was pregnant she didn't need Gabe and she didn't give a fig for who thought what about her. She could do it without him. She was mature and financially secure—two things she hadn't been twenty-three years ago. And she was damned if she'd squander a second chance at being a mother.

Beth stopped in at a pharmacy on her way home that night and bought a home pregnancy test kit. She couldn't stand the speculation any longer. She had to know one way or the other.

She dumped her bag on the dining-room table and headed straight for the bathroom, brown chemist packet in hand. One minute later two pink stripes appeared before her eyes.

Two. Pink. Stripes.

Beth stared at the stick in disbelief. She shut her eyes and opened them again.

Two. Pink. Stripes.

She picked the test strip up and sat on the edge of the bath, looking at it. Her heart swelled with an emotion so overwhelming she felt tears prick her eyes. She smiled and then she laughed as tears brimmed and then fell down her cheeks. She wiped at them as she grinned like an idiot at the stick. She was pregnant. She really was pregnant.

'Hi, there, little guy,' she said, looking down at her flat stomach, cradling it with her hand.

Beth stood and looked at herself in the mirror. She wiped at her red eyes and blotchy face then turned to one side and smoothed her shirt over her abdomen. She took a deep breath and pushed her stomach out as far as it would go. She admired the artificial bump, swinging slightly from side to side to inspect the look from all angles.

She remembered doing the same thing twenty-three years ago. Although she had only been fifteen, she'd been in awe of the changes to her body and had loved how her belly had burgeoned as her baby had grown. She had known she wasn't supposed to be happy about the pregnancy, she certainly hadn't been allowed to want it, but she had loved the little life growing inside her so completely that secretly she'd welcomed every change to her body.

Thoughts of that time put a dampener on her rising joy. The air left her lungs and her stomach returned to its usual flatness. A seed of doubt sprouted roots. Her father's ugly words reverberated through her head. *Easy,* he had called her. *A slut. Irresponsible.* He'd told her repeatedly she'd be *a terrible mother.*

All the taunts and insults that at fifteen had crushed her spirit stirred inside her now. They still burned. As much now as they had back then. Simmered in her stomach like a boiling cauldron. What would her father say now? she wondered. That she hadn't changed? That she hadn't learned anything? Still knocked up and alone?

She looked at herself in the mirror. She looked pale, her red-rimmed blue eyes worried, her father's old ugly words furrowing her brow. She stared hard at her face as the chill of ancient insults battled with the evidence of her eyes. There were things in the mirror that hadn't been there all that time ago. She was older, stronger, confident.

OK, things weren't ideal. But she knew with sudden clarity that her father had been wrong. She would have been a damn good mother. As her body pulsed with the life of another, she knew it with absolute certainty. It would have been tough, sure. But she'd have managed because nothing would have been more important to her than her child. Just as this child was already her number-one priority.

'I'm sorry,' she whispered to her reflection apologising to the child she had never known.

She looked down at her stomach and splayed her hand across it. 'I promise,' she whispered. 'I promise to be the best mother that ever existed. I promise.'

She sat back on the edge of the bath again, her brain

buzzing. So, what now? The urge to tell Rilla and Hailey was amazingly intense. They were her sisters. They may not have been blood relatives but they were sisters in every way that counted and they'd been through too much together to lock them out of such a momentous occasion in her life.

But she knew she couldn't tell them before she told Gabe. And, frankly, she had no idea how she was going to do that. Or how he was going to react when she did.

Her sensible side was urging caution. She was, what? Beth performed a few calculations in her head—about six weeks gone. Realistically, one in four pregnancies ended in miscarriages, the odds worsening the older the mother, so at thirty-eight she was at an increased risk of losing the baby anyway.

The thought caused a physical pain in her chest and she clutched at her stomach. *Please, don't let me lose this baby too.* Beth already knew she'd trade her soul to keep this baby safe.

But telling people, making it public knowledge, seemed pointless until the highest risk period, the first trimester, had passed. Which gave her about six weeks. Six weeks to figure out what she was going to say to Gabe.

And in the interim it would be her little secret. She stood again and hugged her arms around her belly, giving her reflection a furtive smile.

She was having a baby. And no one could take that from her this time. No one.

CHAPTER FIVE

BETH sat in the case conference six weeks later, her hand on her belly, her gaze fixed on the sleeping faces of Brooke and Bridie. She'd just passed the milestone of her first trimester, the morning sickness had settled and she had actually allowed herself to believe that in six months' time she'd be holding her own baby in her arms.

Gabe was chatting with June and Scott and Erica Hamel, the plastic surgeon, about post-separation procedures to close the large residual defects at the back of the twins' heads. She was taking notes for future resource planning but the sweet smell of soap and baby powder kept wafting her way, distracting her.

Gabe's voice was also sidetracking her attention. Their night together two months ago still featured regularly in her dreams but had virtually faded from her head in their day-to-day dealings. Occasionally, though, she was caught unawares and his voice would hit a memory switch and she was back between the sheets with him.

She shut her eyes for a moment to dispel the fleeting but nonetheless entrancing image. June caught her eye and smiled at her. Beth blushed and smiled back. June gave her a saucy wink and Beth paled. Could June read minds? She sat up straighter and returned her attention to her notes and the conversation.

The Fishers left after their usual half-hour and Beth departed also. She was needed to scrub in this morning and she'd spared all the time she could.

'Were you OK in there?' June asked as they waited for the lift. 'You looked kind of daydreamy. Like you had a secret or something.'

Beth blushed again, her hand automatically falling to her stomach. She noticed June's speculative gaze and the urge to share was amazing. They'd got to know each other reasonably well over the weeks and Beth was so happy she wanted the world to know. She had come so close to telling Rilla and Hailey. But she knew she owed Gabe the news first.

'Not that I can blame you for looking a little glazed. Those conversations go right over my head.'

Beth laughed. 'I told you to butt in if you didn't understand anything,' she chided.

'That would make the meetings twice as long.' Scott joked. 'It's OK—we understand the basics. Our girls are in the best of hands. That's all that matters. We have faith in Gabe.'

Beth nodded. They all did. As a neurosurgeon about to separate conjoined twins, there wasn't anyone better. He was definitely *the* man. Beth just wished she could be so sure about his reaction to her pregnancy.

Another week passed, another Monday case conference, and Beth knew it was time. She couldn't put it off any longer. The coward in her wanted to put it off for ever. After all, he didn't have to know. She could probably keep the pregnancy disguised until after he'd left to go back home. But deep down she knew that wasn't fair.

Her baby was Gabe's baby also. And it was his right to know. Keeping it from him would be wrong. She didn't want or expect anything from him. He'd already told her that his career was his priority and that a family wasn't on his agenda. She just had to know that at the end of the day she'd been upfront.

Beth was dealing with the backlog of paperwork that inevitably came with the job. Not that she was actually taking much of it in—her internal dialogue was working overtime, building up the courage to seek Gabe out.

He was working back too, in Theatre Ten, getting in some more practice. At seven o'clock Beth could bear it no longer. *Just get it over with.* She threw her pen on her desk in disgust and marched towards the end of the corridor. Her entire body rocked to the hammering pulse coursing through her veins.

On her way past the storeroom she noticed some movement and stopped abruptly. All the theatres were finished for the day and the cleaning complete. 'Is someone in there?' she demanded at the open doorway.

David poked his head out from behind a shelf. 'It's just me,' he announced.

Beth relaxed. 'Cramming again?' She smiled. After her suggestion, David had practically haunted the storeroom in his spare time. He'd also called in at her office often to clarify things and Beth was impressed by the young man's dedication.

'Big case tomorrow?' she asked, joining him in the space between the shelves

'I'm scrubbing in with Dr Fallon tomorrow. My first neuro case.' He grimaced. 'I'm just going over the instruments.'

Beth gave him an admiring nod. It was nice to see a student nurse take his work so seriously. 'Gabe's a good teacher,' she said. 'You'll learn a lot.'

'I thought my ears were burning.'

Gabe's voice carried towards them and Beth's heart banged loudly against her ribs as she stuck her head out, as David had done earlier. One thing about working in Theatres was that you rarely heard people approach. The bootees that were worn over shoes muffled everyone's footsteps.

'You know what they say about eavesdroppers,' Beth chided, striving for a normal tone in her voice.

Gabe smiled at her and greeted David. 'I see you're scrubbing in with Kerry tomorrow on my morning list?' he said to the student nurse.

David nodded and Gabe noticed the nervous bob of his Adam's apple and the way the younger man constantly sought Beth's gaze. 'I look forward to it,' Gabe said as he brushed past them, looking for some more artery clamps. 'Be sure to ask me any questions.'

Gabe located a packet of clamps and departed, whistling as he went. Beth watched him leave, filling out his scrubs better than any man had a right to, and realised belatedly that she'd been on her way to talk to him. She excused herself from David, her pulse accelerating, knowing if she didn't do it tonight she might never get round to doing it.

She stood outside the swing doors and watched Gabe through the glass panel for a moment. He was behind the operating table, bent over the silicone 3-D model of the girls' fused craniums. Even through the panic that was twisting her stomach into knots she could see his dedication to Bridie and Brooke was absolute.

She took a deep breath and pushed through the door. He glanced up at her and then returned his attention to the vessel dissection he was working on.

'You must know that off by heart,' Beth said.

'Just about.' He grimaced, not looking up from the task. 'That's the purpose. As my father would have said, failure is not an option.'

Beth felt a stab of worry in her thundering heart. Everyone knew Gabe was expecting the operation to be a success but what if it wasn't? How would he react?

'Don't put too much pressure on yourself, Gabe. Everyone knows, including June and Scott that the girls are up against it.'

Gabe stopped what he was doing and glanced up at Beth. 'I know. But, hey, third time lucky, right?' He grinned and raised his crossed fingers.

Beth grinned back, feeling more relaxed now, and crossed her fingers also.

'So,' Gabe said casually, returning his attention to the model, 'David seems to have a little crush on you.'

Beth blinked. And then blushed. She hadn't been expecting that. 'What? Don't be ridiculous.'

Gabe smiled. '"Methinks the lady doth protest too much."'

'That's crazy,' Beth said ignoring his quote. 'I'm old enough to be his mother.' Beth faltered. *Wasn't that the truth?* 'I'm a mentor figure to him, that's all.'

Gabe laughed this time and Beth shot him a withering look. She'd come in here to announce his impending fatherhood and instead they were having a bizarre conversation about a non-existent workplace crush.

'Relax, Beth. I'm teasing.'

She glared at him furiously. 'Well, don't.'

Gabe curbed his smile and tried to look chastised. He'd noticed how often David sought Beth out and didn't think he was too far off the mark. There was certainly more than collegial feelings there on David's behalf. He remembered the crush he'd had as a med student on his first mentor, a professor of oncology. Older, powerful women had always done it for him. *Hell, he'd slept with Beth!*

Gabe returned to his work, a smile still playing at the corners of his mouth, expecting Beth to leave. When she hadn't moved a few minutes later and the weight of her stare was ruining his concentration he put the forceps down. 'Was there something you wanted?'

Beth took a deep breath. His crush allegation had thrown her but, damn it, this had to be done and he'd just given her as good an opening as any.

'I have to tell you something. It's…kind of…big. I want you to promise me you'll hear me out first before you say anything. OK?'

Gabe looked at her. She was twisting her hands in front of her and her voice sounded a little high. 'OK.'

OK. OK. She took another deep breath as the words she'd practiced deserted her. 'I don't really know how to say this.'

Gabe came around the front of the table. Beth looked two shades paler than a moment ago. *This was big.* He put his hands on his hips. 'Beth, you're worrying me now. I don't care how you say it. Just say it.'

Beth nodded. Then swallowed. 'I'm...' Her voice quavered and she cleared her throat. 'I'm pregnant.'

Gabe felt the words fall heavily, like stones, between them. Boulders. He didn't move. He didn't blink. He just stood and stared.

'I'm sorry. I know this wasn't in your plans. It wasn't in mine either. But it's happened. I know it's not what you want. That's fine. I don't want anything from you. I don't expect you to be involved in any way, shape or form. I just thought you should know.'

Beth finished and waited for a response. Gabe was staring at her, unmoving. Like the news had turned him into a statue. He didn't even blink. She couldn't tell if he was angry, upset or...having an absent seizure.

Gabe felt as if he was having an out-of-body experience. Like he'd wake up any moment and be in his bed at the hotel. He didn't feel anything. His mind, his thoughts, his body seemed...frozen.

'Gabe?'

He blinked at the sound of her voice but still his brain was blank.

'Gabe?' Beth prodded again. He was looking at her with an unfathomable expression and she placed a hand on her stomach.

His gaze flicked down to where her hand spanned her flat belly. His child was inside her? He shook his head. 'But...but we used protection.'

Beth heard the disbelief in his voice and could see the comical aspect despite the seriousness. A doctor, a *neurosurgeon* standing there, trying to tell her that condoms were infallible?

'Yes, we did.'

It took a few more moments for Gabe to process the information. 'And you're sure?'

She nodded. 'I'm thirteen weeks.'

Thirteen weeks? Gabe leant back against the table. 'You've known for a while,' he stated, still stunned.

Beth shrugged. 'I didn't see the point in turning your world upside down until I'd carried the baby through the first trimester.'

He nodded. *Made sense*. Gabe rubbed the back of his neck. A kid? He didn't have time for a kid. 'I...I don't know what to say.'

Gabe looked totally horrified. His green eyes were dazed as he stroked his jaw absently. 'It was a shock for me also,' Beth said quietly. Part of her had hoped for a different reaction but deep down she'd known the news wouldn't be welcome.

He looked into her steady blue gaze, her hand still cradling her stomach. It may have been a shock but she seemed quite together about it. Granted, she'd had longer than him to get used to it but she didn't seem panicked or stricken or upset. Surely at thirty-eight this must have been a most unwelcome development?

'So...you want to...have the baby?'

Beth took an involuntary step back, her hands tightening protectively around her stomach. 'More than I've ever wanted anything.'

Gabe stared at her. Her tone brooked no argument, her mouth a tight line. 'But...what about...' He groped around for something to say while his brain tried to make sense of the situation. 'What about your career?'

'My career, Gabe? Or your career?' she asked icily.

Gabe shook his head to clear it. His mind was a jumble. 'I'm sorry…I'm making a bit of a hash of this… I just assumed that as you were single with no kids by now, it was through choice…that children weren't on your agenda.'

Beth felt a well of emotion stronger than her anger rise in her chest and tears pricked her eyes. How many nights had she cried herself to sleep because her arms had ached so much? 'No. It wasn't through choice. It was just the way it panned out.'

Gabe couldn't believe the conversation they were having. To think ten minutes ago, separating conjoined twins had been his biggest worry. It seemed like a walk in the park compared to this.

'You really want to do this…don't you?'

Beth heard the disbelief in his voice. It was obvious he thought being lumbered with a baby was a fate worse than death. She had to make him see that she wanted this baby desperately. That it wasn't some last whim of an almost barren nearly-forty female.

'Twenty-three years ago I had a baby. A little boy. I was fifteen. I gave him up for adoption. It broke my heart.' Beth's voice cracked at the effort it took to suppress the memories of that time and not break down in front of him. 'So, yes, Gabe,' she continued, her voice trembling with the fierceness needed to protect the baby growing inside her. 'I do. I do want to have the baby.'

Gabe stared at Beth, her second shocking revelation in as many minutes hanging between them. It was even harder to absorb than the first one had been. *She'd had a baby?* This was the chunk of information he'd sensed she'd left out that first day at Barney's. It was obviously the reason why she'd run away and why she'd ended up fostered by the Winterses.

Gabe pushed away from the table to pace, feeling like his head was about to explode. *What the hell was he going to do?* He paced for a few minutes, conscious of Beth watching him. He turned and looked at her, one hand on her stomach, the other clenched into a fist by her side.

It was obvious her mind was made up. And given what he now knew, he could understand why. But still…

He lived on the other side of the world. His private practice, his entire career was ten of thousands of kilometres away. A twenty-four-hour trip by plane. Oh, God, did she expect him to propose? Would she even come to the UK?

'Well, of course…I'll…' he swallowed '…support you in anything you want to do.'

Beth shook her head, taking pity on him. She'd just dumped an awful lot of information in his lap. 'No, Gabe. I told you. I don't want you to. And I certainly don't expect you to. I know this isn't what you want. I'm perfectly happy to raise this child alone. Just go back to England when your contract runs out and forget about us. I won't blame you or think any less of you.'

Gabe stopped pacing. He searched her face. He couldn't believe she was being so calm. Giving him an out. She hadn't insisted on a gold band and a white picket fence. In fact, she'd absolved him from all responsibility. Wasn't she supposed to want that? This was too much. It was all too much.

'You really mean that, don't you? You'd raise this baby on your own.'

Beth frowned. 'Of course.'

Gabe reeled. This was madness. 'Doesn't that scare you witless? Isn't that just too…daunting?'

Beth nodded. 'Of course it's scary and daunting and overwhelming and there are a lot of voices in my head, from my past…my father, my stepmother…that make me doubt myself. But I'm not fifteen this time around and I have a supportive family and a home and a stable income. And I want this more than anything.'

'I don't know what to say.' He rubbed the back of his neck again. 'I don't know what to think.'

'Of course,' she replied. 'I've just dumped this in your lap and I'm sorry, you've got enough to worry about, I realise. You need to concentrate on Brooke and Bridie. Don't worry about me. Or the baby.'

She was seriously going to let him walk away?

Gabe knew he didn't want to be a father. He hadn't planned it and he hadn't asked for it. The question was, could he just fly back to the UK and turn his back on his child? Have nothing to do with it? Ever? What kind of a human being did that make him?

Harlon Fallon's son.

He shivered. Even if Beth was as OK with it as she appeared, it just didn't seem right. Didn't his baby deserve two parents? A father as well? One that was around. Interested? Involved? Didn't he want to spare his child the insecurities that had plagued him because of his absent father?

How many nights had he gone to bed with a churned-up stomach knowing that he had a father out there that would rather be in a hospital full of sick people than at home with him? How often had he questioned his identity and his way in life with no father figure as a guide? How miserable had he felt when no matter how hard he had tried to get his father's attention, nothing had ever seemed to work? He'd had to become a doctor before Harlon Fallon had taken any notice of him.

When he looked back at his childhood he could describe it in one word. Incomplete. Could he inflict that on another child? His own child?

'I want to help.'

Beth blinked. 'Wh-what?'

Gabe blinked too, not sure he'd actually said the words. 'This baby…it's my responsibility too.'

Beth felt her pulse slow right down, her blood roar in her ears. He wanted to help? His responsibility? What did that mean? She took a step back. 'I don't understand. I didn't think you'd want to… It's OK, you can walk away, Gabe. I won't judge you. I'm perfectly capable of taking care of this baby. I own my own home, I have good savings, a few investments and a well-paid job. We'll be okay.'

The more determined she seemed to push him away, the more certain he became. It obviously hadn't occurred to her that he'd want any part of it. And, frankly, it scared the hell out of him but as each second ticked by his convictions crystallised.

'I'm not walking. I'm not sure I understand why you're so determined to make me. We both had fathers that left a lot to be desired. They were absent. Emotionally distant. I'm not going to make the same mistake with my own kid. Don't you want better for our child?'

Beth looked at him still dumbfounded by his desire to be involved. 'Of course. I just didn't think you'd want to be involved. I don't want you to feel you have to be out of some stupid sense of propriety or duty.'

'I'm the father,' Gabe said testily. 'It *is* my duty.'

'You know what I mean,' Beth said, her voice tinged with exasperation. 'How do you think it's going to work? Your career is taking off. I can't go to the UK, Gabe.'

Was that what he wanted? Hell, he didn't know. He needed to think things through. All he knew was that he wanted to be part of his child's life. He wanted to be more than a sperm donor and a mysterious gift every birthday.

Gabe shrugged, buying time for his startled thought processes to compute the information. 'Why not?'

Beth felt a knot of tension pull hard in her stomach. 'I can't leave… I have to stay. My son…he may try and get in contact with me one day. I need to be here for that…in case.'

Gabe leant heavily against the operating table. Beth's twenty-three-year-old son. Another angle to consider. Beth had had weeks to think this through, look at it in minute detail. The shocking news had rendered him completely in-capable of anything other than breathing, and yet she had everything planned out.

'I don't know, Beth. I don't know how it'll work. All I know is that I want to be involved. I need time to think about this.'

Beth heard the weary note in his voice, still surprised at his insistence. Shocked, actually. Shocked was a much better word. He hadn't been in any of the plans she'd weaved over the last six weeks. And she wasn't entirely sure she wanted to make room for him. She'd been so sure he'd run. A tremor of apprehension ran through her as she glanced at him uneasily. What did that mean for her future now?

'Of course, Gabe,' Beth said, pulling her straying thoughts back into line. 'There's a lot to take in. And your plate was pretty full to begin with. We don't have to make any concrete decisions at the moment. Nothing has to be decided for ages yet. Let's just get the separation out of the way first.'

Time. They both needed time to think. Adjust.

Gabe leant against the table again, admiring her ability to prioritise calmly. All his focus and energies since arriving in Brisbane had been concentrated on the twins. Every waking moment, even some sleeping ones and certainly every spare minute had been given to the operation. Yet this piece of news had completely obliterated Brooke and Bridie from his mind.

She was right, though—first things first. And the Fisher twins took that honour. He nodded. 'Separation first.'

'I'll let you get on with your practice,' Beth said, backing away.

'Sure,' Gabe said absently. He looked down at the discarded silicone model and knew there was no way he was going to be able to concentrate on that tonight.

Beth reached the door and paused. She looked over her shoulder at a bewildered Gabe who was staring unseeingly at the practice model. He looked like he'd had the stuffing knocked out of him. Maybe she should have kept quiet?

'I'm sorry,' she said. 'I thought you'd want to know.'

Gabe looked up. 'Of course,' he sighed. 'You did the right thing.'

He watched her open the door. It seemed odd that they were parting like this after such news. Finding out their night together had created a life was about as intimate as you could get. An embrace seemed more appropriate.

'When's the baby due?' Gabe called after her.

Beth paused. 'September thirty,' she said, and went on her way, letting the door swing shut behind her.

The silence in Theatre Ten was deafening as a barrage of conflicting thoughts stampeded through Gabe's head. Six months. *Hell.*

A month passed. Beth and Gabe were kept busy with their normal workload as well as the preparations for the separation. Things were initially a little awkward between them again but with their busy schedules and tacit agreement to focus on the twins, their professionalism came to the fore.

Their relationship continued to be that of colleagues. Mutual respect and consideration. In fact, at times it even bordered on friendship. But apart from the odd query after her health, Gabe didn't refer to the pregnancy and there'd been no further discussion about the baby as preparations for the separation ramped up.

But one month shy of the scheduled operation Beth was woken at three in the morning by Gabe's delicious accent. It was brisk and businesslike. No late-night lovers' chat like the last time they'd spoken at this hour of the morning.

'Brooke and Bridie have been admitted to the intensive care unit. Bridie had a prolonged seizure.'

Beth struggled through the layers of sleep, her heart pounding, and not just because of the unexpected turn of events. 'Are we going in?'

'Not yet. I'll keep you posted.'

Beth stared at the dead phone for a few seconds before placing it back on its cradle. She fell back against the pillows, her brain kicking into overdrive, her heart beating crazily. Were they ready for this? Had they practised enough?

She placed a hand over her belly where Gabe's baby was growing safe and well, knowing she'd slay a dragon for their unborn baby. She thought about June and Scott and suppressed the urge to get out of bed and rush to ICU to be with them. They had a very supportive family and Beth knew they'd be rallying around.

Oddly enough, she wanted to go to Gabe more. She knew how much he'd invested in this operation and how much pressure he was under to make it a third successful separation. She'd also seen how close he'd become to the Fishers, as they all had, and knew he'd be taking this development hard.

But, father of her child or not, they didn't have that kind of relationship. In fact, they had gone to pains to maintain a professional distance and she wouldn't ruin that by tearing up to the hospital in the middle of the night to hold his hand. She would see him tomorrow and in the meantime she'd go back to sleep.

Hopefully.

The next few days were fraught for the Fisher twins. Bridie was loaded with anti-convulsants but because the girls shared a blood supply through the intricate meshing of cranial vessels, that complicated things for Brooke.

Bridie went on to develop a pleural effusion and started to show signs of renal and liver impairment. Her blood pressure needed drugs to support it, a tricky balance for ICU doctors who had to consider the effects on both girls.

Gabe was worried that Bridie might not make it, that she would die before separation, flooding her sister's body with toxins that would give Brooke mere hours to live. With Bridie's heart not the strongest, Gabe was reluctant to subject the smaller twin to the rigours of prolonged neurosurgery but he knew they were walking a fine line.

Beth visited regularly. It didn't seem to matter what time she popped in, Gabe was always there. Standing with Scott and June, talking to the ICU doctors or consulting with other specialists. He was upbeat with the Fishers but she could tell he was tense and gravely concerned.

Two days later, Bridie's condition worsened again, with the development of more seizures, and a joint decision was made to go ahead with the op. Gabe knew their hand was being forced but that was just the way it happened sometimes and no matter how much he would have liked both twins to be in optimum shape, life had thrown them a curve ball. He had to operate now or risk losing both of them.

He rang Beth again in the wee small hours. 'We're going in. How soon can we get the team assembled?'

Beth heard the slight huskiness in his voice and knew that Gabe wasn't thrilled about the circumstances. She rubbed the lingering traces of sleep from her eyes her brain racing ahead. 'A few hours.'

'See you then.'

CHAPTER SIX

It was barely seven on Saturday morning as the team members required for the beginning of the operation assembled in Theatre Ten, waiting for the twins to arrive. Half of them had blue scrub tops and gowns, the other half green. Bridie's team wore blue, Brooke's green. They waited silently, rehearsing the steps in their head that they'd honed over the last few months.

The ten-strong anaesthetic team, led by Don Anderson talked quietly, going over their strategies to manage vital signs and minimise blood loss and the logistics of moving the babies once the separation was complete.

Beth scrubbed in, along with several other nurses, and oversaw the set-ups. Circulating nurses opened the mountains of sterile equipment that would be needed, passing them to the scrub nurses, who organised their trolleys methodically. She was hyper-aware of Gabe standing with the other scrubbed surgeons huddled around the numerous images, going over their last-minute plans.

Shortly she would take her place beside him for who knew how many hours. They both wore blue. It had been decided from the beginning that, given his experience, that

Gabe would take the more fragile twin on their separation. And this morning he had insisted she be at his side.

'I want the best neuro scrub nurse on my team,' he'd said. 'Bridie has an uphill battle. More than her sister. I need the best to give her any hope.'

And so now she was wearing blue and hoping, as were they all, she didn't let him down. Gabe turned and looked directly at her.

'Are we ready, Beth?'

Beth looked around at the team and took in their silent nods. 'As ready as we'll ever be.'

The anaesthetised twins were rolled into the theatre. For a few seconds all movement and all conversation ceased. This was what it was about. Two fragile babies, dwarfed by the complex equipment surrounding them and lost in a sea of blue and green strangers who held their fate in their hands.

'Let's get this show on the road,' Gabe announced, and the team kicked into action.

Once plastic surgeons had made the first incision and exposed the area it was Gabe's turn. As he and fellow neurosurgeon Eve Mitchell worked, he could feel sweat building on his brow as his heart hammered madly in his chest. *So far, so good.*

They were about to perform the craniotomy that would open a window into the twins' brains. No 3-D computer image or plastic moulded replica. This was the moment they'd prepared and practised for. The moment of truth. The enormity was almost overwhelming.

'Wipe,' he said.

Beth grabbed one of the folded surgical sponges as

Gabe turned towards her, surprised that he required it already. They'd only been at it for a short while.

She glanced into his peridot eyes, piercingly intense above his mask, and thought she saw a fleeting second of uncertainty. *Poor Gabe*. Bridie's condition had just magnified the pressure on him. She gave him an encouraging smile, even though she knew he couldn't see it behind her mask.

Gabe saw it anyway, reflected in her blue gaze as he bent down slightly for her to mop his brow. Their gazes locked for a fleeting moment and the faith he saw there bolstered his confidence.

The procedure took hours as they slowly and cautiously worked their way through the spaghetti-sized blood vessels. Gabe stopped several times to consult the pre-op scans and diagrams held up for him by circulating nurses.

The anaesthetic team kept a close eye on the babies' vital signs. Gabe asked for regular updates, only too aware that any ongoing blood loss could be catastrophic to patients this size. Transfusions ran to replace the lost volume but it was a delicate balance. Too much could upset the girls' natural clotting factors.

Gabe checked the clock and was surprised to see six hours had passed. His neck and shoulders ached a little from being hunched over the small operating area and he knew it was time to take a break. He and Eve signalled their intention to hand over and allow two fresh surgeons to take their places.

During one of the many pre-op discussions it had been decided that six hours should be the maximum period any member of the team spent in the theatre at any one time unless there was an emergency or the surgery was at a critical stage. Six hours on, maximum. Two hours off, minimum.

Their replacements arrived and all the scrubbed staff, including nurses, degowned and headed for the staffroom for a well-earned break. The team members waiting in the staff room applauded as Gabe entered the room.

'Don't get too carried away,' Gabe warned.

Yes, things were going according to plan and he was cautiously optimistic, but he knew only too well that things could go pear-shaped very quickly. They had a lot of brain to get through still and Bridie's frailty worried him.

Beth, feeling slightly nauseated from lack of food, grabbed a bite to eat. Breakfast of tea and toast seemed an eon ago. Someone had brought in cream buns and she bit into one gratefully. There was a mixture of excitement and cautious optimism in the staffroom and she found it difficult not to be infected by it.

The wall-mounted monitors Beth had arranged previously relayed images and sound from the theatre, and as they chatted and relaxed they could keep an eye on the operation. Being able to watch the proceedings and discuss them was invaluable to keeping them all focused and up to date.

Several shift changes came and went from Theatre Ten. The day was long and night fell without anyone being aware of it. Operating theatres were a windowless world, insulated and artificial. History was being made at the General with each tiny slice of the scalpel and that was all anyone was aware of.

As the night wore on, slow progress was being made on teasing the two brains apart. The staffroom was littered with empty coffee-mugs, discarded food wrappings and staff catching some shut-eye in chairs, while others watched the screens with bleary eyes and murmured quietly among themselves.

Gabe and Beth were back in the thick of it, standing side by side. He was frustrated at the snail-pace progress and worried about the increased bleeding.

They placed special gauze soaked in anti-coagulant as they traveled deeper into the dissection to try and minimise the ooze, and anaesthetic nurses hung bag after bag of blood, platelets and fresh frozen plasma to enhance the twins' clotting factors. But Gabe knew that the longer it took, the worse shape the girls would be in by the end.

Frustratingly, as he meticulously separated the grey matter, the tissues would swell and push into each other again, making the going even more difficult.

Beth could sense Gabe's growing frustration with the un-cooperative brain tissue. He was tired, they all were. Neither of them had slept—too wired to relax. But at their next break she was going to insist. Despite the slowness, they were much closer to the end and the head of the team had to be alert.

An hour later the brain tissue began to bleed heavily. Gabe's fingers worked quickly, accepting instruments from Beth to stem the haemorrhage. Just then the monitor alarm went off.

'What is it?' Gabe asked, without looking away from his task.

'Bridie's pressure's dropping. She's bradycardic,' Don Anderson supplied.

It took thirty minutes to stabilise Bridie again. Luckily Brooke's vitals remained as steady as a rock.

Several hours later they degowned again. 'Get some shut-eye,' Beth ordered. She stopped by the blanket warmer and pulled a deliciously toasty blanket out. 'Go put your head on my desk.'

Gabe shook his head. 'I'll grab forty winks in the staffroom.'

'No,' Beth insisted. 'You won't. You'll sit and yack with fifteen different people about the procedure.' She pushed the blanket into his arms. 'If everything goes according to plan, the separation is imminent in the next few hours. The girls need you rested.'

'I'm fine,' he said abruptly.

'Dr Fallon!'

His head snapped up and their gazes locked. They'd stopped all that ridiculous formality weeks ago.

'You are not fine. Bridie needs the best. You are not at your best.'

Gabe saw the fire in her eyes and appreciated her frankness. She was right. But what about her? She was eighteen weeks pregnant after all.

'What about you, Beth?' He placed a hand against her stomach. 'You must be extra-tired. How are you holding up?'

Beth was surprised by his action. He hadn't mentioned the baby to her once in the last month. His hand there felt so good, so right, so intimate she had to suppress the urge to cover it with her own.

Gabe liked how it felt to touch her there. Operating on the twins made it impossible to ignore he would soon have a baby of his own. Already, despite his conflicting emotions, he felt a weird kind of connection to his child. It enabled him to put himself in Scott and June's shoes. To realise the operating area beneath his hands belonged to somebody's babies.

'I'm OK,' she said, moving away slightly, conscious that

anyone could come out of the staffroom and see them. They'd agreed to keep news of the pregnancy quiet until after the separation. 'I suspect I've had more sleep than you the last few nights.'

Gabe dropped his hand, feeling strangely bereft. God, he must be tired. He smiled grudgingly. 'Sleep has been rather elusive.' He'd been pulling long nights in the ICU. 'You'll wake me if—'

'I will get you immediately if anything happens.'

Gabe rubbed his jaw, a shadow of stubble evident. He gave her a slow, grateful smile. 'Thanks, Beth.'

Beth nodded as he brushed past her and she ignored the mad flutter in her chest. His acknowledgement of their baby had stirred something in her that she hadn't allowed herself to buy into. Gabe as a father figure. And she couldn't afford to buy into it now either.

Beth stood in the doorway to her office, a steaming mug of coffee and several pieces of honey toast on a plate in one hand. Gabe was slumped over her desk, his face relaxed in slumber, his stubble growth more pronounced. His theatre cap was still firmly in place and he'd bunched some of the blanket beneath his face to act as a pillow.

His full lips were parted slightly and she allowed herself the brief fantasy of waking him by placing her mouth on his. He really did have very tempting lips.

'Gabe,' she called quietly.

He didn't move. Beth walked in, placed the food and drink on the edge of her desk and moved closer to him.

'Gabe,' she whispered, and gave his shoulder a gentle shake.

Gabe was awake instantly, his head rising from the desk. 'I'm awake,' he announced loudly. His eyes came to focus on Beth's and he gave her a sleepy smile. 'What's happening?' He sat up fully alert now, pushing the blanket off his shoulders and stretching his neck from side to side.

Beth placed the coffee and toast in front of him. 'They think they're only a couple of hours away but the team is tiring.'

Gabe nodded. 'How long have I been asleep?'

'Nearly four hours.'

'Have the twins been stable?'

'Bridie's required some support for her blood pressure but she seems to be holding her own. Brooke's still soldiering on.'

Gabe took a sip of his coffee. 'OK. I'll eat this then go back in. Did you sleep?'

Beth nodded. 'A little.' He had a mark on his face from the weave of the cellular blanket and she smiled at the criss-cross pattern marring his cheek.

'What? Have I got drool on my chin?'

Beth grinned. 'No. Blanket face.'

Gabe laughed. 'Wait till you see my hat hair after thirty hours.'

Beth laughed too. 'You won't be alone there.' It felt good to laugh after the pressure of the last twenty-four hours and a couple of months of stilted formality.

Gabe offered her one of his pieces of toast. Despite having just had a piece, she took one. High-stakes surgery was not her forte and the baby was letting her know it didn't approve of the extra stress. A vague feeling of nausea had taken up permanent residence in her stomach and, as always, eating helped.

They munched quietly for a few moments. 'Looks like we did get to have breakfast together after all,' he said, and smiled at her. 'Not quite what I'd planned on. Room service at the hotel do the best omelettes and Danish pastries.'

Beth swallowed the toast, which suddenly felt dry and cardboard-like. 'Gabe.'

Gabe heard the note of warning and felt too weary to tease any further. 'I know. Sorry. Inappropriate. Forget I mentioned it.'

'Forgotten.' She straightened, giving her scrub top a firm yank. 'I'll see you at the sinks.'

Gabe sighed as she left, his appetite deserting him. Forgetting their night together, forgetting she was carrying his baby had been a lot easier when they hadn't been practically glued at the hip for the last twenty-four hours.

'Separation imminent,' Gabe announced, looking up into the camera above his head for the benefit of those in the staffroom. 'I need all hands on deck.'

His pulse picked up. In less than thirty minutes Bridie and Brooke would finally be separate and the surgical team that had been operating as one would become two.

The second table was wheeled in by orderlies and the wheels locked in place. More scrub and scout nurses appeared. They draped the new table in preparation to receive Brooke and continue the delicate process of closure. It had been decided that as Brooke was the more stable twin, she was the best candidate to be moved.

The anaesthetic team prepared for the transfer procedure, as they had practised. Brooke's surgeons stood scrubbed and ready to receive her. Kelly, Brooke's scrub nurse, counted instruments and sponges with the circulating nurses. The theatre was now crowded.

And then the moment came. The last bit of tissue and bone was excised and Brooke was gently lifted and slowly transferred across. The manoeuvre was textbook and the collective breaths of nearly thirty people were expelled in one audible exhalation.

But there was no time for self-congratulation as Brooke's team swarmed around the table and the surgeries continued.

'She's bleeding too much again,' Gabe said, his attention only on Bridie. 'How's her vitals?'

'Pressure dropping,' Don confirmed. 'She's getting more tachy. ECG changes.'

'Come on, Bridie,' Gabe pleaded quietly behind his mask. 'Stay with us.'

Beth and the other scrub nurse frantically passed instruments to Gabe and the two other surgeons who were trying valiantly to get the bleeding under control. The anaesthetic teamed push fluids and administered drugs to bolster Bridie's failing heart.

'She's going brady,' the anesthetic nurse announced.

'Come on, Bridie,' Gabe said, his fingers working desperately to control the bleeding.

Don and his team worked continuously to restore the failing twin's circulation, to no avail.

'Surgical staff step back from the table,' Don ordered, as Bridie's ECG displayed life-threatening bradycardia.

Beth and Gabe, along with the others, dropped their instruments frantically and stepped back, hands held slightly in front of them to protect their sterility. Bridie's full anaesthetic team converged on the table, taking turns at external chest compressions.

Fifteen minutes later Gabe moved closer to see what was happening. 'What's her rhythm like?'

The anesthetic nurse stopped compressions momentarily. The line on the monitor barely fluttered.

'It's no good,' Don said to Gabe. 'She's lost too much blood.'

Gabe shook his head. *No*. They hadn't just performed thirty hours of neurosurgery to give up after fifteen minutes.

'More adrenaline,' Gabe said, pushing into the circle surrounding tiny Bridie and taking over compressions.

Twenty minutes passed. Thirty. Forty-five. More drugs. More chest compressions. They even achieved a shockable rhythm at one stage and used the defibrillator twice. Beth stood behind Gabe, watching his erect frame, listening to his orders, her heart breaking for him. He'd invested so much in this operation.

Don's gaze caught hers and she knew what he was thinking. It was no use. Bridie had fought magnificently but it was over. The odds had been stacked against her and it was time to be let go.

But nobody wanted to contradict Gabe. He was the surgeon who had made it all possible, who had so very nearly succeeded, and he was well liked and respected. They all wanted to give Gabe and Bridie every chance. But it was past time.

Beth walked into the circle. 'Gabe,' she said in a low voice.

Gabe ignored her as he pumped at the tiny chest with his blood-covered gloves.

'Gabe,' she said, louder this time.

'More adrenaline,' Gabe said to Don.

The anaesthetist looked at Beth again. 'Dr Fallon…' he said.

'Damn it, Don. I said more adrenaline,' Gabe snapped. *Come on, Bridie, come on.*

'Gabe!' Beth used the voice she always used when dealing with recalcitrant staff. It wasn't loud, she didn't want to draw the attention of the whole theatre, but it had just the right note of don't-mess-with-me.

Gabe looked down at Beth, seeing her for the first time.

'It's time.' She placed her hands over his.

Gabe shook his head, his hands still moving, their gazes locked. *She was just a tiny baby.*

She nodded. 'She's had nearly an hour of downtime,' she said, knowing that even if by some miracle Bridie's heart was to suddenly start, there would no doubt be serious brain damage. 'You've done all you could.'

Gabe knew she was right. Knew she was making sense. But he'd promised June and Scott that he would do everything in his power to give them back two live, separated little girls. How could he break his promise?

'Let her go, Gabe,' Beth said gently staring into his conflicted green eyes. 'Bridie's telling you she's had enough. Her little body can't take any more.'

She was right. Gabe's hands stilled. Her body had been through a huge ordeal and her recent frailty had stacked the odds against her even further. He sighed and withdrew his hands.

He looked at the clock on the wall. 'Time of death fifteen twenty-five hours.'

He peeled off his gloves as the whole theatre fell silent.

Nobody moved for a moment or two as they took in Bridie's pale, lifeless body. She looked so small and defenceless among the green drapes.

Beth raised her hand to touch Gabe on the arm as a wave of sadness overwhelmed her. Everyone looked devastated and she knew Gabe would be feeling the worst of all of them. But she remembered herself at the last moment and dropped her hand to her belly instead grateful for the tiny fluttering movements she felt there.

Gabe roused himself like the true professional he was. This day wasn't over yet. He turned to the table behind him. 'How's Brooke?' he asked.

'We've achieved primary closure,' the plastic surgeon said.

'Vitals?' Gabe queried the anesthetist.

'Stable.'

He looked down at Brooke. Her head was wrapped in a turban-like head bundle. Her eyes were puffy and bruised-looking. Her tiny body was criss-crossed with a multitude of fluid lines and monitoring wires. A bag of blood was running with all the other fluids.

She looked pale, although not as pale as her sister. 'What's her haemoglobin?'

'Ninety.'

Gabe nodded, satisfied with the figure considering all that Brooke had been through and was still to endure. She was by no means out of the woods yet. 'Let's get her to ICU.'

He turned back to Bridie. Beth was assisting one of the plastics team, who was closing the gaping head wound amidst a flurry of clean-up activity. He stood beside her.

'Nearly done,' Beth said.

'Thanks,' Gabe said, admiring the surgeon's neat suturing.

Beth was hyper-aware of him beside her. Being intimate with him had given her a crash course in his body language and, getting to know him and his perfectionism in the last months, she guessed he was reliving those last moments, searching for something he could have done differently. Maybe wondering what his father would have done.

'Why don't you go and talk to Scott and June?' she suggested, knowing there was no use in second-guessing him.

She made a mental note to organise a series of team debriefs. Everyone involved had a huge emotional investment in the case. It would be a bond they'd share for ever. It was important to be able to discuss their reactions to the marathon surgery and the less than ideal outcome.

Gabe nodded, dreading the moment he would have to tell the Fishers that their precious little Bridie hadn't pulled through. It didn't matter that they'd been given a very guarded prognosis and this type of outcome had been discussed at length with them. One of their daughters was dead. No matter how prepared someone was for that, it would still rock them to the core.

CHAPTER SEVEN

THE clean-up was a mammoth task and Beth stayed to help out. The number of instrument trays alone they'd been through added up to the amount they'd normally use in one day for all ten theatres. She slipped into the dirty corridor and gave the staff there a hand before sitting at her desk and reworking the week's roster.

Several of the nursing staff involved in the Fisher case were due back on tomorrow morning and Beth stayed until she'd been able to give them two days off and still cover the roster. It involved ringing staff at home and begging favours and also organising agency cover but she managed it.

She had half expected Gabe to drop by and was absurdly disappointed when he didn't. She was worried about him and needed to reassure herself that he was OK. She decided to drop into the PICU on her way to Barney's for the team get-together, guessing correctly that Gabe would be there.

Brooke was in a side room and her nurse brushed past Beth as she approached, leaving Gabe alone in the room with the surviving twin. Scott and June were absent. Beth stood silently in the doorway, watching Gabe talk quietly to Brooke.

'I'm sorry,' he whispered, stroking the fingers of her tiny

pale hand encumbered by an arterial line. 'I tried, we all did…but your sister was…very weak. She's always going to be with you, though. In here.' Gabe lightly tapped Brooke's chest, expertly avoiding the wires that snaked haphazardly across her tiny body that could trigger an alarm.

Beth backed away, tears in her eyes. The crack in his voice was heartbreaking and it wasn't right to intrude on his private vigil. Her thoughts were jumbled and she knew it was a dangerous moment. A moment when she could have crazy fantasies of love and white picket fences. Beth knew thoughts such as those shouldn't be given any credence at times like this so she quashed them ruthlessly as she left the ICU and walked quickly away.

The sun was setting as she walked across the road to Barney's. The team was meeting for a quick meal and a casual debrief, and Beth knew it was vital to support her staff in this area. All her nurses had been affected by Bridie's death and she knew it was important to lead by example and attend these all important sessions, be they casual or formal.

The mood was subdued. There was satisfaction and immense pride that Brooke had made it but it was overshadowed by Bridie's death. To Beth's surprise, Gabe wasn't there, and she suspected that this contributed to the general gloom.

Gabe had been the leader and his positivity and enthusiasm had buoyed them all whenever the task had seemed too overwhelming. Now that things hadn't gone according to plan, everyone was looking for some reassurance that they hadn't let him down.

Beth's feelings see-sawed from her earlier tenderness to

plain annoyed. And every time the pub door opened and everyone's heads swiveled, looking for Gabe, she got crankier. His no-show had been inconsiderate of the team's needs. The team that had worked their butts off beside him. That were as emotionally invested in the Fisher case as he had been. His absence had left them rudderless.

The group broke up early. Everyone was tired after the marathon surgery and the loss of Bridie had put a dampener on their spirits. Beth imagined that had both twins pulled through, they would have partied late into the night, despite their exhaustion. The gathering felt anti-climatic rather than a celebration of an amazing feat.

Beth headed straight for Gabe's hotel, her irritation having increased as she'd watched her colleagues leave Barney's, their shoulders slumped. He couldn't build them up and then desert them when his grand vision had failed. He'd known the odds had been long from the beginning, and he should have been at Barney's with them, commiserating and assuring them that everyone had done all they'd been able to.

She had a brief thought as she rapped on his door that he might not even be at the hotel, but that was soon proved wrong when he opened the door. Shirtless.

Gabe stared at her. 'You're not room service.'

Beth stared back, her gaze dragged downwards to his magnificently bare chest. 'No.'

He stood aside. 'Do you want to come in?'

With you half-naked? But considering she'd come to give him a piece of her mind, she thought it better to do it in the privacy of his room. She walked through his doorway, taking special care not to brush against him.

'Do you want a drink?' he asked, staring at her very erect back.

'No,' she said abruptly, angrier now that her thoughts had been scattered by the sight of his beautifully hard chest.

Gabe shrugged. 'I'm getting some chips from room service. I can order extra if you like.'

Beth turned. 'I've eaten. At Barney's. With everyone else.'

Gabe saw the accusation glitter in her blue eyes. 'Yeah, sorry about that. I was wrecked.'

He did look exhausted. The shadow of stubble that had been growing at his jaw was more pronounced now. His caramel hair was rumpled. Beth folded her arms across her chest and hardened her heart. 'We were all wrecked.'

Gabe heard the steel in her reply. He took a moment to look at her. Her lips were a tight line. Her spine ramrod straight. Her crossed arms relaying her complete disapproval. 'You're annoyed with me.'

'The team needed you to be there tonight, Gabe. Debrief is mandatory. That's what you told me a few months ago.'

Gabe rubbed his hands through his hair. 'I know. Look, I'm sorry…I just didn't feel like a post-mortem. Talking with the Fishers was hard. I just needed to be alone. To think.'

'How were they?' she asked, her stance softening.

'Distraught,' Gabe said, clenching his fists by his sides as visions of a sobbing Scott reran in his head.

Beth knew from his clipped reply that it must have been bad. He looked so tired, the subdued light in the room making the lines on his forehead look more prominent. He'd always looked younger than his thirty three years but tonight he looked every one of them and a few more. It couldn't have been easy talking to Brooke and Bridie's parents.

She felt her own weariness responding to his. His voice washed over her and with his chest looking all smooth and inviting she could feel her anger dissolving.

She had the absurd urge to lay her head against him and shut her eyes like she had in this very hotel room a few months ago.

Beth sighed. 'I know that must have been awful but all the team needed was a few words of thanks, of encouragement. Every single one of us felt Bridie's death too, Gabe.'

Gabe felt lousy. She was right. He'd been self-centred. There was a knock at the door. 'That'll be room service.'

Beth nodded. 'I'll go. I know you want to be alone. I just wanted you to know you have some fence-mending to do.'

'No,' Gabe said, putting a hand out as she backed towards the door. 'Don't go. I don't want to be alone. Not now you're here.'

Beth felt heat slam into her. Her legs turned to jelly, making any further retreat impossible. She had to go. The emotional roller-coaster of the marathon surgery was still too raw between them. The things he'd said to Brooke still too fresh in her mind. It was dangerous to be near him when they were both still so keyed up.

But the plea in his eyes was hard to ignore and as he brushed past her to answer the door, his male scent wafted towards her and her stomach lurched.

Gabe took the tray from the waiter and set it down on the bed. He noticed Beth still hadn't moved. She was wearing cargo pants and a T-shirt that clung to her breasts and was standing as still as a statue, looking at the bed like it was a monster from the deep.

'How about we eat on the balcony?' he suggested.

Beth knew she was powerless to say no. She'd stood beside Gabe for the last thirty odd-hours, watched while he'd valiantly tried to bring Bridie back from the brink. And he wanted her to stay and she couldn't deny him his request. The balcony was good. *Anywhere but the bed*.

She swallowed. 'As long as you put a shirt on.' She knew her voice was husky and hated herself for it, but there was no way she could sit opposite a shirtless Gabe with his sexy accent and six-pack abs and not think about how she had put her mouth on every inch of him.

The hair at Gabe's neck prickled. Beth wanted him. He felt tendrils of sensation crawl along his spine and shoot to his groin. Despite his professional façade, he hadn't stopped wanting her since their night together, and right now he wanted her more than ever.

He picked his shirt up from the edge of the bed, where he'd slung it when he'd first entered the room. He held her gaze as he pulled it over his head and dragged it down.

'Better?' he asked huskily.

No. 'Thank you,' she said, and commanded her legs to walk out to the balcony.

After some initial awkwardness they settled into small talk. Gabe drank cold beer from the mini-bar and they watched the lights of the River Cats down below, ferrying customers from one side to the other. They avoided any talk of the operation.

'I can't believe you're actually living in a hotel for seven months,' Beth said as she took in the magnificent city view.

He shrugged. 'It was part of my contract. There didn't seem to be any point renting for such a short term.'

Short term. The words reverberated around her head.

She nodded as her gaze fell on his bed. Had he brought anyone else back here? Short-term job. Short-term women? Had she been one of many?

Not that it mattered or was any of her business if he had. Or that she should be thinking about it while he talked about whatever it was that he was talking about.

'And there's this study that I'm involved in...'

His career. Right. He was talking about his career. He had a promising career on the other side of the world. She removed her eyes from the temptation and the memories of his bed, plastered a smile on her face and nodded at him encouragingly.

'I'm sorry,' he said a few minutes later. 'I'm prattling. I guess we really should be talking about the thing we've avoided taking about for too long. The baby.'

Beth felt like she was plunging down a loop on a roller-coaster as her stomach dropped. *Not tonight.* She didn't have the emotional fortitude for that.

'No.' She smiled, placing a hand on her belly. 'Let's not. Not now. It's been a big weekend and we're both tired. I don't have the stamina for a deep and meaningful conversation. Prattling's good.'

An hour later Gabe stifled a yawn as Beth told him about some local tourist spots. He remembered the overwhelming weariness from his last two separations but this time it was different. The success of those ops had offset the tiredness. He couldn't remember having felt more tired.

'I'm sorry,' she said rising to collect the plates. 'You must be exhausted. I'll go.'

No. Don't go. He didn't want to be alone tonight. Gabe shrugged, rising also, his pulse accelerating, humming along with the beat of the city spread out below them. Would she stay if he asked? 'No more than you. We've both had very little sleep in the last couple of days.'

'Yes, but you've borne the brunt of all the pressure. You broke the bad news to June and Scott. That sort of thing takes it out of you more than just physically, Gabe.'

The way she said his name felt like a caress. Like she'd stroked her hand along his belly. 'I like it when you call me Gabe,' he said softly, placing a stilling hand on hers as she reached for his empty beer bottle.

His hand felt warm and vibrant against hers. *No.* This was all wrong. This was too…everything. Too much. Definitely too much.

'Stay.'

Beth felt her mouth turn as dry as ash. A slight breeze ruffled his hair. 'No.' She moved around the table to go inside, dishes in hand, and he stepped in front of the doors, blocking her exit.

'Gabe,' she croaked.

His groin surged again at the ache in her voice as she said his name. 'Please. I need you tonight. I think we need each other.'

Beth could feel her resolve melting. Fast. 'Gabe,' she whispered. She wasn't strong enough for this. 'Don't ask me this. Not tonight.'

Gabe could see she was battling her desire. Knew that an honourable man would stand aside and let her pass. But he wasn't strong enough to deny what he'd wanted every day since that first time.

'You know you want to.'

Beth swallowed. Her eyes fluttered shut for a few

seconds. When she opened them again he'd stepped closer. He took the dishes from her unresisting fingers and set them on the table, allowing him to move closer still. She could feel his body heat enveloping her, his warm breath sweet on her face.

She watched mesmerised as his hand gently pushed back a lock of her hair that had fallen forward. His hand cupped her jaw, his thumb stroking lazily down her neck.

'Beth,' he whispered.

He was staring at her mouth and she ached to feel his lips on hers. She swallowed to moisten her parched mouth as she swayed towards him. She mustered her last remnant of sense. 'We shouldn't be doing this,' she croaked. 'Things are complicated enough.'

'Yes, they are,' Gabe whispered, his gaze not leaving her mouth. She was so close, her mouth so near he could almost taste her, and he wanted her so much his body throbbed.

'Can you walk away?' he asked softly. *I sure as hell can't.*

Beth shook her head, not sure she could articulate a response. His intense gaze on her mouth was breathtakingly erotic.

'Neither can I,' he groaned as he dropped his head and claimed her lips.

All rational thought and reasons for not doing what they were doing fled as Beth melted against him. She felt boneless and weightless and completely unable to support herself. She clung to him as his kiss plundered her mouth and ravaged her body.

He was breathing hard and she was shocked to hear her own ragged breathing match his. She sounded crazed, desperate, dragging in air as the kiss deepened and the whole world spun crazily around her. Gabe was the only thing solid and not moving and she held him tight, anchoring her body to his.

Gabe backed Beth against the glass, the scent of citrus filling his senses, igniting his desire. His need to be surrounded by her, to touch her naked skin was frantic, bordering on reckless. He yanked her shirt out of her waistband and gave a guttural groan as he felt her hands at his fly.

A siren on the street below broke through the sultry city hum and pierced through the haze of lust encapsulating them. Gabe pulled away from the kiss, placing his forehead against hers as he struggled for breath.

'Hell,' he muttered. He would have had her here. Standing against the glass where people in half of the surrounding hotels could watch them. She was tired. And pregnant.

'Gabe?' Beth whimpered, looking at him with a dazed expression, her mouth swollen and moist from their passion. Her head was spinning, her pulse echoing loudly in her head, making coherent thought beyond her. 'Don't stop.'

'Shh,' he whispered, placing two fingers against her mouth. 'Let's go inside.' He opened the sliding glass doors and held out his hand to her.

Beth took his hand without hesitation and he backed in as she followed. Their gazes stayed locked.

'This is better,' he said as the city noises receded. His calves hit the edge of the bed. 'More private.'

Beth nodded. Not that she could have cared. The sight of Gabe looking sexy as hell obliterated everything. His hair was messy and his lips were still moist from her mouth. His fly was gaping and a peak of underwear was visible past his half-untucked shirt.

She stepped closer and reached for the hem of his shirt. 'I want this off,' she said huskily.

Gabe grinned. 'On. Off. Make up your mind.'

'Off,' she said testily, frustrated by her desire to see all of him.

Gabe swallowed at the impatient demand and raised his arms above his head.

Beth inched the shirt up slowly, pressing kisses along the hard planes of his chest as she revealed more and more skin. She stroked her tongue against his nipple and smiled to herself as she heard his swift intake of breath.

Then she pulled it over his head and claimed his mouth in a deep kiss that left them both wanting more.

'My turn,' Gabe said, pulling away reluctantly.

Beth grinned and held her arms above her head. Gabe whisked her T-shirt off in one deft movement. 'My, oh, my,' Gabe sighed, staring at her lush breasts encased in delicate red satin and lace. The front clasp taunted him. 'Sister Rogers…is this what you were wearing beneath your scrubs all weekend?'

He traced the edge of the lace over the ripe bulge of her breast and Beth bit her lip as her nipples scrunched tight. 'No.' She gave a husky laugh. 'I was wearing a pale lemon one actually. I showered before I left work and changed into clean underwear.'

Gabe hadn't looked away from her breasts. He cupped the lacy mounds. They looked bigger, fuller than he remembered, The baby, he supposed. He ran his thumbs in lazy circles over the satin. He heard her breathing go ragged and felt his groin tighten as he looked at her to discover her eyes shut and her teeth biting into her bottom lip.

He traced his finger down into the dip of her cleavage and quickly unclipped her bra. Her breasts swung free and she gasped as the air hit her heated flesh. She moaned out loud when he dipped his head and took a rosy tip deep into his hot mouth.

'Gabe,' she panted.

'You are so beautiful,' he groaned as he lifted his head to claim the other nipple.

'Oh, Gabe,' she whispered, the words no more than a strangled sigh.

He raised his head to claim her mouth and she was more than a match for his ardour and passion. He sank slowly down on the bed behind him, pulling her with him until they were joined from head to hip. Her weight on him felt good as she ground her pelvis against his.

But it wasn't enough for Beth. She wanted more. She wanted to see all of him, feel all of him against her. She wriggled off him, standing a little unsteadily on her feet. He looked sexy as hell, lying on the bed before her, and she smiled at him.

'What?' He grinned.

'Just looking,' she teased.

'Come back here.' He held his arms out for her. She was naked from the waist up and her hair was tousled and her mouth looked thoroughly kissed. And he wanted her.

Beth shook her head. 'No. These off,' she said, and pointed to his jeans. She ran two fingers down his open fly.

Gabe could feel his erection strain against the fabric. 'I'll show you mine if you show me yours.'

Beth grinned. 'Deal.' Her hands flew to the buttons of her cargo pants as she watched Gabe intently. She made short work of her pants as Gabe lifted his hips and slid his jeans down.

His black cotton boxers barely contained him. 'Those too,' she ordered.

Beth felt her eyes widen as he slid his boxers off. She devoured his magnificent proportions. Her hand reached out to touch it.

'Uh-uh.' Gabe grinned, covering himself. 'You next.' He pointed to her matching red satin and lace knickers.

Beth rolled her eyes. 'Spoilsport.' But she gave a few deliberately exaggerated wiggles of her hips and slid her last article of clothing off.

'Now can I touch?' she asked, hand on hip.

Gabe chuckled and removed his hand. 'Now you can do whatever you like.'

And he gave her hand a yank, toppling her onto him. His chuckle was cut off by her mouth. She kissed him long and hard. She kissed him until they were gasping for air and their bodies demanded more.

His length pressed into hers felt divine but it wasn't enough. Beth wanted to feel more. Feel surrounded by him. Dominated by him. She rolled off and pulled him over with her. *That was better.* His weight squashed her against the bed and she revelled in her femininity as his pelvis rocked against hers.

Gabe wanted more too. He wanted to touch her. Taste her. It had been months since he'd sampled the delights of her body and he was starving for her. He trailed kisses down her neck and heard her whimper of loss.

'It's OK,' he said, kissing her mouth. Her eyes were glazed and he felt his erection surge. 'I need to kiss all of you.'

Beth needed his mouth on hers more than her next breath but she also knew what magic he could weave on the rest of her body. *Her mouth could get in line.*

She shut her eyes as he trailed kisses everywhere. Her back arched as he laved her breasts with sweet attention. Her belly clenched and she shivered as he stroked his tongue across her stomach. And when he parted her legs and put his tongue inside her she cried out his name.

'Gabe, please…' She pulled at his shoulders. 'I want you inside me.'

Gabe grinned. 'I thought I was.' He smiled as he kissed his way back up her body.

Their mouths fused as Gabe entered her. Beth groaned and wrapped her legs around his waist as he went deeper.

Gabe, sheathed to the hilt, rose up on his elbows. He didn't move, watching the ecstasy on Beth's face, her eyes closed in pleasure. He didn't want to stop doing this.

Beth felt filled and luxuriated in Gabe's possession. She moved slightly and her eyes fluttered open. Gabe was staring at her intently.

'Tell me you've wanted this since the last time.'

Heat lanced her groin. 'Gabe,' she pleaded.

Gabe withdrew the barest amount and then pulsed into her again. 'Tell me,' he demanded, his voice husky with desire.

Beth felt the craving to have him pull out and plunge in again nearly overwhelm her. She saw the desperation in his eyes. Saw the shadow of the last two days still there. She moved beneath him but he held her firm.

'Gabe, please,' she gasped. 'I need you to…'

Gabe repeated the slight movement again, knowing it was driving him as crazy as her. Fighting the urge to drive in and out of her in wild abandon. 'I've dreamt of this moment every night since that first time. Tell me you want me as much as I want you.'

'Gabe,' she panted, the sensation unbearably erotic.

He pushed into her harder. 'Tell me.'

Beth couldn't bear it any longer. She knew this was about more than their one-night stand. It was about months of denial and hungry looks, about the baby and about breaking his promise to the Fishers and failing probably for the first time in his life.

'Yes,' she gasped. 'Yes. I've thought of us a lot.'

Gabe lowered his mouth and sucked roughly on her nipple. 'Not good enough, Beth.' His voice was ragged. 'I need to hear you say you want me.' He claimed her other breast.

Beth nearly fainted from the eroticism of his teeth grating against her nipple. 'I want you, Gabe,' she whimpered. 'Damn it, I want you.'

Gabe locked gazes with Beth, the desire in her eyes ratcheting his lust up another notch. He pulled out abruptly and plunged back in again. He heard her gasp and watched as her pupils dilated with need. He repeated the movement again and again, their gazes holding steady.

'Gabe.'

He could hear the loss of control in her voice, feel her body trembling against his. Feel his own loss of control roll through him.

'Beth,' he groaned, burying his face in her neck.

'Oh, Gabe,' Beth cried, clinging to his trembling shoulders, her orgasm breaking as quickly as it had built.

'Beth, Beth, Beth,' he whispered as she broke around him and he followed seconds later.

CHAPTER EIGHT

A FEW minutes later Gabe rolled off her and stared at the ceiling.

'I'm sorry,' he said after a while as his heart rate returned to normal.

'It's OK,' she said, turning to look into his troubled eyes. 'It's been an intense couple of days.'

She held out her arms to him and Gabe went to her gratefully. He laid his head against her chest, her heartbeat bounding beneath his ear. She had every right to hate him for the stunt he'd just pulled. But after the surgery, after losing Bridie, he'd needed to feel a connection with her away from their jobs.

Their relationship had been strictly business since that first night. They'd both agreed it was the only appropriate thing to do. But they'd just been through a momentous experience together and she was having his baby, for crying out loud. Tonight of all nights as they faced their uncertain future, he'd needed to know they were more than just colleagues.

Beth cradled his head against her breast and absently ran her fingers through his hair. She tuned into his deep even breathing as the silence stretched between them. 'It wasn't your fault, Gabe. You did everything you could. We all did.'

Gabe heard her voice reverberate through her chest wall. *She could read his thoughts now?* He rolled on his stomach, his chin against her sternum, looking up into her face. 'I know that. I do. Really. I was just thinking, if only we'd had more time to prepare. If only Bridie had been stronger.'

Beth nodded. 'You played the cards you were dealt, Gabe.'

'Yes, but could I have played them better? Could I have done more?'

'Gabe,' Beth reasoned, 'do you always beat yourself up like this after something goes wrong in surgery?'

Gabe dropped his head, pressing a kiss to her chest. He lifted it again. 'I've never lost anyone during surgery. In fact nothing's ever really gone wrong for me intra-operatively. A few hairy moments but nothing I couldn't handle.' He grimaced. 'That's part of the whole Fallons-never-fail thing.'

'Oh.' Her fingers stilled in his hand. Poor Gabe had a whole legacy to uphold. 'You're human, Gabe. And human beings fail. Even your father, I bet.'

Gabe shook his head. 'Oh, no, the great Harlon Fallon never failed.'

Beth stroked a finger down his cheek and cupped his jaw. Gabe's stubble grazed erotically against her palm. 'Yes, he did. He neglected you. His own child. He failed in the worst way.'

Beth knew better than anyone how neglect bruised. How damaging it was.

Gabe gazed into her earnest blue eyes and gave her a gentle smile as he covered her hand with his. He eased it off his jaw and dropped a kiss into her palm and another on her sternum. He turned his head and laid it against her breast again, shutting his eyes as she caressed his scalp and he succumbed to the eroticism.

He opened his eyes a few moments later. The view was pretty damn good. Her pale skin sloped away down the valley between her ribs, smoothing out over her stomach and rising into crescents on either side to cover the jut of her hips.

He trailed a finger down her middle, circling her belly button, his hand coming to rest in the cradle between her hips where his baby was safely nestled. He could feel the slight bulge growing up from behind Beth's pubic bone.

He kept his hand there. His child. He had made her pregnant. Even now, a month down the track, he found it hard to wrap his head around.

'Have you felt it move yet?'

Beth's hand stilled in his hair. She wasn't used to him talking about the baby. She could feel her heartbeat become more forceful in her chest. Surely he could too? 'Some flutterings.'

Gabe waited, hoping to feel something. He barely breathed, reluctant to move a muscle in case he missed the tiniest quiver. The baby didn't oblige but just knowing that they'd created life was particularly poignant given the loss they'd both just experienced. His baby grew safe and snug beneath his hands and yet he knew too well the frailty of life.

He shifted so he was on his elbows again and turned to look at her. 'I'm sorry about how I reacted when you told me about the baby. You kind of…threw me that day.'

Beth shrugged, dropping her hand from his hair. 'I

know. For what it's worth, when I found out it kind of threw me for a while too.'

'So there was a time when you weren't so…together about it?' Gabe grinned. 'That's a relief.'

Beth smiled. 'There was some initial hyperventilating but I always, always wanted it. I've loved this baby from the start.' Beth placed her hand where Gabe's had so recently been. 'I've wanted a baby for a very long time.'

'Since you were fifteen?' Gabe asked, and wasn't surprised to see her nod. 'I guess that's understandable. I wish I could say I've had the same burning desire. But I've never felt like that. Never.'

Beth had got used to Gabe's assertion that he wanted to be around, had started mentally adjusting her plans, so his admission surprised her. Was he trying to back out? 'I've already told you I don't expect anything from you.'

Gabe saw her tense. Heard the strain in her voice. He traced a finger down the side of her face. 'I'm not trying to back out. I'm just trying to explain how…unprepared I was for this. I mean, whenever I think about being a father now and particularly after today, I think how hellish a surgeon's life can be on a child. We don't keep normal business hours.'

Beth nodded slowly, thinking about the marathon thirty hours he'd just been through. But she also remembered his whispered words to Brooke and his fight at the end to give Bridie every chance, and knew that he'd fight just as hard—harder—for their child.

His green eyes were solemn. She could see he was torn. 'We all have choices, Gabe. You can choose to break the mould.'

Gabe sighed. He pushed himself away, rolling onto his back. He remembered that night having dinner at the Winterses' house. Witnessing the balance that John had managed to strike with career and family. But was he capable of that?

'It's not going to be easy to throw everything in I've ever worked for, ditch everything that's important to me and come to Australia to play daddy.'

Beth twisted her neck to look up at him. 'I'm not asking you to.' Though, heaven help her, as the baby fluttered beneath her fingertips, she wanted it more and more.

Gabe rolled on his side and looked at her. 'Come to England with me.'

Beth shut her eyes. If her life was simple, she would. 'I can't, Gabe. You know why.'

Gabe nodded slowly. 'Tell me about him. Your son. About that time.'

Beth stared into his eyes. Maybe if he knew, he'd understand why this was so important to her. She grabbed the sheet.

'Cold?' he asked as he helped her.

She shook her head. She couldn't lie here naked and tell him about her past. Her memories would lay her bare enough. She covered herself and rolled on her side, raising herself up on an elbow to face him.

Beth was silent for a few moments, struggling with the memories. 'It was an awful time. I mean, things had been bad for so long at home but that made it so much worse. My father was furious. He pressured me to give the baby up for adoption. I didn't want to but...I was scared and powerless.'

Her tortured gaze pleaded with him to understand. 'Of

course you were,' he said quietly, stroking a finger up and down her arm.

'I was also underage. He kept telling me it was best for the baby. That I was too young to look after him. That I couldn't do it by myself. That they wouldn't support me. That the baby deserved the best start in life. Two parents who loved him. Not a teenage troublemaker. Didn't I want the best for my baby? he kept asking. He accused me of being selfish and self-absorbed. He just kept at me and at me.'

Beth remembered the arguments and the horrible tension during that time. How she'd been a virtual prisoner in her own home. How she'd cried herself to sleep every night, begging the universe for intervention that never came. How appeals to her stepmother had fallen on deaf ears and she'd felt the loss of her own mother so very acutely.

'Until I caved in.' Beth felt tears build in her eyes and blinked them away. 'Of course I wanted the best for him. He was my baby. I loved him.'

'Oh, Beth…' Gabe murmured, hearing the twenty-odd years of misery in the huskiness of her voice.

'It broke my heart when they took him away.'

Beth recalled the precious minutes she'd had to hold her baby as if they were yesterday. His smell, his newborn curiosity, looking around at the bright new world he'd emerged into. The devastation as he was taken away.

'There hasn't been a day go by when I haven't wondered about him.'

He lifted a hand and stroked a finger down her cheek. 'I'm sorry.'

Beth felt a lump lodge in her throat at his sincerity. 'I've wanted a baby ever since, Gabe. Desperately. I'm sorry it scares the hell out of you but I've been waiting for this for twenty-three years.'

Gabe nodded. They were silent for a while and Beth had never felt so exposed in her life. 'I suppose you must think my adolescent behaviour pretty shocking.'

Gabe stroked her cheek. 'Not at all. I think you were young and sad and desperate for someone to understand you. To love you.' God knew, his own adolescence had been pretty fraught.

Beth nodded. He was right. That was exactly how it had happened. She'd never thought for a minute there'd be such lifelong consequences.

'So he hasn't come forward yet…your son?'

Beth rolled onto her back, the pain in her heart rendering her incapable of supporting herself. 'No. It's been five years since he could have…contacted me…if he wanted to. But…nothing.'

'I'm sorry, Beth.' She sounded so bereft he wasn't sure how to comfort her. And he wanted to. Having her here with him tonight had been immeasurably comforting to him.

'You understand why I can't leave?'

Gabe nodded. He didn't want to, but he did. 'Have you thought about finding him yourself?'

A tear rolled out from the corner of her eye. She wiped it away. 'Yes…often. But I couldn't bear the thought of being rejected. At least if he comes to me, he's seeking me out. I'll know he wants to have a relationship.'

It didn't matter that another baby was growing inside her. Her thoughts, her arms still yearned for the child she'd held for only a few cherished moments.

'I thought maybe this birthday he'd seek me out. But…'

'When's his birthday?'

'January tenth.'

Gabe blinked. January tenth? *Click.* That date was burned into his brain. *The night they'd first made love.* Another piece of the puzzle slotted in. That was why she'd been so upset. Why she'd sobbed in his arms. It had been her son's birthday. The son she'd given up twenty-three years before.

'That was the night of the movies,' Gabe said.

Beth shot him a surprised look. He remembered the date? 'Yes.'

More and more things were making sense. It had been obvious something had been up that night. Obvious that she wasn't someone who usually slept with a man after such brief acquaintance. 'So it wasn't my pure animal magnetism?'

Beth laughed at his faux crestfallen look, grateful for the lighter mood. 'I'm afraid not. Although it was very good.'

Gabe pulled her towards him and snuggled her against him spoon fashion. He kissed her shoulder. 'Actually, I was pretty shocked when you agreed to come with me. I was certain you were going to knock me back. I'd taken you for a straight chick after about two minutes in your company.'

Beth smiled, loving the feel of his contours surrounding hers. 'Why did you even ask, then?'

Good question. Something had appealed to him despite what his instincts had been telling him. 'Nothing ventured, nothing gained. And I was feeling kind of sad myself that night and you seemed like a kindred spirit.'

Beth kissed his arm. 'Your dad?'

He nuzzled her neck. 'My dad.'

They were silent for a few moments and Beth trailed her fingers up and down his firm biceps. She laced her fingers through his. 'You were exceedingly lucky that you got me on that day,' she mused.

'So if it had been the day before or the day after?'

'You wouldn't have stood a chance,' she confirmed.

'Well, I don't know.' Gabe grinned, kissing the curve of her neck, 'I can be very persuasive.'

'So I've discovered.'

Gabe grinned as he trailed a hand down her side, following the dip of her waist and the rise of her hip, and settled it low on her belly. He nuzzled his face into her neck, inhaling her unique Beth scent. Her hair smelled like citrus and her skin like soap and sated female.

He became aware of a slight stirring beneath his fingers. He stopped nuzzling, his head stilling as he realised he was feeling foetal movements. His baby's movements. 'Is that what I think it is?' he asked.

Beth felt goose-bumps feather her neck as his breath fanned her skin. She moved her hand down to cover his so their fingers interlocked. 'Yes,' she said huskily.

Gabe felt incredibly connected with her as they lay sharing the wonder of the moment. He felt truly torn. How could he not want this? It was his child. What kind of a father could be part of such a moment and feel so conflicted? Shouldn't it be clear cut?

'I wish I knew what to do about this,' Gabe whispered, feeling completely out of his depth.

'It's OK, Gabe,' Beth whispered, removing her hand and reaching behind her to stroke his cheek. 'This wasn't exactly on your agenda. You came here on a seven month contract to separate conjoined twins. Not to have a baby with a woman you hardly know. It's OK to not have the answers.'

Her words made him feel even worse. 'I know you,' he protested.

She removed her hand. 'Yes, but not like people who usually make babies together do.' Although, given their short acquaintance, he knew her better than most people she'd worked with for years did. 'There's no commitment. You don't love me, Gabe.'

Beth stalled, amazed at how the realisation hurt. She hadn't expected or needed his love but lying here, cradled against him, the L-word between them, she knew she wanted it. Knew as surely as the sun would rise in the morning that she wanted it as much as the baby growing inside her.

'Neither do I want you to be,' she said automatically, while her brain grappled with the mind-blowing revelation. *This was bad. Really bad.* Not only had she gone and got herself pregnant by him, she'd done something even more stupid. She'd gone and fallen for him. A hotshot, didn't-even-live-in-the-same-hemisphere neurosurgeon whose skills did not include relationships, particularly fatherhood.

'You've still got a few months on your contract and we can use that time to figure out how we're going to work this.'

Gabe was touched by her generosity. He wished he could lay out a plan for her but things were still a big jumble inside him. His entire focus until now had been on the separation. But feeling the tiny movements beneath his hand had highlighted his biggest responsibility yet and how out of his depth he felt.

'You're being very understanding about this.'

Beth felt like a fraud. If only he knew—discovering she

loved him had completely blown her mind. She was on total autopilot. 'A lot's happened in the last few months,' she dismissed. 'In this last weekend. The separation. Bridie.' *And I love you.* That had happened too.

Lying here with him, his hand over her womb, she wondered how she'd been so blind for so long. Especially as now she could pinpoint the exact moment she'd fallen. That first night as he'd rocked her while she'd sobbed her heart out—that had been the moment. She'd been so miserable that day and his gentleness and consideration had touched her more deeply than she'd known.

'You can play whatever part you want in this baby's life, Gabe. There's no pressure. You've still got a few months in the country and now the separation's done, you're freer to think about it.'

Gabe dropped a kiss on her shoulder. 'Thank you, Beth. For everything. For being so understanding and for everything you did for the Fisher case.'

Beth smiled and snuggled in closer. 'I would like to tell my family…if that's OK. I'm not going to be able to hide it for too many more weeks anyway.'

'Of course,' Gabe assured her, not feeling so assured himself. Was he ready for this to go public? But what right did he have to put the brakes on her joy? She'd been more than sensitive to his struggles. 'Stay?' he murmured.

Beth's heart banged crazily in her chest as her love for him swelled to excrutiatingly painful proportions. *She should go.* But he'd asked her to stay. And lying snuggled in the arms of the man she loved while their child lay inside her was too tempting.

She turned in his arms. 'Yes.' *Just a few more hours.*

Their love-making was different this time. Light. Flirty. After the intenseness of the previous time and the seriousness of the last forty-eight hours, laughing and rejoicing in each other's bodies was just what the doctor ordered. They drifted to sleep an hour later totally sated, completed exhausted, smiles on their faces.

Beth called in to the PICU to visit Brooke on her way to work on Tuesday morning. Memories of last night, telling the Winters clan about the baby, curved the corners of her mouth. They had all been so thrilled and she almost skipped into the unit.

Scott was sitting in a recliner at the bedside, an alert-looking Brooke, her head still bandaged, snuggled into his chest. June gave Beth a long hug.

'I'm so sorry about Bridie' Beth murmured.

'We know.' June smiled, her eyes shining with tears. 'We know everyone did all that they could.'

Beth squeezed June's hand as she squatted beside the chair. Brooke was looking pinker and less puffy than when she'd last seen her. Her chest was criss-crossed with a jumble of tubes and wires, her cheeks and nose largely obscured by brown tape where the nasal prongs and feeding tube were secured.

'Look at you,' Beth crooned. 'No breathing tube. You're so clever.'

Beth held out her hand and watched as Brooke's gaze followed and then fixed on her proffered finger. The little girl reached out a tiny hand and grasped it, smiling a toothless grin.

'Nothing wrong with her.'

Gabe's voice was deep and sexy, his accent giving her goose-bumps as it oozed across the distance between them.

'G-Gabe,' she said, looking over her shoulder. Gabe shot her a smile and it went straight to her internal muscles, lancing them with the heat of erotic memories.

'Beth.'

'What do you think of our girl?' Beth asked turning her attention back to the surviving Fisher twin as her pulse rate tripped. If only it wasn't just lust she saw in his gaze.

'I'm cautiously optimistic.'

Beth laughed. 'Do you hear that, sweetie? High praise indeed.'

Scott and June laughed and Gabe joined them. It had been twenty-four hours since he'd kissed her goodbye at his hotel door and he realised he'd missed her. His sleep had been haunted by her face all night. Disjointed snippets of him pushing her on a swing. Them laughing. Her belly swollen with his child.

Beth stood. 'I'd better go. I'll call in later,' she said, addressing June.

'We'd like that,' June said.

The bed area was crowded with four adults and Gabe stood aside so she could get past him. 'See you later,' he murmured as she brushed by.

Beth faltered, his accent and unique scent seducing her to stay longer. Maybe rub her face into his shirt. She barely acknowledged his comment as she fled on trembling legs.

A few hours later Beth sat in her office with David, trying to concentrate on his first evaluation. He'd come in on a day off. As NUM it was her responsibility to appraise all the students. They looked at his written objectives before commencement and assessed his progress.

She went over his scrub sheet and they talked about the different procedures he'd been involved in and mapped out some more objectives for the remaining months.

'You're going really well,' Beth said, wrapping it up. 'You've put in a lot of extra hours. I've given you top marks here, as you can see. I only wish there was a column for ability to catch fainting NUMs. I would have scored you top there as well.'

Beth laughed and David gave her a nervous smile.

'Oh, come on, David, relax.' Beth grinned. 'That was a joke. You're supposed to laugh.'

'Sorry.' David cleared his throat.

Beth looked into the student's face. 'You don't seem yourself today. Everything OK?' she asked, shutting his file.

He gave her another nervous smile and she raised her eyebrows at him, encouraging him to say whatever it was that was obviously still on his mind. They sat for a few moments looking at each other.

'David, was there something else you wanted to discuss?' she prompted.

'Actually, yes…there was.'

Beth watched him shift uncomfortably in his chair. He looked very uneasy. What the hell could he want? Had someone been bullying him? Had he witnessed something sensitive? She gave him an encouraging smile. 'So…'

'Oh, dear,' he said at last. 'I've thought of this moment for such a long time and now it's here I feel all tongue-tied.'

Beth gave him a puzzled look. What on earth was he talking about? 'It's OK,' she said. 'Just spit it out.'

He nodded. 'OK. I think…actually, no, I know. I'm… your son.'

CHAPTER NINE

BETH heard the words come out of his mouth but couldn't actually believe she'd heard them. It was as if everything outside her office had ceased to exist and she and David were sitting in a little bubble, the only two people on the planet.

Could it be true? She desperately wanted to believe it. Had her son finally made contact?

'If this is a joke…' Beth said, finally finding her voice.

'No,' David said, giving his head an emphatic shake. 'The agency gave me the details that you left on record and I have these.' He reached down, dug through his backpack and handed her a small bundle.

She took it, her heart pounding in her chest. Her own strong, neat handwriting stared back at her. They were letters. She didn't have to open them to know they were the ones she'd written him over the years.

'You got these?' she whispered, her eyes filling with tears.

'Yes. Mum and Dad were always up front about me being adopted.'

Beth drank in the sight of him. His height, his blondness, his broad strong shoulders, his long fingers. *Her son.*

Her son had sought her out. She clutched the edge of her desk as her arms ached to embrace him.

'I've imagined this moment since the day they took you from me. I've rehearsed what I would say. But now it's here, I can't think of a single word.'

'It's OK,' David grimaced. 'It's taken me two months to work up the courage.'

'How…how did you know where I worked?' The details she had on record were a name, home address and phone number only.

David shrugged. 'I knew you were a nurse from your letters. I think, actually, deep down, that was my impetus to become one. When I got your details last year—'

'You only got them last year?' Beth interrupted, trying not to feel too hurt. She'd always hoped that her son would have been so eager to know her that he'd contact the agency straight away. But he hadn't.

David nodded and continued. 'It wasn't difficult to track you down after that. When we got to choose our practical electives, I put the General's operating theatres as my top choice.'

'Why didn't you contact me at the number the agency gave you?'

He shrugged. 'I guess I wanted an opportunity to get to know you first.'

Beth frantically tried to think back over the last months. What kind of an impression had she made? She knew she'd developed a good rapport with him but it had been painstakingly collegial. Especially after Gabe's teasing comments. Had she been too distant? Heaven only knew what he thought of her.

Beth's head spun. People bustled by in the corridors either side of her office. She could hear the clatter of instruments as someone walked by with a tray and a trolley being pushed past. She couldn't believe she was sitting in her office with her long-lost son and the world hadn't ground to a halt.

'I suppose you want to know why I did it? Why I gave you up?'

David stood. 'No. I don't. Really.'

What? Surely he must want to now? Surely he'd be curious? Beth opened her mouth to protest. She needed to tell him. She had to explain.

'Look, you obviously had your reasons,' David said. 'You must have been very young. Whatever they were doesn't matter to me. Sure, I went through a long period in my teens when I wondered about you. A lot. Wished you were around. Felt kind of disconnected and rootless. But I always knew deep down you did what you did out of love for me.'

Beth nodded, a lump in her throat making words impossible. Her heart ached, knowing that he'd thought of her. Knowing that he longed for her as much as she'd longed for him. She wanted to weep for his troubled years. It didn't matter that many teenagers went through the same thing. She'd given him up so his teens would be less troubled than hers.

'I'm sorry you went through that. Sorrier than you'll ever know.'

'It's OK,' he dismissed. 'I've matured. I can look back and say I've had a pretty good life.'

Part of Beth was relieved to hear him validate her painful decision. To hear that her sacrifice had been worth it. But part of her wanted to say, *I could have given you a good life too*.

'So do you mind me asking why it took you so long to contact me?' Beth asked.

'I travelled for a few years after I finished school. I think I was trying to find myself. It was good for me. I went to a lot of poorer countries. It put my own petty troubles into perspective. I guess I came away with a bit of a what-will-be-will-be attitude. That things happen if they're meant to happen. After that I started nursing and I don't know if I ever would have sought you out except then I met Andrea.'

Well, thank you, Andrea. Beth didn't know who she was but if she ever got to meet her, she was going to kiss her feet. The thought that this moment might never have arrived was too awful to contemplate. 'Your girlfriend?'

David nodded.

'So Andrea thought you should seek me out?'

He shook his head. 'We've both started to talk long term. I mean, I love her. I know I want to be with her for ever. You know...wedding bells and the pitter-patter of tiny feet.'

Beth blinked. He seemed so young to be so responsible and mature.

'Andrea had a brother who died ten years ago from cystic fibrosis. She carries the gene. And I realised that I don't know anything about my genetic history. I mean, not just about whether there's CF in my genetic make-up. Nothing at all.'

David has sought her out for medical reasons? Beth felt winded as she clenched her hands into fists beneath the desk. She wouldn't have thought such practicality would hurt so much. But it did. It wasn't how she'd pictured this day at all.

A question about his genes was natural, she supposed, but she'd been hoping for something along the lines of— reconnecting with the woman who had given him life. His practicality was like salt being rubbed into wounds that had never fully healed.

'Er, right…' she said, grappling for some perspective, trying to see this from his side. Grateful for anything he was giving her but wanting more. Wanting it all. This was all new to both of them. There wasn't a guide book. She had to let him lead the way. After all, he didn't owe her anything. She'd given up any claim on him and his life when she'd signed the adoption papers.

'Well, there's no CF in my family or in any of the extended family, as far as I know. In fact, I'm pretty sure there are no major genetic illnesses at all.'

'What about my father?'

Beth swallowed. 'I don't know… I'm sorry. I only knew him very briefly.' Someone who had offered her comfort and solace in a world that had been full of uncertainty and conflict. 'I can give you a name if that helps.' She cringed. What must he think of her? Was he judging her?

David shook his head. 'It doesn't matter.'

Would he ever give her a chance to explain the circumstances surrounding his conception and the terrible years that had led up to it? Or the pain of her decision that had left a permanent bruise on her soul?

'I really have to get going,' David said, checking his watch. 'I've got a class starting in half an hour.'

Beth stood. *So soon?* She didn't want him to go.

'Oh…all right, then.' *Let him lead.* She came out from behind her desk. 'Do you think we could…get together away from work some time? I'd like to talk a little more…maybe get to know you?'

'Ah…I'm not sure… Maybe. I'm still wrapping my head around all this.'

Beth knew that feeling. She saw him cast a furtive glance towards the door and took a step closer to him. 'I'd hate to lose contact now.' She placed a hesitant hand on his arm.

'Maybe,' he repeated.

Beth was dismayed when he took a step back and her hand fell from his arm. It was too much. She was rushing him. He'd come to find out his genetic make-up, not play long-lost son. She swallowed a lump of emotion burning like a hot coal in her throat. *Let him lead.*

'Thank you,' he said.

Beth stood aside so he could pass. She balled her hands into fists lest they try and reach for him again. It took all her self-control not to burst into tears and beg him to stay. He paused in the doorway.

'Do you regret you ever had me?' he asked.

He didn't turn so she was forced to address his back. 'The only thing I regret is giving you up,' she said, her voice husky with barely contained tears.

And then he walked out the door and Beth collapsed into the nearby armchair, giving the wall of emotion that had been building inside her its inevitable release. Tears spilled down her cheeks as the enormity of what had just happened hit her squarely in the solar plexus.

The event she'd been waiting twenty-three years for had finally arrived. Her son had reached out to her. And if the meeting hadn't exactly followed the script she'd written in her head for years—it had been a start.

Gabe bustled into Beth's office a few minutes later and found her sitting very still, her eyes red-rimmed.

'Beth?' He crouched beside her. His heart beat frantically in his chest. *Had something happened with the baby?* 'What's wrong?'

Gabe's concern cut through her turmoil. She turned glistening eyes on him. 'Oh, Gabe,' she whispered. 'He was here. My son was here.' She forgot all about professional behaviour and promptly burst into tears, her head falling against his broad shoulder.

'Hey,' Gabe soothed, his hand automatically going to the nape of her neck, his thumb rhythmically stroking the sensitive skin there. 'Shh,' he murmured.

He let her cry, not asking any of the questions that were crashing through his head. 'It's OK,' he whispered. 'It's OK.'

Beth felt the wave of her outburst slowly subside. She left her face pressed into his neck as she fought for control. Firstly because she was so embarrassed she'd cried all over him—again. *This was becoming a habit!* Only this was in broad daylight and they were at work. And also because he smelt so good.

'I'm sorry,' she apologized, reluctantly leaving the shelter of his neck.

Gabe pulled some tissues out of the box on her desk and offered her the swathe. 'Here.'

He stood while she blew her nose and dabbed at her eyes as she prowled around her small office. He sat on the edge of her desk and swung his leg as Beth pulled herself together.

'What happened?' he asked.

'It's David,' Beth said, still pole-axed by the revelation.

Gabe frowned. 'David? The student nurse?'

Beth nodded her head slowly. 'Pretty amazing, huh?' She filled him in on their conversation, noting Gabe seemed as stunned by the turn of events as she was.

'I always thought he was interested in you. I just got the motivation wrong,' Gabe mused as he watched her worry at her bottom lip. 'You seem a little anxious.'

'It wasn't exactly the loving reunion I'd hoped it would be. What if he doesn't want a relationship with me?'

'Give him time, Beth. It took him four and a half years to make contact with the agency and two months to break the news to you. It's obviously not in his nature to be rushed.'

'I know, I know,' she said. 'You'd think I could be patient after all these years of waiting. But there's been so many wasted years. I don't want to waste any more.'

Gabe pushed himself off the desk and stood in front of her. He placed his hands on her shoulders. 'Let him come to you,' he said gently. 'Don't push him. He may not be a confused teenager any more but he's bound to have issues of trust and identity. There's no doubt still a bewildered little boy lurking behind his mature exterior.'

Beth looked into Gabe's serious gaze. She knew he was right. She sighed and nodded, placing her head against his chest. He pulled her close and she allowed herself the luxury of a brief embrace, her heart swelling at his tenderness. Maybe the wait would be more bearable if Gabe was around to share the burden?

She felt so good in his arms that she knew she could stay here for ever. Why did she have to love someone who didn't love her back?

Beth drew in one more lungful of Gabe pheromones and broke away, returning to her seat, struggling for normality. 'I'm sorry, forgive me. Was there something that you wanted?'

Gabe shut his eyes, holding onto the sweet memory of their nearness for a second longer. He turned to face her, their intimacy scattering. 'The media office has been bombarded with calls for a press conference.'

'Scott and June have already released a statement.'

'They want to talk to the team.'

Beth thought for a moment. 'What does John think?'

'He thinks it's a good idea. He's set it up for tomorrow afternoon. I want you there.'

Beth blinked, her heart skipping a beat at his emphatic request. 'What for?'

'All the main players are going to be there. You headed the nursing team as well as looking after all the theatre logistics. We couldn't have done it without you. They might want to talk to you.'

It sounded very sensible when he put it like that but part of her had hoped he'd say, *Because I want you by my side*.

She sighed and flipped her diary to the next page. 'What time?'

Beth gathered in the wings of the auditorium stage with the rest of the medical staff at two the next afternoon. Scott and June were there also and she chatted with them while they waited for the media to assemble and set up.

'Right,' John Winters said, calling the crowd to order. 'I will kick off the conference with a prepared statement. Mr and Mrs Fisher will then field questions before we hand over to Gabe and the surgical team. Everyone will give a brief overview of their part in the process and then there will be more questions.'

Satisfied everyone was on the same page, John led the team out onto the stage, in the middle of which was a long table. Eight chairs and eight glasses of water were set out evenly and everyone took their pre-planned positions as the flashbulbs of a hundred cameras dazzled them. Behind them the General's corporate logo decorated the back wall.

Beth took the end seat, partially blinded by the lights shining down at them. She could vaguely see that an audience had gathered in the terraced theatre-style seating before them. She knew that Hailey was there somewhere, although the lights made it impossible to make anyone out.

The next hour flew in a haze of camera flashes and a barrage of questions. As always, Beth was impressed with Gabe's leadership. He rejected any suggestions that the operation had been a one-man show and deflected questions equally to all members of the team, giving them praise and credit for the roles they'd all played.

For her part, Beth answered the questions that came her way and the few more Gabe kicked straight to her. It wasn't something she felt particularly comfortable with, especially given the loss of Bridie, and she was grateful when things appeared to be drawing to a close.

'Dr Fallon,' a reporter somewhere near the back called, 'you've had a stellar career with two previously successful separations. Given that one of the babies died, do you think this will dent your reputation?'

Beth frowned and squinted, trying to see past the lights to who'd asked such an impertinent question. Was the man trying to imply that his reputation meant more to him than the life of a child?

'I'll let my reputation speak for itself.'

Beth could hear the tightness in Gabe's voice and knew the question had annoyed him.

'Can you tell us a bit about what the differences were with this op and the last two?' another reporter called.

Gabe rattled off an explanation of the differences, their unique anatomies and Bridie's weakened state being the major one.

'As the son of a highly successful Nobel Prize-winning medico, don't you feel, with only Brooke surviving, that you've failed, Dr Fallon? That the surgery was a failure?'

Gabe couldn't really see the face of the persistent reporter, which was probably just as well. He prepared to throw the journalist a noncommittal reply. Comparisons with his father were inevitable.

Beth's blood was boiling and she'd opened her mouth before she'd given it proper thought, beating Gabe to the punch.

'I think I can speak for all of us, including Scott and June, in saying that Dr Gabriel Fallon is a brilliant neurosurgeon who undertook a highly complex procedure in less than ideal circumstances.'

What would the dog-with-a-bone reporter know about the life-and-death decisions people like Gabe made every day?

'I'm sure failing in your job means not meeting your deadline or screwing up a quote. Failing in our business has much more serious ramifications. Patients die and that's a hell of a lot more critical than some headline in a two-bit rag.'

How dared he bandy the word around so liberally?

'I'm sure not even the great Harlon Fallon could have pulled off the outcome we were all hoping for. But nobody worked harder than Gabe Fallon to achieve it.'

The room fell silent. The background murmur ceased. The clatter of lenses stopped. Their retinas were even given a reprieve from the constant flare of flashes. She could see David sitting up at the back but she had no time to process his presence as the entire gathering turned their attention on her.

What are you all looking at? Beth wanted to hurl at them, acutely embarrassed by her outburst, her hands automatically shielding her stomach. She was tired. And pregnant. And in love. And her long-lost son had turned up. And they were messing with Gabe. *She really didn't have the patience for this.*

John Winters recovered first. He'd been shocked to find out about Beth's pregnancy and even more so to learn that Gabriel Fallon was the father. He shouldn't have been surprised to hear his daughter defending Gabe so eloquently. *So much for just being friends.* He pointed to a female reporter in the first row and the show got back on the road with an anaesthetic question for Don Anderson.

Gabe glanced down the line as he leaned forward to take a sip of water, still stunned by Beth's caustic defence of him. She was sitting with her hand covering her belly, her cheeks still tinged with colour, looking like she was hoping the floor would open up and swallow her.

And there was the biggest difference, he realised. Beth. Beth, working with him efficiently in the background. Beth, scrubbing in beside him, anticipating his needs. Beth, ordering him to sleep. Beth, telling him enough, Bridie had

had enough. Beth, staying with him. Beth, sobbing in his arms. Twice. Beth, carrying his child. Beth, understanding.

She'd been the difference. In a few short months she'd become an important presence in his life—constant and steady. From the very first moment, the emotional vulnerability behind her reserved façade had intrigued him. Today, leaping to his defence, she fascinated him even more.

Oh, no. He was falling in love with her!

CHAPTER TEN

BETH couldn't get away from the press conference quickly enough. She wasn't sure who had read what into her little outburst but she wasn't sticking around to answer any more prying questions. She'd barely slept a wink last night after David's bombshell and combined with the little sleep she'd had at the weekend, she wasn't in the mood for petty hospital speculation.

She castigated herself again. She had no doubt her outburst would be juicy gossip this time tomorrow. She might as well have stood up and said, *I love him, back off*. Wait until they found out she was pregnant! She couldn't hide it for ever—another month, maybe two at a stretch. What would they think then?

Beth headed for the main entrance doors. She needed some air. And coffee.

Hailey, Gabe and David rode down in the lift together.

'I didn't realise you were in the audience,' Gabe said to David to distract him from his raging thoughts and Hailey's speculative gaze. How the hell had Beth achieved the one thing no woman had done? And what on earth was he supposed to do about it?

David shrugged. 'My shift had finished. I thought I'd have a sticky beak.'

Hailey looked at Gabe expectantly and it took a second for him to fathom the raised-eyebrow look. He performed the introductions distractedly.

'This is Beth's sister, Hailey,' he said. 'David is one of the student nurses in Theatre at the moment.'

Gabe watched David surreptitiously as the light dawned that Hailey was his aunt. He looked uncomfortable, like Beth had after her outburst during the press conference. Like he'd give anything to be anywhere else.

Gabe felt for the young man. He knew how it was to feel estranged from someone who had given you life and how your identity suffered. But surely he must realise that it hadn't been easy for Beth. If David kept rejecting a relationship with her, it would break Beth's heart. And he couldn't bear the thought of that.

He suspected David was kidding himself. Why had he been at the press conference if he truly wanted nothing more than medical details from his mother? Why all the weeks of seeking her out like an eager puppy, spending as much time with her as possible?

He figured David was just as curious about Beth as Beth was about her son. He just needed encouragement. He could at least do that for the woman he loved. Because he was damn sure anything else was beyond him at the moment. Loving her. Being a father. He didn't know how to do any of those things.

'How about we all go get a coffee?' Gabe suggested.

'Sure,' Hailey chirped.

'Nah, I got to get home,' David said as the lift doors opened onto the ground floor. 'I'll grab one to go, though.'

Beth was at the counter when Gabe, Hailey and David joined her. Her head was pounding and for the second time in her entire working life she contemplated leaving early. She just wanted to crawl into bed and sleep for a week and come back when the talk had died down.

'Hey, you,' Hailey greeted Beth.

'Hi!' Beth turned, plastering a smile on her face that slipped immediately she noticed Gabe and David standing behind her sister. She quickly re-fixed the smile on her face, the throb in her head kicking up a notch as she nodded at her son and her lover.

'Woohoo,' Hailey teased. 'That was quite a performance, Beth. Lucky none of the press knew you and Gabe are having a baby.' She paused to pat her sister's stomach.

'Hails,' Beth warned, knocking the hand away, her gaze flying to David's face.

'Oh, come on.' Hailey laughed. 'A juicy bone like that? The operation would have been totally forgotten.'

'Hailey!' Gabe interrupted abruptly. He too turned to look at David.

'David,' Beth said, reaching a hand out to her son, who was backing away from the circle and looking at her like she'd grown a second head.

'I…I have to go,' he stuttered.

'David…no!' Beth exclaimed as he turned and ran.

Hailey turned to Gabe as Beth ran after David. She looked at him confused. 'Er…am I missing something?' she asked.

Gabe sighed. 'It's…complicated,' he said as he witnessed

Beth catching up with David and managing to halt his flight. He could see how panicked she looked and wished there was something he could do to fix things. His heart swelled with love at her dilemma and it tore him up to know that there was nothing he could do. He wanted to go to her side but knew neither of them needed his interference.

'David, wait,' Beth called finally catching his sleeve and pulling. Her pulse was skittering madly. *Damn Hailey and her impulsiveness!*

'It's OK,' he said, shrugging her off.

'I wanted to tell you,' Beth said, breathing from the exertion of her short run.

'You don't owe me any explanations,' he said. 'Anything you owed me you gave away when you gave me up.'

'No, David,' Beth pleaded, her heart breaking. The look of shock on his face betrayed the confidence he had exuded yesterday. Gabe had been right—there was obviously still an insecure little boy inside. 'I only found out about you yesterday, I didn't want to dump it straight in your lap.'

'I understand,' he said, turning away. 'You have other priorities now.'

His accusation cut when Beth knew it wasn't true. She searched for the right words. 'I have enough love for both of you,' she implored.

David inspected her face for what seemed an age and then backed away again.

'I have to go,' he said.

Beth felt as if the walls were caving in around her and ran after him as he fled. She didn't hear anything other than the sound of her heart beating through her skull, intensifying the throb of her headache. David crossed a narrow internal road and she followed him without thinking, desperate for him to understand, her eyes glued to his retreating back.

She rubbed at her forehead as her foot landed on the bitumen. Her head throbbed as her pulse banged through her temples. She didn't hear the car. She didn't see the car. All she knew was that suddenly it was there and its brakes were squealing and the wheel was turning, but it was too late.

She was vaguely aware of Hailey screaming as she turned to protect the baby. The slow-moving hatchback struck her on the back of the legs. She felt her hip hit the bonnet and winced as her body rolled across the front of the car. In the blink of an eye she'd slid off the other side and was falling to the ground. Her head struck the bitumen as she landed on her side on the road. And then she didn't hear or see anything. Everything went black.

'No!' Hailey screamed.

'Hell,' David whispered.

'Beth!' Gabe yelled, and was running before she even hit the ground. Hailey and David moved a second later.

Gabe reached her first, rounding the now stopped car, and was at Beth's side in an instant. His heart pounded in his chest as her inert form chilled him to the core.

'Oh, God, Beth,' Hailey sobbed, throwing herself on the ground beside her sister.

Gabe felt for a pulse and was relieved to feel a strong carotid. He looked up at David, who was staring down at his mother, pale and shaken.

'Beth!' Hailey cried again.

'Is she OK?' An elderly man knelt beside Gabe. A laceration on his forehead was bleeding and he was clearly dazed. 'I'm so sorry. She just stepped out in front of me,' he muttered.

'It's OK, sir, we know,' Gabe assured him, while Beth's failure to regain consciousness scared the hell out of him.

He took a second to assess the situation. Hailey was practically hysterical, David visibly shocked and the driver obviously traumatised. And he'd never felt more scared in his entire life. The woman he loved had been hit by a car—he wanted to vomit.

Beth murmured and he wanted to sweep her up in his arms and kiss her, but the doctor in him knew she could have serious injuries—broken bones, internal injuries, head trauma—not to mention the baby. *Hell, the baby!* His thoughts crystalised as his hands moved to support her neck. It was imperative she didn't move.

'Hailey,' Gabe said, his voice loud and commanding to cut through the sisterly hysteria. He used one hand to give her shoulder a firm shake. 'Run to Emergency. Get help. I need a trolley and a neck brace. Take him.' He gestured to the driver. 'He'll need checking out. Hurry.'

Hailey saw the urgency in Gabe's gaze and the wave of panic receded. She sniffed and nodded, rising to do his bidding.

'David.' Gabe looked up at the young man who still hadn't moved, his sheet-white face aghast. 'David!' Gabe called again, his voice stern in an effort to snap David out of his stupor. 'I need a hand here,' he said abruptly.

David nodded, his daze clearing as he sank to his knees. 'I didn't mean to—'

'I know,' Gabe said curtly, realising how awful David must feel but too concerned about Beth to be nice.

'Will she be OK?' he asked.

Gabe heard the crack in his voice. *He damn well hoped so.* 'I'm sure she will,' he said, taking pity and nodding with a confidence he didn't feel. 'The car wasn't going very fast.'

Beth groaned and moved her hand to her temple. She hurt everywhere. *What the hell happened?*

'It's OK, Beth,' Gabe whispered, leaning close, his hands still supporting her neck. His nausea was receding and he was so relieved to see her coming round that he wanted to weep. 'You're OK, lie still. Help's coming.'

Beth cracked open an eye and saw David leaning over her, his face worried. She wanted to stroke his brow and soothe away the lines, but pain stabbed into her eyeballs and she shut her eyes. 'What happened?' she muttered.

'A car hit you,' Gabe murmured quietly. 'What hurts?'

The memory returned, the sickening moment of impact, and she groaned. 'Everything hurts.' Her hands, through habit, moved to her stomach. The baby. Oh, God, the baby.

Beth's eyes flew open and she tried to move her head to look down at her stomach. Gabe's hands tightened their hold on her neck.

'Lie still,' he commanded.

'The baby,' she protested. 'Gabe, the baby.' Sudden tears sprang to her eyes and her voice cracked. 'I can't lose this baby.'

Beth reached out to David as her full memory of the preceding events returned. She knew the news had hurt him. Even through her throbbing head and raging thoughts she wanted to reassure him that he wasn't being replaced.

'I can't lose either of my babies,' she whispered, and was so grateful when he squeezed her hand that she started to cry.

They were interrupted by the arrival of a team from Accident and Emergency. No less than the director of the department Ben Stapleton, two orderlies and Rilla. And, of course, Hailey. There was flurry of activity.

'Rilla,' Beth cried, reaching for her sister's hand. Hailey took the other one. 'I need an ultrasound straight away.'

Rilla nodded. 'Be careful, she's pregnant,' she said to the team as they rolled Beth onto a spinal board.

They had her inside the department in ten minutes, an IV in two minutes later and a barrage of tests ordered. The General looked after its own and the NUM of Theatres and daughter of the Chief of Staff was top priority.

'Ultrasound,' Beth said to Ben. 'I need to have the baby checked out.'

'On its way,' he confirmed. 'After that we'll get some X-rays.'

'No.' Beth tried to shake her head but it was secured in a neck brace. 'No X-rays.'

'Beth,' Gabe said softly.

'No X-rays,' she said firmly. 'I'm fine.'

'You are not fine. You've been hit by a car. You were out cold for a couple of minutes.'

Beth gave her limbs a shake. 'I'm fine. Nothing hurts.' She winced. 'More than anything else,' she clarified. 'Nothing's broken.'

'You could have some cracked vertebrae.'

'I don't have pins and needles or numbness in my peripheries. My back and neck aren't sore.'

'You could have fractured your skull,' he said, pointing to the bloodied graze near her temple.

'Listen to him, darling, he's making perfect sense,' an imposing voice interrupted.

'John,' Beth said, smiling as her father pushed through the curtain. She accepted his embrace. 'Who called you? Go back to work. I'm fine.'

'I did,' Gabe said. 'I was hoping he'd pull rank.' Seeing her back to her old in-control self was comforting but she'd scared the hell out of all of them. He wouldn't be happy until everything had been checked out.

'Be sensible, darling. We X-ray pregnant women every day. All care will be taken. Doesn't your head ache?'

'It ached before I got hit,' Beth dismissed. 'All I need is the ultrasound.'

The head of the radiology department popped his head through the curtain. 'Beth Rogers, are you making a scene?'

Beth grinned at the consultant. 'Gordon. This is service. You'd better have the ultrasound machine with you.'

Gordon pulled the curtain back to reveal the ungainly mobile machine. He looked at the crowded cubicle—six adults and a cumbersome piece of equipment were not going to fit. 'I think we need some space in here, folks.'

'Yes, absolutely,' John agreed. 'Gabe, you stay with Beth. Come on, everyone else out.' He noticed David hovering at the back. 'I don't think we've met, young man. John Winters. I'm Beth's father.' He held out his hand and David shook it. 'Thank you for helping out. You probably don't have to hang around now.'

'No!'

Everyone turned and looked at Beth.

'I want him to stay,' Beth said, justifying her vehement rejection. She held out her hand to him and held her breath. 'David's my son.'

Beth only had eyes for David as he walked tentatively towards her and took her hand. She didn't care that by tomorrow not only would the entire hospital know she was pregnant but that she had a twenty-three-year old son.

She turned her gaze to her stunned family. 'He's family. I want him to wait with you.'

It took a few seconds but John, unflappable as always, recovered first. 'Of course, darling,' he said gesturing to David. 'We'll all go and wait outside. Together.'

Beth noticed David hesitate. He'd gone from complete anonymity to full exposure in twenty-four hours. Was he ready for her family? He'd sought her out only through a sense of genetic curiosity and she'd spectacularly outed him. Would he run a mile? Had she totally blown it?

'Actually, I think I'll head on home…now that you're OK… Andrea's expecting me.'

Beth swallowed. *She'd blown it.* David looked like he wanted to run screaming from the room. A new mother. A new sibling. And now an entire new family. Her heart throbbed as painfully as her head as he extricated his hand from hers.

'Of course.' Beth forced a smile onto her face as Gabe's words echoed in her head. *Don't push him.* 'I'll see you later?'

Beth tried not to come across as too desperate, too needy, but the thought of losing contact with him again was unbearable. David gave a noncommittal nod and her heart broke a little as she watched him leave the cubicle. What had she expected? That her banged-up body would make up for years of angst?

Beth lay on the trolley, her gaze firmly fixed on the spot where David had disappeared through the curtains, a hand down low on her stomach. Every part of her body ached and she fought the urge to cry.

'OK,' John said, rounding everyone up, his daughter's misery palpable. 'Let's give Gordon some room to work.'

Everyone trooped out until there were just the three of them. Gabe's heart swelled with love at Beth's obvious heartache and he covered her hand with his. She looked at him with an injured gaze and he gave her hand a squeeze.

'Give him time,' he murmured as he leant forward and kissed her gently on the forehead.

'OK, then,' Gordon said, interrupting their moment. 'Let's check out this baby.'

Beth pulled up her top and shimmied her trousers down a little. The gel was cool against her skin as Gordon placed the transducer on her abdomen. He fiddled with some buttons and the screen flickered to life.

The second their baby appeared on the screen Gabe knew he was lost. It looked like a skeletal alien. All large skull and bones. But he loved it as surely as he loved the woman who carried it. How could he think about a semi-involved role when he was desperately in love with both of them?

'Well, the little tike's certainly kicking a lot,' Gordon murmured. 'What's the gestation?'

'Nearly nineteen weeks,' Beth replied huskily. It was too much. This day had been too much. An emotional roller-coaster that had looped her around until her head spun. And now this. Meeting her baby for the first time.

'Nice strong heartbeat,' Gordon said.

Gabe saw the strong central flicker of his baby's tiny heart. He swallowed hard as a block of emotion rose in his chest. His throat felt tight and he felt like the walls were closing in on him. What sort of a father would a career-orientated neurosurgeon make? What if he screwed it up, like his father had?

'Have you had your routine scan yet?' Gordon asked.

'No, it's booked for next week,' Beth said, unable to drag her gaze away from the monitor.

'I'll just have a quick look at the placenta then we may as well check everything out.'

Beth nodded absently, totally mesmerised by the picture on the screen. She felt another kiss pressed onto her forehead and glanced up a Gabe. He seemed equally entranced by the image and for the first time she began to hope that everything was going to be OK.

'Placenta's intact,' Gordon said. 'Looks like the impact didn't affect the baby at all.'

Beth smiled, her hand trembling as the dark cloud of worry miraculously lifted. 'Really?'

'Really.' Gordon nodded. 'There are no signs of any separation or evidence of haemorrhage. But you need to take it easy for the next few days and see someone straight away if you start to bleed.'

Beth tried to nod but the collar prevented any vigorous movement. Anything. She'd do anything to keep Gabe's baby safe. 'Of course.'

'We'll admit her for observation,' Gabe commented above her head. 'That way we can be sure she's getting bed rest.'

Beth looked up at Gabe. 'Hey,' she said, 'I won't jeopardise this baby's health, Gabe.'

'I know. This will just make it easier for you.'

Beth opened her mouth to protest but Gabe's expression brooked no argument.

'You scared the living daylights out of all of us. You will be admitted.'

She shut her mouth. She could hear the echo of real fear in his voice. She could actually think he cared if she wasn't too careful. But then she thought how awful it must have been to witness someone being hit by the car and realised he'd be as concerned about anyone.

The next half-hour flew by as Gordon looked at the developing baby from every angle. Everything was structurally normal and the baby was growing well. It was certainly active. Beth followed its movements as it moved back and forth. The next twenty weeks stretched before her interminably. She was impatient to hold her baby in her arms.

She risked a look at Gabe. His expression was unfathomable. Had he given too much away earlier when he'd admitted how frightened he'd been? Was he as awed as she was by the sight of their baby or was he changing his mind, desperately trying to think of ways to hightail it back to the UK? She wished she knew what he was thinking.

'Do you want to know the sex?' Gordon asked.

Beth looked at Gabe, her eyebrows arched.

Gabe looked at her and shrugged. Did he? He was too involved already. 'I don't know—do you?'

Beth nodded. She did. Suddenly she wanted to know desperately.

'Girl,' Gordon announced.

A girl. Beth's heart swelled with love. Would she have her father's peridot eyes and caramel hair? Or the same dimple in her chin as her big brother?

Beth grinned at him and Gabe was struck by an image of a little version of Beth. Blonde pigtails and pink ribbons, a little bow mouth and blue, blue eyes. The vision was captivating and he was alarmed by how much it appealed. He didn't know how to be a father to a delicate little girl. He didn't even have a sister.

The ultrasound ended and Gabe left quickly to find her family. Beth brooded while he was gone. She had no idea what Gabe felt about having a daughter.

The arrival of everyone back in the cubicle, including a worried Penny, distracted her from her thoughts.

'Oh, my God. I came straight away,' Penny wailed as she gave Beth a huge hug.

Everyone spoke at once, wanting to know about the accident and the ultrasound and David, and Beth's head throbbed. She suddenly felt a hundred years old. She just wanted to sleep.

Gabe could see the growing weariness in every line of Beth's body. He felt a little overwhelmed himself—no wonder David had hightailed it out of here. The Winters clan was full on. He wasn't used to being around a family that was so tight-knit. His upbringing seemed very…cold in comparison. Still, it was good to know that his child, his daughter, would be surrounded by all this love. By people who cared. By women—lots of women. That's what girls needed, didn't they?

'I think Beth needs some rest,' Gabe said, cutting through the din. 'Let's get her admitted so she can get into bed.'

'Admitted? I thought you said she was OK?' Penny turned to John.

'Just to be on the safe side and because she's refusing X-rays,' Gabe hastened to assure Penny.

Beth shot him a get-over-it look but was exceedingly grateful that he was taking control. It had been a big day. A big few days.

The operation.

Sleeping with Gabe. Again.

Discovering her love for him.

David.

Being knocked flat by a car.

She was so weary she could sleep for a week.

CHAPTER ELEVEN

An hour later she was ensconced in a private room with a spectacular view of the Brisbane skyline. She could also see Barney's and could make out a couple of her staff heading across the road towards the welcoming neon sign.

Her family had just left and she was blissfully alone. The neck brace Gabe insisted she still wear was annoying and she shifted to get comfortable in it. She sighed and shut her eyes. The crisp hospital sheets felt heavenly against her aching body. There was so much to think about so much to process, but within seconds she was drifting away into the blissful folds of slumber.

Gabe found her sound asleep half an hour later. He'd left her in the capable hands of her family earlier. His head was grappling with the revelations of the day and he'd needed some time and space to deal with them. Not that anything seemed any clearer.

He moved into the room and pulled a chair up beside her bed. She looked awful. Her pale skin looked even more so against the backdrop of the white sheets. A dark purple bruise had formed over her right temple and he knew by morning it would spread to encompass her entire right eye area.

She was so still and he felt fear grip him again as his heart rate picked up. His gaze zeroed in on her chest, concentrating on its rise and fall, counting her deep, even respirations. His fingers strayed to the pulse at her wrist and he breathed out, reassured by the strong beat.

His hand shook as he withdrew it, his head playing a rerun of the accident. He saw her being struck by the car, rolling across the bonnet and crashing to the ground. The image of her motionless, crumpled body would be forever implanted on his retinas. He'd thought she'd been killed. His heart still beat madly in his chest hours after the event when he thought about that awful fleeting moment.

That would be a cruel twist of fate. Realising he'd found the one woman who'd managed to get beneath his defences, only to have her snatched away less than an hour later.

She lay with both hands cupped low on her abdomen in a pose peculiar to pregnant women worldwide. Even in sleep she was protecting their child. His hands itched to join hers but he didn't want to disturb her and his feelings were still too jumbled to let his guard down.

Today he'd fallen in love with a woman and met his daughter. It had been momentous, to say the least. And none of it had been on his agenda. God, he could hear his father mocking now. Harlon Fallon would be rolling in his grave to hear a son of his actually thinking about putting family first.

But beliefs ingrained over years cautioned him against diving in head first. How many relationships had he seen break up in his line of work? How many kids played second fiddle to the job? Like he had? Was it fair to act on a whim when he wasn't sure if he was equipped to go the distance?

Was it fair for his daughter to have to settle for being second fiddle?

Looking at Beth lying so still and silent he knew he loved her more than anything. Loved her enough to wonder if she and the baby would be better off without him. She'd already told him she was perfectly happy to do it herself. Maybe he needed to heed that. What made him think she'd even want him anyway? She had what she wanted—a baby. And her son back. Did she even have room in her life for him?

His pager beeped and he quickly pushed the silence button. He needn't have bothered. Beth didn't stir. He checked the message. It was the PICU. He'd been expecting their page. They were removing Brooke's dressing and he'd asked to be notified.

He left Beth's side reluctantly, the dictates of his job warring with his desire to be with her. This was what it would be like all the time if he got involved. Constantly feeling guilty for neglecting one or the other.

He strode down the corridors, eating up the distance between Beth and Brooke with long powerful strides, his head seething. His duty to be with the injured woman he loved at odds with his duty to his patient.

'Hi, June,' he said, plastering a smile on his face as he approached Brooke's bedside.

'Hi, Gabe.'

'So, how's that head looking, sweetie pie?' Gabe crooned, turning his attention to Brooke who gave him a big smile.

Erica Hamel from the plastics team was there also and they were both pleased with how the wound was looking. They spent twenty minutes discussing the next steps in the process for Brooke. Gabe checked his watch several times. He wanted to be there when Beth woke up.

'So, that was quite a press conference,' June said after Erica had left.

'Yes.' Gabe smiled.

'You need to employ Beth as your publicist,' June teased. 'I think she's a bigger fan than even me or Scott.'

Gabe looked at June. There was a shrewd gleam in her eyes. He chuckled. 'Some would say that reporter had it coming.'

'Oh. Absolutely.' June laughed. 'If Beth hadn't said something, I was about to.'

Gabe laughed. 'Well, thanks, I think I can stick up for myself.'

'You shouldn't inspire such loyalty if you don't want your honour defended.'

Is that why Beth had done it? Out of loyalty?

'Of course, I think there was a bit more than loyalty involved,' June said.

Gabe shot June a polite smile. Could she be right? Was there something more that had motivated Beth's outburst? He excused himself, telling June he'd pop into see Brooke in the morning.

He was back at Beth's room eight minutes later, stopping abruptly in the doorway when he realised Beth wasn't alone. David sat in a chair beside the bed, his back to the door.

Gabe approached quietly, crossing to the opposite side of the bed.

'Oh.' David rose. 'Hi. I was just… I'll go,' he said.

Gabe reached across the bed and laid a stilling hand on

the younger man's arm. 'Please, don't. Beth would want you to stay.'

David looked at him and Gabe could almost touch his aura of indecision and conflict. It seemed they would make similar company tonight. Gabe pulled up a chair and was relieved when David resumed his seat.

They sat watching Beth breathe for a long time. Neither of them spoke. It was as if they were both just content to see signs of life.

'So…it's been a big couple of days,' Gabe said eventually.

'You can say that again.' David grimaced.

'You do know how much it means to Beth to have you back in her life?'

David nodded. 'I don't know if I can be what she wants.'

'She just wants a chance to get to know you. That's all. She's your mother—'

'I have a mother,' David rejected quickly. 'I wasn't just on loan to the woman who raised me for the last twenty-three years, you know. Beth can't surely expect us to have the same sort of mother-son relationship.'

Gabe nodded. The younger man's confusion was palpable. He was pretty sure Beth would take whatever David had to offer, but he could sense the younger man had been pushed too much for one day. 'So why are you here?'

David sighed. 'I…don't know. There were so many times as a kid that I wondered about her. Wondered why. How she could have given up her child. And when things were messed up I used to think…to know she'd be able to make it right. But then I grew up and I realised she must have had her reasons and I'd had a good life and what would we really have to say to each other?'

David stopped and Gabe waited for him to continue. He could tell there was so much more David wanted to say.

'But when she was lying there today and she was so still, all I could think was I never got to know her. I was scared stiff she was dead and I didn't get a chance to tell her…I loved her.'

Gabe nodded. Hadn't he had just the same wake-up call? It was important suddenly to try and make David understand about Beth. David was, after all, going to be his daughter's big brother. Hopefully, for Beth's sake, a big part of the baby's life. He knew Beth well enough to know that she just wasn't whole without David.

'Giving you up broke her heart, David. Give her a chance.'

David shook his head. 'She's not going to have time for me now. She has the baby.'

Gabe clenched his hands. David had been put into a situation he hadn't expected and his confusion was more than understandable. But he was wrong if he thought Beth's love was so fickle.

'Love doesn't divide, David. It multiplies. You and Beth are halves of each other's whole. Neither of you are complete without the other. There's a hole in her life that only you fill. No one, not even another child, can fill that space.'

Gabe watched as David seemed to take his words on board.

'Get to know her. You won't regret it. If today demonstrates anything, it's that life's short. My father died without me ever really making an effort to get to know him, and that's just not right. And now I'm about to be a father myself and if there's one thing I've learned in the last little while it's that the bond between a parent and a child is too basic to us as humans to deny.'

Gabe felt the hypocrisy of the words even as he said them. *Do as I say, not as I do?* Here he was urging David to get to know Beth and yet he was contemplating some part-time father status while he still kept an eye on his career.

David nodded and they sat in silence for a while longer. Gabe's brain was working overtime. How stupid had he been? He knew how awful it had been, growing up without a father or one who'd had no emotional investment in him whatsoever. Was that what he was condemning his child to?

Would she lie in bed when she was old enough and wonder about him as David had about Beth? And what would be his excuse when she wanted to know why he hadn't given more? He wasn't a fifteen-year-old from a broken home. Somehow he didn't think *I was too busy with my career to give a damn* would cut it. He'd seen her on the screen today, had felt his heart swell with love for the tiny fragile life. He was fooling himself to think he could just go through the motions.

Everyone had always said he was just like his father. Driven. Focused. Determined. But they were wrong. He wouldn't sacrifice the woman he loved or his child on the altar of his career. He didn't know how but he'd make damn sure there was room in his life for them all.

Just because he'd had a lousy role model it didn't mean it wasn't possible. His father may have been a world-famous doctor but he had been a lousy human being and Gabe didn't intend to follow in those footsteps. John Winters had succeeded. More than succeeded.

David stood. 'Tell her I was here,' he said. 'I'll call again tomorrow.'

Gabe nodded. 'Please, do.' He reached across the bed and offered David his hand. 'She'll like that.'

The two men shook hands and David departed. Gabe sincerely hoped David would be true to his word. He couldn't bear to think of the woman he loved hurting. Looking at her bruised face was making him sick to his stomach. Her broken heart was too much to bear.

It was almost dawn before Beth stirred. She came awake slowly, conscious of every ache and pain. She felt as if her body had been on the rack. Her temple throbbed and her eye felt like it was bulging out of her head. Her stomach grumbled and the baby was kicking like crazy, no doubt demanding that her mother eat.

She brought her hand to her face and tentatively felt the swelling there. Ouch. She had a very bad feeling it was already three different shades of purple. She was going to look very scary for a few days. She opened her sore eye, pleased to find it was still possible and her vision didn't seem to be affected.

Her hand felt heavy and numb and she felt a tremor of alarm as Gabe's warning about a spinal injury reared its ugly head. Beth looked down, no easy task with the collar limiting her range of movement, to check out why. For a brief second her heart stopped. Gabe's head rested against her hand.

He'd stayed?

Beth drank in his features. His eyes were shut, his stubble making him look rakish in the subdued hospital lighting. She wanted to freeze this moment. In this instant she could almost believe they were a couple. A family. The fact that she looked like the bride of Frankenstein and his career was his first priority seemed completely inconsequential.

Her other hand hovered above his head, the urge to rumple his caramel waves almost overwhelming. But the pins and needles in her trapped hand were becoming quite painful, almost a match for the throb in her temple, and she reluctantly removed her hand as gently as she could.

'What?' Gabe roused instantly, his head snapping up.

'It's OK,' she croaked. Her throat felt dry and she swallowed. 'My hand was sore.' She flexed her fingers to encourage the circulation to return.

'Oh, sorry.' He smiled. 'I must have fallen asleep.'

Beth felt herself responding to his sleepy grin and his drowsy voice. She was sore, hungry and no doubt exceedingly frightening to look at, yet her hormones roared to life.

'You should go home, Gabe,' she whispered. 'Have you been here all night?'

He nodded rubbing at a crick in his neck. Her eye looked even worse than it had earlier, and he felt ill all over again, thinking how close he'd come to losing her the previous day. He wasn't leaving until he'd got some stuff off his chest.

'David was here earlier.'

Beth sat forward and then winced, before dropping back against the pillows. 'Really?'

'Easy,' Gabe said.

'Why didn't you wake me?'

'Beth, you scared us both silly yesterday. You were exhausted. Neither of us wanted to disturb you.'

She heard the fear in his voice again and tried not to read too much into it. 'What did he say? How did he seem?'

'He said when he saw you lying on the ground unconscious he thought you were dead and he realised he'd never had the chance to get to know you.'

Beth felt hope flower inside her as tears sprang to her eyes. 'He did?'

Gabe nodded. 'He did. He said to tell you he'd be back to see you later today.'

A tear spilled from an eye and trekked down her cheek. Could it be true? Could her son be taking his first steps towards a permanent relationship? 'Oh, Gabe, I want that so much.'

He smiled at her as he brushed the moisture from her cheek. 'I know,' he whispered. 'I know.'

Beth's mind rushed ahead and she felt a ball of nervousness tighten in the pit of her stomach. *Please, don't let me mess it up.* 'Oh, god, I must look a fright,' she fretted, touching her swollen eye.

'You're alive.' He picked up her hand and kissed her palm. 'Trust me, for an awful moment yesterday none of us thought that was possible.'

Beth's palm tingled and she looked down into his earnest gaze. He was staring at her so intently her belly flopped. 'I'm sorry I scared everyone,' she said huskily.

'Just don't ever do it again, OK?'

'OK,' she whispered. He was still looking at her with those green eyes and she wished she knew what he was thinking. Was this just a concerned friend? A father worried about his baby? Or was this a lover talking?

She couldn't bear to have him look at her like this, so…possessively, if it meant nothing. 'You should go. Get a few hours' sleep in a proper bed. You've got an afternoon list today.'

And just like that she was back-in-control Beth. The Beth that ran the General's operating theatres with efficiency and expertise. The Beth that would manage motherhood with one hand tied behind her back. The one that would be perfectly fine without him. Only he wasn't so sure how fine he'd be.

'I need to talk to you first.'

Gabe had come over all serious and Beth felt a wave of panic rise from the pit of her stomach. She didn't want to hear him talking about future arrangements. Not now. She was tired and aching. She wasn't strong enough. 'Gabe, I'm really not up to much at the moment.'

'Please.'

Beth shivered at the rawness in his tone. 'Gabe,' she pleaded.

Gabe hardened his heart to her plea. He had to say this. 'I was sitting in that press conference yesterday—'

'Oh, God. Look, I'm sorry about that,' Beth interrupted. She cringed, thinking how deranged she must have sounded. 'I don't know what came over me. I was rude and hasty.'

She was trying to take it back? What did that mean? He shook his head—it didn't matter. They weren't in high school, his feelings hadn't changed.

'I…loved it when you said those things.'

Beth's heart stood still in her chest for a few beats. He'd said the L-word.

'In fact, listening to you defend my honour, I realised that I'd fallen in love with you. I don't know when it happened—I think it just kind of sneaked up on me. And I thought, Hell, that's a complication I don't need.'

Beth's heart raced in her chest now. Had he just used the L-word again? In relation to her?

Her hand lay by her side and he picked it up and cradled it against his face.

'And then you got hit by that car and it was the worst moment of my life. And then I saw the baby…my baby.' He placed his hand low on her abdomen. 'And I didn't think it was possible to feel such instantaneous emotion. And I knew I was getting in deeper.'

Beth was holding her breath now. His palm felt amazingly possessive against hers. Was there a 'but' coming?

'And then I was talking to David and telling him how important it was to know the people who had given you life, and I realised I was being a hypocrite. That if I gave any less than my all I was condemning my child to the same fate.'

Beth swallowed. What was he saying? 'Gabe.'

'No, hang on.' He shook his head. 'I want our daughter…' he gave her hand a squeeze '…to know her father. I want to be part of her life. And I realise that you don't need me and I'm not in your parenting plan, but I can't walk away. That's something my father would have done. And I'm not my father. Neither do I want to be. I want to be a father to my daughter. In every sense of the word.'

Beth's brain fizzed with information. Maybe it was the knock to her head but she was finding it all a little hard to process. She was still stuck back at the L-word.

'Beth?' he prompted a minute later. She hadn't said anything. She was just looking at him, clearly confused.

'I'm sorry, did you just say…that you loved me?'

Gabe nodded.

Beth blinked. Truly deep down she'd always felt unworthy of anyone's love. How could someone love her when she'd given her child away? But right now she dared to feel a flare of hope.

'And that you want to be a father?'

He nodded again.

Beth's pulse trebled before she could put the brakes on. 'But what about your career? Your practice in the UK? These things are important to you, Gabe.'

'Yes, they are. And I can have them here.'

Beth still refused to give in to total elation. 'Aren't you worried how you'll manage a career and family? You're the one who told me it didn't work.'

Gabe nodded. 'I'm terrified that I'll get it wrong and I'll make mistakes, but I'm more terrified of how empty my life will be without you in it. I can't promise it'll all be plain sailing, but I can promise I'll always put you and the baby first. Always. Just like John. And Scott and June. Just because my father messed it up, it doesn't mean I will. He was never committed enough. But I am.'

He laid both hands against her stomach. 'I promise on the life of our daughter that I will be committed to make this work every day of our lives.'

Beth couldn't believe what she was hearing. He loved her and wanted to be with her. If it was true, if this gorgeous, successful man truly loved her, despite her baggage, then maybe, just maybe she could start loving herself. Forgive herself.

'I know this is a shock.'

'You can say that again.' Beth gave a half-laugh.

'I realise it'll probably take me a while to win your favour but I'm hoping you'll eventually grow to love me too and we can get married.'

'Oh, Gabe.' It was all too much. Beth felt a wave of emotion well in her throat. 'I can't believe you're proposing to me when I look like I've been pulled through a hedge backwards.'

Gabe smiled and kissed her hand. 'You're alive. I've never seen you more beautiful.' He removed his hands and laid his head against her stomach.

Beth knew tears were coursing down her cheeks but didn't care. She ran a hand through his hair, luxuriating in the feel of it beneath her hands and the weight of his head against her womb.

'Are you sure, Gabe? Really sure? Can you love someone who gave away her child?'

Gabe looked up into her tear-stained face. 'What you did was brave and completely selfless. You were a mixed-up fifteen-year-old and you put his needs first. I love you especially for that.'

Beth's eyes welled with a fresh batch of tears. 'I love you too, Gabe Fallon. I've loved you since that first night when I was so sad and you rocked me in your arms.'

Gabe felt hope for the first time. 'Really?'

Beth nodded. 'Really. And I will marry you and I will keep you to your promise to put me and the baby first. You can count on that.'

Gabe chuckled. 'I have no doubt.' He stood and sat on the edge of her bed. 'You mean it? You really do love me?'

Beth wiped away her tears. 'Really. I really do.'

'You know you've just made my day.' He grinned as he leaned closer. 'God, I want to kiss you very badly at the moment.'

Beth laughed and then winced as it reverberated through

her facial muscles. 'Right—black eye and hard collar. I must look so appealing.'

Gabe grinned. 'I think this is the for-better-or-worse part.'

Beth sobered. She raised a hand to cradle his jaw, his stubble grazing erotically against her palm. 'Are you sure, Gabe? You're giving up a lot here.'

'I'm not giving it up. Just changing direction. It'll take a while to wind things up at home but I've never been surer of anything in my life.'

She caressed his lips with her thumb. 'I love you,' Beth whispered, hardly able to believe she could actually say it to his face. She opened her arms and he went into them.

He gently laid his head against her chest where her heart beat solidly, careful not to hurt her while fighting the urge to crush her to him.

'I love you too,' he murmured against her neck.

And he knew he was going to spend the rest of his life showing her just how much.

EPILOGUE

IT WAS a fine cool winter's day in Brisbane when Beth and Gabe finally tied the knot two months later in a small civil ceremony in the Botanic Gardens. Paperwork and several trips back and forth to England had held them up but nothing had derailed Gabe's determination to get married before the baby was born.

Beth wore a cream, princess-line gown, which accentuated her twenty-eight-week bump. She had a garland of flowers in her hair and a matching posy in her hands. A spectacular peridot necklace adorned her slender neck and complemented her square-cut peridot and diamond ring. Peridot had rapidly become her favourite stone.

'You may kiss the bride,' the celebrant intoned.

Gabe grinned down at his wife. 'At last,' he whispered, and claimed Beth's mouth in a possessive kiss that told all and sundry she belonged to him.

The Winters clan clapped and cheered and then rushed forward to congratulate the newlyweds in a noisy flurry of hugs, kisses and excited exclamations.

Beth held her hand out to David and Andrea and she

accepted her son's embrace gratefully. 'Thank you for coming,' she said huskily.

'He's a great guy,' David said. 'I'm happy for you.'

Beth felt tears spring to her eyes. They'd been making tentative steps towards each other these past couple of months and she'd been so thankful. Andrea and Gabe had been encouraging and with their help she and David were slowly bridging the gap.

'Thanks for coming, you two,' Gabe said as he approached, giving Beth a hug from behind. He held out a hand to David.

'Look after my mother,' David said, grasping Gabe's hand in a firm grip.

Gabe nodded. 'I will cherish her always.'

David nodded as he and Andrea were pulled away by Penny. The extended family had welcomed David and Andrea into the fold with open arms and while there had been some challenges, they were all working together to overcome the obstacles.

'Did you hear that?' Beth whispered, turning in her husband's arms. 'He called me his mother.'

'Yes, darling,' Gabe said, dropping a light kiss on her nose.

'I didn't think this day could get any more perfect,' she said, staring up at her handsome husband, her mind still reeling from David's acknowledgement.

'Stick with me, babe,' Gabe teased. 'Every day is going to be more perfect than the last. That's a promise.'

CARING FOR HIS BABIES

Lilian
DARCY

Lilian Darcy is Australian, but has strong ties to the USA through her American husband. They have four growing children and currently live in Canberra, Australia. Lilian has written over forty romance novels and still has more story ideas crowding into her head than she knows what to do with. Her work has appeared on the Waldenbooks romance bestsellers list and two of her plays have been nominated for major Australian writing awards. 'I'll keep writing as long as people keep reading my books,' she says. 'It's all I've ever wanted to do and I love it.'

CHAPTER ONE

THE phone line between Sydney and Riyadh was far clearer than Keelan had expected it to be, and there weren't the few seconds of delay he sometimes experienced with international calls. He'd had more difficult connections when talking to his cousin two suburbs away.

'Tell me about the babies,' said Jessica Russell, at the other end of the line.

It was four o'clock in the afternoon in Riyadh, but her voice sounded slightly husky as if she'd only just woken. Maybe she was working nights and sleeping days. Whatever her hours, she would be on a plane two days from now, heading home to Australia to meet her tiny new patients and Keelan himself.

'Well, Tavie's a lot better off than Tam at this stage...' Keelan began inadequately.

Keeping the cordless phone against his ear, he paced to the window of his study and looked out into the night. The harbour-scape appeared the same as always—a wide stripe of glittering black water, dancing with blue and red neon reflected from the city on the opposite shore and framed by a huge Moreton Bay fig tree on the right and his neighbour's house on the left.

So much else had changed, however, in just ten days.

'That's why I...we...need you on board so soon,' he continued.

Why had he changed the pronoun to 'we'? he had time to wonder, as he paused for breath. His various cousins, uncles and aunts applauded what he was doing, but had all declared, not without cause, that they had too much going on in their own lives to get involved on a practical level.

His mother had shown more enthusiasm and desire to help. She'd visited the hospital on the weekend, but she lived almost four hours away, north of Newcastle, and technically she was no relation at all to the twins. He wasn't going to foist on her the grandchildren of the woman who'd broken up her marriage twenty-three years ago.

Dad should have stepped forward perhaps, but he seemed frankly terrified—quite paralysed—and ready to run a mile from any involvement. Was it grief, or regret, or the fact that the babies were so fragile and small?

'All going well,' Keelan finished, dragging his focus back to more practical concerns. 'The girl—Tavie— should be discharged next week.'

In a more perfect world the little girl twin would have been discharged into her mother's care, but Brooke— Keelan's half-sister—was dead and...

He revised his thought.

In a more perfect world, twenty-two-year-old Brooke would never have become pregnant in the first place, through one of her many unsuitable affairs, and even if she had, she would have sought the right prenatal care, the twins might not have been born so prematurely and Brooke would certainly have realised that the post-partum bleeding she'd experienced after her discharge from the hospital had been way heavier than it should have been.

Too many ifs.

Too much drama, in too short a time.

The babies were ten days old, having been born at just

over twenty-eight weeks gestation, and the little boy, Tam, was clinging to life by a thread. Brooke had collapsed in a café a week ago, but emergency treatment had come too late and she'd bled out in the ambulance on the way to the same hospital, North Sydney, where she'd given birth. The Hunter clan had survived the funeral—and the publicity—with its usual dignity and repressed emotion.

Keelan's ex-stepmother, Louise—Brooke's mother— had fallen apart in private afterwards, however. She was still heavily medicated, apparently, back home in Melbourne with her new husband, Phillip.

He'd told Keelan categorically, 'We can't take them. It just wouldn't work. Especially if they turn out to be delicate or damaged. I'm too old, and Louise isn't very strong emotionally. Especially now, of course. Some other arrangement will have to be made.'

Keelan had known, at that moment, that there was really only one option. Discounting the babies' father, since he'd disappeared from Brooke's life months ago, and they didn't even know his last name, Keelan was the babies' closest blood relative of an appropriate age for fatherhood. He was a paediatrician at North Sydney Hospital, and knew exactly the kinds of problems that the babies might face now and in the future.

So he'd adopt them himself.

It wouldn't be an ideal solution but, as he'd just concluded, this wasn't a perfect world. He felt uncomfortable about how much the babies' new nurse needed to know about all of this. With four generations of highly successful Hunter lawyers, doctors, politicians and financiers preceding him, Keelan valued privacy and discretion. He wondered uneasily just which boundaries he'd be able to keep in place during the coming months.

'So I'll mainly be settling in until that happens?' Jessica Russell asked over the phone. 'Until she's ready to come home?'

'Spending as much time with both of them at the hospital, I would hope,' he answered firmly. 'I'll be pushing for the earliest discharge that's safely possible, given your experience with preemies, so I'll want you liaising closely with the nurses in the unit and getting familiar with each baby's condition and needs. Settling in can happen in your own time.'

She gave a wry laugh. 'Is there going to be much of that? My own time, I mean. The twins themselves will call the shots on my hours.'

This comment reassured Keelan, yet served to confirm that he hadn't quite trusted her before, and probably still didn't. Wouldn't for a while, if he had any sense. This would be merely a job for her. She could never have the same investment in the twins' well-being as he did.

He'd intended to go through an agency here in Sydney, get someone local. He liked to make his own judgements about people. But a medical colleague in Adelaide had recommended Ms Russell, and when he had gone to a Sydney nursing agency, her name, by coincidence, had come up again.

'She registered with us quite recently, and has first-class credentials and references. I'd jump at her, if I were you. I imagine she'll be looking for a permanent hospital position before too long.'

Jessica had been working in a high-level neonatal unit in Saudi Arabia, but she'd had enough of it after two years and was about to come home. She would be ready to start exactly when Keelan wanted her—that was, immediately.

Keelan was wary of the coincidence rather than reassured by it. He didn't go in for 'signs'. But he couldn't ignore Ms Russell's level of experience when it was coupled with a recommendation from someone he trusted.

'Why's she been in Saudi, though?' he'd asked his colleague, Lukas Cheah, phoning the man for a second time in search of more details. 'It can be a dangerous part of the world for Westerners.'

'Not sure. A bit of a wanderer?'

'A risk-taker?'

'Not necessarily. Saving for a mortgage? Some nurses manage to build a nice bank balance over there. From what my wife has said—' Jane Cheah was also an NICU nurse, Keelan knew '—I don't think she has much family to fall back on.'

Keelan, in contrast, had far too much family. He felt the pressure sometimes. At other times he felt pride.

'Sounds as if you're not worried about working long, erratic hours,' he said to Ms Russell.

'Well, no, since it's obviously a requirement and, I assume, the reason for the…uh…generous salary you've offered. Anyway,' she added quickly, 'I've done it before.'

She sounded uncomfortable about discussing money. Keelan was, too. Probably for different reasons. The Hunter family had a fair bit of it, but he liked to be as discreet about that fact as possible. He went back to the subject of the twins' health and medical status instead.

'Let me give you more details about what you'll be dealing with. They were born somewhere between twenty-eight and twenty-nine weeks. The girl—Tavie— is significantly heavier and stronger.'

'What was her birth weight?'

'She was 1220 grams. Tam was just under a kilo—

990 grams—but we'll get to him later. I'll try and go through this systematically. Tavie is still on oxygen.'

'CPAP?'

'She started on a respirator, but yes, she's up to CPAP now.'

Of course Ms Russell knew the abbreviation—continuous positive airway pressure, delivering oxygen via a tube taped to the baby's face. It was good not to have to explain.

'She's also on light therapy for jaundice as of two days ago,' he continued. 'She had a heart murmur indicative of PDA—' again, it reassured him to use the abbreviation for the common preemie heart problem, patent ductus arteriosus, knowing she'd understand it '—but that's resolved on it's own, fortunately.'

'Sometimes those can re-open.'

'It'll be monitored, of course.'

'Gut problems? As and Bs?'

'Her gut is good, but she's still having recurrent apnoea and bradycardia episodes, yes. With you on board, she can be discharged with oxygen and monitors, if that's still necessary, and I expect it will be.'

'Yes.'

'We want to see her get back up to her birth weight and show some steady gain before her discharge in any case.'

'She's on tube feeds?'

'Yes.'

'And the boy—Tam—isn't so good, you said?'

He couldn't hold back a sigh. 'No, unfortunately. His heart problems are more serious. We…uh…realistically…don't know if he'll make it.'

'Sometimes they don't.' It wasn't an unsympathetic

line. She'd just seen it before, that was all, and knew there wasn't a lot to say.

'We heard a heart murmur when he was a couple of days old,' he continued, keeping to facts, not feelings. 'An echocardiogram showed two ventricular septal defects—VSDs.' It was one of the most common congenital heart defects, more prevalent in boys and more prevalent in twins than single births.

'Serious ones? Can they tell?'

'We're still hoping they may close over on their own, but so far they haven't. Four days ago his oxygen levels began dropping. They did another scan and found a third VSD, large, around 7 millimetres. He also showed co-arctation of the aorta.'

'He wouldn't be strong enough for surgery yet,' she guessed. 'Although that thinned aorta must be a concern for you.'

'Definitely, but yes, before surgery we need to grow him and stabilise him, steer him past a few other risks.'

'Infection, gut problems, jaundice,' she murmured. 'Is he on bili lights, like his sister?'

'Yes.'

'I love bili lights—something we can do for them that doesn't cause them pain.'

'I know what you mean.'

'And they've lost their mother, too... Rough way to come into this world.' The husky note in her voice had deepened. 'I hope someone's told you what a heroic thing you're doing, Dr Hunter, taking them on.'

'There was no choice,' he answered shortly, wondering if he should have saved the story on their circumstances until he'd met the twins' nurse face to face.

She'd rubbed him up the wrong way with her statement, well intentioned though it had clearly been. He didn't want editorial commentary from an employee. A compliment like the one she'd just given him implied that she had the right to criticise as well, and she didn't. She was just a paid carer, chosen for her expertise not for her opinions and feelings.

Except...

Premature babies needed love. It was a medically established fact that fragile infants did better when they had periods of warm, peaceful body contact. Tavie and Tam needed Jessica Russell to care about them.

Keelan wasn't married or seriously involved with any woman right now. There was no other female under his roof to fill a maternal role, and yet he didn't want Ms Russell to get too close, or too indispensable, because eventually, inevitably, she would leave. What would that do to the babies, a few months down the track, if they'd become deeply attached to her?

Lord, this wasn't going to be easy!

Jessie put down the phone after Keelan Hunter's call and squinted out into the glare of the desert's afternoon light. Her eyes ached for the relief of Sydney's lush, almost tropical foliage. Two more days. It would be fun to try a new city, a place she'd only ever seen during a couple of brief holidays. And it might be refreshing to get back to some private nursing for a while, she told herself.

A feeling of restlessness tugged at her heart, dragging her spirits down. She'd been so *good*, so sensible these past two years. She'd lived so frugally, sending as much of her wages back to the investment fund in Australia as she possibly could.

With both her parents remarried, living on opposite sides of the continent, absorbed in their new families, and not particularly keen to be reminded of the miserable marriage they'd endured as their punishment for having conceived her out of wedlock when they'd both been far too young, she'd responded in the most practical way to her realisation that she was essentially alone in the world—she'd saved money.

And then the investment fund had gone bust and she'd lost it all.

If there was a lesson to be learned somewhere in this development, she hadn't yet worked out what it was. The fun-loving, live-for-the-moment grasshopper in the Aesop fable had had it right after all? The serious, hard-working ant should have its legs pulled off for setting such a bad example to impressionable nurses?

Hmm.

She did know one thing, though.

She was homesick. Gut-wrenchingly, tearfully, desperately homesick.

Bit sad that she didn't really have a home to go to. Not Adelaide. Too long since she'd first left, and the in-between experiment of a year she'd spent back there after the stints with Médecins Sans Frontières in Liberia and Sierra Leone, and before the rather crazy time in London, hadn't been enough to re-establish her roots. Jane Cheah was the only friend she missed from that time.

So she was trying Sydney, and a live-in position that offered the dangerous promise of being able to pretend she had a home. From the impression Dr Hunter had given her over the phone, she didn't think he'd do much to foster this illusion, and that was probably for the best. There were many things she liked about a footloose life, perhaps the most important being that you knew exactly where you stood.

She tried to form a picture of Dr Hunter in her mind, based on the way his voice had sounded and the things she knew about him, but couldn't do it. Even his attitude to the babies had been hard to read. She'd just have to wait.

Two days. The long flight. Then Keelan Hunter himself would meet her at the airport and take her...home?

No.

Not home. Not really. Just the next waystation.

Her stomach churned.

Ms Russell looked like what she was—a seasoned Australian traveller returning home after a long absence. Keelan had her name held up on a large piece of card, and when she saw it she steered straight towards it through the crowded terminal, looking tired, relieved, a little dishevelled and wary.

He could match her on three out of those four attributes. Tired because he'd been up half the night at the hospital, relieved because he hadn't been one hundred per cent convinced that she would actually be on the plane, and he was definitely wary.

He would try not to let it show, but the wariness would probably last for weeks. Until he worked out how this was going to operate. Until he knew if Tam would live, and how long both babies might need in-home professional care.

'Hello.' She put down two distinctly battered suitcases and held out her hand. 'Dr Hunter?'

'Yes.' He thought about inviting her to call him Keelan, but held back and said instead, 'How was your flight? This is all your luggage?'

'I've got used to travelling light.' She took it on trust that he remembered the details of her résumé, with its references to periods spent in two different clinics in the developing world, in contrast to the high-level neonatal experience he'd employed her for.

'You need some new suitcases,' he told her.

'And travelling cheap.' She grinned, inviting her to meet him halfway, which he did, because she'd taken him by surprise.

She had an infectious smile, careless and open like a boy's. It went with the liberal splash of freckles across her nose and the red-brown hair, bushy after the flight. Her eyes were a startling blue, and seemed to light up like the flash of sun on water, making the smile dazzling as well as infectious. She was thirty-two, he knew, but she looked younger.

'Fair enough,' he said, and nudged her gently aside so he could grab the pair of shabby handles.

The things weighed a ton, belying her statement about travelling light. Couldn't be clothes. She was wearing a long, modest skirt and long-sleeved top, with a wide white scarf around her neck that she would have used to cover her head in Saudi, and in that part of the world he doubted she would have needed much more than a few repetitions on the same theme. No thick coats or evening clothes or sports gear.

'I'm sorry,' she said. 'Too many books in there. I tended to hoard them in Riyadh, because they were hard to get.'

'Didn't you have someone equally desperate to pass them on to?'

'I passed on all the ones I could bear to part with.' Then she apologised again and finished, 'I hope your car's not far.'

'It's fine. And there's an empty bookcase in the room I've set aside for you.'

She frowned for a moment as if picturing this unfamiliar idea—that she might unpack her books and put them on shelves—then said, 'Something we didn't sort out before—how long are you expecting this arrangement to continue? I mean, once the babies reach, say, one month corrected age, four months since birth, they're hopefully not going to need the level of specialised care I can provide. And a full-time, in-home nurse is…' She stopped.

'Expensive,' he finished for her. 'Look, that's not an issue.'

Another beat of silence. 'No, OK.'

Keelan could almost feel the mental backstep she took as she considered what he'd just revealed. Well, it was pointless to pretend that he struggled for money. The income from his investments competed, to a healthy extent, with his salary as a hospital-based paediatrician, and he'd benefited from an inheritance as well. She'd see all the evidence of his established lifestyle soon enough.

'I'll keep you as long as I feel it's in the twins' best interests,' he said. 'You're right. That'll probably be around four months, from a medical perspective.' In other areas, it was more complex, but he didn't want to thrash this through with her now, when they'd only just met. She might not last a week, if they weren't happy with each other. 'Do you need to know? Do you have a future commitment elsewhere?'

'No, no commitments. Just wondering.'

'Whether it's worth unpacking the books?'

'Something like that.'

A silence fell, slightly awkward. He guessed she was sorting and arranging her first impressions, the way he was, and the way she might, or might not, sort and arrange this forty-kilogram load of books in her new room.

On the whole, he'd had no surprises so far, either

pleasant or otherwise—unless you counted that smile, which was dazzling. Great for Tavie and Tam, when they got to the smiling stage. Or Tavie, anyway. He wasn't letting himself count on little Tam yet.

His gut whipped like a snake suddenly, and his eyes stung. He hadn't wanted these babies in his life, and now, already, he didn't want to lose them. He didn't want to be defeated on this.

If he was going to step in, do the right thing, the thing no one else was prepared or equipped to do—even though everyone agreed that the babies must be kept within the Hunter clan—he absolutely did not want to fail in any part of it.

This, at heart, was why he'd chosen an experienced neonatal nurse as their initial carer, instead of a nanny with a mere first-aid certificate. The babies had to live, and they had to thrive. That was all he needed from Jessica Russell. Her competence, her diligence, her professional care. For around four months.

'Can I take you up to the hospital as soon as you've unpacked?' he said.

'Make that unpacked and had a shower, and you have a deal,' she answered at once.

'I'm sorry. Maybe you need to sleep as well.'

'If I let myself do that, I probably wouldn't wake again for the full eight hours, and then I wouldn't sleep tonight.'

'Right.' He had a fleeting image of her wandering around his house at one in the morning, and didn't like it.

'The shower will do. And I'll unpack later, on condition that you show me where the coffee is.'

She tried her smile on him again, but this time he

didn't respond. He'd got caught up in the implications contained in her mention of coffee.

The two of them would be sharing a fridge and a coffee-maker, living under the same roof.

His house was idiotically large for one adult. He'd inherited it from his grandfather seven years ago, when he'd been twenty-eight. He'd kept it and renovated it, but he'd been married back then, so there had been two people to make use of the space, with the vague prospect of children in the future. The marriage hadn't lasted, however, and Tanya had gone back to New Zealand after the divorce.

He loved the house too much to think of selling it, which meant that now there was plenty of room for an adoptive father, a pair of newborn twins and their nurse. He felt uncomfortable about it all the same. Babies weren't good at boundaries. Some adults weren't either.

'Of course,' he told Jessica quickly. 'I'll give you a tour of the kitchen. I don't eat at home very much, so we shouldn't get in each other's way there.'

'I'll certainly try not to get in yours!'

'Put whatever you want in the fridge and pantry. You have your own bathroom and sitting room. Anyway, you'll see it soon enough.'

They cleared the airport a few minutes later, drove up Southern Cross Drive past bevies of Sunday golfers enjoying the spring sunshine, then swooped down into the traffic tunnels that now ran beneath the city and the harbour. There weren't many cars about, and they turned into his driveway in the North Shore suburb of Cremorne within fifteen minutes of leaving the airport.

They hadn't talked at all during the journey, because Ms Russell had thoughtfully closed her eyes and pretended to be asleep. Keelan appreciated the gesture.

When she shifted in the passenger seat, arching her spine, getting herself comfortable, his skin prickled and stood on end, like that of a tomcat confronting a back-yard rival. She seemed to impinge on his space somehow, and he didn't like it.

He brought her luggage upstairs for her. Since she followed in his wake, he couldn't see from her face and manner what she thought of the house. She'd hardly be able to complain, however. It was a prime piece of real estate, with harbour views, privacy, a large garden and spacious interior.

He'd had the place professionally decorated in a clean, warm yet unfussy style—lots of pale yellow, creamy white and sage green, with accents here and there in rust and teal. There were leather couches, botanical prints, the odd well-placed antique or original painting that he'd acquired from the family. It felt like home to him.

'There's a living room, dining room, study, breakfast room and kitchen downstairs,' he told her, keeping it clipped and brief. 'A terrace opens off the breakfast room and leads into the garden. Oh, and there's a powder room and laundry, too.'

'I'll need the laundry, I'm sure, as soon as Tavie comes home!'

'Up here, there's my master suite, and everything else is essentially yours. Babies' room here, next to your bedroom.'

They both stood in the doorway and looked at it, Ms Russell poised just in front of the arm he rested against the doorframe.

'Looks as if you have some shopping still to do,' she said.

The room contained a couch, a rocking chair and a chest of drawers, and there was still plenty of space, but

he hadn't had a chance to fill it yet. In a spirit of superstition that he privately mocked in himself but couldn't
shake, he wouldn't buy Tam a cot until after his heart
surgery. Well after it.

'I'll get you to buy what we need,' he answered. 'I've
made a list. But if there's anything I've forgotten, you
have *carte blanche*. Clothes, toys. I've noted all the obvious stuff, I think.'

'Do you want to use disposables or cloth?'

'Your choice.'

'Both, probably. Cloth is better for preventing rashes.
Disposables are easier to change when they're still all
wired and tubed.'

'I wish there was a connecting door between your
room and this one. I thought about getting one put in,
but there just hasn't been time.'

'Of course there hasn't,' she murmured. 'Can't imagine…'

He moved on down the corridor, seeking to escape her
empathy. 'Next comes the bathroom, and then the room
you can use as a sitting room. It opens onto a balcony,
and there's a TV. Towels, sheets… I have a part-time
cleaner…housekeeper, really…and she's set everything
up for you. I can increase her hours once Tavie comes
home, if you need extra help.'

'Thanks,' Jessie said.

She stood in the middle of her new bedroom, feeling
a little awkward, while Dr Hunter put down her embarrassing suitcases. She glimpsed his palms, and they
looked reddened and creased by the inadequate, scruffy
handles. Really, next time she took off to some distant
corner of the globe, she needed to invest in new luggage.

'Let me get you that coffee while you have your

shower,' he said. 'Come down to the kitchen when you're ready.'

She nodded. 'I won't be long.'

'No, take your time. I have a couple of calls to make.'

About her, possibly. To announce that she'd safely arrived, thus keeping the twin project on track.

She had the impression, after the flurry of phone calls and e-mails that had passed between the two of them, and between herself and the nursing agency, that the twins were a family obligation which had been delegated to him, and that he would have to report on any developments to certain relatives.

Sad.

Difficult.

Not surprising, though, maybe.

The nursing agency had told Jessie something about Keelan Hunter's very well-established family background, and on first impression he fitted it to a T. With his impressive height went an instinctive confidence and arrogance of bearing. With his brown eyes—not a dark brown, but intense, all the same—went a sharpness of perception that came from looking at the world from a more exalted perspective than most people enjoyed.

And with his strong body, honed from a childhood spent rowing and playing rugby at some top-flight Sydney private boys' school, went expensive casual clothes and a conservative haircut that should have looked anything but sexy.

Hang on.

Sexy?

Well, yes.

This was a dispassionate observation, not a declaration of interest, though, she told herself hastily. He had a well-shaped head and a smooth, tanned neck, and the way his dark hair was cut definitely…surprisingly…qualified as sexy. She'd never be interested in a man like Keelan Hunter on that level, however.

She wasn't that much of a fool, and she knew how to learn from past mistakes. She knew exactly what chasms of difference in outlook and history would yawn between them, and he'd been formal and cool enough to make his own desire for distance quite clear. She could protect herself with the same kind of shield.

In the shower, she felt a rush of almost painful pleasure at being back in Australia. All the little things, the tiny, familiar details told her, You're safe. This *is* home. The sound of the Sunday morning lawnmowers over the distant hum of traffic, the spring scents in the air—eucalyptus and frangipani—the way the taps worked and the fragrance of a familiar brand of soap.

She found clean clothes to dress in—a knee-length summer blue skirt and matching short-sleeved, figure-hugging top that she hadn't worn for two years—pulled a comb through her knotted hair and blasted it with a hairdryer until the bits that framed her face were dry. Then she pulled it up and back into a ponytail, slipped on some flat-heeled black leather sandals and followed that fabulous smell of coffee that wafted up the stairs.

'Much better now!'

Keelan turned. 'Yes, I can see that.' His tone dampened the comment down to the level of understatement, and he managed to hide the fact that he hadn't realised until she'd spoken that she'd arrived in the kitchen. The espresso pot still hissed on the stove and had masked the sound of her shoes on the hardwood floor of the hall.

She flashed her grin at him, and he grinned reluctantly back, then turned to pour the coffee into the two blue and white mugs he'd set on the blue-black granite bench-top in an attempt to hide the discomfort he still couldn't shake.

She was actually very pretty. He hadn't noticed it at the airport, or while showing her to her room. Now the realisation didn't please him. His ex-stepmother, Louise, had been his father's secretary. He didn't trust the illusions generated when a man and his female employee spent too much time in each other's company.

With Ms Russell's hair straight and damp and pulled back from her face, he could see—reluctantly—what lovely bone structure she had. Beautiful skin, too, despite the freckles. The shower had left her face clean and rosy, framed by the shiny silk of hair whose escaping strands contained a dozen different shades of copper and mink and gold.

And her figure was a knock-out, now that the disguising contours of the loose top and long skirt had gone. She had long legs, a rounded and very feminine backside, a long, slender torso and breasts that would comfortably fill a man's hands. Without being too tight or showing very much skin at all, her top and skirt advertised these assets quite plainly. They advertised the grace in her movements, too.

The blue of the new outfit was reflected in her eyes and reminded him again of sunlight on the sea, and he felt as if someone had flung open a window on a breezy day and let in the smell of salt water and the sound of gulls. His breath caught for a moment, and he shoved aside a surge of sensual awareness that he didn't remotely want.

'Milk?' he said.

'Yes, please, a big slurp of it, and please don't tell me

it's that UHT stuff!' Her frankness should have been awkward, lacking in class, but somehow it wasn't.

'No, it's fresh,' he answered.

She was fresh.

'And look,' he went on quickly. 'I'll leave cash in the top drawer, here, for grocery shopping. Buy anything you want, a different brand of coffee. As I said, I eat on the run mostly, but that needn't stop you from cooking, or filling the freezer with microwave dinners, whatever.'

'Thanks.' Another smile. 'I expect Tavie and Tam will limit me to the microwave option.'

'Hmm. I'll leave the menus for the best local take-away places in the drawer as well, shall I?'

They sat in the breakfast room and he offered her a section of the Sunday newspaper, as well as some sweet biscuits he'd found to go with the coffee. She accepted both, which meant they could eat and drink and read and not have to talk to each other. A sense of peace descended over the room and over his spirits, and though he knew it would be temporary, it lightened his outlook a little.

Jessica Russell seemed to be the kind of woman who didn't need to chat constantly, thank goodness. Maybe there was a chance they'd eventually be comfortable with each other after all.

When he looked at his watch, on reaching the paper's sports section, he discovered they'd been sitting here for nearly half an hour. Ms Russell's eyes looked glazed, as if she could easily have slept despite the coffee.

Where were his wits this morning? He'd intended to be at the hospital by now.

'We should go,' he said, standing up with the effort of a much older man as he felt the weight of his new circumstances crush down on him again.

CHAPTER TWO

'THE babies have unusual names,' Jessie said. 'Did you pick them, Dr Hunter? Or...'

She trailed off. Having intended her comment as small talk, she found she'd quickly trespassed into difficult territory. This man had lost his half-sister less than two weeks ago. Jessie couldn't pretend that Brooke Hunter had never existed, but she didn't want to cause her new employer any unnecessary pain.

He frowned, and as they approached the automatic glass doors that led into the main building at North Sydney Hospital, she could see that his reflection showed tense shoulders and a tight mouth.

'Brooke picked them,' he said, his tone clipped and short. There was a stiff silence, and for a moment Jessie thought he wasn't going to say anything more, but then he added in a different voice, much more slowly, 'She was sitting in a café, poring over a baby name book when the full-on haemorrhaging began, and those were the names we found on a sheet of paper folded inside the book. If she was still here, I'd have thought they were...I don't know...too odd and too frivolous, or something.'

'You think so?' Jessie murmured.

'I've been—' He broke off, and muttered something that she didn't catch. 'Hell, pretty critical of my sister, over the years. But as things are, the names seem important somehow. A gift from her. I like them now. I'd never think of changing them.'

'Mmm,' she said, ambushed by a degree of emotion she hadn't been prepared for.

She'd learned a lot about Keelan Hunter in the space of that short, palpably reluctant speech. He'd loved his half-sister, but he hadn't been close to her and held regrets about it now. And he cared a lot more about the twins than he knew. More, probably, than he wanted to care, especially given Tam's fragile state.

It was good to get more of a sense of this man and what made him tick, but that could be dangerous as well. Sometimes, in this sort of situation, you could get way too understanding, and way too involved.

The hospital swallowed them up and engulfed her in warring impressions of familiarity and newness. She'd been in this type of large metropolitan teaching hospital many times before. She'd crossed similar sprawling parking areas, signposted for visitors or reserved for staff.

She'd seen sunsets and sunrises reflected off similar tiered rows of windows in the multi-storey main building, and had imagined Nightingale-like ghosts flitting around similar original colonial buildings. These buildings still existed at many older Australian hospitals, now typically used for things like clinics and support groups. She'd also become lost in a similar maze of extensions and connecting walkways in the past.

Every hospital smelled different, however, and no two hospitals were set out the same way. Dr Hunter led the way to a lift and pressed the button for level seven, which would be easy enough to remember when she came here on her own. He'd already given her the use of his second car, a late-model Japanese sedan, and she had its keys and the keys to his house in her bag. She got the impression he didn't want to have to drive her around, beyond this first trip to see the babies, and that was fair enough.

'Have you had a report on them this morning?' she asked, thinking he might have phoned the unit before picking her up at the airport.

'I was called out to another patient during the night, and spent some time with them after that,' he said. 'Pretty quiet, at that hour. Tam's on a diuretic and prostaglandins, and that treatment is managing his heart condition for the moment. He's being monitored for NEC and IVH. So far so good. I don't think we're out of the woods on those yet, though.'

'Particularly the gut problems.'

Necrotising enterocolitis, in other words. NEC was a jaunty little abbreviation, or you could refer vaguely to 'gut problems' as Jessie just had, but there was nothing fun about the irreversible death of sections of a preemie's bowel.

Dr Hunter, however, focused on what she hadn't talked about—the good news on intraventricular haemorrhage.

'Yes,' he said. 'Statistically, if Tam was going to have a brain bleed it should have happened by now, and even over the past few years they've got better at preventing those. Here we are. Let's take a look at them. I didn't bring the camera today, but I took some pictures a few days ago, and I'm hoping you'll use it sometimes. Louise—Brooke's mother—doesn't want to see photos yet but I hope she may be ready for that in time.'

'Just tell me how the camera works, and of course I'll take some.'

'It's easy. Point and click variety. I'm not expecting artistic shots, and mine certainly haven't been.'

He greeted a couple of nurses on his way in, and Jessie saw that here was another area in which relationships and feelings hadn't quite settled, yet, into their appropriate slots. Keelan Hunter wasn't fully a doctor in this unit, and not exactly a parent either. No one knew quite what he was, at this stage, least of all himself.

One nurse had a vial of blood in her hand, and another was racing for the phone, so Jessie wasn't introduced to anyone yet. The nurses' greetings were polite and respectful—warm even—yet remained formal. No one used his first name.

Something about his bearing didn't invite that, perhaps. He stood out here, taller than the nurses, more upright and contained than a couple of the harried-looking junior doctors moving about the unit. His stride seemed longer than theirs, and his shoulders squarer and stronger.

It was a big place. With techniques in keeping preterm infants alive and healthy improving all the time, NICUs in most major hospitals were a growth area—crowded, like this one was, expensive to maintain, busy and bright and noisy, with different staff constantly coming and going, despite the best efforts of the dedicated doctors, nurses and technicians to give their fragile charges the peace and quiet they really needed.

The two babies weren't together. Even though some studies had shown that twins did better when placed in the same incubator, there were arguments against this practice. In Tavie's and Tam's case, too, the little girl's comparative health and strength classed her as a level one. Tam was with the sickest babies in the unit, at the opposite end—level three.

They reached Tam first. He lay in an incubator, which counted as a 'graduation' of sorts. He would have started out in a radiant warmer, which gave better access to staff when a baby was very unstable and needed constant treatments and tests. Even now, he had equipment and monitors all around him.

He had a cardiorespiratory monitor attached to sensors on his chest and limbs, with alarms set to signal an unsafe change in blood pressure, heart rate, temperature or respiration. He had a pulse oximeter clipped to his foot, measuring the level of oxygen saturation in his blood by shining a light through his skin.

Amazing machine, Jessie always thought. By detecting the fine shadings of colour between red oxygenated blood and blue de-oxygenated blood, the machine could provide an accurate measurement of the blood oxygen level, expressed as a percentage. You wanted to see that percentage up in the high nineties, which Tam's was.

Poor little guy. Little sweetheart.

'Here he is,' Dr Hunter said, his voice hardly more than a growl. He didn't touch the top of the incubator. Some babies found even this stressful, and their nurses had to learn to avoid casually placing charts or pencils there, while going about their work.

Or was her new employer's lack of contact with Tam more a statement about his own distance than his awareness of the baby's needs?

'Hi, Tam,' Jessie whispered.

She was accustomed to babies like this. Most people weren't. Their dry, reddish skin, their spindly limbs, the dark vestiges of downy hair on their shoulders and backs as well as their hat-covered heads, the sheer *smallness* of them. The tip of an adult finger would fill Tam's whole fist when he grasped at it.

'He is jaundiced, isn't he, poor love,' she added.

With the yellow tinge of jaundice on his skin and the blue of the 'bili' lights above him, he looked as if he'd been stained with some strange dye, and his little nappy, a startling white in contrast, was hardly bigger than a folded envelope.

It would get weighed every time he was changed, as a method of calculating his output of urine. You wanted the right amount of fluid going in, and the right amount coming out, and with preemies you measured it all obsessively.

'Have you been able to hold him yet?' she asked.

'No, not yet,' Dr Hunter said. 'Hospital policy is to wait until he hits the kilogram mark.'

Jessie wasn't surprised, although the arbitrary nature of the cut-off point bothered her. Some babies responded very well to being held at nine hundred grams. Others couldn't take it at twelve hundred. Weight was only one way to measure a baby's fitness for certain things. In this case, though...

Tam was still being fed via total parenteral nutrition—intravenous feeding, mainly through a line into his navel. On the plus side, this avoided the digestive problems that could occur if a delicate preemie wasn't yet ready to have its little stomach filled. The down side was that it increased the risk of infection via the entry sites of the different lines, and made a preemie even more difficult to hold—so much equipment in the way.

And a baby like this would tire very easily, too, even through something as simple as being lifted from his incubator into someone's waiting arms. In Tam's case, the no-holding-yet policy was probably the right approach.

'I touch him, though, when he can handle it,' Dr Hunter added. He looked at the baby with narrowed eyes, an expert's judgement and a powerful aura of human will. If he could have pushed a two-ton rock up a hill to increase Tam's chance of survival, he would have done it,

Jessie suspected, whether he cared to call this 'love' or not.

Again, she found herself understanding Keelan Hunter's feelings more than she wanted to.

'Is he showing a lot of stress?' She kept her voice low.

Research on the youngest preemies in recent years showed that they could get dangerously stressed through over-stimulation. Their nervous systems were too fragile and immature. They couldn't listen and look at the same time without tiring themselves. When they were being touched, they didn't want to be talked to. NICU nurses and caring parents learned to read the baby's state.

'He has a couple of great nurses, who try to minimise it as much as possible,' Dr Hunter said. 'They're aware of the situation and looking forward to having you on board. Here's Stephanie now. I'll introduce you.'

He stepped away, and only then did Jessie realise how close the two of them had been standing. A draught of cool air eddied around her bare arm, contrasting with the body heat he'd given off. Thinking back, she wondered if she'd been the one to move closer, without realising it, drawn by some indefinable quality to him that she didn't have a name for yet. The force of will she'd just seen in him, perhaps.

He wasn't as urbane and as civilised as she'd somehow expected, with his classy background. He wasn't as tame or as bland. There was something almost…what…primitive about him. Primitive? That couldn't be the word. Something, though, that left her feeling strangely edgy and stirred up inside.

Just tired, probably.

'Stephanie, here's Jessica Russell, to see the babies,' he said. 'She's just off the plane this morning, so it's only a quick visit today.'

'Welcome to our unit, Jessica,' said the neat, athletic-looking woman. Vincent. Stephanie Vincent. She had some threads of grey in her dark hair and a twinkling, brown-eyed smile.

'Call me Jessie,' she answered at once, realising that she hadn't mentioned the usual shortening of her name to Dr Hunter.

It seemed fairly obvious that he wanted to maintain a more formal relationship. Wise, probably. She wasn't sure if it would be possible in the long run, however, when they'd be caring for two babies together.

'He's looking good, isn't he?' the NICU nurse said. 'Kidneys keeping up, nice steady colour. He's not awake very much. That heart's tiring him out.'

Efficiently, she noted Tam's hourly observations on a chart, checked that the fluid in his lines was flowing as it should, and made some notes about his state. Jessie watched her, aware of the baby's reluctant yet determined adoptive father still standing beside her, as rigid and solid as a tree trunk.

A warm tree trunk. Somehow, they'd moved closer to each other again, and she could feel his heat.

'Well, let's go and see Tavie,' he said after a moment, before she was quite ready to move on. She took a last look at the little boy, wishing she was officially his nurse, wondering if she should let herself feel anything like his mother.

Tam lay on his back, with his head to the side and his eyes closed. His little face looked so still, but then he twitched and grimaced and stiffened his limbs, and she knew he couldn't be very comfortable. Jessie had seen parents weeping in frustration at having to watch their babies like this, and had sometimes cried herself.

You just wanted to hold them against you, take out all

those awful lines, pull the sensors away. It was so hard to accept that the lines and sensors were ultimately keeping the baby alive.

A few minutes later, on the other side of the unit, Tavie looked a lot better, but she was still tiny—the smallest of the level one babies.

'Wednesday, we think, for her discharge, if you're comfortable with that,' Dr Hunter said to Jessie. 'She'll be done with the bili lights by then.'

'How's her weight?' she asked.

'Oh, big milestone when I weighed her this morning,' put in her nurse, Barb McDaniel, who hovered nearby. She looked to be in her late forties, with rounded hips, hair tinted a pretty mid-brown shade and that aura of experience and competence that no one could fake. 'She's hit her birthweight, 1220 grams.'

'Fantastic,' Dr Hunter said. 'That's great.'

And he actually smiled.

He blinked at the same time, twice, as if his honey-brown eyes felt gritty, but his mouth curved and his straight white teeth rested for a moment against his full lower lip, and Barb shot him a curious glance that softened into approval. Clearly, she'd been concerned about how he was handling all this, how involved he was, whether he'd eventually crack.

'Could one of us hold her?' Jessie asked.

'Do you have time, Dr Hunter?' Barb turned to him, tentative and respectful.

But he deferred at once to Jessie. 'Best if you do it, I think. The two of you need to get used to each other as soon as you can.'

'I'd love to,' she answered, and it came out sounding more like a rebuke at her employer's distance than she'd meant it to.

If he noticed, he didn't comment, and his expression didn't change. Jessie tried to forget about him standing there, and focused on the baby instead.

Funny.

In the past, so many times, she'd been the one carefully passing the tiny, swaddled bundle to an eager, tearful parent for that first precious hug. She'd been the one to make sure that feed lines and medication lines and oxygen lines and monitor lines were still firmly taped in place, yet as much out of the way as possible.

She'd been the one to give murmured instructions. Watch for this. Be careful of that. And then she'd been the one to stand back and get choked up herself at the softening in a mother's face, the total focus, the gentle hand movements.

Now I'm on the opposite side of the fence, her thoughts ran, skittish and woolly from fatigue, and from her awareness of Keelan Hunter keeping his distance—and judging this first moment of interaction, probably, behind the mask of his classically handsome face. But I'm not her mother… She's a little darling… How is this going to feel?

Warmth. That was the first sensation.

Tavie was a nugget of feather-light warmth in her arms, like a kitten asleep on her chest. She had that cheesy, salty-sweet newborn smell, and breath so light that Jessie couldn't even feel it. She had her nasal cannula in place, though, giving her oxygen, and her breathing alarm wasn't going off, so she definitely was breathing, despite the lack of evidence.

And then, as Jessie settled into complete stillness, she felt the evidence after all—the tiny, rhythmic movement of Tavie's chest expanding and contracting against her own, so faint that Jessie had to stop breathing herself in order to feel it.

She's going to live, the thoughts ran once more. Whatever it takes, whatever I have to do for her. She's going to thrive, and get strong and smiley and bright and curious, and Keelan Hunter will love her more than he can imagine. Way more than he wants to.

She didn't talk out loud, just let Tavie get used to the feeling of being held. The baby was in a drowsy state, but her little hand moved and tightened in its primitive grasp reflex, and Barb McDaniel warned, 'Watch her oxygen tube, she's going to grab it any minute.'

'Sorry, baby,' Jessie murmured, and carefully lifted it over the baby's head to her other shoulder.

'Might leave the two of you for a few minutes,' Barb said.

'I have a phone call to make,' Dr Hunter came in at once.

He would, wouldn't he? He'd have a repertoire of easy outs, ready for the times when he didn't want to get too close. Jessie thought she might be glad of this fact, too.

'I'll hear if her breathing alarm goes off, but it shouldn't,' Barb continued. 'She's usually pretty good when she's being held.'

'You've been holding her?' Jessie asked. Dr Hunter had already moved towards the door.

'Since last week. Hard to fit it into the routine some days. With these little ones who don't seem to have a mum or dad, I never know if we're doing it for the baby or for us.'

'Both,' Jessie said.

She knew which babies the other nurse was talking about. A disproportionate percentage of premature and low birth-weight babies were born to very young or drug-addicted mothers, who often had trouble bonding with such tiny, fragile infants. A distracted, nervous or uncomfortable visit once every couple of weeks didn't impress NICU nurses, who did their best to compensate.

Apparently the NICU nurses here had judged Dr Hunter in the same way, and found him wanting. For some reason, Jessie felt a strong need to leap to his defence, even though she'd seen his barriers and his boundaries for herself.

'Can you imagine how it must be to suddenly find yourself in his position, though?' she said, her throat suddenly tight. 'I think a lot of people would hold back.'

'Hang on,' Barb said. 'No, I didn't mean him. He's been in here as much as he can, from the day they were born, even when that poor, silly mum of theirs was still in the picture. No, I meant... Even with him around—I wish he was married!—they still don't have a mother.'

'They have me.'

The nurse shot her a quizzical sidelong glance. 'Planning to stick around? How long?'

'As long as he pays me,' Jessie answered, because she had to remember that this was a job, probably lasting around four months, not a labour of love with an accidental salary conveniently attached. She'd blurred that boundary once before, and still bore the emotional scars.

'So there you go,' Barb said gently, and Jessie knew she was right.

It would be a fine line to tread.

Was Ms Russell asleep?

When Keelan returned from phoning a colleague about one of his patients in the paediatric unit upstairs, she still had the baby snuggled against her chest. Tavie's eyes were closed, and so were Ms Russell's. He watched them for a moment, bathed once more in the out-of-body sensation that had become frighteningly common since Brooke's death.

Was this really happening?

Or had he been thrown back in time to the rotations he'd done in various neonatal units during his training? In what sense was that tiny baby *his*? And what bond should he hope for between the twins and their new nurse?

She'd opened her eyes. The nurse, not Tavie. She'd caught him studying her. Had no doubt seen his narrowed eyes and tight mouth.

'Just do your utmost to make her thrive,' he said abruptly. Almost angrily. 'That's all I want. If you need to leave, to move on, give me fair warning. I have no choice but to depend on you. Don't leave me in the lurch.'

She shook her head slowly, her chin raised. She had encountered angry doctors before, and there was a strength to her, radiating like fire. She wasn't the type to be easily cowed. 'Not planning to,' she said. 'I want them to thrive, too. As much as you do.'

Their eyes met, held as if mesmerised, and exchanged a silent promise.

We have two human lives in our hands. We'll work for them, and we'll love them, no matter how hard it is and how much it might hurt, because that's what they need and what they deserve.

'Barb?' he said, finding it hard to break the moment of contact and look away. His throat had constricted, and his whole body seemed flooded with heat.

The older nurse looked up from another patient's chart. These level one 'growers and feeders' didn't need one-to-one care, and she had two more babies to look after today. 'Ready to put her back?' she said.

'Enough for today. Ms Russell—'

'Please, call me Jessie,' his new employee cut in, sounding as if the issue was important.

'Jessie,' he corrected obediently. OK, yes, he had come to his senses about it now. Artificial boundaries wouldn't mean much, if the real ones weren't in place. How hard would it be to keep those? He finished his sentence. 'Jessie needs to get some rest.'

'Bub's looking pretty tired too, aren't you, sweetheart?' Barb cooed softly, and started shifting lines and moving the drip stand so she could lift Tavie back into her incubator.

They took another quick look at Tam on their way out. Oxygen saturation at ninety-four per cent. Heart rate at 150. No mottling, pallor or cynosis in his skin. Keelan searched for something cheery and upbeat to say—about the baby, his appearance, his stats—but a kind of weariness descended over him and he just couldn't do it. Jessica—Jessie—didn't say anything either.

On their way home, he realised that he was hungry, and that he should offer her a chance at lunch, too. It was already noon. When he asked, she admitted she'd been thinking about a meal. He knew of a deli-cum-sandwich shop nearby, open on Sundays, and found a parking place right in front of it.

'We'll pick up some cheese and meat, and some tubs of salad,' he said. 'Want to choose a couple?'

She picked out a Greek salad, and something with artichoke and avocado in it, and he chose a couple more salads, and bought two cottage loaves as well. She might get hungry in the night. She looked like the sort of woman who had an energetic appetite. Her slender arms and legs had a strength to them, despite their grace, which showed she kept herself fit.

He should have thought to stock his kitchen a little better, in anticipation of her needs. Tethered to the house by Tavie as soon as the baby came home—three days from now, if everything continued as they hoped—and committed to visiting Tam whenever she could, she wouldn't have much opportunity for shopping.

He set the various offerings out on the kitchen bench and they served themselves directly from the plastic tubs, then ate together, once again, in his breakfast room. He made himself ask her what she'd thought of the unit at North Sydney, and whether discharge for Tavie on Wednesday seemed too soon.

'I'd be nervous about it,' she answered, 'if I was on staff there, and handing her over to a mum with no medical training. She'll still be under three pounds, and not out of the woods for various complications. But as long as we have the oxygen and breathing alarm here, and if she has no setbacks between now and Wednesday, I think it's a good idea. I'll be able to establish a routine, give her some peace and quiet.'

'That's what I thought, and one of the reasons I opted for someone with your level of skill and training.'

The other reason was Tam.

He didn't want to ask her specifically what she'd thought about Tam. She had too much experience. She would have seen too many babies like him who hadn't made it.

Keelan didn't linger over the meal.

'I'm going sailing with my cousin this afternoon,' he told her. 'Won't be back until fairly late, probably. As I've said, make yourself at home, sit in the garden, use the car, whatever you want. There's a street directory in it, so you can't get lost if you go out.'

'Right now, I'm contemplating the chance that I might get lost between here and my bedroom,' she answered, and that dazzle appeared on her face, that gorgeous smile, radiating out from her sleepy eyes.

'If I come home and find you asleep on the couch, I'll put a blanket over you,' he said. It sounded too personal, almost flirtatious, and Keelan felt his jaw tighten.

She looked like a child about to fall asleep in her plate, her body crumpled and soft, her elbow propped on the table and her hand cradling one pink cheek. Tendrils of slippery clean hair had begun to escape from her ponytail at the front, like a halo in the midday light. She probably even smelled sleepy—warm and sweetly scented from her shower a couple of hours ago.

Keelan felt an idiotic urge to scoop her in his arms, deposit her on the nearest bed and spend a long time tucking her in.

Crushing it, he stood up. She couldn't possibly be as vulnerable as she looked right now. Better remember that. Keep the boundaries in place. An anchorless wanderer like Jessica Russell couldn't possibly be his type, even if *he* was the type who took his staff to bed whenever the opportunity arose.

And he wasn't.

He took his plate to the kitchen and put it in the dishwasher, then changed into his sailing clothes and got out of the house as quickly as he could.

Jessie heroically managed to stay awake until four.

She cleared up the lunch supplies. She phoned her mother in Brisbane and her father in Perth, and got a hearty 'Oh, you're back!' from both of them, followed by a token enquiry about her well-being and a litany of detail on their own news.

In both houses, there was a background of noise from her half-siblings. Mum had eight-year-old Ryan and six-year-old Lucy, while Dad's new three were even younger, just five, three and six months.

Her parents had been seventeen and nineteen, respectively, at the time of her own birth thirty-two years ago. She'd had a messy upbringing, getting handed over to anyone who'd been willing to babysit, encouraged to be as independent as possible from an early age. By eight, she'd had her own key and had come home from school alone to perform a required list of chores—breakfast dishes, laundry, vacuuming.

And she'd apparently been a difficult child—colicky as a baby, stubborn and grumpy as a toddler, fat and giggly in primary school, lacking in confidence in her teens.

Mum and Dad both seemed to be enjoying marriage and parenthood a lot more this time around. When incidents involving spills and fights disrupted both calls, she wasn't sorry to put down the phone.

She went for an exploring walk around the steep, crooked streets that led down to the harbour at Cremorne Point. Back at the house, she drank a glass of iced water while sitting in a jarrah-wood garden chair reading one of Keelan Hunter's suspense thrillers.

She desperately wanted to lie down on that sun-warmed stretch of lush green grass beyond the shady reach of the Moreton Bay fig, but didn't let herself, and when her eyes closed over her book and the sloping back of the garden chair began to feel as soft and comfortable as a down-stuffed pillow, she knew she had to go inside.

She would probably be keeping erratic hours in the

coming months, in any case. Best get her rest when she could.

When she awoke again, after hours of deep sleep, the house was dark and silent, and the clock radio beside her new bed read 11:05 p.m. She knew it was pointless to try and get back to sleep, and she felt starving. Was Dr Hunter asleep, or still out? Dressing quietly to be on the safe side, she crept past his room and, through the partially open door, saw his long bulk in a king-size bed.

She kept going, a little rocked by the reality of sleeping just metres away from a near-stranger—her employer, too. Did he have a girlfriend? She hadn't seen any obvious evidence of anything serious and long term. A bathroom cabinet full of make-up, for example, or pantyhose hung up to dry. What would happen if he brought a woman home? How discreet would they be, with Jessie in the house?

Still, a girlfriend would be better than no girlfriend. Safer, somehow.

As she tiptoed down the stairs, she heard him move and mutter something in his sleep that sounded like 'fluids'.

In the kitchen, she made herself a substantial snack of cheese and tomato on toasted cottage loaf, as well as tea, then considered the seven remaining hours until dawn. There was one place where other people would be awake at this time of night. The hospital. More specifically, the NICU.

She couldn't think of any good reason not to go up there again. There was a slight chance that the noise of the car reversing up the driveway might awaken Dr Hunter, but he was a doctor after all, accustomed to grabbing onto sleep and keeping it.

Different staff were rostered in the unit at this hour,

and she received some questioning looks on her arrival, but was able to present her passport for identification and they found her name in Tam's notes.

'Too jet-lagged to sleep. I'm just going to sit with him,' she told Helen Barry. 'Get to know him.'

'Touch him?' Helen yawned behind her fist, and apologised. 'Sorry, my kids didn't let me sleep today. You might even be able to hold him.'

'But Dr Hunter says hospital policy means I can't do that till he hits a thousand grams.'

Helen looked at her for a moment, her brown eyes steady.

'Yeah, but the really serious hospital policy enforcers aren't around at this hour, are they?' she said very softly.

'Are you including Dr Hunter himself in that statement?' Jessie couldn't help asking. She didn't want to defy her employer's wishes. She also wondered, as she had wondered that morning, how he was viewed here at North Sydney.

'Dr Hunter's good,' the other nurse answered cautiously. 'I don't know him that well. But I get the impression he judges each case on its merits, and that's what you need to do with preemies, isn't it? You can't tell by their stats which ones are going to do well and which aren't. This little guy…'

'Not telling us much yet?'

'See what you think. Have a look at him for a while, keep an eye on his sats and his heart, then we'll think about it,' Helen decided.

Jessie nodded and pulled a chair close to the incubator. In one corner of this part of the unit, a doctor and nurse worked over a very fragile newborn, creating more noise and requiring more light than she would have liked for Tam. Helen had draped a flannel sheet over the top of the incubator, but that didn't provide the baby with much of a shield.

His respirator did some of the work of breathing for him, but it was important to turn the settings down as low as possible to encourage him to get ready to breathe on his own. As she watched, he stirred, grimaced and twitched in his sleep, looking fussy and uncomfortable. His skin drained of colour and his saturation immediately dropped several points, while his heartbeat slowed.

Jessie took in a hiss of breath, waiting instinctively for the alarm, which should kick in if his heart got any slower. Helen heard the sound she'd made and looked at the monitors, but the figures hovered just within the right range.

The other baby's heart alarm went off and the activity from the doctor and nurse got even more frantic. What were they doing? Putting a central venous catheter into an uncooperative vein, by the looks of it, and administering urgent meds. Tam opened his eyes, flailed his arms and tried to cry, but the respirator tube down his throat wouldn't let him.

'Can we mask his incubator with something better?' Jessie asked Helen.

'Always seems it's the noise that bothers him, that's the problem. I've tried a thicker blanket, but he still does this whenever there's a crisis close by. Poor love.'

The other baby, a little girl named Corinne, with a pink teddy in her incubator, continued to give her staff a hard time. Her breathing alarm went off, but at least they had the central line taped in place now. The nurse hooked up a tiny bag of fluid and calibrated its flow rate carefully.

At one point, the doctor—undoubtedly a neonatal resident on call—flung the pink teddy on the floor with a hissing curse, and Tam's limbs went stiff and his eyes panicky. His levels on the monitor were bouncing around, and his own breathing alarm went off. Helen changed the settings on his respirator slightly and frowned at the blood-pressure reading.

She looked across at the resident and opened her mouth as if to summon him to look at Tam, but then she frowned, shook her head and said nothing.

Finally, the doctor left the girl baby alone, while the nurse quietly noted her hourly observations.

'OK, let's see what happens with him now...' Helen said, her voice more breath than sound.

They watched Tam and his monitors. Gradually, his limbs curled up and went still. The oxygen figure climbed back up and so did the heart. Jessie looked at his blood-pressure reading and agreed with Helen's silent, frowning assessment. It was a little higher than she would have liked. She wondered if there was any plan to put him on medication to lower it, as a way of lessening the work-load on the heart.

After half an hour of peace, she asked the other nurse, 'Could I put a hand in there?'

Helen nodded. 'Let's try it. We won't have you hold him tonight, though, after all the fuss.'

'No, it'd be too much, wouldn't it?' Jessie agreed.

She went to the nearest sink and washed and dried her hands carefully, then sat in front of the incubator and carefully reached her right hand in through one of the cuffed ports, making her movements calm and unhurried. Tam remained peacefully asleep.

She didn't touch or stroke him lightly, but cupped her hand around his curled up legs and tiny, padded bottom and kept it there firmly, the way the muscles of his mother's uterine wall should still be doing. She didn't chafe or massage, just held her hand quite still.

She knew how to do this, but it felt different with this baby, and she had an illogical, emotional wish that Dr Hunter could be here to share the moment. Looking at the monitors, she saw a nice, high oxygen saturation and a good heart rate, both of which stayed steady. His colour was far better now, too, an even-toned pink. His jaundice seemed less evident than it had been fifteen hours ago.

The baby liked what she was doing.

Jessie liked it, too.

She responded at once to the sensation of precious life held beneath her hand, and to the miracle of technology, which could chart those small fluctuations in a heart's power to beat and two lungs' power to breathe so that someone who cared could read this tiny baby's well-being the way a healthy baby's parents could read its cry or its smile.

Emotion overwhelmed her, more powerfully than it had done with Tavie earlier today. It might have been sensible to keep reminding herself that this one could still die, that she'd be protecting her own feelings by staying uninvolved, but she just couldn't do it.

She wanted life for Tam so badly—and health, happiness, a sense of belonging and love—that she had no choice but to invest her own heart.

CHAPTER THREE

JESSIE spent much of Monday and Tuesday shopping.

Dr Hunter had told her that she was free to spend whatever she thought necessary, and he'd set up accounts at two different baby shops and an upmarket department store. At first she was tentative about it, comparing prices, telling herself that the cheaper cot was almost as good as the gorgeous one that cost nearly twice as much.

But then he called her from North Sydney's paediatric unit, reaching her on the mobile phone he'd given her, and asked a few searching questions about where she was up to. He then told her categorically, 'If in doubt, go for the top of the line. Don't compromise. I don't care what you have to spend. Please, don't get the cheap cot. I—I really don't want that.'

Family money, she knew.

Something else, too, which she understood just as well—an irrational, unacknowledged fear that if they cut corners and bought the cheap cot for Tavie, Tam might not survive. Interesting that a man like Keelan Hunter should be emotional enough about these babies to submit to that sort of superstition, that sort of irrational bargaining with God. He was complex.

After their phone conversation, she went a bit giddy. She'd never shopped like this in her life. There were such gorgeous things for little girl babies! Stretchy little sleepsuits in pink and lemon and mauve, little tops and pants with lace edges at the cuffs and sleeves, appliquéd dresses and soft cloth bootees. Even the practical pur-

47

chases, like a change table, a baby bath and a nappy bin, were fun to make.

It just seemed a pity to Jessie, at times, that she was doing it all on her own. This was really a task for two people in love, who were thrilled to be parents.

The next day, Tavie left Barb McDaniel's care and came home, with her fixed oxygen tank, her portable oxygen tank, her tank regulator, CPAP cannula, pulse oximeter, nasogastric feed tube, infant weighing scale, apnoea and heart alarms. The hospital kept the baby's medical charts and notes, but Jessie had already set up a similar system to keep track of Tavie's progress, pick up any warning signs and provide an overview for Tavie's father whenever he wanted it.

On discharge, the tiny girl weighed a fraction over her birthweight, and although Dr Hunter had taken the day off, and they'd both tried to make the transition as smooth and unfussed as possible, it must have tired Tavie out. With jet-lag still mucking her body clock around, Jessie felt like a limp rag herself by the time Tavie was set up in her new nursery.

Dr Hunter had been shopping, too. A space heater for the baby's room and a thermometer to keep track of the air temperature. Enough pantry and refrigerator supplies, it seemed, to feed a large family for nearly a month.

'Because I realised you wouldn't get the opportunity,' he told Jessie stiffly, as they stood in the kitchen together, just before lunch. 'I'm sorry, I'm thinking some of this through as I go along.'

'It's fine. You didn't have a lot of time to make plans. Neither of us has.'

'Thanks for being flexible.'

'It's one of the things I'm good at.'

They smiled cautiously at each other, and their eyes

met and held just a little bit too long. Not for the first time. It had happened in the hospital on Sunday, too, and yesterday afternoon when the cot and change table had arrived, and they'd set them up in the baby nursery together.

Now Jessie looked quickly away. The spacious kitchen seemed too small suddenly, and she had to fight to get her perspective and her priorities back in place.

Tavie. Tam. Putting money aside. Making some decisions about her long-term future when she wasn't needed here any more. What was the best way for a woman to go in search of a home?

Tavie was asleep upstairs, and Jessie had a baby monitor clipped to the pocket of her skirt, feeding her a constant stream of little sounds—a high-pitched baby snuffle, birds outside the window, some rattly noises as Tavie kicked. She focused on the sounds instead of on Keelan Hunter's brown eyes.

'I'm going to bring you dinner every night, too,' he continued, after a pause in which he seemed to be listening to the baby monitor noises, too. 'Until we see how you're managing.'

'I thought you didn't eat at home, Dr Hunter,' she blurted out.

'I'm making an exception for a week or two. And I'm not saying I'll cook at home.' He grinned suddenly, unexpectedly, and again something shifted uncomfortably inside her. His smile was much more open and uncomplicated than it should have been. 'It'll come in plastic containers, still steaming,' he finished.

'Well…thanks.'

'Please, let's stick to first names, by the way. You suggested it the other day, and you were right. So it's Keelan, please. It's not that hard to say.'

'Keelan,' she echoed, and liked the feel of it in her mouth. 'You're probably right about the meals. I—' *Bipbipbipbipbip…*

'Heart alarm,' Keelan said, and bolted for the stairs, just as Tavie's breathing alarm began to sound as well. Jessie followed right behind him.

They didn't know what had happened. Something going on in her little stomach maybe. Keelan got to her first and touched her shoulder, and she began breathing again right away. Jessie switched off the alarms and watched the monitor. The heart rate bounced back up too high, and then the baby lost most of her stomach contents in a puddle on the sheet beside her head.

She seemed distressed the whole afternoon. They cleaned up the bed, changed a nappy and slowed the flow rate through the feed tube, so that her twenty mils went in over forty minutes instead of twenty. They checked her monitors and her meds obsessively—she was still on an infant antacid and a couple of other things—then they cleaned the bed again, because she'd lost another feed.

Which was ungrateful of her, because neither of the adults had found an opportunity for lunch.

Through all of this she cried, or slept an exhausted sleep during which she twitched and grimaced and forgot to breathe, setting off her breathing alarm three times.

'Let's try and kangaroo her on your chest,' Keelan finally decided. 'Maybe she'll keep her feed down better if she's more upright, and the body contact should soothe her. We're making classic first-day-home-from-the-hospital mistakes, I think, fussing over her and making her more distressed.'

'I think you're right.'

'Can you change into a top that buttons down the front?'

Jessie almost shot him a panicky look. OK, the accepted 'kangaroo' technique involved having carer and baby in skin-to-skin contact, but...

No, be reasonable, she told herself. As if he'll care. As if he'll even *notice*.

She nodded and went to her room, where she found one of the conservative, long-sleeved blouses she'd worn in Saudi Arabia. Lapping its roomy front panels across her breasts and stomach, she didn't bother with the buttons, since they'd have to be unfastened again anyway. Her pale blue bra was pretty and lacy but decent as far as such garments went. And her breasts weren't that exciting in their dimensions, although she'd had a few compliments in her time.

'Sit down, and I'll give her to you,' Keelan said. 'Ready?'

He unsnapped the fastenings on Tavie's tiny suit, managing her various tubes and sensor lines adeptly. Settling a little deeper into the rocking chair, Jessie parted her blouse and Keelan laid the baby against her chest. His fingers brushed her stomach, just below her breasts, but they didn't linger. In fact, he moved away a little too soon.

'Careful,' she blurted out, and hugged the baby too tightly.

Tavie squirmed for a moment, but she seemed to find the firm contact soothing. Jessie relaxed, loosened her hold a fraction, steadied her own breathing and felt Tavie's delicious warmth mingling with her own. Keelan tucked a cot-size quilt around them both, anchoring it in place between Jessie's back and the back of the chair.

'Comfortable?' he asked a moment later, watching them from several paces away now, his amber eyes narrowed beneath a frown.

'I could do with a pillow behind my back.'

He brought the one from her own bed and slid it in behind her, while she arched the base of her spine. She felt his hand come to rest on her quilt-covered shoulder for a moment, and then the wash of his breath against her bare neck, where the blouse was open and the quilt didn't reach. Her body tingled from head to toe and she felt that magnetism again, that strange, primal pull he'd begun to exert on her senses, beyond her power to control.

She closed her eyes, willing it away, fully aware of how disastrous it could be.

'She seems happier,' Keelan concluded. From the sound of his voice, he'd retreated as far as the doorway. 'I'm going to head up to the hospital in a minute, if that's all right. I have a four-year-old patient going in for heart surgery tomorrow, and Keith Bedford, his surgeon, wanted me to take a final look at him today.'

'That's fine,' Jessie said. She didn't want to mention that she was hungry. The sooner he left, the better.

She held Tavie on her chest for two hours after Keelan had gone, and it felt precious and right. Like this, it seemed as if she could almost feel the baby growing. Tavie's latest feed stayed down and neither of her alarms went off. She slept, and Jessie did, too, in a light doze that still had her able to respond to Tavie's movements.

She didn't open her eyes until she heard the rumbling hum of the garage door, just as the September light was fading from the sky.

Keelan came up the stairs a minute later and appeared as a shadowy figure in the doorway. 'How's it going?' he said softly. 'She looks peaceful.'

'She has been, the whole time,' Jessie whispered back, without moving. 'It's been…absolutely precious, really.

Just delightful.' A little bit scary, this sense of warm delight like a pool of liquid inside her. She'd never sat like this with a baby before, in a home rather than in a primitive clinic or a high-tech hospital unit.

Was it her fault that she'd failed to bond with her much younger half-siblings? she suddenly wondered. Could she have spent this sort of time with them as babies, if she'd pushed?

Thinking back, all she could remember was Dad's wife, Natalie, snatching her babies back after a scant minute in anyone else's arms, and hovering so suspiciously over any attempt to read to them or take them out to the back-yard sandpit that Jessie had soon given up.

Mum, meanwhile, had brought her second brood up on bottle feeds propped on pillows and long periods alone in their cots. 'Don't go in there, Jessie. I'll be furious if you wake him up when he's taken so long to settle.' And a couple of years later, 'Don't get him all excited like that, Jessie. He'll be unbearable after you've gone, and I'll never get him down for his nap.'

But perhaps she'd been too sensitive about it, and too easily put off. She could have tried harder.

'You must be starving,' Keelan said, breaking in on her self-critical train of thought.

'Um, yes, there is that,' she conceded, and he laughed.

He had a surprisingly attractive laugh, so much warmer and more open than she would have expected. Every time she heard it—which wasn't often enough—she felt as if she'd been let in on a delicious secret that he'd shared with no one else. It made her curious, in an illogical and too emotional way, about what other such secrets he might have.

'You should have got me to make you a cheese sandwich before I left,' he said.

'I was hardly going to do such a thing!'

He left a beat of silence before he answered, 'No, I suppose not.' Then he added, 'But I've got dinner downstairs now, so if we can get her back in her cot and hook up another feed...'

'Let me do the feed, and I'll check her nappy, too.'

'Do you want to pass her to me?'

'No, I can manage, but if you could check that her lines are in the right place...'

By shifting her own weight, Jessie tipped the rocking chair forward enough to stand easily, without jolting the baby. Keelan twitched various tubes and sensor lines out of the way.

Jessie leaned over and laid Tavie in her cot, brushing the baby with the open front panels of her blouse. The tops of her breasts felt cool and heavy above the edges of her bra. Straightening, she did up the blouse, glad that she had her back to Keelan. It was her own awareness that troubled her, however, not any potential signals coming from him.

'Come and eat as soon as you can, then,' he said. 'I'll set it out. How about we forget the formal approach and have it on the coffee-table, in front of the TV? We can pull out some videos, find a movie neither of us has seen.'

'Sounds good!'

Tavie didn't seem to need a change. Jessie swaddled her as tightly as her tubes and sensors would allow, then held her breath. Monitors looked fine. Face looked peaceful. Room was warm, but not too hot and dry. She'd hear those alarms again through the audio monitor if they went off.

She went downstairs to greet the delectable smell of Italian food, and found Keelan with a stemmed glass and an open bottle of white wine in his hand. 'Could you use some of this?' he said.

'Not to sound like a lush, but could I ever!'

'Me, too, actually. Not to sound like a lush,' he parroted on a drawl. 'It's been...quite a day.'

He'd bought a salad, garlic bread and minestrone soup, as well as fettucine with a creamy salmon and caviar sauce, and a big slice of spinach and mushroom lasagne, and it was all set out on the table in front of wide, brightly coloured Italian ceramic plates and cream cloth napkins.

Jessie felt giddy with hunger, and surrendered any awkwardness about sitting down to another meal with Keelan, after he'd been so careful to stress that their personal lives wouldn't intersect very much. She would eat, then retreat to her own sitting room. She doubted very much that he'd try to hold her here until the end of the movie.

He put it on straight away, as soon as he found one in his cabinet that she said she hadn't seen. It was an American romantic comedy, fun but forgettable, and with it burbling away in front of them, the wine and food slipped down very easily.

Tavie's alarms stayed quiet. Jessie forgot that she hadn't planned to watch the whole movie. The end credits began to roll just as she was wondering how that last piece of garlic bread would taste now that it had grown cold, if she washed it down with the three inches of wine still left in her glass.

Three inches? Had she drunk less than half a glass?

No, Keelan must have topped it up. Possibly more than once. He had the bottle in his hand again now, and she grabbed the stemmed piece of crystal beneath the hovering green glass rim to pull it away before he could waste another drop.

'It's fine,' she blurted. 'I'm fine with this.'

Both of them moved clumsily. The bottle connected with the glass and it tipped and spilled, splashing Jessie's hand and Keelan's knee. They spoke in unison.

'Sorry, I shouldn't have—'

'I'm sorry. That was—'

'No, it's all right,' Jessie said. 'My fault.'

While her hand still dripped with wine, she grabbed a paper napkin and pressed it onto his knee, imagining the unsightly stain that might be left on what were undoubtedly expensive trousers. The napkin soaked through, so she took another one and put it on top, curving her palm over the knob of bone and solid muscle beneath the fabric.

Keelan's knee, warm and hard. Her hand, moving like a frightened bird. Several layers of paper and a layer of cloth separated his skin from hers, but the contact still mesmerised and magnetised her.

This was the first time they had really touched.

She looked up, past his long, solid thigh and angled torso to his face, where she saw the same electric prickle of alarm that he must be able to read on her own features. His eyes gleamed darkly, and his lips had parted. She could see the tip of his tongue held between his teeth. She pulled away from his knee too fast, and the wine on the back of her hand splashed several more drops onto his thigh.

'Hey,' he said. 'Let's deal with this properly.'

For a second, she thought he meant the attraction. It frightened her, the way they could both see so clearly what was going on, reading each other's body language like a newly revealed and fascinating code. She didn't want it, but she didn't know how to rein it in.

But no, he wasn't talking about that.

To her relief.

Spelling it out could only make it worse. More real, somehow. And it was clear that he didn't want it either.

He took a napkin and dropped it onto her hand. 'There. Soak it up, then go and wash, before…' He stopped. 'It'll be sticky.'

'I'm really sorry.'

'And stop apologising. It's as much my fault as yours.'

He could equally have been talking about the spill, or about what they felt.

She jumped to her feet, feeling giddy and awkward, and had time to see a flash of relief in his eyes and a dropping of tension from his shoulders. Her whole body crawled with awareness.

In the kitchen, with the taps running, she couldn't hear what he was doing, but when she turned to dry her hands, she found that he'd brought in a pile of containers and the plates from their meal.

'I'll stack it here,' he said tersely. 'Mrs Sagovic can deal with it in the morning.'

'Oh, she comes Thursdays?'

'Sorry, didn't I tell you?' He paused in the doorway, at a safe distance of several metres. 'And I'm going to talk to her tomorrow about coming Mondays and Tuesdays as well from now on. She's very willing to help with Tavie's care as the baby gets stronger, and she'll handle the laundry for you.'

'See how I manage, first.'

'No,' he told her decisively. 'I don't want you to get exhausted. Without her help, it'll be very difficult for you to get to the hospital to see Tam, and that's too important to let slide.'

He seemed angry—trying to hide it, obviously, but not totally succeeding. Jessie had the impression that he was reminded at every turn about details in this new life of his that he didn't like, and that one of those details was her.

'Let me check the baby now,' she murmured.

'Yes,' he answered at once. 'I'll finish down here. Goodnight,' he added, just in case she hadn't picked up on the fact that she'd been ordered upstairs.

'Goodnight, Keelan,' she echoed in the same firm, distant tone.

Tavie slept peacefully in her cot in the warm nursery.

'I'm going to enjoy interpreting your signals more than your dad's,' she told the baby softly.

Moving carefully, she checked temperature, heart rate and oxygen level, and noted the readings down in the chart she'd started, adding her observations on Tavie's colour and state as well. The familiar task settled her fluttery stomach and cooled her down inside, and she didn't see anything to be concerned about in her tiny charge.

Preparing another feed and setting its flow rate through Tavie's nasogastric tube, she considered a nappy change, but decided to wait until the baby woke up.

Tomorrow, she would try a bottle feed—just a small one, so that Tavie could practise. Her sucking reflex had been weak at the hospital, and she'd tired very quickly when she'd tried to feed, but she would get stronger every day. They didn't want to keep her on tube feeds for longer than necessary.

Next week or the week after, all going well, they'd try some spells without oxygen and maybe even a trip outside, a little push in her pram on a sunny afternoon. Only a few weeks after that, Tavie should begin to smile…

In the middle of the night, at around 2:00 a.m., the smiling, feeding and breathing milestones seemed a long way off.

Jessie dragged herself out of a deep sleep in response to the piping of the heart alarm and reached Tavie's darkened room just after Keelan. He hadn't put on a robe, and wore dark silk pyjama pants and a white T-shirt that looked warm and rumpled from his bed, just the way Jessie felt. She wore pyjamas, too—a women's fashion lingerie version of classic male blue-striped flannel, with navy piping and a drawstring waist.

They eyed each other, and Jessie searched for some clever, downplaying, soufflé-weight comment.

Love the PJs.

Must get some slippers.

Is it cold in here, or are you just pleased to see me?

Um, no. Not that.

Not anything. She couldn't come up with a word.

'What's wrong, princess?' she said instead, to the baby. Her voice came out creaky. 'Jumping the gun on your next feed?'

Help me out, Tavie. Play chaperone for us. OK, yes, fill your nappy. That'll do, for a distraction.

The baby was apparently locked in a titanic battle with her digestion. She screwed up her face, then opened her eyes wide and forgot to breathe. Her oxygen alarm went off, and Keelan reset it while Jessie tapped Tavie's feet to encourage her to breathe properly again.

'Nothing serious, I don't think,' Keelan said. He blinked the sleep out of his eyes.

'No, she's just being a preemie.'

'Can you handle the rest?' He hid a yawn behind his fist.

The nightlight plugged into the wall socket etched a gold sheen onto his skin, highlighting the fine, dark hairs on his bare forearms. Again, Jessie was slammed with an awareness of just how male he was. She'd never met a man before who had drawn her with quite this instinctive, sensual power, particularly when she didn't want it at all.

'It's fine,' she answered. 'She's still not happy, though. I'd…um…close your door.'

'It was closed,' he drawled. 'And I think her cry is louder than the alarm.' He didn't leave, however. He hovered, frowning and square-jawed, clearly unable to let go.

'I'll close this one as well,' Jessie offered.

Her steps towards it had the effect of chasing him out, and he muttered over his shoulder, 'Thanks. I've got a couple of tough patients at the moment, and some decisions to make tomorrow. A case conference I'm not looking forward to.'

'Sleep, then.'

But he'd already disappeared into his dark bedroom and didn't reply.

Jessie set up the next feed, took some routine observations, changed a full nappy and discovered skin which had begun to look a little inflamed. Debating on the best approach to head off a serious case of nappy rash, she patted the area gently with a pad of cotton wool dipped in clean, lukewarm water.

Apparently she hadn't been gentle enough. Tavie shrieked, Jessie winced and Keelan appeared in the doorway again, just seconds later. He looked as if he'd once more been dragged from sleep.

'Problem?'

'Her bottom's looking a bit sore. I hate waking her to

change her, but I'll have to if her skin's this sensitive. I'm going to try a cloth nappy this time. Sorry, sweetheart, I'm sorry.'

'You're using something, though? A barrier cream? An antifungal ointment?'

She shook her head, and began, 'I don't think—'

But he cut her off. 'Surely. Wasn't she prescribed something at the hospital? Isn't it obvious that this would happen?' His tension shrieked at Jessie far louder than the baby.

'No, it's not obvious,' she answered, calm but sure of herself. Doctors often extrapolated a simple problem to its worst-case scenario. She could understand Keelan doing so, but she would resist his attitude all the same. 'Some babies never get nappy rash, and others do worse if they're slathered with creams and ointments.'

She turned to Tavie again and started folding the soft piece of gauze cloth in place, ready for pinning. Keelan stood and watched her.

Still angry.

She could sense it.

'I'll keep a close eye on this,' she promised, with her back to him. 'I won't put her in plastic pants. In fact, I didn't even buy any. I bought these open weave nappy covers—which I'm not going to use tonight either. Just the gauze will be fine. If there's any sign that it's thrush, or something else that needs medicinal treatment, I won't let it slip, Keelan, I really won't.'

'Hmm.'

He was still watching her. With her back to him again, she completed the change and wrapped Tavie up, checked her oxygen and her heart and her skin colour. The baby seemed ready to settle, and the feed was going in as it should.

Now, if the baby's dad would just go back to bed…
She turned.
Nope. Still there.

'What is it about me that you don't trust?' It came out before she could stop it. 'This shouldn't be so complicated and so difficult for both of us, should it? Don't we feel the same about most things?'

'What things?' he asked, and it seemed like a dangerous question when he was standing so close, looking at her like this, in his night attire.

'That it's important to keep our own personal space. That I'm just here to do a job, even if it's a pretty intense and emotional one. That the needs of the babies come first. That neither of us is really prepared for everything this situation might entail, because no one ever is. No parent ever is.'

'I don't feel like a parent yet. I don't feel remotely like a parent.' He pressed his fingers into his tired eyes, suddenly. 'I feel…numb half the time.'

'That's OK, isn't it?'

He ignored her. 'Like a doctor, the rest. Wanting to win against death, not out of love but because that's what doctors do. We win against death. How is it going to be for these babies if I can't care for them? Love them? Really fit them into my life? What's wrong with me?'

'Nothing's wrong.' She stepped forward, flooded with an intense need to reassure him, to tell him that she understood and that he was expecting too much of himself too quickly.

She even reached out a hand, not thinking about the magnetism between them but about giving him support and human warmth. He did have the capacity to love them. She was sure of it, having read some of his reactions more clearly than he could read them himself. Her fingers made contact with his cheek and jaw, and the magnetism was instantly there, but he flinched away at once, shook his head and stepped back.

Jessie felt as if she'd been burned.

Or as if she'd burned him.

'My marriage broke down several years ago,' he said, speaking quickly. 'One of those relationships that only works when it's fresh and new and sunny, and can't withstand any of the pressures of day-to-day reality.'

'There are quite a few of those around,' Jessie murmured. She didn't know quite where this was going.

'Yes, too many! Tanya was the one who got bored first. She went back to New Zealand straight away—she was a doctor, well situated in her career, we had no children, we could make a very clean break. I hardly ever think about her. Only now I'm suddenly regretting that she, no, *we*—I'm not going to let myself off the hook— that both of us didn't try harder, so that she'd be here now. On paper we had everything going for us, everything in common. Similar careers, similar backgrounds and priorities and goals—which was, I always assumed, why my father's marriage to Brooke's mother failed, because they didn't share those things.'

'What are you saying, Keelan?'

He shook his head. 'I don't know. Just retracing my route, wondering where I went off track.'

'I don't think you should conclude that you did. I'm not sure you should conclude anything at all at this point.'

'In my life?'

'At this hour of the night!'

He said nothing for a moment, then sighed through a tight jaw. 'You're right. I shouldn't have said any of that,' he told her.

'Well, that's not what I meant,' she murmured, although perhaps it should have been. If he hadn't spilled his tortured feelings, she would never have reached out like that, earning not only another moment of hot, reluctant awareness but also his swift rebuff.

'Look, let's agree that in future we'll have a system to this,' he said. 'We'll prearrange which nights I'll go to Tavie and which nights it'll be you. There's no sense in both of us having every night disrupted.'

'There's no need for you to get up in the night at all. It's my job.'

'No, it's a parent's job as well.'

Hearing the distancing way he'd worded the sentence, Jessie ached for him, but he'd just denied her any right to involve herself in his feelings and his struggles, so she said nothing.

'Given my responsibilities at the hospital,' he went on, 'I'm not pushing for a fifty-fifty arrangement, but I'll do two nights a week.'

'That would be good.'

'Let me know if you have a preference for any night in particular.'

'It's up to you. You have on-call nights at the hospital to consider, too. I'm flexible.'

He nodded. 'OK, I'll let you know. For now, let's both get some sleep.'

Keelan's pager sounded at 4:00 a.m., and the readout on the illuminated panel showed the extension number of the neonatal unit.

Full, instant wakefulness broadsided him like an unexpected wave and he felt nauseous as he flung the covers aside and shot out of bed onto his feet. He was dressed within a minute, knowing that the unit wouldn't have paged him at this hour unless it was urgent.

He didn't page them back. If it was bad news—and in relation to Tam, he couldn't imagine any other kind—he didn't want to hear it over the phone, when he'd feel even more powerless than he felt already.

Across the corridor, Jessie had both her own door and Tavie's shut tight. She must have the one-way baby audio monitor switched on, so that she'd hear the baby or her alarms through that and give Keelan himself a better chance of staying asleep.

Now he attempted to show her the same consideration, creeping down the stairs with his shoes in his hand, while a cold draught from the open window on the landing chilled his neck. He scribbled a note to her, to leave on the front hall table in case he wasn't back by morning, then let himself out of the house.

They'd had a difficult night, beginning with that deceptively pleasant interlude over dinner and the video. He wished they hadn't spilled that wine—and he didn't give a damn about the stain on his trousers. Her hand on his knee had been the big problem.

Driving down the street, damming back a need to floor the accelerator pedal, he realised he'd always considered his father to have a vein of weakness in him, because of the whole disaster over Louise.

Keelan's former stepmother had carried a torch for Dawson Hunter for a good two years before their professional boss-secretary relationship had progressed to an affair. Couldn't Dad have seen it coming, exercised some self-restraint and sacked the woman before things got out of hand?

It wasn't as if their eventual marriage had been a success, as he'd told Jessie tonight. It had lasted for eight years, long enough to produce Brooke, whom Louise had always spoiled while claiming, 'She's far too strong for me. I can't understand her, or manage her.'

And then the infatuation had worn off, for both parties. Dad found Louise endlessly irritating, while she was constantly getting hurt over some imagined insult or slight, often involving Keelan's rather strong-minded mother, whom Louise seemed to fear.

In his late teens by this time, and living on campus at Sydney University, Keelan stayed out of the whole thing as much as possible, with a young man's smug confidence that he'd never get his own life into the same mess as his father's.

Now, sixteen years later, he found himself divorced from a fellow doctor, not interested in any of the women he'd met socially over the past couple of years and in danger of developing the same kind of raging, unsuitable, *unworkable* attraction that had ultimately set his father adrift from family life and left his mother on her own.

If it *was* a vein of weakness, then he feared that he might share it—feared it to the extent that he'd gone too far the other way tonight. He'd got angry, he'd questioned Jessie's judgement, he'd launched into an unburdening of his inner feelings that was quite inappropriate, then he'd flinched away from her touch as if her fingers could cast magic, hypnotic spells.

He needed to get back on a straight course. He knew that. He'd gone to sleep on a very firm resolution about it. But now something was going on with Tam, and his whole body felt stiff and cold with terror.

Turning into the doctors' parking area beside the hospital, he found himself making the kind of classic bargains with the universe that ill people and their loved ones made all the time.

If Tam is OK, I'll do everything I can to get close to Dad again.

If Tam is OK, I'll tell Jessie she's free to resign, no questions asked. Before something else happens.

If Tam is OK, I won't ask for anything more.

The lift was waiting for him, and he jabbed the button hard, as if that might make the doors close faster. The fluorescent lighting of the corridor on the seventh floor seemed garish and harsh as it always did at this hour. He couldn't hear any commotion coming from the unit, which gave him an absurd and totally illogical rush of reassurance.

Seconds later, his spirits crashed again when night nurse Andrea Stanton met him in front of the nurses' station and told him, 'We didn't want to wait until morning before calling you in, in case—'

'No, I'm glad you didn't.'

'Look, he's not in good shape, Dr Hunter. His heart is failing, he's showing evidence of a major candida infection, and Dr Nguyen has concerns about his kidneys. He's here now, and he wants to talk to you about options.'

'Let me look at the baby first.'

She nodded, her face betraying the helpless empathy she'd given to desperate parents so many times before. 'Of course,' she said. 'Of course, Dr Hunter.'

CHAPTER FOUR

'THE heart is having a tougher time than we had hoped, I'm afraid, Keelan,' neonatologist Dr Daniel Nguyen said.

Keelan knew the other doctor quite well. They were around the same age, and they'd shared patients in the past. Sometimes a chronically ill baby graduated directly from the neonatal unit to the paediatric ward upstairs. In such cases, the prognosis was rarely good, so they'd had bad news to communicate to each other before.

This time it felt so different.

'Tam's not strong enough for that sort of surgery yet,' Keelan answered.

The tiny boy struggled visibly for life. He had a urinary catheter in place now, and his body was still swollen with fluid, although he'd been started on a medication to help his kidney function. His muscle tone was floppy and his stats on the monitor should have been a lot better.

'No, he's not,' Daniel Nguyen agreed.

'So what's left?'

'We treat the symptoms of his heart condition more aggressively, we combat the yeast infection, we continue intravenous feeding and increase support for his breathing.'

'A stronger diuretic for his kidneys, something to lower his blood pressure, a couple of heart stimulants, antifungal agents, antibiotics, oxygen settings turned up higher...' Keelan trailed off, extrapolating all of this into multiple problems down the track.

Broncho-pulmonary dysplasia, if Tam remained on a ventilator for too long. Eye problems for the same reason, especially if he continued to need these high oxygen settings. A brain bleed, due to side-effects from the blood pressure and heart drugs. With or without the antibiotics, bowel problems remained a possibility. And antifungal medications were nasty at the best of times.

All of this, and more, even if everything they did to help the heart was sufficient to hold it up until Tam was big enough and strong enough for the surgery he would need.

Daniel watched Keelan in silence for a moment, then said quietly, 'I've seen babies in worse shape than this one come through in perfect health, no developmental delay, happy personalities, only the most minimal long-term problems with their eyesight or their size.'

'But you've seen babies in this kind of shape who didn't make it at all.'

'Yes, I have. Which is why I called you in.'

'To say goodbye?'

'To OK the aggressive treatment. Is this what you want, Keelan?'

'Yes!' He said it without hesitation, and felt a wash of anger towards Brooke that he knew wasn't entirely fair. There was no guarantee, even with perfect prenatal care, that she would have carried the twins for longer than she had.

The thing that angered him, though, was that she hadn't tried. She'd coasted along, taking for granted that her path would be strewn with rose petals, the way she always had, the way Louise had always encouraged her to, despite everything Louise had said about 'not being able to manage her'.

Even if Brooke had still been around, Keelan doubted

she'd have known what to do in a situation like this, where to find the courage and the commitment.

Tam needed someone to fight for him.

No, that wasn't quite right. Even at this tiny size, the fight had to be Tam's. Keelan had heard nurses talk as if this was how it happened. 'She decided to live.' 'He found the strength for one more fight, and then he didn't look back.' 'She just didn't want to do it any more, and so she let go. We couldn't bring her back this time.'

Tam had to decide to fight, and he had to know that someone—Keelan himself—applauded him for it, loved him for it.

'Keep doing everything you can, Daniel,' he told his colleague. 'I'm going to sit with him for a while.'

'You're going to watch those monitor figures?'

'No, I'm going to watch him. Touch him. I—I really want him to know I'm here tonight, if that's possible.'

Dr Nguyen yawned. 'Not much night left.'

He stepped towards Andrea, Tam's nurse, and gave her some low-voiced instructions, and they both fiddled with ventilator settings and IV flow rates for a while. Tam's chart rustled as they added several more lines of scrawled, cryptic notation.

Keelan watched them at work, then vaguely realised that if he wanted to put his arm inside Tam's incubator, he should wash his hands again. When he came back, Andrea was ready for him and he sat amongst all the machinery that surrounded the baby, and cupped his hand around the tiny head, capped in thick, pale blue knit cotton.

He lost all track of time, all awareness of the other activity in this section of the unit. And he didn't watch the monitors.

Just live, OK?

Fight, Tam.

Choose life.

*   *   *

Tavie's thin, high-pitched crying awoke Jessie at just after five.

On her way to the baby's room, she saw Keelan's open door and his empty bed. The covers had been flung to one side in a heap, as if he'd projected himself out of them at speed.

She put up a new feed and changed the baby's nappy. Tavie's skin in that area no longer looked such an angry red, thank goodness, and there were no raised areas and no sections of broken skin. In her judgement, it wasn't thrush, or any other cause for concern.

Next, she went downstairs, but Keelan wasn't there either, and his car had gone from the garage.

To the hospital?

Where else?

The callout could have been for one of his own patients, or it could have been because of Tam, and Jessie couldn't put her mind at rest when she didn't know. She thought of phoning the hospital...actually picked up the telephone from the hall table to dial...but didn't feel it was her right. If they'd lost Tam in the night, Keelan would deal with the formalities and with the grief, and her own responsibility lay in caring for the twin that was left.

After all, Tavie remained frail, too.

Waiting for news, Jessie made a pot of coffee in the chilly kitchen, then carried her mug up to the much warmer nursery, setting it down carefully where there was no chance it could spill even a drop on the baby. She found Tavie awake, alert and quiet, with her feed still running easily through the tube that passed through her nose and throat, down to her stomach. No alarms went off, and her colour was perfect.

Seizing this ideal opportunity, she checked the baby's weight gain—ten grams, which deserved a cooing congratulation. 'You good, beautiful girl!' She gave Tavie a sponge bath, with tiny gauze pads and cotton buds dipped in clean, warm water, and went through the tiny girl's mouth care routine.

'Still awake, sweetheart, even after all that?' she cooed again. 'Can you see how tense I am? I'm really trying to hide it, little girl. Look, I'm smiling at you, giving you a big, important smiling lesson, and you don't know how thumpy my heart is. Wouldn't your dad phone us if something was going on with your brother? Or does he actually think you've let me sleep?'

Thinking she heard a noise, she paused for a moment but, no, that wasn't the automatic garage door opening. The house stayed silent. Jessie considered trying Tavie on a bottle feed, but the baby had to be tiring by now. Yes, her semi-translucent lids looked heavy... She was drifting off...she was asleep. The bottle feed could come later.

Jessie grabbed a quick shower, but the clammy feeling wouldn't wash from her skin. If Keelan hadn't called by seven, she'd phone the unit. She had a bad feeling about the way those bundled covers lay like a discarded crash test dummy on his king-size bed.

'Hey, Baby Hunter, did you pee?' Keelan heard Tam's nurse say, breaking his reverie. She glanced at the new fluid that had appeared. 'Hey, you did! Good boy!'

Keelan looked up, eyebrows raised, and she nodded. 'That's what we want.' She weighed the nappy and announced, 'Twelve mils. Wonder Boy!'

Outside, dawn had broken, and the humming sound of morning traffic had begun to build. A clock on the wall read six-fifteen. Keelan uncupped his hand slowly from Tam's head, feeling a spot begin to burn in the top of his spine.

'He looks better,' he observed out loud, sliding his wrist back from the warm, moist incubator. 'His colour is definitely better.'

Less mottled, more even and pinker.

'Stats have improved, too,' Andrea said. 'Sats are up, blood pressure's down. Prettier pattern on the heart graph.'

Keelan looked at the monitors. The figures hadn't changed all that much in an hour, but at least they'd changed in the right direction.

Tam had decided to keep fighting.

For the time being.

A wave of limp-muscled fatigue washed over him, and the rest of his life rushed back into his awareness like a flood tide. He had paediatric unit rounds at eight, the toughest of two tough case conferences at eight-thirty...

Did he have time to get home first? Sleep was out of the question, but he could manage breakfast at least, a look at Tavie and a chance to report to Jessie on what had happened with Tam.

'I'll be back later,' he promised Andrea Stanton vaguely, although Stephanie Vincent would be covering Tam's care by then.

In the car, he drove on autopilot, scarcely aware of streets still blessedly quiet at this hour.

At home, at just after six-thirty, Jessie must have heard the garage door. She met Keelan in the front hallway, already dressed in neat stretch jeans and a figure-hugging blue top. In any other state he would have struggled not to appreciate the way the outfit casually emphasised her ripe, healthy body, and the way she seemed at ease within it. Today, though, the male stirring in his loins was a brief irritant and nothing more.

The ends of her bright hair were damp, as if she'd just showered, he noted, and her eyes were wide and concerned.

'When I woke up at five and realised you weren't here...' Her voice sounded shaky, reflecting his own emotion. 'Was it Tam?'

Keelan nodded. 'I left you a note,' he said, in a voice made of cardboard. 'You didn't see...?' He looked past her. 'Oh, there it is, on the floor under the sideboard.'

The window on the upstairs landing was open, and he remembered the draught streaming down from it two and a half hours ago, chilling his neck. It had blown the piece of paper off the table.

The lost note didn't seem important right now, but all the same he promised vaguely, 'Next time, I'll...' He stopped, wondering what kind of a next time there might be. The very idea made his stomach liquefy.

Jessie just stood there, waiting for him to say more, to say something that mattered. He could see that she was too scared to ask, and that something in his face had made her think the worst. Or maybe she'd been thinking the worst ever since she'd woken up to find him gone.

And she was too close to the truth.

He didn't know how to reassure her, and rasped out finally, 'He's still alive.'

'But he's not...'

'Not great, no. I need...' He trailed off, trying to work out what he did need, which way he should move, what he should do first. 'Coffee. Breakfast.' No, not yet, even though he didn't have a lot of time. 'How's Tavie?'

Switching his trajectory to head up the stairs, he almost barged into Jessie, still standing close with those wide blue eyes fixed on him, and she grabbed his arm to fend him off.

Looking up into his face from just inches away and gripping a fistful of his sweater sleeve, she said, 'Tavie's fine, putting on weight, had a bath... Um, Keelan, you feel as if you're shaking, and I— Tell me what happened with Tam. You're making me scared. How bad is he? What does his doctor say?'

He closed his eyes for a moment, then opened them to find her still there. And against all good sense, he wanted her to be. Exactly this close. Exactly this needful. He wanted *someone* to share in this. It touched him to the depths that she'd spent the past hour and a half worrying, sweating, imagining dire things, just as he had.

Her care and concern linked them.

'Heart's failing further,' he said, 'And he's battling infection. He's on all the drugs now, all the support they can give him. They can't do anything more, short of surgery, and he's not well enough or strong enough for that. It's up to him.'

'And you don't think he's going to do it?'

'I'm not sure how to bear the wait, or my own helplessness, even if he does.'

They looked at each other again, finding nothing to say. Jessie reached blindly around to the back of his neck and tucked in the escaping label of his sweater with tender fingers. She seemed to realise how tightly she'd scrunched his sleeve, and smoothed that out, too, then ran her hand up to his shoulder and rested it there, as if she didn't know what else to do with it.

Neither of them said a word.

Keelan knew he should push her away, regain control,

go and get coffee or see Tavie or something—anything other than standing here letting Jessie touch him, console him, share in all this—but he couldn't do it.

He cupped his hand beneath her elbow, then moved to splay his fingers across her back. He felt warmth, and the even, regularly spaced knobs of her spine marching up between her shoulder blades. His gaze lost itself on her lips, which were pale and make-up free but looked so soft and full, parted in wordless concern.

He touched his other hand to her hip, felt the hint of bone beneath a firm curve of muscle and skin, and let himself settle deeper into the contact. She watched him, her eyes beginning to narrow and soften, and he could see the moment when she reached a decision—the same moment that he did.

Her palm came to lie against his jaw, and she lined up their kiss with the precision of a potter shaping the pouring lip on a jug. There was plenty of time for him to turn away, but he didn't do it. The responsibility was as much his as hers. *More* his. She was only acting on his wordless invitation and need. He knew the signals he'd been giving out.

The first touch of her mouth brought the blood rushing through him in male response. Those lips felt every bit as good as they looked, every bit as right, moving against his. The balance of initiative shifted between them at once, from her to him, and he tightened his arms around her, nudged her lips apart with his mouth and deepened the kiss until they were both gasping for breath.

Keelan stroked her shoulders, her back, the curve of her rear, the tops of her thighs, claiming and exploring each part. He felt the generous press of her breasts against him, and a slow, sinuous rocking of her hips that she might not even have been aware of. Her hair smelled sweet and fragrant, its tumbling strands silky on the skin of his cheeks and temples.

She felt so warm and giving and real, and so utterly responsive. Beneath the snug blue knit of her top, he could feel her pebbled nipples thrusting against him as she arched her spine. He knew she'd be as moist as he was hard, and that they would be very, very good to each other if they took this further.

He forgot his reasons for not wanting it.

He even forgot the babies.

He simply drowned himself and this new, sweet-smelling woman in the sensual magic of touch and taste and discovery. He didn't want to take this anywhere, he just wanted to be in it now, the one pleasurable refuge, the one piece of selfishness he'd allowed himself since hearing the news about Brooke.

Jessie was the first to come to her senses, minutes later, but even so she couldn't push Keelan away and end their kiss without a painful struggle inside.

He felt and tasted so good, like cold water for a dry thirst, like home after too long away. His body was hard and strong, every bit as male as she'd known it would be, yet he moved tenderly against her, his mouth and hands searching and sensitive, not demanding or rough.

She had to remind herself in the harshest terms that something like this could feel right, even when it wasn't. Hadn't she been through a beginning like this once before? Hadn't it felt necessary then, too? John Bishop was a very different kind of man to Keelan Hunter, but both men had called forth her empathy and her care.

She didn't stop to analyse any deeper similarities, or to look for any deeper differences, she just found the strength, finally, to twist her head and push her hands against Keelan's chest and say, 'Stop!'

He didn't. Not right away.

He didn't seem to hear her. His mouth landed on her jaw and her neck, sending thrills of perfect sensation coiling and chasing each other down across her peaked breasts, her tingling skin, into her swollen inner heat. He made a sound low in his throat, like a man protesting against being wakened from a dream.

'You don't want this,' she told him. She locked her arms straight, with her hands hard on his shoulders. 'I know you don't. I know why it's happening, too. We're sharing something, all this fear about Tam, as if we were both his parents, but we're not, and we don't want this…this baggage, this complication, either of us. I am really not in the market for something like this with a temporary employer! It's not part of the professional package on offer!'

A pair of brown eyes as hard as polished stones met hers, Keelan's fatigue and stress etched in tiny lines that fanned out from their corners and criss-crossed beneath his lids. His mouth looked almost numb.

'If you're so clear on that, why let it happen at all?' he demanded. 'Why start it? Didn't you start it?'

Her confidence faltered. 'Yes… In a way. But I was…' She shook her head impatiently. 'Does that matter?'

He let a beat of silence hang in the air, then admitted, 'No. You're right. I'm looking for excuses.' His arms slid from her body and he pressed his palms to the sides of his head, as if he could push out the craziness of what had just happened. 'I won't do that. That's wrong. I'm sorry,' he said.

'So am I. I should have known better.'

'No. It was my responsibility not to let something like

this…' He paused. 'Travel any further. Totally mine. And it won't happen again.'

'No. OK. No arguments there.' Her voice sounded thin, even to her own ears. She firmed it. 'I'll stay well out of your way.'

'Yes.'

Nothing like this had happened with John, Jessie realised vaguely in the back of her mind. There'd been no attempt to undo the initial mistake, by either of them. John had taken everything she'd offered at once, without looking back, and she'd offered it without question.

Then in the end, months later, when she'd realised what a self-destructive limbo she'd become locked in and had found the courage to leave, he'd told her that the whole thing had been her own fault—the fact that it had happened in the first place, and the fact that she was unable to follow it through.

The really hard part was that she still believed him.

Less than three years ago. She'd been old enough to know better.

'I'm making coffee,' Keelan growled, and turned towards the kitchen.

'None for me, thanks.'

Her employer paused before he reached the kitchen door.

'I'm due back at the hospital at eight,' he said.

'Yes, and I know you have a full day.'

Just go, for both our sakes.

'Mrs Sagovic should get here at around nine. She's caring, and she's pretty bright. If you think it's possible to train her in how Tavie's alarms and monitors work over the next week or so, please start. I can't help feeling… I really got the feeling during the night that Tam gained some strength from having me there. That might be—' He broke off and swore under his breath. 'You know, I really understand what the parents of my patients do to themselves now. The wishful thinking. The mind games and the bargains with God. The placebo effect, in full, living colour.'

'It's not wishful thinking, Keelan,' Jessie told him, believing it. 'It *is* important that Tam knows we're there.'

He shrugged, distancing himself yet again. 'We'll act on that assumption. We'll do this right. We'll make sure at least one of us spends some good time with Tam every day, which means that Mrs Sagovic needs to know how to take care of Tavie.'

'She's already looking stronger, and she's gained weight since Barb weighed her at the hospital yesterday. If all goes well, she'll be off her alarms soon. A few weeks.'

'Time seems to run on a different scale for Tam. I'm not thinking beyond a few days.'

'No.' Jessie controlled a sigh. 'I suppose not.'

Over the following two weeks, Tavie continued to grow and strengthen, while Tam continued to hold on, with the help of aggressive treatment and a barrage of drugs. Keelan brought home the first set of photos he'd taken, and there was already a marked difference between Tavie as a newborn and Tavie now. The contrast in Tam's appearance wasn't so encouraging.

On most days Jessie saw more of Keelan's fifty-six-year-old housekeeper than she did of Keelan himself—not surprising, since she deliberately kept out of his way and knew he was doing the same. Sometimes she could laugh about it—an edgy, cynical kind of laugh like a two-edged sword.

He left notes for her in the kitchen now, pinned safely beneath the tea canister on the granite benchtop.

'I'm going to stay right through and sit with Tam tonight. Probably until around ten. Can you get something delivered for dinner, whenever you want to eat, and leave enough for me? Thai or Vietnamese, for preference. Pizza's OK, too. Suit yourself.'

'Mrs S. is coming in all day today. If Tavie looks good, can you plan to spend the afternoon in the unit with Tam?'

'On hospital call tonight, so I won't be home. Plenty of pizza left. I'll phone some time for a report, so switch off the ringer if you're sleeping. Tam a touch feverish in the night, but fine now—6 a.m. Dr N. trying nasogastric feed today, if all well.'

When they did see each other, they were polite and careful, like new colleagues in a hospital unit who didn't want to tread on each other's toes. What a pity they couldn't have fallen into this pattern from the beginning!

When Tavie had been home from the hospital for three weeks, Dawson Hunter came to visit his tiny granddaughter. He must have arranged to meet his son here at a specific time, as the two of them came in together.

When she heard their voices, Jessie was upstairs, sitting in the rocker with the baby in her lap, attempting a bottle feed. Tavie's suck had strengthened, but she still tired quickly, and her nasogastric tube remained in place. Without it, she wouldn't have received all the nourishment she needed. Fortunately, unlike many preemies, and especially the formula-fed ones, she had a strong stomach valve for her size and kept most of her feeds down.

She had celebrated her one month birthday last week, but her gestational age had not yet reached thirty-four weeks. She no longer forgot to breathe when she got startled or stressed, but it still happened sometimes when she fell into a deep sleep.

Mrs Sagovic—getting more and more clucky over Tavie every day, and shocked at the photos of Tam, who remained so fragile in contrast—had become adept at tickling the little girl's feet or stroking her forehead to rouse her when the breathing alarm went off, and Jessie had begun snatching an increasingly precious hour at the hospital with Tam every morning, and occasionally in the afternoon as well.

Little fighter.

He clung to life, and he'd put on a tiny amount of weight—real growth, not retained fluid—but no one wanted to relax yet.

'I'm not!' said a man's voice downstairs, mid-conversation. Jessie knew it must be Keelan's father, but they didn't sound alike. Dawson Hunter, QC, had a voice like cement rattling in a mixer, exacerbated at the moment by an emotion she could detect but couldn't name. 'This will be easier. With the other, there's no point.'

Two sets of footsteps echoed on the hardwood stairs.

'He's doing better than he was,' Keelan said.

'That, I can't imagine! But it's your area.'

'I'm speaking as a parent, not as a doctor.'

'Yes, well…a parent… Dear God! How did we get to this?'

'Jessie?' Keelan called from the landing, lowering his voice.

'Yes, we're here,' she called back. 'She's feeding. Falling asleep, naughty girl.'

She looked up as the two men appeared in the doorway, Keelan's father first. Not quite as tall as Keelan, but close, he had to be in his mid-sixties, with a commanding head of grey hair, a prominent nose and weathered skin.

His mouth was pressed tightly shut and he bristled with tension and reluctance.

'Dad, this is Tavie's nurse, Jessie.'

'Hi,' Jessie said. 'It's good to meet you, Mr Hunter.' She tapped Tavie's cheek gently, hoping she'd stay awake long enough to meet her grandfather properly.

Dawson raised his eyebrows slightly in greeting and gave a short nod, then unglued his white-lipped mouth to say in apparent disbelief, 'And this is the big one! The strong one! I can't even imagine…'

'She's growing as hard as she knows how,' Jessie answered with a smile, even though he'd probably been talking to his son, not to her. The two men seemed like magnets with their poles positioned to push each other away.

Keelan hadn't fully explained why his father had been unable to put in an appearance before this. 'He couldn't,' he'd said a couple of days ago, during a brief conversation on the subject.

That hadn't told Jessie much. There were many different kinds of 'couldn't'. Now that she was face to face with the man, she suspected the emotional kind, and her heart went out to him, despite his brusque, instinctively arrogant manner…or perhaps because of it. He found this whole thing agonising, and he'd just lost a daughter.

Understanding clicked inside Jessie like a camera coming into focus—something she already knew at heart but had been in danger of forgetting. Beyond the trappings of wealth and success, the members of this family struggled with the same complex, difficult emotions as anyone else.

You didn't have to let someone's different background create barriers. If you tried, you could break those barriers down.

'I'm sorry,' she said, and began loosening the blanket away from Tavie's little face with her finger. 'It's hard for you to get a good look at her like this, and this chair's too low.'

'No, I can see.' The older man hesitated, then stepped closer and bent lower. 'I can see,' he repeated, in a softer tone.

He crouched and his knees cracked. Jessie tapped Tavie's cheek again, and the baby opened her dark blue eyes, crinkled up one side of her nose and pursed her lips, with their tiny, translucent pink sucking blisters. She seemed nicely alert, interested in what she could hear and see, even if the sights were blurry.

Keelan's father rocked forward on his haunches, and put his hand on the rocking chair's wooden arm. 'She's beautiful…and she looks so much like Brooke,' he said in his gruff voice, and then his shoulders began to shake.

He stood up blindly and turned away from Jessie and the baby. Keelan put an angular arm around his shoulders and squeezed. 'Dad?' he said, sounding at first confused, then comprehending. 'Dad…'

They were the tears of a man who hadn't cried in half a century, rusty and painful and deep. Jessie caught one glimpse of Keelan's face, appalled and concerned, then the two men left the room together without speaking, their arms still locked together. Once more, Jessie heard their footsteps on the stairs.

Tavie didn't understand what all the fuss was about. She just thought that the light patterns she could see in the window were very interesting and pretty. And she had no idea how precious and important she was, and what a good, difficult thing she'd just done, unlocking her grandfather's pent-up grief.

'There's still a long way to go, darling girl,' Jessie told

the baby. 'But your grandad's going to be OK, with you around. The two of you are going to think each other are pretty special, I think.'

She felt a wash of tenderness, and when Tavie drifted off to sleep, she kept the baby snuggled on her lap for a long time.

CHAPTER FIVE

WHEN Dawson had left, after indulging in a stiff whisky out in the garden, Keelan stood in the front hallway for some seconds, debating with himself what to do next.

He still felt very emotional, pained by the amount of grief his father had displayed and yet hopeful in a way he hadn't been before that some unexpected blessings might come from Tavie's birth and his own involvement in her life. His complex, angry grief over his half-sister's death had eased a little.

By becoming the twins' father, he realised, he might enable Dad to find comfort and satisfaction in his new role as a grandfather.

'I should have come before this,' Dad had said, as they'd stood together in the driveway beside Dawson's latest luxury car. 'I'm sorry. I'll come again soon. And I'll stay longer. Hold her, or something. Give her a bottle. I just didn't want to...in front of that...you know, the girl, Tavie's nurse.'

'I understand, Dad.'

'Do you?' He'd collected his feelings again with difficulty, and had asked in a much more matter-of-fact tone, 'Is she good, the nurse? Do you have faith in her? Because I can't help thinking, such a fragile little girl in the wrong person's care...'

'No, Jessie is very good,' Keelan had answered at once. 'No doubts on that score.'

Except for his growing doubt as to how he and the twins would manage when she eventually left. This was

86

just a job for her after all, not a lifetime commitment. As far as lifetime commitments went, he had no evidence that she'd ever made any of those, with all those years knocking about from London to Adelaide to Liberia to Saudi Arabia.

They hadn't talked much over the past couple of weeks, of course. He hadn't learned much more about her than he'd read in her résumé or discovered during her first three days under his roof. You could view the fact that they hadn't talked in one of two ways. First possibility—that they'd sensibly decided to keep an appropriate professional distance after one unfortunate lapse of judgement. Second possibility—that they were running scared.

The second possibility was ridiculous even to consider, Keelan revised immediately as he headed up the stairs. What power could one kiss have to scare him? He'd kissed women before.

OK, so 'scared' was the wrong word. He didn't want to scare *her*, more to the point—ruin any possibility of a healthy working relationship, so that she'd leave and he'd have to start again with someone new. He sensed she might bolt, just decamp, if things went too sour between them. Her career history suggested she might have done so in the past, and he just didn't want that. Tavie was thriving. Tam was…still here.

Stephanie Vincent had said to Keelan the other day, 'His oxygen sats are definitely better when you or Jessie are touching him. I love that!'

And it was true. He'd noted those levels himself. You couldn't fake the tenderness that Jessie showed, or the attention to detail. The charts she still kept to record Tavie's progress were meticulous, yet frequently softened and personalised with little notes to the baby, accompanied by forests of exclamation points.

'Wow, Tavie!!!' or 'Bad girl!!! How come you don't like breathing at 3 a.m.!!!'—as if she expected that the baby's charts would be kept down the years as mementoes, to show to Tavie herself when she was old enough to understand.

In the baby's nursery, he found Jessie relaxed and dozing, with Tavie snuggled in her arms. The baby stayed asleep, but the nurse opened her eyes as soon as she heard Keelan in the doorway.

'Dad's left,' he said.

'It was great that he came,' she answered.

'Yes, it was.' He added after a moment, 'To be honest, I didn't expect him to break down like that. I hope it didn't make you—'

'No! Oh, no! Uncomfortable? Of course not. It seemed as if he really needed it, Keelan. That Tavie might really help.'

Unconsciously, she tightened her arms around the tiny, blanketed bundle, and something shifted inside Keelan as he took in the tender picture—Jessie's shoulders protectively curved, the baby's dark little head, the light from the window making the fine hairs on Jessie's arms gleam like white gold.

'I thought maybe you might have gone out together to eat or something,' she finished.

'No, he had a business dinner.'

'And did he see Tam?'

'No. He didn't feel ready for that yet.'

'Mmm. Sometimes people can't make a commitment to the baby until they know if the baby's committed to life,' Jessie said.

'One way of putting it. Accurate, probably.'

Keelan shifted his weight, oddly unsure of his next move. The unsure feeling irritated him. In seventeen years of successful adult life, it remained a rare experience, but it had become much more familiar since his sister's death.

Striding across the room, he pulled a second chair out from the wall and sat down. 'My turn to hold her? Can you pass her across without waking her?'

Jessie smiled. 'I think she's out for the count. She had a good feed.' She rose carefully, mindful of the nasogastric tube and the wiring for the alarms.

When Tavie was settled in Keelan's arms and still safely asleep, he asked, 'How many times did her breathing alarm go off last night? Really go off, I mean, rather than a false one.'

Those could happen often if the baby shifted position too much. It had to be tiring for Jessie, getting up several times a night to reset the device after a false trigger, in addition to running Tavie's tube feeds, checking her vitals and responding to her cries.

'Just once,' Jessie said, her face brightening, because this was an achievement for Tavie.

Jessie did look tired, although Mrs Sagovic had told Keelan that the nurse tried to find time for a nap each day. The nap must be adequate compensation for the disrupted nights, in Jessie's own view at least, because she never complained. And the fatigue around those dazzling sunlight-on-water eyes suited her, in an odd way.

'Is that a personal best for her?' Keelan suggested, smiling back.

He watched Jessie as she sat down again in the rocking chair. She kicked off her sandals and lifted her feet to the seat, hugging her arms around her knees.

Pretty feet, he noticed. Neat, soft heels and tapering

toes, painted in clear polish. She used the motion of her body to rock the chair gently back and forth. Didn't look as if she was thinking about it, probably because she instinctively did the same thing whenever she held Tavie there.

'Yep,' she answered Keelan. 'She's getting stronger every day. How long do you want to keep the alarm in place once the genuine triggers taper off to zero?'

'You're asking me how nervous I am, right?'

'Seeing if your nerve level matches mine. To be honest, Keelan, I—I won't sleep any better without the alarm's false triggers, if I'm even the slightest bit afraid we've taken her off it too soon.'

'No.' He felt a frown crease his forehead. 'And I want you to know how much I appreciate your level of care.'

'Oh, of course. Thanks. As if I'd give anything less, though, when it's so important.'

She was a study in contrasts, he decided. Sitting there with her legs curled up and her feet bare, her hair scraped back in a ponytail that needed brushing, she looked as if she took life pretty casually. Yet she'd had the commitment not only to work in the highly specialised and emotionally demanding area of neonatal care, but to take on two separate stints for Médecins Sans Frontières in between. Had those simply been passports to travel for someone who wanted to see the world?

On an impulse, wanting to understand her better, he said, 'Tell me about Liberia and Sierra Leone. What was the hardest part about working in that sort of situation?'

'Um, the infrequency of hot showers?' Her smile was impish this time.

'No, seriously.'

'Seriously?' She sighed. 'In some ways, the hardest part was stepping back, afterwards, into a world where people take hot showers for granted. And good medical care. And water. And food. The sheer *plenty* jars more when you return to it than the scarcity jars when you first encounter it.'

'And then you worked in London for a year.'

'It's what Australian nurses are supposed to do—use their qualifications as passports to travel.'

Just as he'd thought. She'd even used the same expression.

'Storing up life experience?' he suggested.

'Definitely!' Her expression was complicated, and he guessed that not all of the experiences had been good ones. Would have asked more, except that it would have seemed like prying, given the clouded look that still lingered in her eyes.

'But not putting down roots,' he said instead.

'I thought I might have done, for a while, but that turned out to be wrong.' Again, her tone and her expression suggested he shouldn't go any further in that direction—which, of course, made him want to do just that. She thought for a moment, then added, 'I don't have high expectations regarding roots, I guess.'

'No, I think I'd got that impression already,' he drawled.

She gave him a sharp look. 'That's not a problem for you, is it? As a philosophy of living, it's not something that impinges on the way I do my job. In some ways, it probably helps. I couldn't be so committed to these babies if I had a lot of competing demands in my personal life.'

'True.'

And he'd met nurses like that before. Doctors, too, for that matter. They seemed to live for their work, and you'd swear someone simply took their batteries out and stored them in a box whenever they weren't haunting their particular domain, obsessing about patients or protocols or professional politics. They could be scary people.

Jessica Russell didn't quite seem to fit that profile somehow, but Keelan couldn't put his finger on the difference. It shouldn't matter to him, in any case.

Tavie snuffled in her sleep. She was turning into a noisy baby. On the nights when Keelan was scheduled to get up for her and therefore had the monitor in his room, she sounded like a piglet or a kitten. It disturbed his sleep, but he forgave her for it because, in fragile contrast, Tam usually lay so still and quiet.

With all the noise in the NICU, the sound of crying babies was eerily absent. They had tubes between their vocal cords, they were too heavily medicated, or they just didn't have the strength.

'Is she waking up?' Jessie asked.

'No, just pigletting.'

She laughed. 'Pigletting. I like that. It fits.' She stretched her legs down to the floor again, and slipped her sandals back on. 'Want to put her in her cot?'

'I should. I have a couple of calls to make. And I'm getting hungry. Any preferences?'

She made a face. 'I was going to...' She stopped, as if rethinking her quick response, and took a breath. 'Actually,' she continued slowly, 'I was going to hide in my room until you'd eaten, then sneak downstairs and cook myself scrambled eggs on toast. I'm ready for a break from container food. Would you mind?'

'You don't need to sneak, do you? Or ask about using our eggs?'

'No, but you know what I mean. I'm poking fun at the way we've been avoiding each other. Maybe I shouldn't.'

'Avoid me?'

'Poke fun at it.'

'I guess it has had its comical elements at times,' Keelan conceded. 'But, no, I don't think we should avoid each other. That was a difficult day, the night Daniel Nguyen called me up to the hospital to talk about Tam. What happened was…' he searched for the right phrase '…out of character for both of us, I imagine. We're scarcely candidates for a successful affair.'

'No. Poles apart. Backgrounds, for one thing. Lifestyles. Priorities.'

'I'm glad you agree.'

Their eyes locked, and they both understood that there was one area in which they weren't poles apart and hadn't acted out of character three weeks ago. The chemical attraction between them remained, volatile and intriguing, even while it was unwanted and uncomfortable.

'So,' he went on. 'Scrambled eggs. Want to make some for me?'

'Bacon on the side? Grilled tomatoes and mushrooms? Toast triangles?'

'Sounds great.'

'You go and make your phone calls, then, Keelan.'

'I'll open some wine, and we can eat outside. It's early, and it's warm.'

She'd had evenings like this with John many times, Jessie remembered half an hour later as she and Keelan sat on the stone-paved rear terrace, with steaming plates and chilled white wine in front of them.

Deceptively beautiful evenings, those London ones had seemed—innocent and romantic and poignant.

But in the cold light of day they hadn't been any of those things.

She'd taken on a private nursing assignment while

looking around for something in the hospital system, and she hadn't minded that it had been very different work to what she'd done in the past. She'd ended up staying with them quite a bit longer than originally planned.

During that summer, she would spend long days nursing John's wife Audrey at home while John was at work, running his successful management consultancy. By eight or nine in the evening, Audrey would be lying in a restless, medicated sleep upstairs. Jessie would have spent the previous hour fussing around in the kitchen, eagerly planning to spoil John with a delicious, private meal. More often than not, he would get home late, just as she was beginning to abandon hope.

'Business drinks. Mind-numbing. Sorry, my darling. And you've cooked? Audrey's asleep?'

Having been stricken with multiple sclerosis sixteen years earlier, Audrey had endured her worst exacerbation phase during the four months Jessie had nursed her. From her first days in the Bishops' employ, Jessie's heart had gone out to both of them. To Audrey because of what she suffered with so little complaint, and to John because he was heroically, stoically committed to a marriage which, he'd made clear, could no longer provide him with companionship or stimulation...or sex.

And he'd milked and manipulated Jessie's empathy from the first.

Why had she taken so long to see it?

He was good at manipulation, but she blamed her own naïvety and idealism and woolly principles more.

'Not as hungry as you thought?' Keelan's question cut across her thoughts, and she realised she'd been too deeply locked in memories to eat properly.

'Just as hungry as I thought,' she answered, obediently

heaping bacon and tomato onto her fork. 'Just savouring the evening, taking my time, because it's so nice.'

Too nice.

Like London.

They had Tavie's monitor on the wrought-iron table in front of them, but she was quiet at the moment. Keelan was quiet, too, apparently in the same sort of thoughtful mood as Jessie was. The way he sat opposite her, and so close, it was hard not to be aware of him. He half filled her field of vision every time she looked up.

Physically, he'd become so familiar to her now. The shape of his head, as smooth and regular as a classical sculpture, with its straight Grecian nose. The colour of his skin, a light, even-toned olive. The muscular mass of his torso, not over-developed but impressive all the same, because he sailed and swam. The way the dark hairs soft-ened the contours of his forearm.

It would be very easy just to keep looking, to remem-ber the way he'd felt against her body, to imagine how it might feel to be in his arms again, skin to skin, to crave his woody, living, masculine scent in her nostrils.

Music drifted to their ears from the compact disc Keelan had put on inside the house. Some folky, Celtic thing. Jessie didn't know what it was, but she liked it. The Sydney spring evening felt like a summer evening in suburban London, warm and green and filled with bird-song.

The Bishops had had a beautiful home, and with no children in their lives it had always looked perfect, filled with antiques and works of art and surrounded by a man-icured garden perfumed by flowers. Jessie had assumed at first that John's consultancy must be very successful indeed, but she'd later learned that the real money had been Audrey's, inherited just after she and John had married.

Jessie had also come to understand that John's affair with herself hadn't been his first, and hadn't been the momentous, miraculous bonding she'd believed it to be, but only the latest in a long string, with some strands in that string running parallel.

Many women fell for the vibes John put out, and for his subtle allusions to the fact that his marriage was an empty shell, that Audrey's life would not be long and her death a merciful release. Tragically, he would someday be free to marry again. In the meantime…

'You can't know how much this means to me,' he told Jessie, more than once. 'To have you here, to know how much you care. God knows, I'd never do anything to hurt Audrey. She must never know about us, and I can't make you any promises. Not yet. It's a poor bargain for you. For me, it's everything.'

Hmm.

What an idiot I was.

She hadn't come to her senses, or rediscovered her principles, until she'd found the evidence of another love interest in John's life—convenient to act upon, thanks to the many business trips he'd taken. She'd played the wronged, cheated woman in a horrible emotional scene, and he'd been derisive in response to her naked hurt.

Wake up and smell the gravy, Jessie.

Surely Audrey was the only woman who had any right to complain about his fidelity? he pointed out, his urbane, civilised logic as slippery as eel skin. Wasn't there a teeny-weeny double standard going on here?

Although Jessie didn't buy that argument, she knew she was in no position to take the moral high ground.

How could she have suffered such a disastrous loss of perspective?

She left a week later, racked with guilt when Audrey told her, in her effortful, indistinct speech, 'I'll miss you. You've been the best.'

Never, never, never again.

Never fall for a man because his troubles make him seem like a hero. Never take him at his own valuation. Keep your ideals and your empathy for your work.

John had risked nothing, and had lost nothing. Like Keelan, he was too well set up in life to be cast adrift when an ill-advised relationship failed. For someone in her own situation, Jessie understood now, the risks were much greater. She hadn't had a lot to begin with. Not much money. Not much security. Not many close emotional ties. At the end of the wrong affair, she could lose even the little that she had.

'Is there any season of the year when Sydney isn't beautiful?' she asked Keelan quickly, struggling to pick up a conversational thread. She didn't want to dwell on the past.

'When it's raining,' he answered. 'Which can happen in any season, so I haven't really answered your question.'

'When it's raining,' she echoed.

It had rained a lot in London.

She finished her meal quickly after this, and although she accepted his offer of decaf coffee, she took it up to her sitting room and drank it while reading a book—one of those he'd commented on—from her suitcase. She'd unpacked them and arranged them on the bookshelves in her bedroom, but that had probably been a mistake. She should have left them in storage, to emphasise the transience of her life here.

* * *

Two weeks after Dawson's first visit to Tavie, he came again, in the middle of the day. Keelan was held back at the hospital, and Mica Sagovic had gone grocery shopping, so it fell to Jessie to usher him in and play hostess.

For a man of his position, he seemed awkward and lacking in confidence, and Jessie understood that she was probably seeing a side to him that few others had ever seen, and that the man himself might not have known he possessed until recently.

'Tea or coffee?' she offered at once, then after a sideways glance she added, 'Or something stronger?'

While looking distinctly tempted by the 'something stronger', he settled for coffee, and she suggested, 'Why don't I take you upstairs so you can see Tavie, and I'll bring the coffee up to you in a few minutes when it's ready?'

'Oh. Yes. Is she awake?'

'Not right now.'

'I thought you might bring her down.'

'We tend not to do that. It's still awkward to move her, although we're hoping she'll come off tube feeds and oxygen next week, and then it'll be easier.'

'Right.'

Jessie led the way upstairs, aware of Mr Hunter following her. Her neck prickled, and she felt unexpectedly emotional—the safe, generous yet distant form of tenderness that she should have felt for John Bishop, and should feel now for Keelan. She really wanted this second meeting between grandfather and granddaughter to go well.

When they reached the baby's room, Tavie was awake and beginning to fuss, and Keelan's father said, 'Oh. What does that mean? Is she hungry?'

'I expect so. And bored. She's starting to want a bit of entertainment now.'

Jessie thought for a moment. Tavie had begun to be weaned off the supplemental oxygen for set periods each day. She took half her feeds by mouth. It would be possible...

'Since she's awake,' she added, 'would you like to help me with a milestone for her? Her first trip outside? We could take her into the back garden.'

'Would that be safe? If you haven't done it before...' He looked around the room as if it was a fortress that only just managed to keep hidden dangers at bay.

Two weeks ago, he'd only submitted to a three-minute visit before fleeing. This time Jessie was determined to keep him longer, and to make the interlude more rewarding for both the man and the baby.

'I think I've been waiting for the right moment.' She touched his arm briefly. 'It would be a celebration, don't you think?'

'I'm in your hands,' he answered gravely. 'If you know what to do with all this equipment.'

'We can leave most of it behind for a short period,' she assured him.

He stood back and watched while Jessie detached the lengths of tube and wire. She thought of giving him Tavie to carry downstairs but guessed the idea would terrify him. Tavie had her new, unused pram sitting in the little storage room beneath the stairs. If Dawson could bring that outside for her, they could put Tavie in it and park her under a shady tree, safely bundled in blankets. She'd love it.

'This much effort,' Keelan's father murmured at one point, when Jessie had had to send him back upstairs for a lambskin to pad the pram with. 'Is it worth it?'

'It'll be lovely,' she answered confidently.

And it was.

Jessie settled Tavie in the pram and left her in her grandfather's care while she made the coffee and found some biscuits to go with it. Waiting for the liquid to drip through the filter, she tiptoed to the back door to see how they were getting on, and saw that he'd positioned his chair right beside the pram.

He had his eyes fixed on the tiny girl, who gazed up at the moving patterns of the green leaves, waving her little hands around excitedly, as if she thought she might catch one.

Way too much to read into a seven-week-old preemie's random arm movements and blurry gaze, but Jessie knew she wasn't reading too much into the body language that Dawson Hunter displayed. He found his granddaughter fascinating, and she'd brought him to a level of contemplation and stillness that he would rarely achieve in the rest of his busy, high-profile life.

When Jessie appeared with the coffee and biscuits, Dawson shifted his chair several inches away from the baby's pram, as if he'd been caught out in some sinful display, sitting so close, watching so intently. She didn't comment, just handed him the cup and saucer with a smile and offered the biscuits a short while later.

'Tam's getting a little stronger,' she told him.

'Keelan says his heart may yet give out before he's strong enough for the surgery.'

'His doctors are walking a knife edge with the timing,' Jessie agreed. 'It's been a battle to get his infections under control. Tam needs us to be hopeful, I always think.'

'New Age mumbo-jumbo,' the older man growled. 'It would have been better to let him go. To spare all of us this nightmare.'

He passed the back of his hand across his forehead, as if brushing away a fly. Jessie pretended not to notice. Tavie started fussing. 'She's ready for her bottle. I'll go and warm it up.'

'What about the tube?' The business end of it was still taped to Tavie's face and threaded up through her nose and down into her stomach, although Jessie had detached and capped the other end.

'She likes the bottle better now. Doesn't like the tube one bit. We're holding our breath because a couple of times she's looked as if she was trying to pull it out.'

'She couldn't do that!'

'Some NICU people say that if a baby is strong enough to pull out the tube, she's strong enough to do without it. Would you like to give her the bottle?'

'I could give it a try. I was never much of a hands-on parent.'

'Second chance, then,' Jessie suggested lightly, then realised that her comment had far more meaning than her tone had conveyed, in the light of his daughter's recent death. She winced inwardly.

I'm usually more tactful than that!

But Keelan's father seemed to take her words differently. 'Yes, I've been extraordinarily lucky,' he said soberly. 'I'm only just beginning to understand that.'

Jessie left him alone with Tavie again while she mixed and warmed the forty mils of special preemie formula that the baby could now manage at one feeding session. She brought some pillows to help Mr Hunter and his granddaughter get comfortable together in the outdoor chair.

Keelan appeared on the terrace while she was still helping his father and Tavie get their positioning right.

'Starting to wonder where everyone had got to,' he said. 'Dad, I'm glad you got here. Sorry I was held up.'

'We've been managing pretty well,' his father said. 'Haven't we, Jessie?'

'Very well. Her first trip into the open air, Keelan, and she loves it. I knew she would.'

She saw him take in the fact that his father had the baby on his lap, bottle included, and couldn't help deliberately seeking eye contact to telegraph her satisfaction. She raised her eyebrows at Keelan and gave a tiny nod that said, Isn't he doing well?

Keelan nodded back, and mouthed, 'Thanks.' And just that one, tiny, secret communication between them, that warm, short connection with his dark eyes, was enough to shatter any illusion on her part that she'd kept her attraction to him under control over the past few weeks.

She hadn't. It had only grown.

Any further along this path, and she'd be a mess.

No, thank you. I'm not going there again.

She flashed her gaze down to the baby instead, and watched the tiny, singing stream of bubbles rising against the bottle's clear plastic sides.

CHAPTER SIX

'YES, of course I'd like you to come and see Tam, Dad, but I'm not going to push,' Keelan told his father.

'No, well, once he's home, all right? I don't like hospitals.'

'He won't be home for a while yet. Christmas if he's lucky.'

'We'll see.'

Not for the first time, they seemed to be having the most important conversation of the day while standing next to Dawson's car in the driveway, driver's side door hanging open, when they'd supposedly already said goodbye.

This didn't score as a coincidence, Keelan was sure. Unconsciously, Dad did it on purpose. At the last moment, he got up half the necessary courage—enough to ask the hard question, while still hoping he could run away from the answer by jumping behind the wheel and gunning the engine up the street.

Simple honesty was the best response to this strategy, Keelan had decided. He wondered, sometimes, if successful men of his own generation were as startling a mix of strength and weakness as were successful men of his father's age. He thought perhaps they weren't, that there had been some progress, some balance achieved. He hoped so.

Another car approached down the quiet street. Looking up, he recognised his mother's blue Volvo and the silhouette of her neatly coiffed head. His heart lurched side-

ways, and he almost elbowed his father out of the way
so he himself could take the vehicular escape route Dad
had been looking for. So much for emotional progress...

My lord!

His parents—his bitterly divorced parents—were about
to encounter each other, out of the blue, for the first time
since their very precisely choreographed and ultra-polite
meeting at his own wedding to Tanya nine years ago.
He'd had no idea that Mum was coming down today.

He froze.

Dad hadn't seen Mum yet. She parked under a tree on
the opposite side of the street, a little further up the hill,
and started across towards them, waving cheerfully.
Apparently she hadn't recognised Dad's car, and he'd
slid into the driver's seat now, masked from her view by
the glare of the sun on his windscreen.

'Surprise!' she trilled, smiling, still some metres away.
'Love, I didn't want to tell you that I was coming. Just
in case. Because there's been this kerfuffle over—' She
broke off suddenly, her eyes fixed on the red Mercedes,
and added in a very different tone, 'Dawson!'

'Susan,' he growled back, and slid awkwardly from
the car into a standing position again.

Neither of them said anything further, and neither of
them took their eyes from each other's face. Keelan seriously contemplated pushing past his father, sliding into
the driver's seat of the Mercedes, turning the key that
was still in the ignition and getting the hell out of the
situation.

He restrained himself and broke the ice with the scin-
tillating word, 'Well...'

As the wronged partner in the long-ended marriage,
Mum had the right to her son's loyalty and the right to
snub her ex-husband to an extent limited only by her

imagination. Typically, though, she didn't. Instead, after a yawning pause, she reached out a rather shaky pair of hands, gripped the man's shirtsleeves and hugged him.

'Oh, Dawson, I'm so sorry.' Her voice shook, too. 'I can only imagine how these past weeks have been for you. For Louise, too.'

'Hasn't been easy,' he said, that gravelly gruffness filling his tone. 'I haven't spoken much to Louise.'

'No…'

'I think Phillip has been very good. And his girls.' Louise had two stepdaughters, since her recent remarriage, aged in their mid-twenties.

'I'm glad.'

Keelan's parents let each other go, slowly.

His mother went on, 'Are you coming or going, Dawson?'

'Going. She's absolutely beautiful, Susie. It's good of you to take an interest.'

'Take an interest?' Her eyes blazed. If she'd been a cat, you could have seen her fur standing on end. 'Dawson Hunter, she's…my…granddaughter!'

Keelan's scalp tingled at the implacable rebuke in those five words.

His father looked unutterably shocked. 'But—'

'My son has adopted her. That makes her his daughter. My granddaughter. Yours, too, of course. And Louise's. But mine just as much. Never, ever think otherwise, Dawson.'

'My God, Susan, of course, if that's the way you see it, and the way you feel…'

'It is. Keelan, can we go inside? Let's not keep your father standing here when he wants to get on his way.

I'm sure we'll see more of each other now, Dawson. I…uh… That'll be…interesting, won't it?'

Keelan's father could manage only the briefest of nods. Keelan ushered his mother inside, but when he looked back, before closing the front door, he saw that Dawson still sat motionless behind the wheel, as if he didn't have the co-ordination skills to start the engine.

'She'll be asleep, and tired out. It's a pity. You just missed her first experience of the big, wide world.'

Laying Tavie back in her cot, Jessie heard Keelan's voice in the front hallway and wondered who he had with him now.

'I'm staying for several days,' said a female voice.

'Here?'

'If you'll have me, dear. I wanted to let you get settled before I came down, to give you time to, well, start feeling like a parent, but now I'm feeling selfish and I couldn't wait any longer to see her properly. So will you have me?'

'Of course I'll have you, but you might prefer better accommodation than I can offer. There's no spare room any more. Tavie has her nursery, and I've given Jessie a bedroom and a sitting room.' Keelan's voice got closer as he spoke.

Keeping her curiosity down to a simmer, Jessie set up the alarms again and clipped the pulse oximeter to Tavie's foot. Ninety-eight per cent, the monitor indicated, which was great after the baby had been breathing regular air for a whole hour with no respiratory support.

'You are so good and strong, little girl,' she told the baby, even though she'd fallen asleep.

'Jessie, my mother's here,' Keelan said, from the doorway. 'She had some strange idea that it would be more ''convenient'' if she didn't tell us she was coming. Convenient for whom, I'm not sure, but anyhow here she is.'

'With a very warm, thoughtful introduction from my son,' said a trim-figured woman of about sixty. She had Keelan's dark eyes, and they twinkled, framed by beautifully tinted light brown hair. 'It's good to meet you. I've heard all the right things.'

'Um, tell me what those are, and I'll be flattered, shall I?' Jessie murmured, softening the cheeky response with her tone. Keelan had set up this mood, and his mother had followed through, but Jessie wasn't sure if she was allowed to join in.

'Keelan, have a look out the front and tell me if your father has left yet,' Susan Hunter murmured. 'He acted as if I'd kneecapped him with the granddaughter thing. I don't know why he thought I'd feel differently.'

'Some women would have.'

'And deprived themselves of a grandchild?' She caught sight of the baby, still dwarfed by the expanse of the cot mattress, and bundled in a white cotton blanket. 'Oh, and she's gorgeous! Oh, she is! So much bigger and stronger than the first time I saw her! I don't want to hold her, she's asleep, but, oh, I wish I could!'

Keelan stepped back into the corridor and went to the landing, where the window looked out onto the street. Coming back a few seconds later, he reported, 'Dad's still there.'

'Well, he's not my responsibility,' Keelan's mother said, sounding very firm about it.

Jessie got the impression, however, that at some level Susan felt he still was. Possibly, she even wanted him to be.

'Well, she *was* screaming, Dr Hunter,' the A & E nurse said in an apologetic tone, 'until two minutes before you got here.'

Her gesture presented a tranquil tableau of mother and toddler looking at each other as if not at all sure what to do next. No one was crying. No one appeared to be in pain, although the little girl did look rather pale and wrung out.

Keelan approached the bed in the paediatric section of the emergency department, and got an apology from the mother as well. She was in her early forties, rather tired-looking, but with a pretty face and Snow White colouring that her little daughter also shared.

'I'm sorry, she seems fine now.' The mother smiled and spread her hands. 'I do tend to panic with her a bit, because of her having Down's. She started screaming at home, and then she stopped, and then she screamed again and I brought her straight in. We're not far. She's hard to interpret sometimes, and she only has a couple of words. She'll be two next month. I guess she just got herself into a state, or ate too fast, or— But she really did seem to be in such a lot of pain!'

'Hang on, we won't let her off the hook just yet, now that I'm here,' Keelan said.

The child had shown some other symptoms, according to a report from the resident who'd examined her—rigid, tender abdomen, low blood pressure, flaccid body; pale, septic and very sick appearance, as well as the strong evidence of serious pain that her mother had mentioned.

He examined the little girl. She had several classic Down's traits—a flattened head, a slight heart murmur which her parents had been told was minor—and seemed like a lovable and loving child. Loved, too.

'She's our only one,' the mother said, still apologetic. 'I do panic.'

With reason this time. Without warning, little Laura stiffened and began to scream again, in severe and unmistakable pain. Tears streamed down her cheeks and her mother could do nothing to console her.

'Let's have another look at her BP,' Keelan murmured, and sure enough it had dipped again. 'I think she probably has an intussusception,' he said. 'A sort of telescoped segment of the intestine. It'll pouch into the adjacent intestine, and while it's happening it's very painful. Then it'll push out again and everything seems fine. You'd swear they've forgotten all about it, and nothing's wrong.'

'So you're saying…' The mother frowned, waiting for the other shoe to drop, hugging her child and soothing her. Experience with a Down's baby had taught her never to take good news for granted.

'It does mean surgery,' he had to tell her. 'Straight away, so that she doesn't have to go through many more bouts of this. That vulnerable segment of the intestine will have to be taken out. But it's not a complex operation, and you should have no ongoing problems. It's very rare to find this condition in a child over two.'

'So it's not related to the Down's, or—or indicative of any other problem, or something we'll have to watch for…'

'She should be absolutely fine, Mrs Carter. I'll arrange a bed for her upstairs and talk to the surgeon straight away.'

The surgery didn't take long to set up, and there were no more children in the emergency department that Keelan needed to see. He looked at his watch. If he could get out of here before someone else collared him, he could manage a side trip to the NICU on the way back to his own unit. Jessie would probably be there at this time of day.

He tried not to think of this as an added inducement, but knew he was kidding himself.

He could give himself a mental pep talk about it.

He should!

Having given himself numerous such talks over the past few weeks, he had the lines down by heart and could play them in his head like a tape. He could also choose to visit Tam this afternoon, instead of right now, by which time Jessie would be home again with Tavie. That way, she wouldn't be a distraction.

Or he could just forget the avoidance strategies and enjoy the pleasure of her company.

Why didn't the two of them launch into a hot affair, in fact?

They were both single, sensible adults, and they were living under the same roof, with all the privacy they needed, and a king-size bed. The attraction existed on both sides. His senses told him this, not any particular arrogance about his male magnetism. And yet he was pretty convinced that if he tried to get her into bed, she'd turn him down. A large part of her wouldn't want to, but she'd do it anyway.

Because…?

She had more self-control. She had a clearer perception of their differences, and of all the ways in which a relationship between the wrong people could turn sour. She'd been bitten before, and she'd be twice as shy this time around.

Pick one answer. Pick all of them.

She was probably right.

He sighed through the corner of his mouth and hit the

lift button for the seventh floor. Saw her as soon as he got halfway into the unit, and all the tension and awareness and intuition between them flooded back into the air again.

'Hi,' she said. She smiled, then looked away too quickly, the turn of her head a little giddy and the angles of her body self-conscious.

'How's he looking today?' Keelan asked her, wondering if he betrayed as much as she did with his body.

What did Jessie pick up? What did other people see? It shouldn't hit them this hard when they saw so much of each other. Familiarity should have rubbed off some of the heady, unsettling glow after nearly three months.

But it hadn't. The glow only got worse.

Stephanie had Tam's chart resting on top of the respirator while she added some notes, but glanced at all three of them when she heard Keelan's question. She made a little sound with her tongue and her teeth that he didn't like.

'He's hanging in there,' Jessie answered. 'Struggling a bit. I don't want to say that. Do I, Tam, sweetheart? But he is. The weight's not going on the way we want. Slowed to a standstill this week—you looked at his numbers yesterday, didn't you?'

Keelan nodded. Today was Thursday, and he'd had a busy week. He'd barely managed to see the baby and he felt out of touch, remorseful and newly anguished about Tam's slight but definite downturn over the past few days, as if his necessary preoccupation with his own patients was to blame.

In contrast, Tavie's health had gone from strength to strength. After Keelan's mother's visit, Jessie had steadily weaned the little girl onto longer and longer intervals of breathing room air, and bigger and bigger mouth feeds. Tavie had conformed to the unwritten preemie rule about readiness for oral feeds, and had finally pulled out her nasogastric tube one day.

During the three days that followed, Keelan and Jessie had debated whether they might need to put it back in. If she fell asleep during too many of her bottle feeds and couldn't finish them... If her weight gain slowed or stalled...

No, thanks, Tavie had told them very clearly, via her stats and her observations and her behaviour. I hate the tube. And I can handle this. See, I'm staying awake because this sucking stuff feels very nice, and I'm still growing. Probably a good idea if you keep me on the breathing alarm at night for a bit longer, though.

Keelan's mother had been absolutely captivated and had stayed for four nights. She and Jessie had got on well. They'd kept certain boundaries in place, but the boundaries were friendly ones.

'Come for a visit with Tavie as soon as she's strong enough,' Susan had begged Keelan, on the morning of her departure, a month ago now. 'And bring Jessie to share the load. She'll need a change of scene soon. You couldn't have asked for a better carer for the baby.'

The invitation still hovered in the back of Keelan's mind, but he hadn't planned a time to take his mother up on it yet.

'And he's retaining fluids again,' Jessie finished. Her hand rested lightly and protectively on top of Tam's incubator. 'Dr Nguyen increased the diuretic this morning.'

'Is he around?'

'Parent conference,' Stephanie put in, using a tone that conveyed too much. Shut away in the privacy of the unit's tiny conference room, some baby's parents were getting bad news.

Meanwhile, the flurry of nervous yet happy activity at the far end of the unit told Keelan that a different set of parents would be leaving with their baby in a few minutes. Home. Healthy. Safe.

A wave of sick envy poured down on him, tightening up his throat, making blood beat in his head, and for the hundredth time he thought, And every day there are parents feeling like this, getting torn apart like this. It's horrible. And there's nothing to do but suffer it...

'Yikes, Ethan!' another nurse suddenly exclaimed behind him. 'Are you just trying to scare me, or—? No, you're for real! You're not supposed to do this! And not this fast! *Yikes!*'

Keelan whipped around, his whole body yanked like a marionette by the urgency in her tone. Stephanie asked with the same urgency, 'Get a doctor?'

'Who's around?'

Keelan zapped his focus across the unit, seeking to answer this question for himself. He already knew that Daniel was in conference with those poor parents. Dr Cathy Richler should be here... Yes, but fully involved in a procedure on another very ill baby. Residents? Busy or absent. Even doctors needed bathroom breaks and occasional nourishment.

'What's going on?' he asked the other nurse. Carol something. He didn't waste time checking her badge. Should know her last name, but it had flown from his head. Hardly heard her answer, because he could observe the evidence for himself.

The baby boy had paled to parchment white, his skin textured like paper. On the monitor, his heart numbers had fallen, and they kept falling, while his blood pressure had climbed to dangerous heights. This had to be the aftermath of an IVH—an intraventricular haemorrhage.

A brain bleed, if you wanted to be totally blunt about it. Sometimes you didn't, because it sounded too scary, but the baby's parents weren't here right now, so there was no need to pretend.

The real problem was that the evidence only showed up, as now, after the event. You could treat the symptoms, but you couldn't prevent damage to the brain that might already have happened.

'So fast!' Carol said. 'He was at risk. They're always at risk, these ones—he's a twenty-eight-weeker, four days old—but he'd been looking so good and stable. Now...'

'I'm not calling Nguyen out of that conference,' Stephanie said.

Keelan cold-shouldered the technicality that this wasn't his domain.

'He needs something to boost his heart rate,' he said. 'And look at those sats.' He dredged his mind and found the weight-to-dosage figures he'd known by heart during his times in the NICU in the past, scaled down from the figures he usually needed upstairs but not so very different in principle.

He announced the result out loud, then added, 'That right, Stephanie? Carol?' They'd both nursed in this unit for years. They'd know if he'd somehow got it wrong, although he was sure he hadn't. Double-checking in his head, he saw both nurses nod.

Jessie also agreed. 'Yes, that's right.' Then she added, 'But let me tell Dr Richler what's going on.'

'You should,' Keelan said. 'I'm not waiting for her, though.'

This could have been Tam.

In the few seconds it had taken Keelan to react Carol had already begun to prepare the minuscule doses of medication while Stephanie had grabbed the equipment they'd need to bag oxygen into the baby boy in order to get those saturation figures on the monitor back up. Keelan snatched the bagging equipment from her and began to work on the baby. If he responded quickly to the treatment, they could cross their fingers that the bleed had been mild, no long-term effects, a small piece of bad luck instead of a terrible tragedy.

Because this could so easily have been Tam during his first days of life.

Jessie disappeared from Keelan's field of vision, her walk calm and steady and graceful as always. He forgot about her in the urgency of getting this baby right again, absolutely determined that one set of parents, at least, would be spared his own anguish today.

Lord, this blue-white, papery little face was so tiny and crumpled! He'd forgotten just how much delicacy of movement you needed. He held the bag in place, squeezed, counted, squeezed.

Come on, baby! Do this for me. For us. For your mum and dad. For *my* boy, Tam.

'Yep,' Carol said a few minutes later. 'Look. Sats are climbing. Colour's getting better.'

Ethan's blood pressure had fallen to a safer level, too, and his heart rate had improved. Another ten minutes and he had fully stabilised. You never would have known the bleed had happened, looking at his stats. They couldn't know for certain about the long-term consequences, but the outlook was promising, the way he'd bounced back so quickly.

Stepping back, letting go, Keelan found Cathy Richler standing there, the corner of her mouth quirked.

'Branching out?' she drawled.

'Call it a refresher course.' The closest he planned to get to an apology. 'I did consider this specialty, you know. And I have graduates of yours—' infant graduates, he meant '—in my care.'

'OK, I won't tell anyone,' she said. She and Keelan had always respected each other. 'Particularly since you got the right result. How bad did it look?'

Carol answered for him, reeling off the rock-bottom figures Ethan had reached seconds before they'd begun treatment.

'Hmm,' Cathy said, then leaned close to the incubator and addressed the baby, face-to-face. 'Drama king! What are we going to tell Mum and Dad, hey? They've gone out to lunch together, and I was the one who made them do it. They're going to think it was all their fault for not being here, little guy, you know that, don't you?'

Yeah, Keelan knew how that felt!

He decided to stay on until Daniel had a moment for him. Jessie sat in the one chair beside Tam, but when she saw the way he hovered, she stood up and said quietly, 'Can I get you something, Keelan? Coffee and a sandwich?'

'Mmm, please. That'd be nice,' he answered, feeling the usual wash of tenderness and magnetism that flowed between them.

That was what made it so hard. Magnetism…physical, chemical attraction…was one thing. You could box that up, keep it in its place, act cynical and call it raging animal libido. But when it came pre-blended with an equal mix of tenderness, the whole thing got a lot harder. Blame the babies, who made both him and Jessie feel like parents.

'Ham and salad?'

'Whatever comes.' His stomach felt hollow, but the hunger seemed distant and unimportant. He honestly didn't care. Cared far more about the look in her blue eyes, the little frown, the soft, concerned mouth. 'Just whatever,' he finished, the words like a reluctant hand pushing her away.

Daniel showed up before Jessie got back, and obviously knew from Keelan's face what he wanted to talk about. 'You want to take another look at the issue of surgery?'

'This isn't working, Daniel. It was for a while, when we were getting him over the infections, but now it's just the heart and we're going—he's going—one step forward and another step back. I'm not seeing what we're going to achieve here. He's so tired. He needs more help. Even with the risk.'

'Have you seen Keith? Said any of this to him?'

Keith Bedford was the paediatric heart surgeon who, with a junior surgeon assisting, would perform the operation to close the holes in Tam's tiny heart. Keelan knew him well, because he had paediatric heart patients of his own upstairs.

'No,' he answered. 'I wouldn't skirt your involvement on that. Let's present a united front. He's not going to be very keen.'

'Would you be?'

'I'd rather—I couldn't stand just watching him slide and slide, a little each day.'

'So is this about you? What you can stand?'

'No, it's about what Tam can stand. And I think he'd stand an aggressive boost, even with the risks, better than he's standing this wait-and-see, growing and feeding routine. It isn't working. I want to conclude that now, not wait to conclude it when it's definitively too late to act. And the harder the heart has to work, the more I'm concerned about the ticking time bomb of that thinned aorta wall. He needs the surgery.'

'Let's schedule a meeting with Keith. You want to be there?'

'Yes. Make it today, if we can. I can rejig most of my schedule, make the time. If we agree on this, Keith can operate Monday. I'm getting the worst feeling about waiting longer. And that's as a doctor, not a parent.' He stopped and frowned, heard the uncertainty vibrating in his own voice. 'Lord, I *think* that's as a doctor. Who the hell knows any more?'

He felt a soft touch on his sleeve. Jessie. With his sandwich and his coffee. She'd obviously heard enough of what he and Daniel had said to be able to put together the whole conversation. She looked very worried.

About him or about Tam?

Suddenly, he wanted her at the meeting with Keith and Daniel as well. For support. Input, even.

But then he braked hard on his emotions and got his perspective back. She had to get back to Tavie. She wasn't Tam's mother, or even officially—yet—his nurse. She didn't need to be there, and it wouldn't be fair to give her any responsibility for the decision.

He took the sandwich in its white paper bag and the coffee in its lidded styrofoam cup, and said, 'Thanks. Do you want to head off now?'

'Will you tell me when something's been decided? As soon as you can get to a phone?' She added quickly, 'Sorry, that's not fair of me, but I'm going to be thinking about it all afternoon.'

'It's fine. Of course I'll phone. It depends on Keith. I'm not sure of his schedule, when we'll be able to meet. And I'll try and get home for dinner, too.' It sounded like a promise from a busy husband to a neglected wife, but he didn't care.

She nodded, said goodbye to the nurses and Tam, and

left. He watched her go, and if Daniel and Stephanie and Carol were watching him watching her, and wondering why he couldn't drag his eyes away, he didn't care about that either.

At five-thirty, Jessie heard the rumble of the garage door when she'd just tiptoed into the baby's room to check that Tavie was still sleeping nicely. She'd been wakeful and fretful in the early afternoon, then she'd had a good feed and had settled down at around two. She would probably wake up again within the next half-hour.

At the familiar sound of Keelan's arrival home, Jessie felt a spurt of unreasonable anger—the channelling of a tension she'd been suffering under all afternoon.

Keelan had promised her that he'd phone as soon as he had any news, but she'd heard nothing, and she'd been on tenterhooks, wondering if the meeting had taken place. She couldn't imagine that Keelan would be home this early if he hadn't yet cornered Keith Bedford. He'd have waited at the hospital.

Entering the house, he saw her poised at the top of the stairs and said at once, 'I'm sorry, I know I told you I'd phone, but Keith and Daniel and I have only just finished our meeting. I didn't have anything else urgent, so it seemed best to come straight home and tell you in person.'

'Tell me…what?'

'He's willing to operate. He agrees that the real danger now is in waiting too long. Barring any unforeseen developments over the weekend, they'll do the surgery on Monday morning.'

'Whew!'

'You think that's the right decision?'

'Why are you asking me that, Keelan?' Jessie started down the stairs, as Keelan started up. 'I don't—'

'Because you said "Whew", as if you were relieved. As if you'd been waiting for this, and wanted it.'

'I— No, I mean, if you're relieved, then I'm relieved for you. I'm just...overwhelmed a bit. That's why the "Whew". It's—'

'Hey.' They reached each other in the middle of the stairs and stopped awkwardly. The treads were wide ones, but there wasn't a lot of room all the same. He brushed a strand of vibrant hair from her face. 'I'm treating it as good news. Don't fall apart on me.'

Jessie laughed, and it came out breathy and awkward. 'Sorry, is that not in my job description?'

'Most of this is not in your job description. None of this.'

The air vibrated, and Keelan put his hand on her arm to steady them both.

To keep that treacherous air in place.

Or something.

Jessie knew she ought not to look at his face. It wasn't safe. She couldn't help it, though. She wanted to—to drink in the painful pleasure of seeing him this close, feeling herself enveloped in his unique aura, sharing so much with him, watching his mouth when she was close enough to kiss it and his eyes when she could feel his gaze on her skin like radiant heat.

Every nerve ending in her body trembled and sang, and hot liquid seemed to pool inside her. The strength drained out of her legs like water from an open pipe. She really felt as if she couldn't stand and sank to the carpeted stairs, her fingers circled around his hard forearm, clinging to him for support.

She thought he'd follow her, sit beside her and consummate the touch of mouth to mouth that she could already taste, but he didn't, which left him towering over her, leaning a little because she still held onto his arm.

'You're just exhausted, aren't you?' he said.

'No. Yes. Of course.'

'Why didn't I see it?'

'Because you're exhausted, too.' She propped her elbow on her thigh and pillowed her cheek on the heel of her hand, waiting for something definitive to happen.

The kiss. Or the deliberate creation of distance.

Neither event did. Keelan and Jessie both simply stayed where they were on the stairs, clinging awkwardly to each other's arms. If he was looking at her the way she'd looked at him just now, she didn't know, because she'd at least managed to focus her eyes on the stair rails instead of his face.

'Listen, Mum wants us to bring Tavie up to see her,' he said finally. 'She told me when she was here that we'd both need a break within a few weeks, and she was right. We do.'

'But Tam's going into surgery on Monday.'

'Which means this weekend is our last chance until... Well, our last chance for a while.' He stopped, clearly fighting the spectre of possibilities that he didn't want to put into words, and that Jessie didn't even want to think about. If Tam didn't survive the surgery, they'd have plenty of chances to get away for a weekend in future.

'My schedule's pretty clear,' he went on after a moment. 'Tavie's strong enough to travel, if we're careful. Tam's in good care. Let's do it. I don't like the way you look today. Pale and wrung out and totally on edge. This weekend will be tough otherwise, hanging around waiting for the surgery on Monday. I don't think it'll do Tam any good at this stage to have us there, and these next weeks are going to be…'

Again, he stopped and didn't finish. They could only hope that the weeks ahead would be tiring, too, with all the time they'd be spending at the hospital, because if they weren't spending time at the hospital, it could only mean that the surgery on fragile Tam had failed.

'We could head up to Mum's late tomorrow afternoon,' Keelan continued. 'Take some snacks in the car and have a late meal when we get there. It's a great place, right on the beach, plenty of space and air. Bring a book and a swimsuit.'

Jessie laughed, somewhat shakily. 'You can stop, Keelan. I'm sold, OK? I'm packing. I'm digging out the swimsuit.'

He let her go at last and stepped carefully back down the stairs. 'It'll be good for both of us. I can work my schedule tomorrow so we can leave at four, if you can have Tavie ready.'

'If she co-operates.' Jessie hugged her arm against her chest, still feeling the sensation his touch had left on her skin. 'She was a bit fussy this afternoon, for a while. I didn't get much done until she finally fell asleep.'

'What would you like for dinner?' He stepped down another three treads, sliding his broad shoulders against the pale lemon-cream wall. 'Shall we eat late, take Tavie out for a stroll first, if she wakes up? It's a warm evening, and I think she's ready for another milestone.'

'A stroll would be great. Mica made a batch of pasta sauce yesterday. How does that sound?'

'Nice. With salad?'

He'd retreated all the way to the bottom of the stairs, and since both of them had just been gabbling at each other, with a tenth of their brains engaged, about the minutiae of their plans for the next two hours, the whole atmosphere felt safer now. Lighter. The air had stopped vibrating, and contained only the faint echo of all that awareness, like the echo that followed the dying sound of cathedral bells.

Jessie could breathe.

CHAPTER SEVEN

TAVIE took the journey to her grandmother's in stride like a veteran traveller…until the last twenty minutes of driving, when she suddenly decided that enough was enough and cried loudly for it to be over.

'She can't be hungry. Her nappy is fine. She's not sick.' Keelan ticked off the options for the fifth time.

'She's just frazzled,' Jessie said, also for the fifth time. 'And so are we.'

'Do you want to stop?' she asked.

They'd had a seductively pleasant drive until now. Hard to maintain any sort of distance when cocooned together in a moving car on a highway. It hadn't seemed particularly dangerous. They'd simply talked, or listened to music and news, or stayed silent.

But Jessie had no illusions. It wouldn't take much. The right touch or the right look at the wrong time, and the air would sing as if criss-crossed with firing bullets. Her heart would sing, too, no matter how much she tried not to hear it.

There had been an unspoken agreement that they weren't going to talk about Tam. Jessie had spent some time with him that morning, and they would see him again late Sunday afternoon when they returned to Sydney. Meanwhile, they knew he was in good hands, and they wanted this weekend to be about enjoying Tavie and getting a break.

By this time Jessie had grown used to the feeling of knowing where every bit of Keelan's body was positioned in relation to her own, of catching movements or gestures or voice tones from him that made her insides melt with wanting. She thought she could probably endure it, if she was careful, until it went away.

Which it would.

Surely.

It had with John Bishop, quite suddenly, after that telling argument about fidelity. She'd been left with regret and shame, but no longing or pain.

'What, you think we should set up camp by the side of the road?' Keelan said, in answer to her question about stopping, above the sound of Tavie's piercing cries. 'No, we have to get there, just get her peaceful and settled.'

They spilled noisily into Susan Hunter's spacious beach-front house some minutes later, bringing an atmosphere of chaos that Keelan's mother took cheerfully in her stride. 'And here's your Aunt Lynette, Keelan.' Another woman, clearly Susan's sister, hovered in the background. 'She's here to give me grandmother lessons, and I'm obviously going to need them.'

'I'm sorry, Mum. We think she's just stressed from the drive. She slept most of the way, until just this last…month, it feels like. Year.'

'Twenty minutes,' Jessie corrected, squeezing out a smile. 'We fed her halfway, and had a snack ourselves. I think we should try a bottle, Keelan, just to soothe her, even if she's not very hungry. Can I sit somewhere quiet with her?'

'Let me show you where I've put you all,' Susan said. 'There's an armchair in the baby's room.'

'I can make up her bottle,' Keelan's aunt offered.

'Here's her bag,' he said and tossed it to her like a rugby ball, without even looking to see if it had found its mark. His eyes were on crying Tavie again. 'The formula's in the tin, should be near the top. Don't overheat it.'

'If I could have a couple of pillows in the chair...' Jessie suggested.

'Four adults, one baby, and it still feels like we don't have enough pairs of hands,' Susan said.

But it broke the ice, and by the time Tavie finally settled, stopped crying and went to sleep, Jessie had forgotten that she didn't quite know how she fitted in here in Susan Hunter's lovely home, and whether she was viewed as a friend or an employee...or some other option she hadn't even considered, because she didn't dare to.

The house was gorgeous, with views, through its huge windows, over the dunes to the beach. On a wide wooden deck that looked silver in the moonlight, there was an awning for daytime shade, an outdoor table and chairs, and a big gas barbecue. Inside, the floors were tiled in cool ceramic or glowing polished cork, and the decor had a relaxed, summery feel, with lots of blue and white.

You could hear the ocean in the background, eternally washing and crashing onto the sand.

As well as Keelan's mother and aunt, Lynette's husband Alan was also there for the weekend. A keen fisherman, he warned everyone not to expect much in the way of baby-care from him, but possibly they'd get something nice and fresh from the ocean for breakfast. He'd be rising before dawn to try his luck on the rocky tidal shelf just to the south.

Keelan didn't attempt to persuade him to take more of an interest in his little adoptive great-niece. Tavie's immune system would still be fragile, so it didn't make sense to have too many people closely involved in her care.

Keelan and Jessie hadn't eaten yet, even though it was

now after nine, but the delectable aroma issuing from the kitchen suggested that dinner had been saved for them— a chicken and white wine casserole with mushrooms, sour cream, herbs and vegetables, served on a bed of fluffy rice.

After the delicious meal, Keelan's mother and aunt both pushed Jessie in the direction of an enormous bath-tub in a palatial bathroom. Susan even lit candles and an aromatherapy oil burner, then produced a huge, fluffy blue towel and told her, 'Don't you dare fight this, be-cause you're here for a break. I'm not having my grand-daughter's primary carer collapse in an exhausted heap.'

She finished in a different tone, over the sound of hot water plunging into the porcelain tub, 'And Tam's going to need your strength and energy over the next few weeks. Keelan, too.' Another pause. 'Keelan, most of all.'

Tavie only woke up once during the night, and they'd already agreed that Keelan would go to her, so Jessie didn't even hear about it until breakfast. She'd slept won-derfully, and felt as cosseted as a pedigreed cat.

Keelan's aunt brought her a late breakfast of coffee, pink grapefruit, croissants and grilled tailor-fish that had still been swimming a couple of hours ago, with fresh bread, butter and lemon, and she ate it out on the deck. She couldn't remember ever being spoiled like this in her life.

'We have the day all planned out,' Lynette Schaeffer said. 'Morning here on the sun deck with the weekend newspapers, while Sue and I take the baby for a stroll. A simple lunch. Tavie has a big nap in the afternoon, after all the fresh air, and you and Keelan head for the beach. Tonight, we'll babysit, while he takes you to a wonderful Italian restaurant in Handley Head, overlooking the water.'

'Has Keelan signed off on this?' Jessie had to ask. 'Where is he?'

'He's in the shower. And he will sign off on it. His mother can be very persuasive! And when I tell her you've agreed…'

'But I haven't. Have I?'

'Your face is speaking for you. Don't fight it, dear.'

On the strength of this cryptic comment, Jessie wondered, with a fluttery stomach, just how much Susan had seen and guessed during her Sydney visit, and how much conspiring she and her sister had done.

I *am* fighting it, though, she thought. I have to…

But then, just a little while later, Tavie stepped in and joined the conspiracy, and at that point Jessie couldn't pretend to herself any longer about anything.

They had the baby girl all ready to go for her morning walk, as per the plan, lying on her sheepskin in the pram, swaddled in blankets, shaded by the canopy, protected with netting and recently fed. She still seemed tiny to her great-aunt Lynette, who was used to her own very robust grandchildren, but the way she kicked and looked so alert, no one could doubt that she was getting stronger every day.

And the two older women, Keelan and Jessie were all grouped around the pram, down on the path that ran in front of the house, when Tavie reached a milestone they'd all been talking about and waiting for, but hadn't yet seen.

She smiled.

'At me!' Jessie said, emotion flooding her in a painful rush. 'Oh, you're smiling at me!'

Tavie didn't just smile with her mouth and her eyes

when she saw that familiar human shape bending over her. She seemed to smile with every muscle in her body. Her little hands stretched like pink starfish, her breathing went fast and excited, and her whole face lit up.

'Oh, let's see!' Susan said. 'Keep doing it for Grandma, darling. Grandma wants to see, too.'

Tavie obliged. Her dad got one, and even her great-aunt. But the best and longest smile came when she looked at Jessie.

How can I ever let this go? Jessie wondered, her stomach rolling at the thought of what she'd lose when Keelan didn't need her any more, just a couple of months from now. She'd lose far more than she could put into words, far more than she even dared to think about. The baby, the man, a home that was warmer and better than anything she'd ever imagined.

She wouldn't think about it. She couldn't afford to…

The realisation came anyway, despite the desperate fire wall she'd tried to construct inside her head.

She'd fallen in love with Keelan, and all her barriers lay in ruins.

When? How?

She could try to map it all out, pinpoint each subtle or sudden change in her perceptions, but even if she succeeded, it wouldn't change the basic fact, she knew. Love didn't operate that way.

Suddenly one day it was just there, as much a part of you as, say, your taste for spicy food or your aversion to the smell of mint toothpaste. And it could feel as frightening inside you as a newly diagnosed disease or an unexpected stab of pain.

Beside her, standing close, Keelan laughed. 'Wow! Oh, wow!'

He sounded choky and tight in the throat, as if he

couldn't risk more words without breaking down. Jessie wanted to reach out for him, hug him and hold him and lean on him while they watched the baby together, but this wasn't her right, or her role, and that felt more frightening than ever, now that she understood what had happened inside her.

How can I let any of this go? she thought. It's going to tear out my heart.

A minute later, Susan and Lynette set off with the pram, leaving Keelan and Jessie free.

And alone.

Neither of them was used to it. In Sydney, they always had something or someone to hide behind. Keelan's work. Mica Sagovic's cheerful, slightly bossy presence. Tavie. Now they both stepped back from each other instinctively, as if they needed greater distance now that their three chaperones were gone. Keelan's uncle had also gone out—to the local bait shop to discuss tides and other fishing-related topics.

'We're supposed to read the paper now, I think,' Jessie murmured. She still felt shaky inside, dizzy and sick and hugely off-balance, as if she'd been tumbled over and over through the water by a rogue wave.

'On the deck,' Keelan agreed. 'Sipping cool drinks when the sun gets hotter.'

She manufactured a laugh. 'Oh, you got the bulletin, too?'

'I did.' He shrugged, and gave that delicious smile of his, suggesting its usual shared secret.

They turned and began to walk back towards the house, still keeping carefully apart.

'I wonder,' Jessie said, speaking too fast, 'if you could ask your mother and your aunt to stop treating me like family.'

And you and me like a couple.

'Is that what they're doing?' Keelan opened the door for her, and let her precede him up the stairs that opened beyond the entranceway. Passing him, her skin tingled and she couldn't breathe. 'They claim they're only treating you like a friend who needs a break.'

'But you don't buy that either, do you?' Still a little breathless, she flung the question over her shoulder on her way up the stairs.

'Not entirely.'

'So you've talked to them about it already.'

He shrugged, skirted around her and picked the weekend newspapers off the coffee-table. 'I had a word or two.'

'When?'

'Last night.'

'Well, then, it hasn't done any good, because they're still doing it this morning.'

And I like it too much. I'm greedy for everything I want it to mean.

'We can ride it out,' he said calmly, as if it didn't matter much. 'It's only until tomorrow. Here, have the *Herald.*' He handed her the thick fold of newsprint, but their fingers didn't touch. 'I'll take the *Australian.* We can ignore each other all morning, if you want.'

'I don't want—I'm not avoiding you. I just don't want—'

'Them thinking what they're thinking?' His voice dropped. 'About us?'

He'd come right out and said it.

'Yes,' Jessie answered. 'That.'

She hugged the paper to her chest like a shield, and they stared at each other, all pretence dropping away. An electric charge filled the air, softening every bone in her body. Keelan put the second newspaper back on the coffee-table in an untidy heap and stepped towards her. He was close enough to touch her, but he didn't. The possibility that he soon would seemed like both a promise and a threat.

'What exactly is it that's stopping us from acting on this, Jessie?' he said. 'Remind me. Because I'm not sure that I know the reason any more. I did know, but it's been swamped by...other things. Left behind in Sydney, or something. I kept thinking this would go away, that we could push it away by avoiding each other, but it hasn't gone at all.'

'Yet,' she insisted, hugging the newspaper tighter against her body.

'So you still think it will?'

'Oh, yes!'

For him, if not for her.

'You're quite a cynic, aren't you?' His eyes dropped to her mouth, as if to suggest that she told sweet lies from time to time as well.

Was she a cynic? she wondered.

In regard to John, yes, but only because of how badly he'd hurt her, how unscathed he'd been at the end of it in contrast, and how much she regretted her own decisions. In too many other areas of her life she wasn't nearly cynical enough. She only pretended.

Her heart was a puppy asleep in front of a tractor wheel, completely vulnerable unless it woke up in time.

One whole, huge, naïve part of her desperately didn't want this feeling for Keelan to *ever* go away. It felt too good and too important—nourishing her, making her dizzy, giving her hope and home, and terrifying her, all at the same time.

The rest of her winced and shuddered, waiting to get

crushed, and she didn't want him to know anything about how she really felt.

The depth of it. The strength of it.

'I suppose I am…somewhat cynical in some areas,' she answered him coolly, because this answer seemed safest.

'So tell me why we shouldn't just go with it, give in to it, enjoy it,' Keelan said.

His brown eyes raked over her again, touching on her lips, which she scraped nervously with her teeth, and her wrists, bent across the newspaper.

'Cynicism is an asset in a situation like this, isn't it?' he went on, and his voice had the texture of raw silk. 'Plenty of people launch into relationships they know have zero likelihood of lasting, and surely that's part of the appeal.'

'Zero likelihood…' She gave a cautious little laugh. 'Yes. My track record isn't good, is it? Personally or professionally. If it was, I wouldn't be here in the first place. I'd still be…somewhere else.'

Adelaide. She'd had a relationship there that hadn't lasted. London. Or somewhere in the developing world with the doctor who'd been her lover in Sierra Leone and who was still, judging from the occasional postcard, totally wedded to his work. She couldn't even remember, now, how she'd felt about him.

Nothing like this.

Nothing anywhere near as dangerous and turbulent as this.

'Plenty of people see that as a plus,' Keelan was saying. 'The fact that it has to be short term. And it seems as if you're one of them, so present your case.'

'I have no case to present. I'm not sure what you're saying, Keelan, or what you want.'

'Oh, you know what I want.' He moved closer, his open hands hovering lightly near her elbows, which were angled outwards because of the wad of newsprint she still clutched against her chest.

'Sex,' she suggested bluntly, because the word was practically written across his face in big block capitals.

'For starters,' he agreed, just as bluntly. 'To be honest, you've got me so close to the brink I'm not going to be able to think straight until we get that out of the way. If we do.'

Their eyes met once again, and she knew that he could have left off those last three words. They weren't necessary. They didn't apply. There was no 'if' any more. Sometime between driving up from Sydney last night and standing here with Keelan right now, 'if' had evaporated completely. Now there was only 'when'.

'Let's talk about it,' he suggested, his voice dropping to a growl. 'You've sampled different professional environments on several continents. Big, richly endowed hospitals, tiny, primitive clinics, attractive private homes. I'm not going to assume that you've sampled relationships in the same way, but…have you?'

'A couple of times.' What did she want him to think? What would protect her best? 'Yes, several times.'

'With no intention of looking for something that might last? You have no desire for that?'

'Sometimes things do last,' she said. 'But I'm a realist. Haven't we talked about this? I'm sure you'd only get serious about a woman who has a lot more to offer than I do.'

'Hell, do you doubt yourself that much?'

'I don't doubt myself.' She lifted her chin instinctively. 'But I do have a healthy awareness of our differences. You're not going to risk messing up your life with a relationship that doesn't fit the mould. You're not going to risk squandering your assets.'

'My assets?'

'Your family, your background, your reputation, your rock-solid position in every area of your life.' She spoke as dispassionately as she could, wondering if he would argue. 'The assets you want for the twins, too. You'll want a capital gain when you marry, an advantageous alliance, someone you're sure of on paper, as well as someone you love.'

'I've been married before, you know.'

'Yes, you've mentioned it. Tanya.' She said the name with a deliberate sourness, even though she felt no genuine hostility towards Keelan's ex-wife. 'And wasn't she a doctor? From a very well-established New Zealand family?'

'Yes, she was. And it didn't last. I've been thinking about that lately.'

'And you've concluded that this time around you're looking for a serious commitment with a lower middle-class, footloose nurse, with a fractured, uncaring family and a dubious sexual history on three continents? I don't think so!'

He pivoted on his heel and made a sound deep in his throat that she couldn't interpret. 'Don't put yourself down! Don't you think you're insulting both of us with that statement?'

No, I'm just putting some essential protection in place before I give in, trying to find out where you stand. Being realistic.

'If we're going to do this, let's shatter the illusions before, not after, Keelan,' she said coolly, burning up inside.

'Right. Go ahead. Shatter away. Because we're definitely doing this.' He stepped close again, and laced his arms loosely around her. She felt the power of her body's response, like water dragging on a rudderless boat in a strong current. 'And soon.'

'It's an affair,' she said, giving him what he wanted. 'It's not going to last.' Time for greater honesty now. 'It's going to hurt at the end...'

'Yeah?'

'I already know that. And it's...nothing to do with you in a way. Part of it. It's because of the way Tavie smiled at me just now. I—I couldn't care *for* her without caring *about* her, and she's not mine, so—'

'No reason you can't stay in her life, is there, even if you don't meaningfully stay in mine? Get a hospital job in Sydney, and visit her whenever you want. Tam, too. Be their Auntie Jessie.'

Jessie closed her eyes and shook her head. 'I'm not staying in Sydney.' She looked into his face again. 'I'll take another assignment with Médecins Sans Frontières probably.'

Again, she said it in as cool and practical a tone as she could, making it sound like a positive plan instead of a blind escape and a desperate bid to get her priorities back. She couldn't stay in Sydney purely in order to fill a peripheral role in another family's life, once Keelan's inappropriate, inconvenient attraction to her had flared and burned out.

Now, feeling as she did, she knew there had to be more. If she gave herself to this, was she opening a tiny chink of hope that one day there might be, or was she sabotaging that hope forever?

'What about hurting me?' Keelan asked lightly. 'Any predictions on that?'

'Men can get hurt, too. Of course. I think there'll be

some regret. Of course,' she repeated ineptly. Her voice didn't come out nearly as cool as she wanted it to. 'Endings are often messy, and while some men don't mind mess in their living space, most run a mile from it in their emotional lives. They want everything clean and uncluttered. My prediction? You'll be thoroughly glad if I get on a plane and fly far, far away. Like Tanya did.'

'You don't think you'll break my heart?'

'No. I don't. You're too sensible for that. Too much else on your plate. And too much in control.'

He had to be in control, because she certainly wasn't.

They stared at each other again.

'OK,' he said, after a moment. 'You've shattered the illusions. Now I'll set out the ground rules.'

'I guess there would have to be a few of those.'

'This ends when you leave—and when you leave is a decision either of us can make. But while it's happening, it's not half-hearted. It's exclusive. Nothing on the side. It's intense. Sexually, and in every other way. It's not something we hide, and it's not something we flaunt. It just is.'

'Those aren't quite the rules I expected.'

'No?'

She shrugged, aware that she'd flushed a little. She felt the slide of his hands across her skin.

'I thought there might be more about boundaries,' she said. 'No waking up in the same bed or something. And discretion. Not letting anyone get the wrong idea. Never getting seen at certain restaurants.'

'Nope, there's none of that. Are you ever going to put down that newspaper? I think it's safe now.'

Jessie laughed, and blurted out the most honest statement she'd made in minutes. 'There's nothing safe about this.'

'No,' he said slowly. He pried her arms loose and took the newspaper. Looking down, she saw that the ink had left black smears on her pale blue top, darkest where the print had pressed against her breasts. 'That's one thing we might both agree on without further negotiation. Seems like part of the attraction. That we're heading into the danger of the unknown.'

Right now.

Right at the moment when his mouth touched hers.

The newspaper rustled as it dropped onto the table, and Jessie didn't give it another thought. The first time Keelan had kissed her, it had been blind, rather desperate, full of an uncertainty that had come from both of them. This time it was intensely sensual—no, *sexual*, why beat around the bush?—and both of them knew that they weren't willingly turning back.

Keelan held Jessie's shoulders and printed her lips with the heat of his mouth, like some potent, fiery liquor. Her whole being seemed to arrow into this one seamless, endless point of contact. Every sense channelled into it, like a high tide funnelling into a deep, narrow strait. And every emotion channelled into it, too—the love she'd discovered, the passionate need to stay in his life, to mother his babies and to belong. All of this, in one kiss.

Gradually, however, their bodies shifted closer, fitting together like a hand sliding into a glove. Her breasts against his chest, her hips against his groin, two pairs of thighs like jointed woodwork.

His arms wrapped around her, cradling most of her weight. She felt as boneless as a piece of fabric, her body held together only by the beating of the blood through her veins.

'Keelan…' His name made a sigh in her mouth.

She sounded as if she was begging for the next step,

and this was the meaning he took from that one breathless word. 'Yes,' he said. 'We'll go to my room.'

She didn't argue, didn't even want to.

They moved as far as the corridor, pulling on each other's arms, but then he groaned and stopped, pressed her shoulder blades up against the wall and pulled her hips roughly towards him with both hands. She arched her back, gasped and swallowed and kissed him fiercely again, wanting him to feel the way her nipples jutted, and to understand the pleasure she felt when she kneaded the muscles of his back with her fingers.

Impatient and clumsy, she dragged his sage-green polo shirt up to his armpits, until he completed the action for her, reaching around to pull it forward over his head. He tossed it through the open doorway of his room, and then she ran the palms of her hands down his chest, exulting in the hard, hair-roughened planes she'd known she would find.

In this moment, those planes of skin and muscle belonged only to her, and she explored them in naked appreciation of her new right of possession.

'Take your top off, too,' he told her.

His words were rough and careless, and he didn't try to disguise the way he kept his eyes on her body, waiting for what he'd see next. His open need aroused her even further, made her pulse and crumble inside.

Every inch of skin on fire, she complied with what he'd asked, crossing her arms, taking the fabric in her grip and pulling it upward. She heard rather than saw the moment when he caught sight of her breasts, cupped in a dark blue lace bra. His breath hissed across his teeth and shuddered into his lungs.

Above her head, the top tangled around her wrists,

handcuffing her arms back against the wall and jutting her upper body forward.

Keelan took full advantage of her temporary imprisonment. He splayed his hands over her stretched ribs and buried his face in the valley between her breasts. Her torso twisted with pleasure and he slid his hands higher, cupping the lace and thumbing the edge of the fabric down to release her nipple into his waiting mouth.

She writhed and flapped ineffectually at the twisted top, didn't much care if she had to stay like this a bit longer. Be honest, she could have freed herself if she'd wanted to. She wondered if she'd ever want to, but couldn't imagine it right now.

Keelan slid his hands inside the back waistband of her jeans and traced the taut contours of her cheeks beyond the high-cut edge of her underwear, and the sensitive crease where thighs and bottom joined. He kissed her mouth and her neck, then came back to her breasts and ravaged them, making them swell and ache.

'I'm stuck in this top,' she breathed. 'Let me get free, because I want to—'

Women's voices sounded outside, and Keelan suddenly stilled at the same moment that Jessie's unfinished sentence cut out. They both listened, and recognised his mother and his aunt, locked in chatty, sisterly talk, as well as something about Tavie's nappy-change bag.

They hadn't brought it with them, but should have done. They didn't want to disrupt Keelan's and Jessie's tranquil morning, but it couldn't be helped.

The doorknob downstairs rattled a little as it opened.

Keelan didn't say a word at first. Eyes fixed on Jessie's face, he nudged his thigh between her legs to press into the swollen heat that pulsed against the centre seam of her jeans. Then he gave her one last, searing kiss, eased back and lifted his arm to lower her hands and twisted sleeves down in front of her.

'Later,' he finally muttered. 'I guess this has to happen later.'

'Yes,' she agreed, not knowing how either of them would stand the wait.

CHAPTER EIGHT

THE cold salt water felt fabulous on Jessie's over-heated body. She wore a navy and white tank-style swimsuit that seemed to cling far too closely and reveal far too much today, although by any Australian standard it wasn't a provocative garment.

There were only a few other swimmers on the beach, since the water in November still contained the chill of winter. Beside her Keelan body-surfed, launching himself forward in the curve of each wave just before it broke and powering towards the shore amidst the tumbling white foam.

Lunch had seemed like one long ache of awareness between the two of them. A couple of times Jessie could have sworn she'd seen a significant, satisfied look pass between Susan and her sister. But then she had come to her senses and realised that they'd just been smiling at Tavie, fast asleep in her canopied pram between the two older women, knocked out by the fresh sea air just as Keelan's aunt had predicted she would be.

There had been no earth-shattering understanding passing between the two sisters in regard to what had happened between Keelan and herself. Jessie was the only person in Tavie's life whose world had completely shifted on its axis today.

'Off to the beach, you two,' Lynette ordered, a little later. 'It's getting quite hot. We'll feed her if she wakes up.'

'The bottle is—'

'I know all about bottles, Jessie, don't worry.'

So here they were, herself and Keelan, pretending that all they could think about was the water, the sun and the salt, when really...

Oh, dear heaven, Keelan's body was gorgeous!

Jessie had taken this in from day one as a simple fact. His whole frame was so strong and so confident and so beautifully built. Any woman with breath in her body would have to see it. Now her awareness of him was very different, however. So much more personal, so much more detailed, and filled with a hunger and a need that she didn't know how she'd ever assuage, no matter how heated and intense their affair became.

They had claimed ownership of each other this morning, and that had seemed so right and inevitable and necessary, but now she felt a little frightened again, wondering if it might be possible to put on the brakes, wondering if she should want to.

There was a term for it in the area of commerce, she thought—the cooling-off period. Some kind of contractual window during which the buyer could change his or her mind and not make the purchase after all.

Tavie's urgent need for a nappy change this morning had given Jessie and Keelan a cooling-off period. They needn't go through with this after all. They could cool their heated libidos and renege on the entire agreement.

But, no, she didn't want to renege, or to cool anything.

She wanted Keelan more than ever, her senses pushed to the brink by what had happened between them this morning, and by what had happened so powerfully in her heart. The sea might be cooling her skin, but it couldn't cool her feelings. Every time he looked at her, she got that helpless, boneless, light-headed feeling again, and it both exulted and terrified her.

So this was what love felt like.

'Had enough?' he asked finally, as they stood in the shallows with the foam still churning around their legs. Water glistened and streamed on his chest and arms, and down his thighs below the baggy black board-shorts he wore. 'Your lips are going blue, and my ears are aching.'

'It's great,' she answered breathlessly. 'But, yes, I've had enough.'

'Next on the agenda, we're supposed to go for a walk.'

'Right.'

'But we can stage a revolution, if you want, and refuse to submit to this dictatorial conspiracy.'

'I'm OK with a walk,' she drawled, through closed lips.

'Beach to the north is pretty deserted, especially once you get to the headland.'

'So are you saying you want to head south?'

'No. I'm not.' His eyes were fixed on her face, and filled with a light that Jessie couldn't misinterpret or ignore. 'I'm voting for north.'

She couldn't find words or breath to answer.

They left the water, found their towels and buffed the salt water from their bodies. Keelan put on his polo shirt and Jessie slipped into her strappy lemon yellow sundress, still without speaking. At first they walked just where the highest-reaching waves sank their frilly edges into the sand, but Jessie had had enough of the cold water and soon moved to where the sand was dry.

'Still chilly?' Keelan asked her, and her nod gave him the cue they'd both been looking for.

He put his arm around her and pulled her close against his side. She laid her head on his shoulder, and felt his mouth press her temple and her hair, both places sticky with drying salt.

'You're very quiet,' he said after a moment.

She laughed, knowing he wouldn't understand her odd, upside-down source of amusement. 'Nothing to say.'

Everything to say.

That would have been more truthful, and that was why she had laughed.

She simply didn't dare to open her mouth, for fear of what might spill out—foolish words of love that she knew he would never say in return, feverish demands for a reassurance that he would never give.

Perhaps he'd been right earlier.

She did doubt herself.

Or she doubted her place in the universe. Why should *she* be blessed with something miraculous and right and lasting, when so many people got it wrong, and when she'd got it so disastrously wrong herself, with John Bishop, in similar circumstances? Whatever the magic ingredient was that allowed someone to find that kind of love, she wasn't at all convinced that she had it, or knew it.

'Silence is nice,' Keelan said.

'Mmm.'

Because I can put all my energy into remembering to breathe, she added inwardly.

'I won't ask what you're thinking, but I'll tell you what I'm thinking,' he offered.

'Yes?'

'Wondering just how secluded it is…in the lee of that headland. If there's no one there, and if there's a sheltered patch of grass…'

'It's not that secluded!'

He laughed this time. 'Putting me and my male needs firmly in place?'

She took a steadying breath and confessed, 'And mine. My needs are just as— But I'm being…practical.'

Cool-headed.

As far as that was possible.

'I guess sand is not an ingredient we really want this time around,' he conceded. He brushed some grains of the stuff from her forearm as he spoke.

'Other times, though?' She smiled, turned to him and did the same, where some adhered to his jaw. 'Have to admit, it hasn't ever entered my fantasies.'

'Next time we'll bring our towels. And you can tell me a bit more about those fantasies of yours. Show me a couple.'

Her fantasies? There was really only one, at this moment—the fantasy that, strong as it was, this shared desire for each other was just one part of a complete package.

Jessie closed her mouth firmly again and pressed her lips tightly against her teeth, to make sure she didn't say it.

They kissed, of course, in the secluded lee of the headland Keelan had talked about. Waiting for it, she could have thrown herself against his chest and begged, but managed to retain enough control to spare them both such an embarrassing degree of emotion.

Instead, he was the one who took the initiative.

'The breeze has dropped here,' he said. 'We're protected by the cliff. You feel much warmer now.' He ran his hand lightly down her arm. 'Delicious. Radiating heat.'

'So do you,' she managed to answer, as he turned her in his arms.

His skin had been buffed by the wind and the waves, and felt as smooth as polished stone baked in the sun.

She slid her hands up inside his shirt at once, splaying her fingers across his back.

'Your mouth has turned pink again.' He touched it lightly with his lips, just a soft brushstroke of sensation. 'And you taste...warm, salty.'

'So do you,' she repeated.

She closed her eyes as he tasted her again, his mouth still soft and light on hers. She had to fight to hold herself back to his lazy, leisurely pace, and it made her ache in impossible places. He wasn't planning to rush this, to go too deep, too soon, yet she was already trembling.

A sound of need escaped from her throat like a bubble rising in water, and she would have whimpered if she hadn't dammed the feeling back. Was this really as easy for him as it seemed?

No, perhaps it wasn't.

His control suddenly seemed to break, and their kiss deepened the way a flowing stream could suddenly deepen into a dark, spinning pool. His arms tightened around her, the bruising press of his mouth parted her lips and drew her tongue into a sinuous dance. She lifted her hand to the back of his head and ran her fingers up through his hair, loving the shape and the texture and the scents of sea water and shampoo that she released into the air.

'You're fabulous...beautiful,' he said raggedly. 'I want you right now, and the only way, let me tell you, that I'm going to stand the wait is by promising both of us that it will be even better that way. If we've held back just a little. If we've had to dam this inside us. It will be...better...even better than what we have now.'

'Yes. Oh, yes.'

Sliding her dress up her thighs, he cupped her bottom through the still-damp fabric of her swimsuit, and Jessie felt the weight and heat of his arousal hard and insistent against her.

Yes. She had this, at least. This proof of need and connection.

With a shock, she realised she'd never wanted a man quite this nakedly, this physically. Giving herself to John, she'd surrounded herself with a misty glow of romance and sacrifice. Only in hindsight had she acknowledged that their love-making had often been a disappointment to her on a sensual level. A few years earlier, when she had assuaged the fatigue and stress of work in an African clinic with Gary, they had both been looking for time out and release more than a truly passionate connection.

This felt different.

This felt like something she should run a hundred miles to avoid because it might so easily shatter her into pieces, only she didn't have the will or the strength to run anywhere. Instead, she shored her weakened limbs more firmly against Keelan and gave him everything she had with her kiss.

By the time they stopped, both were breathless and dishevelled. Jessie's dress and swimsuit straps had slipped down her arms until the tops of her breasts threatened to spill into Keelan's demanding hands, or his even more demanding mouth. Her hair, already tangled by the sea, whipped across her face in salty strands so that he had to push it aside with impatient fingers to keep his delectable contact with her lips.

When his hold on her finally eased, she felt the shuddering breath he drew and heard the edge in his laugh.

'I'm starting to repeat blatant lies to myself about sand,' he said, mocking himself. 'And beachcombers. Wouldn't be so bad, would it? If our skin got chafed? If someone wandered past? With a camera? And no one's going to, are they?'

'Keelan—'

'Don't worry. Not serious here. Very serious, but not about here. Later. We're going to dinner, and—'

'Yes, dinner's in the plan. But there's nothing mentioned about after dinner.' Jessie didn't know if she was teasing him or what. Looking into his brown eyes, she saw the suffering, and the amusement, and wondered what her own expression said back to him. More of the same, she guessed.

'Dinner's an ambiguous word,' he answered, 'and it fills an open-ended slot. I could feast on you. Cover you in whipped cream and lick it off. Or put a chocolate-coated strawberry between our lips and—'

'Mmm!' She closed her eyes, almost tasting the sweet red juice of the fruit, mingled with the taste of him.

'That would be dinner,' he claimed. 'Dessert. Definitely in the plan.'

Weakly, she leaned her forehead into his shoulder and told him, 'I'm not going to argue this with you on the basis of what the word "dinner" means.'

'But you're going to argue?'

'Maybe. I don't think so. I don't know.'

'Have to warn you, I'm going to take that as a challenge. By the end of the evening, you'll know.'

'Hello?' Keelan murmured, as they came along the path between the dunes half an hour later and arrived within sight of the house. 'There's another car out the—' He stopped and swore. 'That's Dad!'

Jessie sensed his immediate wariness, although they weren't touching. She could almost hear the questions jangling inside his head as well. After a moment of strained silence, he began to speak them out loud, answering most of them himself in the same breath.

'What's he doing here? Did Mum know he was coming, I wonder? Can't imagine she did. What's the time? Must be well after four. I should have worn my watch. He's not planning to stay, surely?'

Jessie listened to the litany until this last question, then cut in with one of her own. 'He knew we were coming up?'

'Yes, I mentioned it to him Thursday evening when he phoned.'

Since Dawson Hunter's first two visits to Tavie, he'd begun to drop in a couple of times a week to spend time with his granddaughter, and he expected regular reports from his son by phone as well.

Keelan didn't say anything more, and they reached the house a minute later. Upstairs on the sun deck, they realised that Dawson must have only just arrived.

The atmosphere seemed strained, though he looked relieved to see his son, as if counting on him as an ally. Alan offered his ex-brother-in-law a beer, but apparently no one heard. Dawson himself said in a tone of mingled defensiveness and belligerence, 'I knew this would be a big weekend for her, and I wanted to see for myself how she was doing. I dropped in. Is that wrong, Susan?'

'Dropped in? It's a four-hour drive.'

'Hmm. I can do it in three and a half, if the traffic co-operates,' he muttered. 'Send me straight back, if you feel so strongly about it.'

'I—I don't.' Susan spread her hands. 'Not really. I just wish you'd—'

'Warned you?'

'Yes, if I'm honest!'

'So you could, what?'

'Make up a bed for you in the laundry alcove downstairs, because that's about all the room we've got left.'

'And that's where you'd put a visiting dog.'

'Dawson…'

'Dad,' Keelan said, stepping into the fray. 'Specialist in knocking us all for a loop.' He clapped his father on the back. 'Tavie's doing really well, if you were worried.'

'Of course I was. She's so small for a long car journey.'

'She got a bit frazzled by the end, but she settled down as soon as we got her into a quiet environment and gave her a feed. She's been great today, hasn't she, Mum?'

'She had a bottle at three, but now she's back asleep, like a little lamb,' his mother confirmed.

'Beer, Dawson?' Alan repeated, and this time he got a grateful nod.

Lynette and Susan exchanged significant looks, and this time Jessie knew her imagination wasn't playing tricks when she read their meaning.

Lynette's look said, Why don't you just kick him out right now?

Susan's answered, Because I have a horrible feeling I don't want to, even though I probably should.

Next, after a strained pause, Lynette announced aloud, 'Alan and I were thinking of going to the club for dinner tonight, by the way, Susan, as long as you're feeling comfortable with Tavie.'

'Club?' Alan queried, not quick enough on the uptake to please his wife. 'What club?'

'Any club, Alan, for heaven's sake! The RSL, the Surf Lifesavers, the golf club. Wherever we like.'

'I thought we were— Oh. Yes. Give other people a quiet night, if they want one.' He telegraphed a hunted look towards Susan and Dawson that told everyone he'd got the point now. Leave the two of them alone to sort something out, whether they wanted to or not. 'Of course. That was the plan, wasn't it? You're going out, too, aren't you, Keelan? Jessie?'

'Yes, but they're not going to the club,' Lynette answered for them, in a tone decisive enough to sharpen a blunt axe. 'They're going to that lovely Italian place, just the two of them. Early. So they can start with a relaxed drink at the bar. And that's what we're doing, too. And since it's almost five, those of us who are showering had better start.'

'That's me,' Keelan said.

'And me,' Jessie added. There were two bathrooms.

'We don't need to, do we, Alan?' Lynette decided. 'I'll change—it'll take thirty seconds—and then we can head off. Phone me on my mobile, Sue, if you need me home again.'

'I...uh...' Keelan's mother trailed off, looking helplessly at her ex-husband, her pushy sister, her unhelpful son. 'I imagine Dawson and I will be able to manage between us.'

'Her two grandparents,' Dawson said, then turned to his ex-wife. 'Susie? Will you give it a try?'

It was so painfully apparent that he was asking about far more than just a single evening of shared babysitting that every molecule of air in the room suddenly seemed as fragile as spun glass. Jessie held her breath, unbearably moved by the naked, vulnerable appeal in such a large, arrogant and successful man, and by the emotion and uncertainty that Susan showed.

She couldn't answer her ex-husband at first. Her hands worked and twisted in front of her, and her mouth fell open, though no sound came out.

'I need…a lot of time,' she finally said in a strangled voice. 'I need…a lot more than this.'

'But it's a start, Susie,' came Dawson's hoarse voice. Jessie had already begun her retreat into the house, with Keelan, Lynette and Alan close behind her. 'Just tell me it might be a start.'

If Susan answered, it wasn't audible from this distance.

'How would you feel about it, Keelan, if they did get back together?' Jessie asked, two hours later.

He thought about her question for a moment, his fingers laced in hers across the restaurant table. He'd brought the subject of his parents up on his own, without prompting, just as they'd finished their main course, and Jessie had to fight not to read too much into such a personal topic. He needed someone to listen, that was all, and she was the person he happened to be with.

They shouldn't be touching like this, caressing each other's hands, yet she couldn't bring herself to ease hers away. All they'd done since they'd arrived at this beautiful waterfront restaurant had been talk and touch. As for eating and drinking, she'd hardly noticed any of that! But all of it felt impossibly intense, as if the talking was laying a foundation for the body magic that they could hardly wait for, and much more.

'Protective, I think,' he answered her finally. His finger stilled in hers. 'Towards both of them. Mum, in particular. If Dad hurt her again…'

'Is that what's holding her back, do you think? The risk of getting hurt?' Jessie couldn't help leaning towards him, couldn't take her eyes from his face.

'I don't know. I imagine it's more complicated than that. Their history together is so complicated after all.' He looked down, putting his eyes into shadow and making the thick crescents of his lashes look darker. 'She's a very sensible woman, my mother, but she has the capacity for strong feelings as well, and that's a difficult combination sometimes. She'll look very carefully before she leaps, because she has such a keen eye for the consequences, and such good memory for all the good and bad there was in their marriage. It's a hard ask, on his part.'

'Do you think he's aware of that?' Jessie sipped some wine absently.

Keelan looked up, and she watched his mouth—the way it pouted for a moment into a kiss shape on certain words, the way his tongue rested for a moment against his lower lip. 'Not fully. Not yet. But Mum will make damned sure that he is before she makes him any promises.'

'You sound as if you're still on her side.' She squeezed his hand, and ran the ball of her thumb lightly across his knuckles.

Again, he thought for a good while before he answered. 'I've tried not to make that too apparent to Dad, since his divorce from Louise, because that was such an admission on his part that he'd made a huge mistake. Actually, I'm just trying to be fair, and to look at the whole thing with my eyes open.'

The way he'd said his mother would. Jessie suspected they were alike in many ways, although superficially he resembled his father more. Talking with Keelan about his family on this level held a dangerous satisfaction for her. It created the illusion that she belonged.

She recognised the feeling. She'd had it before.

Last time she hadn't even tried to fight it. This time she kept up the struggle, even though she knew she'd already lost. And suddenly she found herself spilling everything to him about John, in the context of questions she and Keelan both had about marital infidelity and forgiveness, comparing what had happened between Keelan's parents with what *hadn't* happened between Audrey and John.

'And, of course, I played Louise's part.' Her hand rested on the table now, a willing prisoner beneath his.

'Not really,' he said. 'I don't think that's true, from what you've just told me.'

'The other woman? The woman who was prepared to betray someone I respected and cared about for the sake of what I thought was love?'

'Louise never respected or cared about Mum. She was terrified of her. But that's irrelevant. What I'm interested in is the fact that you still blame yourself to such an extent.'

'Shouldn't I? I was terribly in the wrong.'

'At first, I guess, but—' He switched tack suddenly. 'Did you see it coming?'

'See…?'

'What you felt. And his response.'

'No, I didn't.' She stared down at her empty plate, hardly noticing when the waiter took it away, while she was speaking. 'It blind-sided me completely. I was still calling it empathy and admiration, when suddenly he and I were alone in the kitchen one day and he took me in his arms and I discovered just how much I'd been kidding myself.'

'You might have managed to put up some barriers if you'd had more warning,' Keelan suggested.

'Maybe.'

'And you were the one who ended it.'

'For the wrong reasons.'

'No. The right ones.' He stroked a strand of uncooperative hair back from her face. 'Without Audrey herself ever knowing, and that was right, because in her situation knowing wouldn't have helped. I might concede that your wake-up call came from the wrong direction—that other woman—but when it did come, you got everything into perspective very quickly, from the sound of it.'

'Why are you working so hard to let me off the hook, Keelan?' She frowned and shook her head, unsettled by the intent way he still watched her. 'Telling you all this was supposed to be about giving you some insights into what's happening with your parents.'

'Yes?' He tilted his face, sceptical and almost teasing. She flushed. 'Yes, I—I think so.'

'Nope.' He sounded very decisive now. 'We're not doing that at all. We're doing something else. Clearing our emotional in-trays, I think. So that there's plenty of room.'

'Room?'

'For so much else, Jessie. For holding each other, skin to skin, without any baggage getting in the way. It's my turn now—to tell you about my divorce.'

'Keelan, I don't want to weasel out anything from you that—'

'Shh… Let's just talk.' He took her hand again, and leaned across the table. 'Let's do this. Let me tell you about Tanya, and what broke us apart. I've only glossed over it to you before.'

Deep down, she wanted to hear everything and anything he wanted to tell her, so she didn't argue. He wasn't long-winded about it. A couple of years into their marriage, an old crush of Tanya's had come back into her life. Not someone she'd ever been involved with, but someone she'd wanted.

'And they had an affair?' Jessie said, when Keelan paused.

'No, they didn't. But she must have been getting signals from him. It would have been against her principles to leap into bed with him while she was still married to me, but it wasn't against her principles to sabotage our marriage in every other way she could think of. I was...totally bewildered for a long time, didn't understand that she was deliberately driving me away to leave her own slate clean.'

'Driving you away?'

What woman in her right mind could possibly do that?

Me, came an insidious little voice inside her.

Isn't that what I'm trying to do, a part of me, because I'm so sceptical and scared?

'Suddenly, everything I did was wrong,' Keelan said. 'Ranging from petty things like not buying her flowers often enough to major issues like "you don't communicate, you close yourself off," which I couldn't see the...' He stopped, then continued, 'Maybe it's a guy thing. These vague accusations, the suggestion that I was clueless because I couldn't even get a bead on the accusations, let alone address them.'

He shook his head and went on. 'I really thought, for months, that they were genuine grievances I should work on, or we should work on together. But when I tried, she upped the ante. 'Now you're just bringing me flowers because I complained. Don't you get it?' Well, no. I didn't. But it worked in the end. When we split, I thought it was a mutual decision. Amicable separation. Irreconcilable differences. You know the drill. I really thought we'd both tried. Until she flew back to New Zealand to move in with Rick just a few weeks later. He owns a big construction company there. Doing very well. They have

two little girls, and I wish them well. At the time, I felt...'
He shrugged.

'Conned,' Jessie suggested, because she knew about feeling conned.

Something they had in common that she would never have suspected without all the talking they'd done tonight.

'Most definitely conned,' he answered. 'Wondering why I hadn't seen what was happening while I was in the middle of it.'

'Because people don't. So often, people don't. It takes hindsight. Don't blame yourself for that, Keelan.'

'And I'm going to tell you the same thing. Don't keep racking yourself over Audrey and John. Don't see all that as a pattern you're bound to repeat.'

He said their names as if they were people he knew, and Jessie understood what a lot of ground they'd covered tonight. It felt good, but deeply dangerous as usual.

'Our waiter is hovering,' he said a moment or two later. 'Do you want dessert?'

'Real dessert?' she blurted out at once, remembering what he'd said on the beach about chocolate-dipped strawberries and whipped cream. 'Or...?'

He sat back and laughed, then leaned close again and said in a low voice, 'Believe it or not, yes, I was actually talking about real dessert. But if you're too impatient for the other kind...'

She blushed at once. 'No! I mean...' She trailed off, then took her courage in her hands, fixed her eyes on him steadily and said, 'I'm up for both.'

The house was very quiet when they got back at almost eleven. The sky had clouded over, the air had cooled and freshened, and there was no moon. Jessie thought she could smell rain in the air. She hoped everyone would sleep well tonight...

Inside, the bedrooms were dark, with doors ajar. Tavie 'pigletted' in her sleep, the sound coming through louder on the monitor in Susan's room than it did from the baby herself. In the big, open-plan living room, they discovered Dawson asleep on the couch, which had been made up with sheets, a quilt and pillows.

Their arrival had woken him, unfortunately. He stirred, sat up and said croakily, 'Back safe? That's good. She had a fussy period, but Susie got her settled.'

'Sorry to wake you, Dad.' Understatement on Keelan's part. His tone sounded a little strained.

'I should have gone for the alcove outside the laundry, but I thought your mother might need help with the baby if she woke up again before you got back, and I might not hear down there. Changed her nappy tonight,' he added, trying but failing to sound offhand about the feat. 'She kicks beautifully, doesn't she?'

'Dawson, you're not giving them a blow-by-blow description, I hope!' Lynette said, appearing in a robe from the bedroom she and Alan were using. 'Keelan and Jessie are supposed to be...' She stopped. 'Well, getting a break.'

'Hardly preventing that with a bit of a report, am I?'

But he was, of course.

Jessie felt as self-conscious as if they'd both been caught naked. Her whole body, which had been swimming with anticipation and nerves and aching, terrifying need, now felt bathed in floodlights. She hugged her arms around herself as if touching Keelan was the furthest thing from her mind.

'You're fine, Dad,' Keelan assured him, his throat rasping. 'No problem. Goodnight, now.'

Along the corridor, a minute later, he muttered darkly to Jessie, 'Are you getting a sense of *déjà vu* here?'

He brushed his knuckles from her ear to her neck to her collar-bone, painting her with a hot trail of awareness and desire. Leaving the restaurant half an hour ago, they'd paused for a long time beside the car to kiss. Here in the driveway, they'd reached for each other at once, every touch containing impatience and promise.

'I will get a very strong sense of *déjà vu* if you tell me "Later", like you did this morning,' she admitted. 'And you're going to, aren't you?'

'Is there a choice? The layout of this house does not facilitate privacy.' He pinned her against her bedroom door and traced the contours of her lips with the tip of one finger, his imposing body almost menacing her with the strength of his desire, and hers. 'Pity they didn't put one of us in the end room. I wasn't planning for this to have to be quiet and stealthy. Not at all. I want it to be anything but.' He brushed his mouth against her ear and whispered, 'Have to tell you, Jessie, I've been wondering all day if I could get you to make a lot of noise…'

'Keelan…' she breathed, throbbing deep inside.

'Thought Dad would be downstairs, and the others asleep with their doors closed.'

'There's tomorrow,' she said. 'When we get home.'

It seemed too far away, both physically and emotionally.

'There'd better be tomorrow,' he answered.

'Or there's the beach.'

Her words were punctuated by the sound of rain beginning to spatter onto the roof, and all they could do was sigh and shrug and laugh.

CHAPTER NINE

KEELAN and Jessie pulled into the hospital parking area at five the following afternoon, after an easier journey than Friday's northbound one had been and a relatively relaxing morning. They'd talked a lot, looked at each other a lot and said an impossible amount to each other with their eyes.

'She didn't wake up,' Keelan said.

'She's starting to.'

'Her first visit to her brother. Maybe she's getting excited about it.'

'The nurses will love seeing her. I want to see them deeply impressed at how much she's grown and how strong she looks.'

Impressing the nurses wouldn't be hard when they had Tam for comparison.

Back in the familiar environment of the hospital, the reality of Tam's impending surgery came crashing down on both of them again, and the fact that they didn't talk about it was more significant than if they had. Jessie knew that Keelan's thoughts would be running along the same tired, difficult track as hers.

They'd had their weekend away, and Susan and her sister, and even Keelan's father, had been unflagging in their efforts to make it easy and pleasant for the two of them and for Tavie, but this was the world they really inhabited. Jessie felt the first tinge of inner questioning about the depth and meaning of what had flared so powerfully between herself and Keelan.

Would it hold up *at all* here in the city?

Or would it all vanish, no more than a brief illusion?

Keelan had phoned the NICU late yesterday afternoon and again this morning, to receive cautiously positive reports about his little boy. Tam was hanging in there. His surgeons were confident that the planned procedure would take place. They didn't talk about the percentage chance of success, and Keelan told Jessie that he hadn't asked.

Percentages weren't relevant when there was no choice.

Nurse Barb McDaniel, who'd been one of Tavie's main carers during her stay, was rostered to look after Tam on this shift, and she was delighted to see Tam's sister again, after the two adults had been through the necessary hand-washing routine in the big sinks just beyond the unit's swing doors.

'Oh, she's amazing!' Barb said. 'Well, they always are, but this one! No, I'd love to hold her, but I won't. Keep her in her car capsule. What does she weigh now? And she's not on any oxygen or supplemental feeds any more? That's fantastic! See what your sister's given you to live up to, little man? All we need is that heart ticking over nicely, and you'll be powering along, threatening to catch up and overtake her.'

Tavie delivered a fabulous smile. She'd get hungry soon. Jessie wondered how long Keelan would want to stay. She could prepare the baby's bottle down in the car, if necessary, feed her and wait for Keelan there.

'Has he had a good weekend?' Keelan asked, standing beside the transparent humidicrib.

'Hanging in there.'

Jessie felt Keelan stiffen, wanted to run her hand down his arm in a gesture of support, but didn't dare. He swore.

'You don't know how I hate that expression now! I'm sorry, I'm not blaming you for using it, Barb. I just wish we could hear something different for a change. His colour's not very good today, is it?'

'No, he's fighting to keep those lips looking pink, and his hands are a bit too mottled for my liking. He's put on a few grams.'

'Which he could shed just as easily.'

'Did you sign the consent forms on Friday, Dr Hunter?'

'Yes, all of that.'

'And Dr Bedford outlined how he's planning to proceed?'

'In more detail than I wanted, to be honest.' Like any doctor, he knew too much, and he'd seen failure as well as miracles.

As was often done with preemies, the surgeons would perform the surgery here in the unit, tucked away in a tiny annexe room, rather than tiring Tam with a long trip down to the basement-level operating suites. It would be a lengthy process—several hours—and the apparent size and position of the largest hole, as well as its complex arrangement of entry and exit points, would dictate open heart surgery through the side of the organ.

Jessie could only imagine, but she could imagine far too vividly. She'd been in NICU units during surgery on a baby and, even though she hadn't been directly involved, she knew what it would be like.

There would be two surgeons, two nurses and an anaesthetist, all jostling for space around the tiny child. He would need minuscule doses of the required drugs— a sedative to put him to sleep, an agent to numb the surgical site itself and a narcotic for pain. As with any surgery, he'd be draped, taped and painted with a sterilising solution, and the planned line of the incision would be marked. It would no doubt look like a huge swathe of territory on his tiny torso.

When his skin had been pulled back, and the armature of muscles that stretched over his tiny ribs had been cut and folded, he would be at the mercy of surgical instruments hardly bigger than sewing pins, in the hands of a grown man's fingers that could, despite their size, move with the delicacy of a bee dancing.

The blood vessels in a baby this young and this small were not much stronger than sodden paper. Even a tiny tear in one of the really important ones could be fatal—a death dive via sudden, irreparable blood loss. The holes would be patched with a special synthetic fabric, as would the thinned section of Tam's tiny aorta. Dr Bedford would be soaked in sweat by the time he finished, even if everything went perfectly to plan.

Jessie knew how long those hours would seem for both herself and Keelan tomorrow. She'd be at home with Tavie. Keelan had commitments with his own patients. Knowing that there was nothing he could do for Tam, he hadn't tried to postpone those. They'd provide a more productive focus for his thoughts. Doubtless he would be called down to the A & E department more than once as well to give his verdict on a potential admission.

'Going to be a long day,' Barb McDaniel said, summarising, in just six short words, the track Jessie's thoughts had taken.

'Keith is starting at eight, he told me,' Keelan said. 'I'll be in here during my lunch-break—if I get one. He's hoping the surgery will be done by then.'

Tavie started to fuss a little.

'I'll take her down to the car,' Jessie said. 'Stay as long as you want, Keelan. She'll take her feed on my lap in the passenger seat. It's in the shade, nice and peaceful. Take an hour, if you want.'

'I'd like to spend some time with him,' Keelan said. 'But I'd like you to as well.'

'We'll fit that in this evening, if we can. If Tavie co-operates.'

He nodded, reached out, squeezed her hand, and like so many times before, it felt as if they were parents, sharing all of this completely, only the sensation was so much stronger today, so much more physical, buried deep inside Jessie and radiating out to her fingertips and to the sun-bleached ends of her hair.

She wanted to kiss Keelan, hold him, tell him, It's going to be all right. And she wanted to cry with him, bury her face in his shoulder and feel their bodies shaking together with inextricably mingled emotion.

Instead, all she could say in a husky voice was, 'See you in a while. Just when you're ready. Don't hurry.'

Down in the car, she cuddled little Tavie and sang to her, gave her the bottle she'd prepared earlier—which Tavie was generous enough to take colder than usual—and even played peek-a-boo.

'This is probably a little too advanced for you, sweetheart, but it's keeping *me* entertained, and I need that right now!'

Tavie was fast asleep again by the time Keelan appeared. He looked very strained, and didn't say much in the car. Jessie didn't need to ask why. Tavie had one of her fussy periods in the evening, which turned a simple dinner of ham and cheese omelettes into a lengthy process during which the two adults never got to sit down at the same time.

'Let me take care of her now,' Jessie said at eight o'clock.

'No, I really want you to go back up to the hospital.'

And she knew that in the back of Keelan's mind, although he'd never say it out loud, was the fear that if she didn't go and see Tam tonight, she'd miss out on her last chance to say goodbye.

Keelan was shameless in his need to anaesthetise himself after Jessie had gone to the hospital. He got Tavie ready for bed and tried rocking her in the chair in her room, but she remained fussy so he gave up and went back downstairs, found himself a beer and the junkiest television on offer.

Maybe the baby had been sensing his tension. Now that he sat sprawled on the couch, absorbed in the nth repeat of a paint-by-numbers, G-rated action movie, Tavie seemed ready to sleep more peacefully. She lay in a warm little bundle with her body on his chest and her head on his shoulder, and he could feel the tiny puffs of her warm, milky breath on his neck. The pictures on the television screen provided the only light, and her little face lay in shadow.

He didn't want to have another try at putting her in her cot. Just didn't want to move. So they both stayed put.

What a weekend!

Two major undercurrents of unresolved feeling still twisted together inside him even now. Tam was having life-or-death surgery tomorrow, and he and Jessie were desperate to sleep together, with the entire universe apparently conspiring to prevent it.

He'd learned a lot more about her over the weekend—her doubts, her vulnerabilities and her strengths. He knew, now, how much of that footloose attitude of hers was just a protection. And he also knew that she was nothing like his father's second wife.

Which left him with very few barriers in place in his feelings about Tam and his feelings about Jessica Russell.

Pretty tough to live through.

He still wondered about his parents, too, and whether they'd really have a second attempt at their marriage. It looked distinctly possible, after what he'd seen yesterday and today.

Meanwhile, by one definition, he and Jessie were already up to the third attempt at theirs.

Tonight? When she got back from the hospital?

No. Hardly seemed possible that she'd want to. He wasn't crass enough to toss Tavie into her cot like a football so that he had his hands free for ripping off the nurse's clothes.

He ached.

Focus on the movie, Hunter. Pretend you don't already know exactly what's going to happen in every scene.

His eyelids began to feel heavy and his limbs relaxed. Tavie had the right idea. Jessie would be back soon. She'd wake him up if necessary. Sleep was a refuge that had eluded him for most of last night, and he knew he'd wake early in the morning. If he could flick off the television with the remote control and snatch some now…

The first he knew of Jessie's return was the feel of her hands as she gently lifted the sleeping baby from his chest. He dragged his eyes open, but she told him in a whisper, 'Don't move. I'll take her upstairs. Just stay right there.'

Tavie stirred a little but remained asleep, and Jessie wasn't gone long. When she returned, Keelan was still groggily attempting to wake up enough to move. Within two seconds he was as awake as he'd ever been in his life, and one part of him, at least, was moving just as nature intended.

Jessie's lush, firm rear end had planted itself squarely and confidently on his thighs, and two soft arms had wound around his neck. 'I'm sorry I was at the hospital so long. It was—Tam was…hard to leave. But I'm…'

She stopped, must have sensed the initial tensing of his muscles in sheer surprise. Her voice faltered. 'Keelan? Isn't this…?'

'Yes.' He swore. 'Yes! It's what I wanted, and want. Painfully. But after a long day—after *this* day—I thought that you might have changed your mind, lost your—'

'No,' she said, without hesitation. 'No.'

Keelan's whole body surged, charged with electricity, burst into flames. He stole the initiative from her openly at once, slipping one hand between her thighs and curving the other around her neck to pull her against his mouth. Her lips were warm and sweet and hungry.

He kissed her until they were both breathless and dizzy and half-drunk with the taste of each other, and he kept on kissing her because it felt so fabulous to get utterly lost in her like this.

Eventually, with eyes closed and fingers gripping his shoulders for support, she pivoted to straddle him. He loved her impatience, and the way it was so obvious how much more she wanted, how much closer she wanted their contact to be. Her knees pressed into the back of the couch, and her breasts felt heavy and powerfully erotic against his chest. He cupped his hands around her hips and wondered how they'd get upstairs, then just a few seconds later, *if* they'd get upstairs.

When she eased herself back from his touch, crossed her arms across her front and pulled off that same thin, figure-hugging blue sweater she'd worn yesterday morning and got herself tangled in against the corridor wall of his mother's house, Keelan abandoned any more thought of moving anywhere.

This was going to happen right here and now. Only…

'We have no protection,' he managed to say.

'Yes, we do…' She pulled something from her pocket, pressed it into his hand, then blushed and looked touchingly uncertain. 'I thought of it. Is that…?'

Shameful? Was that the word she couldn't quite say?

'It's enough reason for my lifelong gratitude, Jessie,' he told her seriously.

Her breasts were fabulous, and swollen dramatically with passion, their nipples hard through her skin-toned bra. Deftly, she unclipped it and he pulled it down, loving the way the cups fell from her body to release her weight into his hands.

She closed her eyes again, hair spilling over her face like a drift of autumn leaves caught by a breeze. Her body shuddered at every touch he made, and her breath went in an out like that of an athlete after a race.

Her responsiveness made the electric charge in his own body even stronger.

Somehow they moved until they lay horizontal on the long couch, again with Jessie poised over him, hair hiding her face, rock-hard, darkened nipples pushing on him, sending their message of pleasure and need.

'How much patience do you have?' he growled at her.

'None.' The word hardly counted as speech, it had so much breath in it.

'Good.'

He snapped open the fastening on her jeans and began to drag them down. She helped him, shimmying her hips in a way that had his own dark trousers stretched painfully tight across the front. Her body could rock like a belly dancer, and he wanted to rock with her. After a little clumsiness, a little laughter and a lot of distracted, desperate caresses, they had nothing getting in the way any more, except that small piece of latex she'd been so unsure about, and he strained against the soft heat of her lower stomach which pressed on top of him, making him crazy every time he let himself slip.

'You're so perfect,' he told her. 'Your skin, your shape, the way you move.'

'So are you. Don't wait. Let me feel you.'

They rolled and she held up her arms, shaped herself for him and made his entry effortless. He shuddered and she held him, her breath coming in time to his own rhythm, her warmth enfolding him in an ecstasy that clawed higher and higher. It seemed impossible that the peak they surged towards could be any steeper, any further, yet the climb continued and every second of it felt better than the last.

He felt the exact moment when her world spun out of control, felt the dig of her nails in his back, moved in unison with the whip of her hips and spine, and heard the cries from her that vibrated like the soundbox of a cello. Then his own cries overtook hers, the last remnant of his control shattered into a million pieces, and his senses blurred and merged into one dark, headlong current.

They lay tangled together afterwards for a long time, too overwhelmed to speak. And, anyway, hadn't their bodies already said everything about how perfect and earth-shattering their love-making had been?

Keelan kissed Jessie's hair, her temple, her shoulder, deeply savouring his right of possession, the way he could hold her and touch her wherever he wanted, without any fear of protest or of overstepping her boundaries.

There was something so generous about her. Courageous, too. To have given herself like this, to the babies and to him, without the promise of anything in return. Keelan knew he'd short-changed her in suggesting a cool-headed affair. Tavie was at least giving smiles in payment now, but Tam hadn't yet even promised to live.

A sour jet of fear surged inside him as he thought this, giving his mouth an unpleasant taste, and he shut his eyes blindly to any consideration of the future. He could make no promises right now. Not to Jessie, and not to himself. Maybe everything they both felt had far more to do with Tam than either of them had realised.

In all honesty, he couldn't discount this possibility, because he knew it happened to people all the time. In war, in grief, in crisis. When your gut was churning with fear about the future, about the prospect of gut-wrenching loss, you didn't know what you would feel about each other this time next year, or next month, or even next week.

Kissing her one last time, in the soft curve of her neck, he murmured, 'It's late, Jessie.'

Her eyes looked soft and sleepy and full of questions. She wanted more.

Women usually did, and in the past he'd always been happy to give it, and say it. 'I'll phone you tomorrow evening,' or 'That was amazing,' or 'Can't wait till I can see you again.' After he and Tanya had slept together for the first time, he'd said, 'I love you,' without hesitation.

Tonight, however, he couldn't think of anything that would be safe or fair. He knew he didn't want to hurt Jessie. Or himself.

In the end, all he said was, 'Sleep well,' hearing the inadequacy of the line but knowing he had nothing better.

She nodded and gave a tentative smile. 'You, too.'

Then she disappeared up the stairs on soft feet, her bundled clothing gathered in her arms and her bare, pale body vulnerable in a way it hadn't been as they'd made love.

Keelan listened in the darkness and heard the movements she made as she prepared for bed. Water ran through the pipes, and a couple of floorboards creaked. A faint light came from her room and reflected against the wall that flanked the stairs, but then it ebbed away as she closed her bedroom door.

He waited another few seconds until no more sounds filtered down, and only then did he make a move himself.

Jessie had known that the following morning would be endless, and it was.

The night hadn't exactly passed in the blink of an eye either. Having dozed and dreamed for long, delicious minutes in Keelan's arms on the couch, she had lain awake as restless and jittery as a caffeine addict once she'd reached her own bed.

She'd wanted Keelan beside her so badly, but he hadn't come.

Why?

Regret, already, about what they'd just done?

Or was it only women who felt that kind of remorse? Maybe he'd simply felt a replete and very male sense of release which had launched him into an excellent night's sleep.

Oh, and he probably needed it!

She couldn't be selfish enough to wish her own restlessness on him when he must be so worried, as she was, about Tam. And she couldn't expect that the way they'd made love had tilted his whole universe, the way it had tilted hers.

At six in the morning, Tavie announced loudly that she was awake and hungry and ready to play. Jessie went to her and tried to gain a sense of peace and contentment from the feel of that warm, delicious little body, and the huge smile that came in the middle of Tavie's feed so that milk pooled in the baby's pink mouth and ran out at the corners.

'Angel sweetheart,' she whispered to the little girl. 'Precious darling. Gosh, I love you!'

Tavie thought that was fine.

Tavie didn't know what her brother had to go through today.

Jessie still had the baby on her lap when she heard Keelan in his room, and then the faint, rhythmic thrum of water piping into his shower. He appeared a few minutes later. 'I'm heading straight to the hospital,' he said. 'I'll grab breakfast there later.'

'And you'll phone me as soon as—'

'Of course. I can't promise when you'll get to see him, though.'

'That's all right.'

'You should be there. This is so...' He stopped, opened his hands. 'Backwards somehow. Wrong.' He scraped his fingers across his newly shaven jaw, and they almost looked as if they were shaking. 'But I don't know what to do about that.'

'It's OK.' She had to tell him so, because the last thing he needed was a litany of all the reasons why it wasn't OK at all.

'I'll be home when I can. If Mica is free this afternoon, get her to stay on. Leave Tavie with her and come up. See you some time.'

'Yes. See you.' She couldn't manage more than this, and he didn't wait.

She heard him leave the house just a few minutes later.

Mrs Sagovic arrived at eight-thirty. She hadn't been here on Friday, so she didn't yet know that Tam was scheduled for surgery today. When Jessie told her, she threw up her hands then clasped them together, her eyes bright with tears. 'That tiny boy!' She'd seen how fragile he was in the photos that Keelan and Jessie had both taken. 'I can't believe it!'

'There was no choice, Mica. It's the last throw of the dice.'

'And you're not there?'

Jessie shrugged. 'I'm here. With Tavie. I couldn't have stood in on the surgery, and I wouldn't have wanted to. And what's the use of just pacing the corridors outside? If it goes badly…' She didn't even want to say it.

The housekeeper hugged her, and murmured something in her mother tongue.

'Keelan did wonder if you could stay this afternoon so I can go up there then,' Jessie said.

'And where is he?'

'With patients.'

'Of course I can stay. Whether I can push myself together to clean Dr Hunter's house is another story!' She threw up her work hardened hands again and cried, 'That little boy…'

'Keelan is going to phone when there's some news. He doesn't think it'll be before lunch.'

'Then that's when you should go to the hospital. At lunch. That man needs someone with him.'

'His mother wanted to come down, but he wouldn't let her, in case—in case the surgery went—'

'What does "let" mean?' Mrs Sagovic cut in. 'She should have come anyway!'

The housekeeper's manner suggested that these

Australians of northern European origin didn't have the slightest idea when it came to family relationships, compared to people who shared her own Mediterranean heritage. She probably wouldn't have been impressed with Jessie's parents, or with Brooke Hunter's mother, Louise.

But she'd underestimated Keelan's mother, as it turned out.

Susan arrived at just before noon. 'I couldn't wait for a phone call.' She hugged Jessie, seeming warm and a little shaky—tired, too, after the drive.

Dawson had driven back to Sydney yesterday afternoon, and Jessie took a moment to wonder whether the two of them would see each other while Susan was down.

'I can't wait for a phone call either,' Jessie answered frankly. 'But no one's taking any notice of that. He hasn't phoned.'

'Which can only mean the baby's still in surgery. Can't believe it can take that long and still have any chance of success.'

'Can I drive you up, Susan? Mica's ready to push me out of the house. She'll think we're incurably wrongheaded if we don't go.'

'Yes, can you drive me? Please? We *are* incurably wrong-headed if we don't go, but I'm not sure that I could get back behind the wheel. I would have gone straight there, only…I'm terrified. I'm so scared.'

'Mmm.' Jessie nodded, her throat tight.

'Let me bring in my bags…'

Jessie helped, and then the two of them took Keelan's second car, ushered there by approving nods and pats from Mrs Sagovic. 'Yes, I know the baby is waking up. I can take care of her. You must go.'

*   *   *

The unit seemed quiet when they arrived, and the door to the annexe was still firmly closed. 'The team's still in there?' Jessie asked Stephanie.

'Yes, they are.'

'I thought surely...'

The other nurse shrugged and smiled, then said, 'Dr Hunter was called down from Paediatrics about ten minutes ago. He'll be here soon.'

'So we wait,' Susan murmured.

'We wait,' Jessie confirmed.

The wait wasn't long. Only about six hundred heartbeats, every one of which Jessie felt like a painful blow in her chest. Keelan arrived, and didn't seem all that surprised to see his mother. He managed a pale smile and a few token words of greeting, and he hardly seemed to look at Jessie at all.

Which in the greater scheme of things didn't matter right now, but...

Then suddenly Keith Bedford appeared, surgical mask still in his hand and clothing darkened with moisture. He put his hand on Keelan's arm. 'We had some problems, I'm afraid,' he said.

CHAPTER TEN

'WHAT problems?' Keelan's white lips hardly moved.

Having beat so painfully for ten minutes, Jessie's heart now didn't seem to be beating at all, and that was worse. She couldn't speak, but heard the stricken sound that came from Susan's throat, beside her.

'Well, the surgery itself went better than expected in many ways,' Dr Bedford said. 'One of the holes was small enough to leave alone. It'll close over on its own. The biggest, yes, was very tricky but we made a successful repair, as we did with the other two moderate-size holes and the thinned section of aorta. Unfortunately, right in the middle of it all, Tam developed a third-degree AV block.'

Susan cast a terrified, questioning look at Jessie, but she could only shake her head. She knew what Dr Bedford was talking about. The electrical impulses in the baby's heart had been slowed or blocked somehow, and had ceased to take their normal path through the heart's conduction system, resulting in compromised or, in the most extreme scenario, non-existent electrical communication between the heart's upper and lower chambers— the atria and the ventricles.

Sometimes the lower heart chambers generated electrical impulses on their own, but these weren't enough to keep the heart muscle at full function. There was a serious risk of full cardiac arrest. Had this happened to Tam?

But she couldn't explain something so complex and

technical to Susan now, not while the heart surgeon was still speaking, not while she didn't yet know what the outcome had been.

'We've put in an external pacemaker wire,' the surgeon said.

'And he's survived? He's...' Keelan slowed and shaped his mouth carefully around the phrase Jessie knew he hated. 'Hanging in there?'

'Yes. He's doing well. But you know the consequences of this, Keelan. If his heart doesn't resume its natural pacing on its own, he'll need further surgery to implant a permanent pacemaker.'

'OK.' Keelan gave a brief, jerky nod. 'How long will you give him before a decision on that is made?'

'If it hasn't happened within a few days, then it's not going to. After that has become evident, if it becomes evident, we'll wait until he's recovered from today's surgery and then go in again. Obviously, it's a much more minor procedure.'

Jessie heard Susan give a cautious, shaky sigh of relief at this final piece of comparative good news.

'Can we see him?' Keelan asked.

Dr Bedford narrowed his eyes. 'Not all three of you. Not yet. Two of you. And I want you in masks, caps, gowns and shoe covers. I'm keeping him in the annexe until someone else needs the space, basically. At least twenty-four hours, I hope, and preferably longer. This has been touch and go for him the whole way. And it still is.'

'Two of us,' Keelan muttered.

'For a couple of minutes. Bevan's still monitoring the reversal of the anaesthesia. Page me if you have any questions. I'll be in again to look at him later this afternoon. But you know what to look for yourself, what to expect.'

Keelan only nodded. His eyes flicked to Jessie, and then to his mother.

'You see him, Susan,' Jessie said quickly. Her throat felt as if there was a bone lodged in it, sideways.

'No, Jessie. I want you to go.'

Jessie closed her eyes. Susan was being incredibly generous, but a grandmother took precedence over an employee, and officially that was all she was. 'No,' she said. She had to fight so hard to keep her voice firm that it sounded almost angry. 'I'm not. You must. With Keelan.'

This time nobody argued.

Nervously, Susan accepted Keelan's guidance in putting on the sterile garments Dr Bedford had required. The bright royal blue of the stiff disposable fabric cap seemed to suck the colour away from her face. She wasn't a large or imposing woman, but Jessie hadn't really registered her slightness of build until now. Normally she carried with her such a strong sense of life, but at this moment she looked shrunken in trepidation.

And, of course, she was the right person to go.

Keelan touched the heel of his hand lightly to his mother's back, propelling her in the direction of the annexe where Tam still lay, and within a half minute they had disappeared, leaving Jessie alone.

She felt empty, frozen, grief-stricken. Keith Bedford's casual decree that Tam couldn't yet be crowded with more than two visitors had only emphasised the uncertainty that coloured everything she felt.

It surely wouldn't have eased her fears over Tam if she had known exactly where she fitted into Keelan's life—his present and his future. And yet, perversely, she felt that nothing could be harder than the way she felt now.

She was so scared for Tam, and yet she didn't remotely know if she had the right to take comfort in the love for Tavie that grew stronger inside her every day, let alone the love for Keelan that felt like something she'd known since she'd entered this world, and would know, just as painfully as this, until she left it again.

All of that might end in a matter of weeks, when Keelan decided he didn't need her any more.

Keelan and Susan weren't with the baby for long. He had his hand on her shoulder when they came out, and Jessie could see that Susan had found it very emotional, and very hard, to see the way her little grandson must look—motionless enough to seem frozen, lost in wires, his chest seemingly weighed down and lopsided with a dressing that would be huge and terrifying on such a tiny body.

'The monitors say he's alive. That was the only way I knew,' Susan said.

'His colour looked good,' Keelan said. 'He looked good.'

Jessie nodded. Colour was important. You clung to things like a baby's colour at a time like this.

'Can I take these things off now, love?' Susan asked.

'Yes, Mum, that's fine. There's a bin just outside.' He pressed his fingertips to the bridge of his nose. 'Then, do you need me to…? What do you need me to do?'

'Tell me where the cafeteria is, because I need some tea.'

'Something to eat, too. You look pale.'

'A sandwich. Just show me where it is.' She hung on his arm, apparently in need of the support.

Not knowing what was expected of her, Jessie went

down with them in the lift. She let them get out first, then peeled off quietly in the direction of a visitors' bathroom. She didn't think they'd noticed.

Later, she would find Susan in the cafeteria, because the older woman would probably want to be taken home. Meanwhile, not the slightest bit hungry, Jessie decided she would go outside for a bit and find some fresh air and some sun for her face, out by the little piece of garden that flanked the hospital's original colonial-era building.

It must have been ten or fifteen minutes before Keelan found her, and one look at him striding across the grass towards her told her how angry he was. Tight lines etched his face, and his shoulders had tensed and lifted as if padded like an American football player's.

'Where the hell did you get to?' he demanded. 'I looked around and you'd disappeared. Not a word. When? Why?'

'I wasn't hungry.'

He swore. 'Is that an answer?' His hands closed hard around her upper arms. 'You came down with us in the lift, and then you disappeared.'

In a shaky voice, she tried to make light of it. 'I'm here now, aren't I? Didn't vanish forever.'

'Made me realise, once and for all, how I'd feel if you did,' he growled, so low that she wasn't convinced she'd heard him right.

'How you'd feel if I…?'

'Vanished forever.'

'Abducted by space aliens?'

'Stop!' He bent and pressed his forehead against hers. 'Jessie, last night…last night…'

'Was pretty good, I thought,' she murmured.

He had his arms around her now, chafing her softly,

squeezing her as if he couldn't hold her tightly enough and never wanted to let her go. It was the best feeling she'd had all day, and it gave her just a little bit of courage—enough to let him know just a little bit about how she felt. She looked up into his face, and saw the light and the determination there.

'It was more than good,' he said. 'It was amazing. Fabulous. Unique. Perfect. And I didn't say that.'

'No, you didn't.'

'Because I didn't want to send the wrong message. What might be the wrong message,' he corrected himself quickly. 'I couldn't think straight, didn't trust anything about how I felt—last night, the whole weekend, weeks ago. And I'm still not sure if—'

'I understand, Keelan,' she cut in. 'I understand how impossible it is for you to be sure about anything right now.'

'No.' He pressed a finger to her lips. 'Now I'm sure about quite a few things. I'm not sure, though, if I was right to hold back last night. How much did that hurt, Jessie? How much did that leave you in the lurch?'

'Well, it did,' she admitted. 'Both those things.'

'Will it undo the hurt if I don't leave you in the lurch any longer?' He didn't wait for her to answer. 'I love you. That's the only way any of this fits together. I couldn't see it, couldn't feel it properly before, for so many reasons. And when I did feel it, I didn't trust it. But now… I was burning to say it as soon as we'd seen Tam, wanted to point out the cafeteria sign to Mum and tell her, "Follow that." But then I turned to check on you, and you'd just gone.'

'Only to the bathroom. You didn't notice.'

'No, I damn well didn't! But that doesn't mean—When I had to choose between you and Mum coming in to see Tam just now, and you jumped in and chose for me, and you chose Mum, it was so wrong.'

'No. Tam's grandmother…'

He ignored her. 'Totally my fault. I could see that. It stuck in my throat, too late to do anything about it then, until I could get you alone, as soon as I'd got Mum to the damned cafeteria. I hung back last night, doubting the best love-making of my life, and in doing that I denied you the right to see the baby you should be able to call yours, and I didn't want to wait a moment longer to give you that right.'

He stopped, as if suddenly unsure.

'If you want it,' he continued. 'If you want to call him yours. Do you, Jessie? Will you be my wife? Can we make a family together, so that Tam and Tavie can be yours for the rest of their lives?'

'Ours,' she whispered, holding him more tightly and pillowing her head against his chest. 'That's what I want. For them to be ours.'

'Ours. Yes. Ours.' He pressed his face into her neck and hair, and time seemed to stop in the hospital garden, even though the shadow on the old sundial crept several degrees around the tarnished bronze face.

'It's not an easy way to start,' Keelan told Jessie finally.

'I've never looked for things that were easy.'

He pulled back a little and looked at her, his face set and serious. 'No. I know. But you've made everything so much easier for me from the moment you walked off that plane nearly three months ago. Can't imagine how I'd ever do without it.'

'Neither can I. Keelan, I've come home…'

'Just where I want you. Can't believe I'm this lucky.

Can't help hoping it's part of a pattern, and that Tam's going to be this lucky, too.'

'Oh, yes.' She pressed her cheek against his, then instinctively they both turned so that their mouths met in the kiss of two people in love, sharing their hope and their fear, knowing this was only the beginning. 'He has to be this lucky. He's fought so hard.'

At almost the same time, high up in the hospital building, a little boy's heart remembered how it was supposed to beat. The pacemaker wire came out that same afternoon. After that day, Tam never looked back, never took a backward step, and neither did his parents.

Three months later, Tam and Tavie both attended a Sydney garden wedding that made everybody in the Hunter clan very happy. The bride looked radiant. The groom looked as if he'd discovered the secret to eternal youth...

And the bride and groom's thirty-five-year-old son stood with his fiancée at his side and a healthy baby girl in his arms, and had a hard time keeping his feelings in check.

'Are you taking notes?' Keelan whispered to his future bride as he watched his parents saying their vows. 'We have our own wedding coming up pretty soon, and you keep telling me I haven't got long to decide on the wording of the ceremony.'

'Thirty-five days. Not that I'm counting,' Jessie whispered back.

'I'm counting. Can't wait.'

'We haven't waited for very much, as far as I can work out,' she teased him. 'We're living under the same roof. We're already parents.'

'Can't wait for the honeymoon.'

'Oh, that. Oh, yes, that! We do have to wait a bit longer for that.'

Jessie blushed and laughed and closed her eyes to receive Keelan's kiss, while baby Tam cooed in her arms and closed his little fist against her heart.